A Child for
Christmas

A *baby in their Christmas stocking!*

Look out for these brand-new books
by three bestselling authors

HIS CINDERELLA MISTRESS
the first in *The Calendar Brides* trilogy
by Carole Mortimer
On sale January 2004, in Modern Romance™!

THE FRENCHMAN'S BRIDE
an emotionally compelling romance
by Rebecca Winters
On sale next month, in Tender Romance™!

THE PREGNANT SURGEON
the latest book in the *Practising and Pregnant*
mini-series by Jennifer Taylor
On sale next month, in Medical Romance™!

A Child for
Christmas

MARRIED BY CHRISTMAS
by
Carole Mortimer

THE NUTCRACKER PRINCE
by
Rebecca Winters

A REAL FAMILY CHRISTMAS
by
Jennifer Taylor

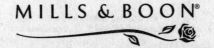

MILLS & BOON®

*MILLS & BOON and MILLS & BOON with the Rose Device
are registered trademarks of the publisher.*
Harlequin Mills & Boon Limited,
Eton House, 18-24 Paradise Road, Richmond, Surrey, TW9 1SR

A CHILD FOR CHRISTMAS
© by Harlequin Enterprises II B.V., 2003

Married by Christmas, The Nutcracker Prince and *A Real Family
Christmas* were first published in Great Britain by Harlequin Mills &
Boon Limited in separate, single volumes.

Married by Christmas © Carole Mortimer 1998
The Nutcracker Prince © Rebecca Winters 1994
A Real Family Christmas © Jennifer Taylor 2000

ISBN 0 263 83597 9

05-1203

*Printed and bound in Spain
by Litografía Rosés S.A., Barcelona*

Carole Mortimer was born in England, the youngest of three children. She began writing in 1978, and has now written over 120 books for Mills & Boon®. Carole has four sons, Matthew, Joshua, Timothy and Peter, and a bearded collie dog called Merlyn. She says, 'I'm in a very happy relationship with Peter senior; we're best friends as well as lovers, which is probably the best recipe for a successful relationship. We live on the Isle of Man.'

MARRIED BY
CHRISTMAS
by
Carole Mortimer

CHAPTER ONE

'WHO *is* that gorgeous-looking man over there?' Sally gushed eagerly at Lilli's side.

Until that moment, Lilli had been staring sightlessly at a barman across the room as he quickly and efficiently served drinks to the multitude of people attending what had so far been a pretty boring party.

Or maybe it wasn't the party that was boring; maybe it was just Lilli who felt slightly out of sync with the rest of the people here: if the babble of noise was anything to go by they were having such a good time.

She hadn't attended a party like this in such a long while, and so much had happened in the preceding months. Once upon a time, she acknowledged, she would have thought this was a great party too, would have been at the centre of whatever was going on, but tonight—well, tonight she felt like a total outsider, rather as the only sober person in a room full of inebriates must feel. Except she had already consumed several glasses of champagne herself, so that wasn't the reason she felt so out of touch with this crowd with which she had once spent so much time.

As for gorgeous men, the house was full of them— gorgeous and rich. When Geraldine Simms threw a party, this a pre-Christmas one, only the rich and beautiful were invited to attend, in their hundreds. Geraldine's house, in a fashionable part of London, was as huge and prepossessing as its neighbours, and tonight it was bursting at the seams with bejewelled women and handsome men.

Lilli dragged her gaze away from the efficient barman, obviously hired for the evening. It was time she looked away anyway—the man had obviously noticed her attention several minutes ago, and, from the speculative look in his eyes, believed he had made a conquest! He couldn't have been further from the truth; the last thing Lilli was interested in was a fling with any man, let alone someone as transient as a hired barman!

'What gorgeous man?' she asked Sally without interest. Sally was the one who had persuaded her to come in the first place, on the basis that a Geraldine Simms party, an event that only happened twice a year, was a party not to be missed.

'Over by the door— Oh, damn it, he's disappeared again!' Sally frowned her irritation. She was a petite blonde, with a beauty that could stop a man in his tracks, the black dress she almost wore doing little to forestall this.

Lilli had met her several years ago, during the usual round of parties, and, because neither of them had any interest in becoming permanently entangled with any of the handsome men they encountered, they often found themselves spending the evening together laughing at some of the antics of the other women around them as they cast out their nets and secured some unsuspecting man for the evening. Rather a cruel occupation, really, but it had got Lilli and Sally through many a tedious occasion.

'He must be gorgeous if you've taken an interest,' Lilli said dryly, attracting more than her own fair share of admiring glances as she stood tall and slender next to Sally, her hair long and straight to her waist, as black as a raven's wing, eyes cool and green in a gaminely beautiful face, the strapless above-knee-length red dress that she wore clinging to the perfection of her body. Her legs were long and shapely, still tanned from the summer months, the red high-heeled shoes she wore only adding to her height—and to the impression of unobtainable aloofness that she had practised to perfection over the years.

'Oh, he is,' Sally assured her, still searching the crowd for the object of her interest. 'He makes all the other men here look like callow, narcissistic youths. He— Oh, damn,' she swore impatiently. 'Oh, well,' she sighed, turning back to Lilli with a rueful grimace. 'That was fun while it lasted!' She sipped her champagne.

Lilli's eyes widened. 'You've given up already?' She sounded surprised because she was. On the few occasions she had known Sally to take an interest in a man, she hadn't given up until she had got him! And, as far as Lilli was aware, her friend had always succeeded...

'Had to.' Sally grimaced her disappointment, taking another sip of her champagne. 'Unobtainable.'

'You mean he's married,' Lilli said knowingly.

Sally arched her brows. 'I'm sorry to say that hasn't always been a deterrent in the past.' She shook her head. 'No, he belongs to Gerry,' she explained disappointedly. 'As far as I'm aware, no woman has ever taken one of our hostess's men and lived to tell the tale. And I'm too young to die!'

Lilli laughed huskily at her friend's woebegone expression. Sally was exaggerating, of course, although Geraldine's succession of lovers was legendary. In fact, Lilli doubted there were too many men in this room the beautiful Geraldine Simms hadn't been involved with at some time or other during the last few years. But at least she seemed to stay good friends with them, which had to say something about the bubbling effervescence of their hostess!

Sally glanced across the room again. 'But he is *so* gorgeous…' she said longingly.

Lilli gave a shake of her head. 'Okay, I give up; where is he?' She turned to look for the man who was so attractive that Sally seemed to be about to throw caution to the wind and challenge Gerry for him, on the other woman's home ground, no less!

'Over there.' Sally nodded to the far side of the elegantly furnished room. 'Standing next to Gerry near the window.'

Sally continued to give an exact description of the gorgeous man but Lilli was no longer listening to her, having already located the intimately engrossed couple, feeling the blood drain from her cheeks as she easily spotted the man standing so arrogantly self-assured at Geraldine's side.

No!

Not him. Not here. Not with *her*!

Oh, God…! How could he? How dared he?

'Isn't he just—? I say, Lilli, you've gone very pale all of a sudden.' Sally looked at her concernedly.

Pale? She was surprised she hadn't gone grey, shocked she was still standing on legs that seemed to be shaking so badly her knees were knocking together, surprised she wasn't screaming, *accusing*. What was *he* doing here? And so obviously with Geraldine Simms, a woman with the reputation of a man-eater.

'Are you feeling okay?' Sally touched her arm worriedly.

She wasn't feeling at all, seemed to have gone completely numb. It wasn't an emotion she was unfamiliar with, but she had never thought he would be the one to deal her such a blow.

Oh, God, she had to get out of here, away from the noise, away from *them*!

'I'm fine, Sally,' she told her friend stiltedly, the smile she forced not quite managing to curve her lips. 'I—I think I've had enough for one night. It's my first time out for months,' she babbled. 'I'm obviously out of practice. I—I'll call you.' She put her champagne glass down on the nearest available table. 'We'll have lunch.'

Sally looked totally bewildered by Lilli's sudden urgency to be gone. 'But it's only eleven-thirty!'

And the party would go on until almost morning. In the past Lilli would probably have been among the last to leave. But not tonight. She had to get out of here now. She had to!

'I'll call you, Sally,' she promised distantly, turning to stumble across the room, muttering her apologies as she bumped into people on the way, blind to where she was going, just needing to escape.

She had a jacket somewhere, she remembered. It was in a room at the back of the house. And she didn't want to leave without it, didn't want to have to come back to this house again to collect it. She didn't want to ever have to see Geraldine Simms again. Not ever!

Where had they stored the coats? Every room she looked in appeared to be empty. One of them turned out not to be as empty as it at first appeared, a young couple in there taking advantage of the sofa to make love. But there were no coats.

She would just abandon her damn coat in a minute, would send someone over tomorrow for it, would just have to hope that it was still here.

She thrust open another door, deciding that if this

room proved as fruitless as the others she would quietly leave and find herself a taxi.

'Oh!' She gasped as she realised she had walked into what must be the main kitchen of the house. It wasn't empty. Not that there were any chefs rushing around preparing the food for the numerous guests. No, all the food, put out so deliciously on plates in the dining-room, had been provided by caterers.

A man sat at a long oak table in the middle of the room, his dark evening suit and snowy white shirt, with red bow-tie, tagging him as part of the elegant gathering in the main part of the house. Yet he sat alone in the kitchen, strong hands nursing what looked to be a glass of red wine, the open bottle on the table beside him, the only light in the room a single spotlight over the Aga.

But Lilli could see the man well enough, his dark, overlong hair with distinguished strands of grey at the temples, grey, enigmatic eyes in a face that might have been carved from granite, all sharp angles and hard-hewn features. From the way his long legs stretched out beneath the table, he was a very tall man, well over six feet, if Lilli had to guess. She would put his age in the late thirties.

She also knew, from that very first glance, that she had never seen him before!

She really was very much out of touch with the party scene! Once upon a time she would have known all the other guests at any occasion she went to, which was ultimately the reason they had become so boring to attend. But tonight there were at least two men present that she hadn't encountered at one of these parties before—one she didn't know at all, the other she most certainly did!

Her mouth tightened at her thoughts. 'I'm sorry to

have disturbed you,' she told the man distractedly, turning to leave.

'Not at all,' the man drawled in a weary voice. 'It's quite pleasant to meet another refugee from that free-for-all out there!'

Lilli turned slowly back to him, dark brows raised. 'You aren't enjoying the party?'

His mouth quirked into a humourless smile, and he took a swallow of the wine before answering. 'Not particularly,' he dismissed disgustedly. 'If I had known—!' He picked up the bottle and refilled his glass, turning back to Lilli and raising the bottle in her direction. 'Can I offer you some wine? It's from Gerry's private stock,' he explained temptingly. 'Much preferable to that champagne being served out there.' He waved the bottle in the direction of the front of the house.

Gerry... Only Geraldine's really close friends shortened her name in that way. He also knew where Geraldine kept her cellar of wine.

Lilli looked at the man with new interest. He obviously was—or had been—a close friend of Geraldine Simms. And, while Geraldine might remain on good terms with her ex-lovers, she certainly didn't give them up to another woman easily...

Lilli entered the kitchen fully, aware of the man's gaze on her as she moved across the dimly lit room, able to tell by the cool assessment in those pale grey eyes that he liked what he saw. 'I would love some wine,' she accepted as she sat down at the table, not opposite him but next to him, pushing a long swathe of her dark hair over her shoulder as she did so, turning to look at him, green eyes dark, a smile curving lips coloured the same red as her dress. 'Thank you,' she added huskily.

'Good.' He nodded his satisfaction with her answer, standing up to get a second glass.

Now it was Lilli's turn to watch him. She had been right about his height; he must be at least six feet four, the cut of his suit doing nothing to hide the powerfully muscled body beneath. It also did nothing to mask his obvious contempt for these elegant trappings of civilised company!

She had no doubt that Sally would also have described him as gorgeous!

Her smile faded somewhat as she vividly brought to mind that image of the other man Sally had called gorgeous tonight; her last vision had been of Geraldine Simms draped decoratively across him as the two of them talked softly together.

'Thank you,' she told the man as he sat down beside her to pour her wine, picking up the glass when it was filled to swallow a grateful gulp. She could instantly feel the warmth of the wine inside her, merging with the glasses of champagne she had already consumed.

'Patrick Devlin.' The man held out his hand.

'Lilli.' She shook his hand, liking its cool strength, his name meaning absolutely nothing to her.

He raised dark brows, still retaining his light hold on her hand. 'Just Lilli?'

Her gaze met his, seeing a wealth of experience in those grey depths. Some of that experience had been with Geraldine Simms, she felt sure. 'Just Lilli,' she nodded, sensing his interest in her. And she intended to keep that interest...

'Well, Just Lilli...' He slowly released her hand, although his gaze still easily held hers. 'As we're both bored with this party, what do you suggest we do with ourselves for the rest of the evening?' He quirked mocking lips.

She laughed softly, well versed in the art of seduction herself. 'What do you suggest we do?' she encouraged softly.

He turned back to sit with his elbows resting on the table, sipping his wine. 'Well…we could count how many patterned tiles there are on the wall over there.' He nodded to the wall opposite.

Lilli didn't so much as glance at them. 'I have no interest in counting tiles, patterned or otherwise,' she returned dryly, drinking some of her own wine. He was right—this wine was much nicer than champagne. It was taking away the numbness she had felt earlier, too.

'No? Oh, well.' He shrugged at the playful shake of her head, refilling her glass. 'We could swap life stories?'

'Definitely not!' There was an edge of bitterness to her laugh this time.

He pursed his lips thoughtfully. 'You're probably right,' he said. 'We could bake a cake? We're certainly in the right place for it!' He looked about them.

'Can you cook?' Lilli prompted; he didn't look as if he knew one end of a cooker—or Aga!—from the other!

He grinned at her, showing very white and even teeth—and unlike most of the men here tonight, she would swear that he'd had none of them capped. 'No one has yet complained about my toast,' he drawled. 'And I've been told I pour a mean glass of orange juice!'

She nodded as he gave her the answer she had expected. 'And a mean glass of wine.' She raised her glass as if in a salute to him.

He poured the last of the wine into her glass. 'I'll open another bottle.' He stood up, moving confidently about the kitchen, walking to the cupboard at the back of the room, emerging triumphantly seconds later with a second bottle of the same wine.

Which he then proceeded to open deftly, refilling his own glass before sitting down next to Lilli once again. 'Your turn. To make some suggestions,' he elaborated huskily at her questioning look.

His words themselves were suggestive, but at this particular moment Lilli didn't care. She was actually enjoying herself, and after the shock she had received earlier this evening that was something in itself.

'Let me see…' She made a show of giving it some thought, happily playing along with the game. 'Do you play chess?'

'Tolerably,' he replied.

'Hmm. Draughts?'

'A champion,' he assured her confidently. 'That's the one with the black and white discs—'

'Not draughts, either,' Lilli laughed, green eyes glowing, her cheeks warm, whether from the effect of the wine and champagne, or their verbal flirtation, she wasn't really sure.

And she didn't care, either. This man was a special friend of Geraldine Simms', she was sure of it, and at this moment she had one hundred per cent of his attention. Wonderful!

'Snakes and ladders?' she suggested lightly.

'Yes…' he answered slowly. 'Although my sister always said I cheated when we played as children; I used to go up the snakes and down the ladders!'

Lilli laughed again. Either the man really was funny, or else the wine was taking effect; either way, this was the most fun she had had in a long time. 'I used to do that too,' she confided, lightly touching his arm, instantly feeling the steely strength beneath his jacket. 'And there's no way we can play if we both cheat!'

'True,' he agreed, suddenly very close, his face mere inches away from hers now. 'You know, Just Lilli, there's one game I have an idea we're both good at— and at which neither of us cheats!' His voice was mesmerisingly low now, his aftershave faintly elusive, but at the same time completely masculine. 'What do you say to the two of us—?'

'Patrick!' A feminine voice, slightly raised with impatience, interrupted him. 'Why aren't you at the party?'

He held Lilli's eyes for several seconds longer, a promise in his own, lightly squeezing her hand as it still rested on his arm, before turning to face the source of that feminine impatience. 'Because I prefer to be here,' he answered firmly. 'And, luckily for me, so does Lilli.'

'Lilli…?' The woman sounded startled now.

So much so that Lilli finally turned to look at her too. Geraldine Simms! She looked far from pleased to see the two of them sitting so close together, Patrick's hand still resting slightly possessively on Lilli's.

Lilli looked coldly at the other woman. 'Geraldine,' she greeted her hardly.

'I didn't realise you were here,' Geraldine said faintly.

She could easily have guessed that! 'Sally Walker telephoned me earlier and persuaded me to come with her.' Lilli finished abruptly, 'Wonderful party,' her sarcasm barely veiled.

'So wonderful Lilli and I were just about to leave.' Patrick stood up, lightly pulling Lilli to her feet beside him, his arm moving about the slenderness of her waist now. 'Weren't we,' he prompted.

As far as Lilli was aware—no, but it did seem like an excellent idea.

She turned her head slightly to give Geraldine a triumphant look. 'Yes, we were just about to leave,' she agreed brightly.

'But—' Geraldine looked flustered, not at all her usually confident self. 'Patrick, you can't leave!' She looked at him beseechingly, not at all certain of herself—or him.

His arm tightened about Lilli's waist. 'Watch me,' he stated determinedly.

'But—' Geraldine wrung her hands together. 'Patrick, I threw this party partly for you—'

'I hate parties, you know that.' There was a hard edge to his voice that hadn't been there when he'd flirted with Lilli. 'I'll come back tomorrow when all of this is over. In the meantime, I intend booking into a hotel for the night. Unless Lilli has any other ideas?' he added, looking at her with raised brows.

'Just Lilli' had realised, from the conversation between these two, that the original plan must have been for Patrick to spend the night here. And, considering Geraldine's intimacy with the man she had been draped over in the other room, that was no mean feat in itself; what did this woman do, line them up in relays? Whatever, Patrick had obviously decided he would rather spend the night with her, though the house she shared in Mayfair with her father was not the place for her to take him; she felt hurt and betrayed, but not *that* hurt and betrayed!

'A hotel sounds fine,' she accepted with bravado, green eyes challenging as she looked across the room at Geraldine.

The other woman's stare relaxed slightly as she met that challenge. 'Lilli, don't do something you'll regret,' she cautioned gently.

Geraldine knew she had seen the two of *them* together,

knew why she was doing this! All the better; there was no satisfaction in revenge if the person targeted was unaware of it...!

Lilli turned slightly into Patrick's body, resting her head against the hardness of his chest. 'I'm sure Patrick will make sure I don't regret a thing,' she said huskily.

'Lilli—'

'Gerry, just butt out, will you?' Patrick told her impatiently. 'Go and find your ageing lover and leave Lilli and me to get on with our lives. I'm not a monster intent on seducing an innocent, and you aren't the girl's mother, for goodness' sake,' he added disgustedly.

Lilli looked at the other woman with pure venom in her eyes; she had never disliked anyone as much as she did Geraldine Simms at that moment. 'Yes, Geraldine,' she said flatly. 'Please go back to your lover; I'm sure he must be wondering where you are.'

'We'll go out the back way,' Patrick suggested lightly. 'Unless you want to fight your way out through the chaos?'

'No, the back way is fine.' Her coat didn't matter any more; no doubt it would be returned to her in time!

'Patrick!' Geraldine had crossed the room to stop them at the door, a restraining hand on Patrick's arm now. 'I realise you're angry with me right now, but please don't—'

'I'm not angry with you, Gerry,' he cut in contemptuously. 'No one has any ties on you; they never had!' His face was cold as he looked down at her.

'This isn't important just now,' the beautiful redhead dismissed impatiently. 'Anyone but Lilli, Patrick,' she groaned.

So the woman did have a conscience, after all! Unless, of course, she just didn't want Lilli, in particular, walking off with one of her men…? In the circumstances, that was probably closer to the truth.

'Please don't worry on my account, Geraldine.' Lilli deliberately used the other woman's full name. The two of them had never been particularly close in the past, although Lilli did usually call her Gerry; but after this evening she hoped they would never meet again. 'I know exactly what I'm doing,' she affirmed.

Geraldine looked at Lilli searchingly for several long seconds. 'I don't think you do.' She shook her head slowly. 'And I'm absolutely positive you don't, Patrick,' she added firmly. 'Lilli is—'

'Could we leave now, Patrick?' Lilli turned to him, open flirtation in the dark green of her eyes. 'Before I decide snakes and ladders is preferable!'

He looked at her admiringly. 'We're leaving, Gerry,' he told the other woman decisively. 'Now.'

'But—'

'Now, Gerry,' he insisted, opening the back door for Lilli to precede him. 'Enjoy your party,' he called over his shoulder, his arm once more about Lilli's waist as they stepped out into the cold December evening.

The blast of icy cold air was like a slap on the face, and Lilli could feel her head swimming from the amount of champagne and wine she had drunk during the evening. In fact, she suddenly felt decidedly light-headed.

'Steady.' Patrick's arm tightened about her waist as he held her beside him. 'My car is just over here. Don't you have a coat?' He frowned as she shivered from the cold while he unlocked the doors of his sleek black sports car.

She suddenly couldn't remember whether she had a coat or not. In fact, she was having trouble putting two thoughts together inside her head!

She gave a laugh as he opened the car door for her to get in, showing a long expanse of shapely leg as she dropped down into the low passenger seat. 'I'm sure you'll help me to get warm once we reach the hotel,' she told him seductively.

His mouth quirked. 'I'll do my best, Just Lilli,' he assured her, the promise in his voice unmistakable.

Lilli leant her head back against the seat as he closed her door to move around the car and get in behind the wheel. What was she doing here...? Oh, yes, she was getting away from Geraldine and him!

'Any preference on hotels?' Patrick glanced at her as he turned on the ignition.

Hotels? Why were they going to a hotel...? Oh, yes...this man was going to make love to her.

She shook her head, instantly wishing she hadn't as it began to spin once again. 'You choose,' she said weakly.

She wasn't actually going to be sick, was she?

God, she hoped not. Although she had no idea where they were going as Patrick turned the car out onto the road. And at that moment she didn't care either. Nothing mattered at the moment. Not her. Not him. Not Geraldine Simms!

'All right?' Patrick reached out to squeeze her hand reassuringly.

She didn't think she would ever be 'all right' again. She had felt as if her world had shattered three months ago; tonight it felt as if it had ended completely.

'Fine,' she answered as if from a long way away. 'Just take me somewhere private and make love to me.'

'Oh, I intend to, Just Lilli. I intend to.'

Lilli sat back with her eyes closed, wishing at that moment for total oblivion, not just a few hours in Patrick Devlin's arms...

CHAPTER TWO

'YOUR jacket.' The garment was thrown over the back of a dining-room chair.

Lilli didn't move, didn't even raise her head. She wasn't sure that she could!

She had been sitting here at the dining-table for the last hour, just drinking strong, unsweetened black coffee; the smell of food on the serving plates sitting on the side board had made her feel nauseous, so she had asked for them to be taken away. There was no one else here to eat it, anyway. At least, there hadn't been...

'Did you hear what I said?'

'I heard you!' She winced as the sound of her own voice made the thumping in her head even louder. 'I heard you,' she repeated softly, her voice almost a whisper now. But it still sounded too loud for her sensitive ears!

'Well?'

He wasn't going to leave it at that. She should have known that he wouldn't. But all she really wanted to do, now that her head had at least stopped spinning, was to crawl into bed and sleep for twenty-four hours.

Fat chance!

'Lilli!' The impatience deepened in his voice.

At last she raised her head from where it had been resting in her hands as she stared down into her coffee cup, pushing back the dark thickness of her hair to look up at him with studied determination.

'My God, Lilli!' her father gasped disbelievingly.
'You look terrible!'

'Thank you!' Her smile was merely a caricature of
one, even her facial muscles seeming to hurt.

She knew exactly how she looked, had recoiled from
her own reflection in the mirror earlier this morning. Her
eyes were a dull green, bruises from lack of sleep visible
beneath them, her face chalk-white. Her tangled hair she
had managed to smooth into some sort of order with her
fingers, but the overall impression, she knew, was not
good. It wasn't helped by the fact that she still had on
the revealing red dress she had worn to the party the
night before. A fact Grimes, the family butler, had definitely noted when she'd arrived back here by taxi an
hour ago!

But if her father thought she looked bad now he
should have seen her a couple of hours ago, when she'd
first woken up; then she hadn't even been wearing the
red dress! And the rich baritone voice of Patrick Devlin
had been coming from the bathroom as he'd sung while
he took a shower…!

Her father dropped down heavily into the chair opposite her. 'What were you thinking of, Lilli?' He looked
at her searchingly. 'Or were you just not thinking at all?'
he added with regret.

He knew; she could tell by the expression in his eyes
that he did. Of course he knew; Geraldine would have
told him!

Because her father had been the man at Geraldine
Simms' side last night, the gorgeous man that Sally had
referred to so interestedly, the man Geraldine had been
draped over so intimately, her 'ageing lover', as Patrick
had called him.

'Were *you*?' Lilli challenged insultingly. 'Yes, I saw

you last night,' she scorned as a guarded look came over
her father's handsome face. 'With Geraldine Simms,'
she continued accusingly, so angry she didn't care about
the pounding in her head at that moment. 'But I suppose
you call her Gerry.' Her top lip curled back contemptuously. 'All her *intimate* friends do!'

He drew in a harshly controlling breath. 'And is that
why you did what you did?' he asked flatly. 'Went off
with a man you had only just met? A man you obviously
spent the night with,' he added as he looked pointedly
at her dress.

'And what about you?' Lilli accused emotionally. 'I
don't need to ask where *you* spent the night. Or with
whom!' She was furiously angry, but at the same time
tears of pain glistened in her eyes.

Her father reached out to touch her hand, but she drew
back as if she had been burnt. 'You don't understand,
Lilli,' he told her in a hurt voice. 'You—'

'Oh, I understand only too well.' She stood up so
suddenly, her chair fell over behind her with a loud clat-
ter, but neither of them took any notice of it as their
green eyes locked. 'You spent last night in the bed of a
woman everyone knows to be a man-eating flirt, a
woman who has been involved with numerous men since
her brief marriage—and equally quick divorce!—five
years ago. And with my mother, your wife, barely cold
in her grave!' She glared across the table at him, her
breathing shallow and erratic in her agitation, her hands
clenched into fists at her sides.

For that was what hurt the most about all this. After
a long illness, her mother had died three months ago—
and now her father was intimately involved with one of
the biggest flirts in London!

It was an insult to her mother's memory. It was—it

was— God, the pain last night of seeing her father with another woman—with that woman in particular!—had been almost more than she could bear.

Her father looked as if she had physically hit him, his face as pale as her own, the likeness between them even more noticeable during those seconds. Lilli had always been so proud of her father, had adored him as a child, admired him as an adult, had always loved the fact that she looked so much like him, her hair as dark as his.

Now she wished she looked like anyone else but him—because at this particular moment she hated him!

'You're right, Father; I don't understand,' she told him coldly as she rose and walked away from him. 'But then, I don't think I particularly want to.'

'Lilli, did you spend the night with Patrick Devlin?'

She stopped at the door, her back still towards him. Then, swallowing hard, she turned to face him, her head held back defiantly. 'Yes, I did,' she told him starkly.

He frowned. 'You went to bed with him?'

Lilli stared at her parent woodenly. She had woken up in a hotel bedroom this morning, wearing only her lace panties, with Patrick Devlin singing in the adjoining bathroom as he took a shower, the other side of the double bed showing signs of someone having slept there, the pillow indented, the sheet tangled; so it was probably a fair assumption that she had been to bed with him!

But the real truth of the matter was she didn't actually remember, couldn't recall anything of the night before from the moment she had closed her eyes in the car— and even some of the events before that were a bit hazy!

Her mouth tightened stubbornly. 'What if I did? I'm over twenty-one.' Just! 'And a free agent.' Definitely that, since the end of her engagement. She had barely been out of the house during the last six months—which was the reason the champagne and wine she'd drunk last night had hit her so strongly, she was sure. At least, that was what she had told herself this morning when she'd finally managed to open her eyes and face the day. 'Who was I hurting?' she added challengingly.

Her father gave a weary sigh, shaking his head. 'Well, I believe the intention was to hurt me. But the person you've hurt the most is yourself. Lilli, do you have any idea who Patrick Devlin is?'

Why should she? As her father had already said, she had only met the man last night. And her nonsensical conversation with Patrick in the kitchen had told her nothing about him, except that he had a sense of humour. But then, she had told him nothing about herself either, was 'Just Lilli' as far as he was concerned. She never expected to see or hear from him again!

'I only wanted to go to bed with him, not hear his life story!' she scorned dismissively.

Her father drew a harsh breath. 'Perhaps if you had done the latter, and not the former, this conversation wouldn't be taking place. In fact, I'm sure it wouldn't,' he rasped abruptly. 'You really don't have any idea who he is?'

'Why do you keep harping on about the man?' She snapped her impatience. 'He isn't important—'

'Oh, but he is,' her father cut in softly.

'Not to me.' She gave a firm shake of her head, wincing as she did so.

She just wanted to forget about Patrick Devlin. Last night she had behaved completely out of character, mostly because, as her father had guessed, she wanted to hit out at him. But also at Geraldine Simms. Well, she had done that—more than done that if her father's reaction was anything to go by!—and now she just wanted to forget it had ever happened. She couldn't even remember half of last night's events, so it shouldn't be that hard to do!

'Oh, yes, Lilli, he is important to you too.' Her father nodded grimly. 'Patrick Devlin is the Chairman of Paradise Bank.'

She thought back to the man she had met last night in Geraldine Simms' kitchen—she couldn't count this morning; she had left the hotel before he'd stopped singing and emerged from the bathroom! She remembered a tall, handsome man, with slightly overlong dark hair, and laughter in his deep grey eyes. He hadn't looked anything like a banker.

She shrugged. 'So? Is he married, with a dozen children; is that the problem?' Although if he were he must have a very understanding wife, to have gone off to a party on his own and then have felt no compunction about staying out all night. No...somehow she didn't think he was married.

Her father gave a sigh at the mockery in her tone. 'Okay, let's leave that part alone for a while. Do you know what else he is, Lilli?'

'A Liberal Democrat,' she taunted.

'Oh, very funny!' Her father, a staunch Conservative voter, wasn't in the least amused at her continued levity.

'Look, Father, I don't—'

'And will you stop calling me "Father" in that judgemental tone?' he bit out tautly.

'I'm sorry, but you just don't seem like "Daddy" to me at the moment,' she told him in a pained voice, unable to look at him at that moment, too.

Her father had always been there for her in the past, she had always been 'Daddy's little girl', and now he suddenly seemed like a stranger...

'I'm really sorry you feel that way, Lilli.' He spoke gently. 'It wasn't meant to be this way.'

'I'm not even going to ask what you mean by that remark,' she said scathingly, turning towards the door once again.

'I haven't finished yet, Lilli—'

'But I have!' She swung round, eyes flashing deeply green. 'To be honest, I'm not sure I can listen to any more of this without being sick!' This time she did turn and walk out the door, her head held high.

'He's Geraldine's brother,' her father called after her. 'Patrick Devlin is Geraldine's older brother!'

She faltered only slightly, and then she just kept on walking, her legs moving automatically, that numbness she had known the night before thankfully creeping over her once again.

'Where are you going?' Her father now stood at the bottom of the stairs she had half ascended.

'To bed,' she told him flatly. 'To sleep.' For a million years, if she was lucky!

'This mess will still be here when you wake up, Lilli,' her father told her fiercely. '*I'll* still be here!'

She didn't answer him, didn't even glance at him, continuing up to her bedroom, closing the door firmly behind her, deliberately keeping her mind blank as she threw off the clothes she had worn last night, not even bothering to put on a nightgown before climbing in between the sheets of her bed, pulling the covers up over the top of her head, willing herself to go to sleep.

And when she woke up maybe she would find the last twelve hours had been a nightmare...!

Geraldine Simms' brother!

She didn't know what time it was, how long she had

slept, only that she had woken suddenly, sitting up in the bed, her eyes wide as that terrible truth pounded in her brain.

Patrick Devlin wasn't a past or present lover of Geraldine Simms, but her *brother*!

No wonder he had been so familiar with the house, with where the wine was kept. And he hadn't been going to spend the night there with Geraldine, but was obviously her guest at her house during his visit to London.

Lilli had thought she was being so clever, that she was walking away with a prize taken from under Geraldine's nose. But all the time Patrick was the woman's brother! No wonder Geraldine had tried to stop the two of them leaving together; considering her own involvement with Lilli's father, any relationship between Lilli and her brother was a complication she could well do without!

Lilli had been to bed with the enemy…!

But she wasn't involved with Patrick Devlin, had no 'relationship' with him; one night in bed together did not a relationship make!

One night in bed…

And she didn't even remember it, she inwardly groaned. But Patrick had been singing quite happily to himself in the shower this morning, so he obviously did!

With the exception of her ex-fiancé, she had spent the majority of the last four years ignoring the obvious advances of the 'beautiful men' she met at parties, not even aware of the less obvious ones. But in a single night she had wiped all of that out by going to bed with the one man she should have stayed well away from.

Her father was right—this was a mess!

She fell back against the pillows, her eyes closed. A

million years of sleep couldn't undo what she had done last night.

Her only consolation—and it was a very slight one!—was that she was sure Patrick had been involved in a conversation with his sister this morning very similar to the one she'd had with her father. She wouldn't be 'Just Lilli' to Patrick any more, but Elizabeth Bennett, daughter of Richard Bennett, of Bennett International Hotels, the current man in Geraldine's life. No doubt her identity as the daughter of his sister's 'ageing lover' had come as much of a shock to him as it had to her to realise he was Geraldine's brother.

Lilli opened her eyes, her expression thoughtful now. Patrick hadn't seemed any more pleased than she was at his sister's choice of lover, which meant he wouldn't be too eager ever to meet the lover's daughter again, either. Which meant she could forget the whole sorry business.

End of mess.

Of course it was.

Now if she could just make her father see sense over this ridiculous involvement with Geraldine Simms—

She turned towards the door as a knock sounded on it. She hadn't left instructions that she wasn't to be disturbed, but even so she was irritated at the intrusion. 'Yes?' she prompted impatiently, getting out of bed to pull on her robe.

'There's someone downstairs waiting to see you, Miss Lilli, and—'

The young maid broke off in surprise as Lilli wrenched open the door. 'There's someone to see you,' the maid repeated awkwardly.

'What time is it?' Lilli frowned, totally disoriented after her daytime sleep.

'Three-thirty,' Emily provided, a girl not much

younger than Lilli herself. 'Would you like me to serve tea to you and your visitor?'

She wasn't in the mood to receive visitors, let alone sit and have tea with them. 'I don't think so, thank you,' she replied distractedly. 'Who is it?' She frowned.

'A Mr Devlin,' Emily told her chattily. 'I asked him to wait in the small sitting-room—'

'Devlin!' Lilli repeated forcefully, causing the young maid to look alarmed all over again. 'Did you say a Mr Devlin, Emily?' Her thoughts raced.

Patrick was here? So much for her thinking he wouldn't ever want to see her again either once he realised who she was!

'Yes.' The young girl's face was alight with infatuation—all the evidence Lilli needed that indeed it was the handsome Patrick Devlin downstairs.

Thinking back to the way he had looked last night—tall, and so elegantly handsome—she found it easy to see how a woman's breath could be taken away just to look at him. And she had just spent the night with him!

Lilli drew in a sharp breath. 'Please tell him I'll be down in a few minutes.' Once she was dressed. His last memory of her must be of her wearing only cream lace panties; she intended the memory he took away of her today to be quite different!

It took more than the few minutes she had said to don a black sweater, fitted black trousers, apply a light make-up to hide the pallor of her face, and to braid her long hair into a loose plait down her spine. But at least when she looked in the mirror at her reflection she was satisfied with the result—cool and elegant.

Nevertheless, she took a deep breath before entering the room where Patrick Devlin waited for her. She had no idea what he was doing here—didn't a woman walk-

ing out on him without even a goodbye, after spending
the night with him, tell him that she didn't want to see
him again—ever? Obviously not, if his presence here
was anything to go by…

He was standing in front of the window looking out
at the winter garden when she entered, slowly turning to
look at her as he became aware of her presence.

Lilli's breath caught in her throat. God, he was handsome!

She hadn't really registered that last night, but in the
clear light of day he was incredibly attractive, ruggedly
so, his hair so dark a brown it almost appeared black,
with those distinguished wings of silver at his temples.
His skin was lightly tanned, features so finely hewn they
might have been carved from stone, his eyes a light,
enigmatic grey.

He was dressed very similarly to her, except he wore
a fine checked jacket over his black jumper. Which
meant he had been back to Geraldine's house this morning—if only to change his clothes!

He moved forward in long, easy movements, looking
her critically up and down. 'Well, well, well,' he finally
drawled. 'If it isn't Just Lilli—alias Elizabeth Bennett.'
His voice hardened over the latter.

'Mr Devlin.' She nodded coolly in acknowledgement,
none of her inner turmoil—she hoped!—in evidence.

She had chosen to go with this man the evening before
for two reasons: to hurt her father, and hit out at
Geraldine Simms. And at this moment Patrick Devlin
seemed very much aware of that!

His mouth twisted mockingly. 'Mr. Devlin…? Really,
Lilli, it's a little late for formality between us, isn't it?'
he taunted.

She moved pointedly away from him; his derisive

manner was deliberately insulting. 'Why are you here?' She looked at him across the room with cool green eyes.

Dark brows rose at her tone. 'Well, I could say you left your bra behind and I've come to return it, but as you weren't wearing a bra last night…!'

'That's enough!' she snapped, two bright spots of embarrassed colour in her cheeks now.

'More than enough, I would say,' he agreed, his eyes glittering icily. 'Lilli, exactly what did you hope to achieve by going to bed with me?'

To hit out at her father, to hurt Geraldine Simms. Nothing more. But certainly nothing less. At the time she hadn't realised the man she had chosen to help her was actually the other woman's brother. She accepted it complicated things a little. Especially as he had come here today…

She deliberately gave a careless shrug. 'A good time.' It was half a question—because she couldn't remember whether or not they'd had a good time together!

He gave an acknowledging nod at her reply. 'And did you? Have a good time,' he persisted dryly at her puzzled expression.

She frowned. 'Didn't you?' she instantly returned. Two could play at this game!

His mouth quirked. 'Marks out of ten? Or do you have some other method of rating your lovers—?'

'There's no need to be insulting!' Lilli told him sharply.

'There's every need, damn you!' Patrick advanced towards her, his hand on her arm, fingers warm against her skin.

'Don't touch me!' she told him angrily, pulling away, and only succeeding in hurting herself. 'Let me go,' she ordered with every ounce of Bennett arrogance she possessed. This was her home, damn it, and he couldn't just come in here—uninvited!—and insult and manhandle her!

He thrust her away from him. 'I ought to break that beautiful neck of yours!' he ground out fiercely, eyes narrowed. 'You looked older last night... Exactly how old are you?' he bit out, his gaze sweeping over her scathingly.

She looked startled. 'What does my age have to do with anything?'

'Just answer the question, Lilli,' he rasped. 'And while you're at it explain to me exactly how the haughty Elizabeth Bennett ended up with a name like Lilli!'

Her own cheeks were flushed with anger now. 'Neither of those things is any of your business!'

'I'm making them so,' he told her levelly.

This man might be as good-looking as the devil, but he had the arrogance to match! Why hadn't she realised any of this the previous evening when she had met him? Because she hadn't been thinking straight, she acknowledged heavily, had been blinded by the fury she felt towards her father and the woman he was obviously involved with. This man's sister... She still had trouble connecting the two—they looked absolutely nothing alike!

'Well?' he prompted at her continued silence.

She glared at him resentfully, wanting him to leave but knowing he had no intention of doing so until he was good and ready—and he wasn't either of those things yet! 'I'm twenty-one,' she told him tautly.

'And?' He looked at her hardly.

'And three months,' she supplied challengingly, knowing it wasn't what he had been asking. But she had no intention of telling him that she had acquired the name Lilli because the baby brother she had adored, the baby brother who had died when he was only two years old, hadn't been able to manage the name Elizabeth. Just as she had no intention of telling him that she knew to the day exactly how old she was, because her mother, the mother she had also adored, had died on her twenty-first birthday... It was also the day her fiancée, her father's assistant, had walked out of her life...

He grimaced ruefully at her evasion. 'A mere child,' he ground out disgustedly. 'The sacrificial lamb!' He shook his head. 'I hate to tell you this, Lilli, but your efforts—enjoyable as they were!—were completely wasted.' His gaze hardened. 'If my own sister's pleadings failed to move me, you can be assured that a night of pleasure in your arms would have had even less effect!'

Lilli looked at him with haughty disdain. 'I don't have the least idea what you're talking about,' she snapped.

'No?' he queried sceptically.

'No,' she echoed tartly. 'I don't even know what you're doing here today. We were at a party, we decided to spend the night together—and that should have been the end of it. You came here, I didn't come to you,' she reminded him coldly.

'Actually, Lilli,' he drawled softly, 'I came to see your father, not you.'

Her head went back in astonishment. 'My father...?' she repeated in a puzzled voice.

Patrick nodded abruptly. 'Unfortunately, I was informed he isn't in,' he said grimly.

'So you asked to see me instead?' she realised incredulously.

'Correct,' he affirmed, with a slight inclination of his head. 'Sorry to disappoint you, Lilli,' he added.

She swallowed hard, quickly reassessing the situation. 'And just why did you want to see my father?'

Patrick looked at her with narrowed eyes. 'I'm sure you already know the answer to that question.'

'Because he's having a relationship with your sister?' Lilli scorned. 'It must keep you very busy if you pay personal calls on all her lovers in this way!'

Anger flared briefly in the grey depths of his eyes, and then they became glacially enigmatic, that gaze sweeping over her with deliberate assessment. 'I'm sure you keep your father just as busy,' he drawled.

After her comment about Geraldine, she had probably deserved that remark. Unfortunately, both this man and his sister brought out the worst in her; she wasn't usually a bitchy person. But then, this whole situation was unusual!

'Perhaps he's paying a similar call on you at this very moment?' Lilli returned.

'I very much doubt it.' Patrick gave a smile. 'It hasn't been my impression, so far in our acquaintance, that your father has ever deliberately gone out of his way to meet me!'

Her eyes widened. 'The two of you have met?' If they had, her father hadn't mentioned that particular fact earlier!

'Several times,' Patrick confirmed enigmatically.

Exactly how long had her father been involved with Geraldine? Lilli had assumed it was a very recent thing, but if the two men had met 'several times'...

'Perhaps you could pass on a message to him that we will be meeting again, too. Very soon,' Patrick added grimly, walking to the door.

Lilli watched him frowningly. 'You're leaving...?' She hadn't meant her voice to sound wistful at all—and yet somehow it did. In the fifteen minutes Patrick had been here he had made insulting comments to her, enigmatic remarks about her father—but he hadn't really said anything. She wasn't really sure what she had expected him to say... But the two of them had spent the night together, and—

He turned at the door, dark brows raised questioningly. 'Do we have anything else to say to each other?' he questioned in a bored voice.

No, of course they didn't. They had had nothing to say to each other from the beginning. It was just that—

'Ten, Lilli,' he drawled softly. 'You were a ten,' he explained dryly as she gave him a puzzled look.

He laughed huskily as his meaning became clear and her cheeks suffused with heated colour.

She hadn't wanted to know—hadn't asked—

'I'll let myself out, Lilli,' he volunteered, and did so, the door closing softly behind him.

Which was just as well—because Lilli had been rooted to the spot after that last statement.

Ten...

And she didn't remember a single moment of it...

CHAPTER THREE

'I WANT to know exactly what is going on, Daddy,' Lilli told him firmly, having waited in the sitting-room for two hours before he came home, fortified by the tray of tea things Emily had brought in to her. After Patrick Devlin's departure, Lilli had felt in need of something, and whisky, at that hour of the day, had been out of the question. Although the man was enough to drive anyone to drink!

She had heard her father enter the house, accosting him in the hallway as he walked towards the wide staircase.

He turned at the sound of her voice, his expression grim. 'I was left in no doubt by you earlier that you didn't want to hear anything more about Geraldine.'

'I still don't,' Lilli told him impatiently. 'Her brother, however, is a different matter!'

'Patrick?' her father replied.

Her mouth twisted. 'Unless she has another brother— yes!'

Her father stiffened, striding forcefully across the hall-way to join her as she went into the sitting-room, closing the door firmly behind him. 'What about him?' he said warily.

She gave an impatient sigh. 'That's what I just asked you!'

'You spent the night with him, Lilli,' her father reminded her. 'I would have thought you would know all

36

there is to know about the man! We none of us have defences in bed. Or so I'm told…'

She bit back the reply she would have liked to make; that sort of conversation would take them absolutely nowhere, as it had this morning. 'I'm not talking about the man's prowess—or otherwise!—in the bedroom,' she snapped. 'He said the two of you know each other.'

'Did he?' her father returned with studied indifference.

'Daddy!' She glared at her father's back as he stood looking out of the window now—very much as Patrick had done earlier. He was trying to give the impression that the subject of the other man bored him, and yet, somehow, she knew that it didn't…

He sighed. 'I'm sorry. I just didn't realise the two of you had spent part of your night together discussing me—'

'We didn't,' Lilli cut in. 'He was here earlier.'

Her father froze, slowly turning to face her. 'Devlin came here?'

She wasn't wrong; she was sure she wasn't; she had never seen this emotion in her father before, but he actually looked slightly fearful. And it had something to do with Patrick Devlin…

'Yes, he was here,' she confirmed steadily. 'And he said some things—'

'He had no right, damn him!' her father told her fiercely, his hands clenched into fists at his sides.

'I'm your daughter—'

'And this is a business matter,' he barked tensely. 'If I had wanted to tell you about it then I would have done so.'

'Tell me now?' Lilli encouraged softly. Her father had mentioned this morning that Patrick Devlin was the

chairman of Paradise Bank—could that have something
to do with this 'business matter'? Although, as far as she
was aware, her family had always banked with
Cleveley…

'I told you, Patrick Devlin *is* Paradise Bank,' her father grated.

And she was none the wiser for his repeating the fact!
'Yes?'

'Don't you ever read the newspapers, Lilli?' her father
said tersely. 'Or are you more like your mother than
I realised, and only interested in what Bennett
International Hotels can give you in terms of money and
lifestyle?'

The accusation hung between them, everything suddenly seeming very quiet; even the air was still.

Lilli stared at her father, barely breathing, a tight pain
in her chest.

Her father stared back at her, obviously mortified at
what he had just said, his face very pale.

They never talked about her mother, or baby Robbie;
they had, by tacit agreement, never talked about the loss
of either.

Lilli drew in a deep breath. 'I know Mummy had her
faults—'

'I'm sorry, Lilli—'

They had both begun talking at the same time, both
coming to an abrupt halt, once again staring at each
other, awkwardly this time. The last three months had
been difficult; Lilli's grief at her mother's death was
something she hadn't been able to share with anyone.
Not even her father.

She had known that her father had his own pain to
deal with. The years during which her mother's illness
had deteriorated had been even more difficult for him

than they had for Lilli, her mother's moods fluctuating
between self-pity and anger. It had been hard to cope
with, Lilli freely acknowledged. But she had had no idea
how bitter her father had become…

'I shouldn't have said that.' Her father ran a weary
hand through dark hair liberally peppered with grey.
'I'm sorry, Lilli.'

She wasn't sure whether he was apologising for the
remarks about her mother, or for the fact that he felt the
way he did…

'No, you shouldn't,' she agreed quietly. 'But a lot of
things have been said and done in the last twenty-four
hours that shouldn't have been.' She included her own
behaviour with Patrick Devlin in that! 'Perhaps it would
be better if we just forgot about them?' She certainly
wanted to forget last night!

'I wish we could, Lilli.' Her father sat down heavily
in one of the armchairs, shaking his head. 'But I don't
think Devlin will let either of us do that.' He leant his
head back against the chair, his eyes closed. 'What did
he have to say when he came here earlier?' He opened
his eyes to look at her frowningly.

Besides marking her as a ten…?

'Not a lot, Daddy.' She crossed the room to kneel on
the carpet at his feet. 'Although he did say to tell you
the two of you would be meeting again. Soon. Tell me
what's going on, Daddy?' She looked up at him appealingly.

He reached out to smooth gently the loose tendrils of
dark hair away from her cheeks. 'You're so young,
Lilli.' He sounded pained. 'So very young,' he groaned.
'You give the outward impression of being so cool and
self-possessed, and yet…'

'It's just an impression,' she acknowledged ruefully.

'How well you know me, Daddy.' She gave a wistful smile.

'I should do,' he said with gentle affection. 'I love you very much, Lilli. No matter what happens, I hope you never forget that.' He gave a heavy sigh.

Lilli once again felt that chill of foreboding down her spine. What was going to happen? And what did Patrick Devlin have to do with it? Because she didn't doubt that he was at the root of her father's problem.

Her father straightened determinedly in his chair, that air of defeat instantly dispelled. 'Devlin and I are involved in some business that isn't going quite the way he wishes it would,' he explained briskly.

Lilli frowned, realising that, with this blunt statement, her father had decided not to tell her anything. 'He called me a sacrificial lamb,' she persisted.

'Did he, indeed?' her father rapped out harshly. 'What the hell does he think I am?' he cried angrily, rising forcefully to his feet. 'Devlin is right, Lilli—it's past time the two of us met again. Damn Gerry and her diplomatic approach—'

'About Geraldine Simms—'

'She's not for discussion, Lilli,' her father cut in defensively, those few minutes of father-daughter closeness definitely over.

Obviously Geraldine Simms was too important in his life to be discussed with her! It made Lilli question exactly how long this relationship with the other woman had been going on. Since her mother's death—or before that? The thought of her father having an affair with a woman like Geraldine Simms while her mother was still alive made Lilli feel ill. He couldn't have—could he…?

Lilli stood up too, eyes flashing deeply emerald. 'In

that case,' she rebutted angrily, 'neither is the night I spent with her brother!'

'Lilli!' Her father stopped her as she was about to storm out of the room.

She turned slowly. 'Yes?' she said curtly.

'Stay away from Devlin,' he advised heavily. 'He's trouble.'

He might be, and until a short time ago she had been only too happy with the idea of never setting eyes on him again. But not any more. Patrick Devlin was the other half of this puzzle, and if her father wouldn't tell her what was going on perhaps Patrick would!

She met her father's gaze unblinkingly. 'Stay away from Geraldine Simms,' she mocked. 'She's trouble.'

Her father steadily met her rebellious gaze for several long seconds, and then he wearily shook his head. 'This is so much deeper than you can possibly realise. You're playing with fire where Devlin is concerned. He's a barracuda in a city suit,' he added bitterly.

'Sounds like a fascinating combination,' Lilli replied.

'More like deadly,' her father rasped, scowling darkly. 'Lilli, I'm ordering you to stay away from him!'

Her eyes widened in shock. This was much more serious than she had even imagined; she couldn't remember the last time her father had ordered her to do anything. If he ever had. But the fact that he did it now only made her all the more determined.

The real problem with that was she had no idea— yet!—how to even make contact with Patrick Devlin again, without it seeming as if she was doing exactly that. Because she had a feeling he would react exactly as her father was doing if she went to him and asked for answers to her questions: refuse to give any!

Well, she might be young, as both men had already

stated quite clearly today, but she was the daughter of one man, and had spent the previous night in the arms of the other—she certainly wasn't a child, and she wasn't about to be treated like one. By either of them!

'Save that tone of voice for your employees, Father,' she told him coldly. 'Of which I—thankfully!—am not one!' She closed the door decisively behind her as she left the room.

It was only once she was safely outside in the hallway that she allowed some of her defiance to leave her. But she had meant every word she'd said in there, she would get to the bottom of this mystery. And she knew the very person to help her do that...

'Sally!' she said warmly a few minutes later when the other woman answered her call after the tenth ring. She had begun to think Sally must be out. And that didn't fit in with her plans at all. 'It's Lilli.'

'Wow, that was quick,' Sally returned lightly. 'I didn't expect to hear from you again for weeks.'

Lilli forced a bright laugh. 'I said I would call you,' she reminded her.

'It's a little late in the day for lunch,' Sally said dryly. 'Although to be honest,' she added confidingly, 'I've only just got out of bed. That was some party last night!'

Lilli wouldn't know. 'Any luck with that gorgeous man?' she said playfully—knowing full well there hadn't been; her father had spent the night with Geraldine Simms.

'None at all.' Sally sounded disappointed. 'But then, with Gerry on the hunt, I never expected it. She monopolised the man all night, and then—'

'Are you free for dinner this evening?' Lilli cut in sharply—she knew what came 'then'!

'Well...I was due to go to the Jameses' party this

evening, but it will just be like every other party I've been to this month. Christmas-time is a bitch, isn't it? Everyone and his cousin throws a party—and invites exactly the same people to every one! In all honesty, I'm all partied out. And there's another ten days to go yet!' Sally groaned with feeling.

'Does that mean you're free for dinner?' Lilli prompted.

'Name the place!' The grin could be heard in Sally's voice.

Lilli did, choosing one of her own favourite restaurants, knowing the other woman would like it too. She also promised that it was her treat; Sally knew 'everyone and his cousin', and anything there was to know about them. Lilli didn't doubt she would know about Patrick Devlin too...

She wasn't disappointed in her choice of informant!

'Patrick!' Even the way Sally said his name spoke volumes. 'Now there *is* a gorgeous man. Tall, dark, handsome— He's Gerry's brother, you know—'

'I do know,' Lilli confirmed—she knew now!

'He's also intelligent, rich—oh yes, very rich.' Sally laughed softly.

'And single.' It was almost a question—because Lilli wasn't absolutely sure of his marital status. She had been to bed with the man, and she didn't even know whether he was married!

'He is now,' Sally nodded, nibbling on one of the prawns she had chosen to start her meal. 'Sanchia wasn't the faithful kind, and so he went through rather a messy divorce about five years ago. Sanchia took him for millions. Personally, I would rather have kept the man, but

Sanchia settled for the cash and moved back to France, where she originally came from.'

Sanchia... Patrick had been married to a woman called Sanchia. A woman who had been unfaithful to him. She couldn't have known him very well if she had thought he would put up with that; Lilli had only known him twenty-four hours, but, even so, she knew he was a man who kept what he had. Exclusively.

But at least he wasn't married now, which was a relief to hear after last night. Although there was still so much Lilli wanted to know about him...

'What does he do?' Lilli frowned; chairman of a bank didn't tell her anything.

'I just told you.' Sally laughed. 'He makes millions.'

'And then gives them away to ex-wives,' Lilli scorned; that didn't sound very intelligent to her!

'One ex-wife,' Sally corrected her. 'And he didn't give it away. It was probably worth it to him to get that embarrassment out of his life. Sanchia liked men, and made no secret of the fact...'

'She sounds a lot like his sister,' Lilli said bitterly. How could her father have been so stupid as to have got mixed up with such a family?

'Gerry's okay,' Sally said grudgingly. 'Although Patrick is even better,' she added suggestively.

Lilli gave her a guarded look. 'Sally, you haven't— You and he haven't—'

'I should be so lucky!' Sally laughed again ruefully. 'But Patrick doesn't. Not any more. Not since Sanchia,' she amended wistfully.

Lilli hoped she succeeded in hiding the shock she felt at this last statement. Because Patrick most certainly did! At least, he had last night. With her...

Sally gave her a considering look. 'You do realise I'm

going to have a few questions of my own at the end of this conversation?' she teased. 'And the first one is going to be, just when and where did you get to meet Patrick? As far as I'm aware, he's lived in New York for the last five years, and he's very rarely seen over here.'

Lilli kept her expression deliberately bland. 'Hey, I'm the one buying you dinner, remember,' she reminded her. She liked Sally very much, found her great fun to go out with, but she was also aware that her friend was the biggest gossip in London—that was the reason she had been the perfect choice for this conversation in the first place! 'Besides, just what makes you think I have met him?' She opened widely innocent eyes.

Sally gave a throaty chuckle, attracting the attention of several of the men at adjoining tables. Not that she seemed in the least concerned by this male interest; she was still looking thoughtfully at Lilli. 'Only a woman who had actually met Patrick would show this much interest in him; he's a presence to be reckoned with!'

Well, from all accounts—his account!—Lilli had met that challenge all too capably. 'I'm more interested in the business side of his life than his personal one.' Now that she had assured herself he wasn't married or seriously involved with anyone!

Sally shrugged. 'I've just told you he's based in New York. Chairman of Paradise Bank. Rich as Croesus. What else is there to know?'

His business connection to her father! 'English business interests?' she prompted skilfully.

'Oh, that one's easy,' the other woman returned. 'It was all in the newspapers a couple of months ago.' She smiled warmly at the waiter as he brought their main course.

Lilli barely stopped herself grinding her teeth together

in frustration. What had been in the newspapers months ago? 'I was a little out of touch with things at the time,' she reminded Sally once they were alone again.

'I'm sorry, of course you were.' Sally at once looked contrite. 'Paradise Bank took over Cleveley Bank.'

Cleveley Bank... Her father's bank. But that still didn't make a lot of sense to Lilli. Bennett International Hotels had shown a profit since before she was born, so it couldn't possibly have anything to do with them.

'Personally, I thought it was wonderful news.' Sally grinned across at Lilli as she gave her a puzzled glance. 'It means Patrick will probably start spending more time in England. More chance for us eager women to make a play at being the second Mrs Patrick Devlin,' she explained. 'I could quite easily give up this round of parties and the bachelor-girl life if I had Patrick coming home to me every evening!'

'It wasn't enough for the first Mrs Devlin,' Lilli said sharply as she realised she was actually jealous of Sally's undoubted interest in Patrick. Ridiculous! The man was arrogant, insulting, dangerous. And she had spent last night in his arms...

'Sanchia was stupid,' Sally rejoined unhesitatingly. 'She thought Patrick was so besotted with her that he would forgive her little indiscretions with other men.' Sally shook her head disgustedly. 'What Patrick owns, he owns exclusively.'

Exactly what Lilli had thought earlier! 'Not even Patrick Devlin can own people,' she said quickly.

'You have met him!' Sally said speculatively.

She could feel the guilty colour in her cheeks. 'Perhaps,' she acknowledged grudgingly. Obviously Patrick hadn't spent any time at the party last night, otherwise Sally would have seen him there too...

'But you're not telling, hmm?' Sally said knowingly. 'Oh, don't worry, Lilli.' She lightly touched Lilli's arm. 'I wouldn't be telling anyone about it either if I had Patrick tucked away in my pocket. But you will invite me to the wedding, won't you?'

Lilli drew back in shocked revulsion at the very suggestion. 'I think you've misunderstood my interest, Sally—'

'Not in the least.' The other woman gave her a conspiratorial wink. 'And if you have him, Lilli, hang onto him. There are dozens of women out there—including me!—who would snap him up given the chance!'

'But—'

'I won't tell a soul, Lilli,' Sally assured her softly. 'It will be our little secret.'

Perhaps her choice of informant hadn't been such a wise one, after all. Lilli had forgotten, in her need to know more about Patrick Devlin, just how much Sally loved what she considered a tasty piece of gossip—and how she loved sharing it with other people, despite what she might have just said to the contrary! The news of Lilli's interest in Patrick Devlin would be all over London by tomorrow if she didn't think of some way to avert it!

Her only hope seemed to be to give the other woman such a good time she wouldn't remember where they had spent the evening, let alone what they had talked about at the beginning of it—least of all Patrick Devlin.

A bottle of champagne later and Lilli wasn't sure what they had talked about either! Sally's suggestion that they go on to a club seemed an excellent idea. The restaurant staff seemed quite happy to see their last customers leave too, ordering a taxi to take them on to the club.

'I know I'm going to regret this some time tomorrow

when I finally wake up,' Sally giggled as they got out of the taxi outside the club. 'But what the hell!'

Lilli's sentiments exactly. It seemed like years, not just months, since she had been out and enjoyed herself like this. Last night certainly didn't count!

She was enjoying herself, couldn't remember when she had had so much fun, dancing, chatting with friends she hadn't seen for such a long time, once again the life and soul of the party, as she always used to be.

'Well, if it isn't Just Lilli, come out to play once again,' drawled an all-too-familiar voice close behind her. 'It's our dance, I believe,' Patrick Devlin added forcefully—and before Lilli could so much as utter a protest she found herself on the dance floor with him.

And it wasn't one of the fast numbers she had danced to earlier, the evening was now mellowing out into early morning, and so was the music. Lilli found herself firmly moulded against Patrick's chest and thighs, his arms about her waist not ungentle, but unyielding nonetheless.

And Lilli knew, because she tried to move, pulling back to look up at him with furious green eyes. 'Let me go,' she ordered between gritted teeth.

God knew what Sally was going to make of this after their earlier conversation! Not that Lilli could be in the least responsible for this meeting; she hadn't even realised he was at the club, certainly hadn't seen him amongst the crowd of people here. But he had obviously seen her!

For all that she was tall herself, the high heels on her shoes making her even more so, she still had to tilt her head to look up into his face. 'I said—'

'I heard you,' he returned unconcernedly, continuing to move slowly in rhythm to the music, his warm breath stirring the loose tendrils of hair at her temples.

She glared up at him. 'I thought you didn't like parties,' she said accusingly. He had no right being here, spoiling her evening once again.

He glanced down at her. 'This isn't a party,' he dismissed easily. 'But you're right—I don't particularly like noisy clubs like this one. I came here to conclude a business deal.'

Business! She should have known he had a calculated reason for being here. 'Like last night,' she said waspishly.

His mouth tightened. 'Last night I expected a quiet dinner party with my sister, with perhaps a dozen or so other guests. Not including your father,' he bit out tersely. 'Or that madhouse I walked into—and as quickly walked out of again! To the kitchen, as it happens. Which was where I met you.'

Lilli stiffened in his arms. 'Earlier today you seemed to have the impression that *I* had deliberately found *you*,' she reminded him.

He shrugged unconcernedly. 'Earlier today I was talking to the haughty Elizabeth Bennett. Tonight you're Just Lilli again.' He looked down at her admiringly. 'I like your hair loose like this.' He ran one of his hands through her long, silky black tresses. 'And as for this dress…!' His eyes darkened in colour as he looked down at the figure-hugging black dress.

All Lilli could think of at that moment was that they were attracting too much attention. Obviously Patrick was well known by quite a lot of the people here, and the speculation in the room about the two of them was tangible. Especially as Sally was in the midst of one particular crowd, chatting away feverishly, Lilli sure their 'little secret' was no longer any such thing!

'I wouldn't worry about them if I were you,' Patrick

followed her gaze—and, it seemed, her dismayed thoughts. 'Gossip, true or false, is what keeps most of them going. It's probably because they lead such boring lives themselves,' he added scornfully.

She knew he was right; it was one of the aspects of being part of a 'crowd' that she hadn't liked. But, even so, she wasn't sure she particularly liked being the subject—along with Patrick Devlin—of that gossip, either.

Patrick made no effort to leave the dance floor as one song ended and another began, continuing to guide her smoothly around. 'Forget about them, Lilli,' he suggested as she still frowned.

She would have liked to, but unfortunately she had a feeling that by tomorrow half of London would believe she was involved in an affair with Patrick Devlin. And the other half wouldn't give a damn whom she was involved with—because they had never heard of her or Patrick!

'Lilli and Elizabeth Bennett are one and the same person.' She coldly answered his earlier remark.

'No, they aren't. Just Lilli is warm and giving, fun to be with. Elizabeth Bennett is as cold as ice.' He looked down at her with mocking grey eyes. 'I'm curious; which one were you with your ex-fiancé?'

How did he—? Not a single person she had met this evening had so much as mentioned Andy, let alone their broken engagement. Surely Patrick hadn't done the same as her—spent part of the day finding out more about her…?

If so, *why* had he?

'Don't bother to answer that, Lilli; I think I can guess.' Patrick grinned. 'If you had been Just Lilli with him then he would probably still be around—despite his other interests.'

Lilli deeply resented his even talking about her broken engagement. She had been deeply distressed by her mother's death, and then for Andy to walk out on her too…! It had seemed like a nightmare at the time.

She had just started to feel she was coming out of it when she had been plunged into another one—with the name of Patrick Devlin!

'Just Lilli is a pretty potent woman, you know.' Patrick's arms tightened about her as he moulded her even closer against his body, showing her all too forcibly just how 'potent' he found her! 'In fact, I haven't been able to get her out of my mind all day.'

She swallowed hard, not immune herself to the intimacy of the situation, her nipples firm and tingling, her thighs aching warmly. 'And Elizabeth Bennett?' she prompted huskily.

'A spoilt little rich girl who needs her bottom spanked,' he replied unhesitatingly.

Lilli gasped. How dared he—? Just who did he think he was, suddenly appearing in her life, and then proceeding to arrogantly—?

'And if I had been her fiancé that's exactly what I would have done,' he continued unconcernedly.

They were still dancing slowly to the music, the room still as noisy and crowded, and yet at the moment they could have been the only two people in the room, their gazes locked in silent battle, grey eyes calmly challenging, green eyes spitting fire.

Finally Lilli was the one to break that deadlock as she pulled away from him, ending the dance abruptly, the two of them simply standing on the dance floor now. 'I would never have agreed to marry you in the first place,' she told him insultingly.

Patrick shrugged, totally unmoved by her anger. 'But you will, Lilli,' he said softly. 'I guarantee that you will.'

'I—you— Never!' She spluttered her indignation. 'You're mad!' She shook her head incredulously.

'But not, thank God, about you,' he said calmly. 'I've been there, and done that. And I've realised that loving the person you marry is a recipe for disaster. I've found qualities in you that are infinitely more preferable.'

'Such as?' she challenged. She still couldn't believe they were having this conversation!

'Loyalty, for one. A true sense of family.' He shrugged. 'And, of course, I find you very desirable.' This last was added, it seemed, as an afterthought.

Loyalty? A sense of family! Desire! They weren't reasons for marrying someone—

She was *not* going to marry Patrick Devlin!

He was mad. Completely. Utterly insane!

His mouth quirked with amusement as he saw those emotions flashing across her expressive face. 'A month, Lilli,' he told her softly. 'You will be my wife within the month.'

Lilli looked up at him frowningly; his gaze was enigmatic now. He sounded so sure of himself, so calmly certain...

She was not going to marry him.

She was not!

CHAPTER FOUR

'HE WHAT?' her father gasped as he once again sat across the breakfast table from her.

Lilli sighed, still slightly shell-shocked about last night herself. She had walked away from Patrick, and the club, after his ridiculous claim, still had trouble even now believing he could possibly have said what he did. But the bouquet of red roses, delivered early this morning, told her that Patrick had indeed stated last night that he intended marrying her.

Her father had been intrigued by the delivery of the roses when he'd joined her for breakfast, especially since there was no accompanying card with the flowers to say who they were from. But Lilli had no doubts who had sent them; only someone as arrogant as Patrick Devlin could have red roses delivered before the shops were even open!

'Your business associate, Mr Devlin, has decided he wants to marry me,' she repeated wearily, pushing her scrambled eggs distractedly about her plate. She couldn't possibly eat anything after the delivery of the roses!

Her father had lost interest in his bacon and eggs too now. 'What the hell did you do to him the other night?'

Lilli could feel the blush in her cheeks. She couldn't remember being with Patrick Devlin the night before last; she only wished she could. Well...part of her wished she could. The other part of her just wished it had never happened at all. Because Patrick wasn't going to let her forget it, that was for sure!

'I don't think his marriage proposal has anything to do with that,' she dismissed hurriedly.

Or did it? After all, he *had* said she was a ten...

Her father looked at her through narrowed lids. 'What does it have to do with, then?'

Lilli met his gaze steadily. 'You tell me?' She arched questioning brows.

'I have no idea.' Her father stood up, obviously having trouble coming to terms with this strange turn of events. *He* was having trouble coming to terms with it? *She* found it totally incredible.

'Why ever does he want to marry you?' Her father scowled darkly.

'Having already "had" me?' Lilli returned dryly.

'I didn't mean that at all!' Her father looked flustered. Dressed in a dark suit and formal tie and shirt, he was on his way to his office. Although he seemed in no hurry to get there... 'The two of you barely know— The two of you only met two days ago,' he hastily corrected as Lilli's expression clearly questioned his initial choice of words.

'Oh, don't imagine this proposal is based on love,' Lilli assured him. '"Loyalty" and "desire" were the words Patrick used.'

'Loyalty and—! Do you have "loyalty" and "desire" for him?' her father said incredulously.

She didn't even know the man!

Patrick Devlin was obviously a successful businessman, so she supposed he was to be admired for that, but whether or not he was an honest one was another matter. If her father's state of anxiety at being involved in business with him was anything to go by, then he probably wasn't.

As for desire… She supposed she must have wanted him the other night…

If she were honest, she had felt a stirring of that attraction towards him last night as well—

'The whole thing is ridiculous!' She stood up abruptly too. 'The man has obviously tried marrying for love, and it was not a success, so now he seems to have decided to marry for totally different reasons.' Loyalty and desire…

Her father shook his head. 'Why does he want to marry at all?'

'It's time I provided the Devlin name with a couple of heirs,' drawled that all-too-familiar voice. The two of them turned to confront Patrick Devlin, a flustered Emily standing in the doorway behind him.

'I did ask Mr Devlin to wait, but—'

'Who knows?' Patrick continued softly. 'After the other night, perhaps Lilli is already pregnant with my child.'

Lilli gasped, her father went pale—and poor Emily looked as if she was about to faint!

Which wasn't surprising, in the circumstances. How dared Patrick Devlin just walk in here as if he owned the place? And make such outrageous remarks too!

Lilli turned dismissively to the young maid. 'That will be all, thank you, Emily.' She had no intention of giving the young girl any more information for gossip among the household staff.

'Perhaps you could bring us all a fresh pot of coffee?' Patrick Devlin smiled disarmingly at Emily before she could make good her escape. 'I'm sure we could all do with some,' he added dryly as he sat down—uninvited— at the dining-table.

Emily hesitated in the doorway, looking uncertainly

at Lilli. Patrick Devlin might be behaving as if he owned the place, but Emily, at least, knew that he didn't!

'A pot of coffee will be fine, Emily,' Lilli said, waiting for the maid to leave and close the door behind her before turning to Patrick Devlin. 'What are you doing here?' she demanded, this man, with his arrogant behaviour, didn't deserve customary politeness!

He met her question unconcernedly. 'Waiting for fresh coffee to arrive,' he replied easily. 'Good morning, Richard. Has Lilli told you our good news?'

'If you're referring to that ridiculous marriage proposal,' her father blustered, 'then—'

'It isn't ridiculous, Richard,' Patrick cut in steadily. 'Ah, I see the roses arrived,' he said with satisfaction. 'I hope you like red roses?' He smiled across at Lilli.

There probably wasn't a woman alive who didn't, especially if you happened to be the lucky woman who received them. But in this case it depended who the sender was!

'You can't marry Lilli,' her father told the other man fiercely.

'Why not?' Patrick returned lightly. 'She isn't married already, is she?'

'No, of course not,' her father denied impatiently. 'But you—'

'I'm not married, either,' Patrick told him firmly. 'In which case, I can see no obstacle to our marrying each other.'

'But you don't know each other—'

'I know Lilli is beautiful. Popular—if last night is anything to go by. Well educated. And, as your daughter, an accomplished hostess. There's no doubting she's young, and she certainly seems healthy enough—'

'To provide you with those Devlin heirs you mentioned?' Lilli broke in disgustedly. 'You sound as if you're discussing buying a horse, or—or arranging a business contract, not considering taking a wife!'

'Marriage is a business, Lilli,' Patrick told her evenly, eyes coldly unmoving. 'And anyone who approaches it from any other angle is just asking for trouble. Not that it will be all business, of course,' he continued smoothly. 'I'm well aware of the fact that women like a little romance attached to things. I'm quite willing to play my role in that department too. If you think it necessary.' His derisive expression was indicative of his own feelings on the subject.

'Hence the sending of the roses,' Lilli guessed scornfully.

'Hence the roses.' He nodded in acknowledgement. 'Ah, coffee.' He turned to Emily as she came in carrying the steaming pot. 'Thank you.' He nodded to her, looking back at Lilli and her father once they were alone again. 'Shall I pour? Although you look as if you're on your way to your office, Richard, so perhaps you don't want another cup of coffee?' He quirked dark brows.

This man's arrogance was like nothing Lilli had ever encountered before; he had already taken over the staff, and now he appeared to be telling her father what to do too!

'Sit down and have some coffee, Daddy.' Lilli looked at Patrick pointedly as she resumed her own seat at the table—on the opposite side to him. 'I'm sure Patrick won't be staying very long.' She looked challengingly at the younger man.

'Oh, I'm in no hurry to leave,' Patrick replied, completely unperturbed by the fact that he obviously wasn't welcome here. 'I have nothing to do today until my business appointment with you this afternoon, Richard.' He

looked across at the older man. 'You did ask my secretary for a three o'clock appointment, didn't you?' he
queried pleasantly, pouring the three cups of coffee as
he spoke.

Her father sat down abruptly. 'I did,' he confirmed
gruffly.

'Good.' Patrick grinned his satisfaction. 'That means
I'll have time to take Lilli to lunch first.'

'I—'

'You have to eat, Lilli.' Patrick gently forestalled her
refusal.

'Not with you, I don't,' she told him heatedly; he
wasn't being polite, so why should she be?

'What do you think, Richard?' He looked at Lilli's
father. 'Don't you think Lilli would enjoy having lunch
with me?'

Richard Bennett looked frustrated once again. 'I—'

'As my father won't be the one having lunch with
you, his opinion on the subject is irrelevant!' Lilli
snapped frostily.

Patrick raised dark brows at her vehemence. 'There
speaks Miss Bennett,' he drawled, his expression innocent.

Too damned innocent! Lilli remembered all too well
what his opinion of Elizabeth Bennett was!

'Mm, this is good coffee,' Patrick said appreciatively
as he sipped the hot brew. 'I think I must have drunk
too much champagne last night,' he opined ruefully.

Lilli glared at him. 'Is that your excuse for your outrageous announcement last night?' she said contemptuously.

'Do I take it you're referring to my marriage proposal?' He frowned.

'Of course.'

'Sorry for the confusion, but I don't consider it an "outrageous announcement",' he returned. 'Especially as I've made it again this morning. Several times,' he added in a bored voice.

'And I have dismissed it as ludicrous—several times!' Lilli told him with feeling.

'You know, Richard…' Patrick looked calmly across the table. 'You really should have taken Lilli in hand years ago—you've made the job of becoming her husband all the more difficult by not doing so!'

Lilli was so enraged by this last casually condemning remark about her independent nature that for a moment she couldn't even speak.

And her father laughed!

Considering he hadn't done so for some time, it was good to hear—but not at her expense! There was nothing in the least funny about this situation.

Her father looked a little shamefaced, sobering slowly. 'I'm sorry, Lilli.' He touched her hand in apology. 'It was just that—well—'

'He knows I'm right,' Patrick put in. 'Although I'm probably the first person brave enough to actually say as much.'

She had realised the first night she met him that he was very direct, but she hadn't known it was to the point of rudeness. What on earth had she been thinking of two nights ago, becoming involved with such a man? The trouble was, she hadn't been thinking at all, had just wanted to hit out and hurt, the way she had been hurt when she saw her father with Geraldine Simms.

How that had rebounded on her! Spending the night with Patrick had changed nothing—except that the man now seemed to think he was going to marry her! Oh, she had hurt her father, but he was still seeing Geraldine, and now she, it seemed, was stuck with the infuriating Patrick Devlin!

'Although I can quite easily see how it happened, Richard.' Patrick continued his conversation with her father. 'Lilli is the sort of woman you want to spoil.'

'Thank you.' Laughter still gleamed in her father's eyes. 'She was incredibly endearing as a little girl.'

'I can imagine.' Patrick nodded, turning back to Lilli. 'Make sure you stop me from spoiling our daughters, Lilli, because they're sure to look like you, and—'

'Daughters!' She gasped at the plural. 'How many children do you want?'

'You see, I knew you would come round.' Patrick grinned at her approvingly. 'I would like you to be mother to two sons and two daughters.'

Four children. 'You said "a couple of heirs" earlier,' she reminded him.

He shrugged. 'Four sounds a much better number. Besides, I'm sure you'll look even more beautiful when you're pregnant than you do now, so I'll—'

Her father stood up noisily, effectively cutting off the indignant reply he could see Lilli had been about to make. 'I'll leave the two of you to continue discussing this,' he said. 'And the outcome, as I've told you before—' he turned to Patrick with narrowed eyes '—will have no bearing whatsoever on our—business arrangement.'

'Agreed,' the other man conceded easily. 'Although, as your son-in-law, I could be more helpful to you...'

'I don't think so,' Lilli's father replied slowly, giving Lilli a considering look. 'As my son-in-law, you're likely to end up with a knife sticking in your back on your wedding night!'

Patrick's mouth twisted humorously. 'All the more

reason for you to encourage the marriage, I would have thought,' he drawled.

'Ah, but then I would have to explain to Gerry how I let this happen to the older brother she so obviously adores. And, as I know to my cost,' Richard dramatically added, 'an angry and upset Gerry is a force to be reckoned with!'

'But you have no personal objections to this marriage?' Patrick prompted.

'None at all—because it will never happen,' Lilli's father returned easily. 'I know my Lilli.' He kissed her lightly on the forehead in parting. 'I'll see you later, Devlin,' he said hardly before leaving the room.

Patrick turned back to Lilli with calm grey eyes. '*Does* he know you?' he asked. 'Did he really believe you could go off and spend the night with a man you had only just met?'

She could too easily recall the pained expression on her father's face yesterday morning. No, her father hadn't believed her capable of that. But then, neither had she!

Her head went back in haughty dismissal. 'No one has to spend a lifetime paying for the mistake of one night of stupidity any more.'

'Don't they?' Patrick said softly, standing up to move round the table to stand at her side. 'The other night wasn't stupid, Lilli,' he told her huskily as he pulled her easily to her feet to stand in front of him. 'I wouldn't still have it on my mind if it had been. You were warm and responsive, gave yourself—'

'Stop it!' she cut in desperately, not wanting to hear about what she couldn't even remember. Or did she…

Even as he spoke she had images flitting in and out of her head, of the two of them in bed together, of their bodies entwined, of Patrick's lips and hands on her body, of her own pleasure in those caresses—

No! She didn't want to remember. It had been a mistake, and not one for which she intended paying for the rest of her life.

'But you were, Lilli,' Patrick told her, suddenly very close. 'And you did.'

He was too close! She could smell his aftershave, see black specks amongst the grey in his irises, feel the warmth of his breath on her cheek, knew—

His mouth, as it claimed hers, was warm and gently caressing, his arms enfolding her against the hardness of his body, moulding her to each sinewed curve, deepening the kiss, desire and wanting suddenly taking over.

Lilli felt the same need, her body responding instinctively to the caress of his hands down her spine, shivers of delight coursing through her body, her mouth opening to the intimacy of his kiss, a feeling of hard possession sweeping over her.

It was the force of that feeling that made her at last struggle to be free of his arms. Yes, she responded to him. Yes, she could feel the heat in her body for him, for the need of him. But she didn't want to be possessed, by him or any other man. Especially not by Patrick Devlin!

Patrick felt her struggles and at once released her, his eyes dark with his own emotions as he looked at her. 'It would work between us, Lilli,' he whispered. 'What further proof do you want?'

Heated colour warmed her cheeks. 'Physically we—'

'Match completely,' he completed for her.

Lilli looked at him. 'We have a certain response to each other,' she allowed. 'But when you came here yesterday afternoon you believed I had spent the night with you for devious reasons of my own—reasons I'm still not fully sure of. Although I do know they involve my father, in some way.' She frowned. 'Last night when we met, your attitude towards me had changed yet again. For some reason you announced you wanted to marry me!' She shook her head, not acknowledging for the moment the fact that she had needed to see him again, anyway. His arrogant announcement about marrying her had made null and void any intention she might have had of asking him for the truth about his business dealings with her father. She would rather never know the truth about that than have to be nice to this man! 'You're inconsistent, as well as—'

'Not in the least, Lilli,' he interrupted smoothly, his eyes coolly grey once more. 'The things you just spoke of are the very reasons why I've realised you will make me an excellent wife.'

She became very still. 'I don't see how…'

'I'm under no illusions where you're concerned, Lilli,' he explained. 'I even respect the fact that you tried to help your father—'

'By—as you think—going to bed with you!' Her eyes glittered deeply green at the accusation.

He shrugged. 'By whatever means were at your disposal,' he countered. 'It shows loyalty to your father. And loyalty, if not love, is something to be admired in a wife. My wife,' he added softly.

That word again! She was not going to be his wife, no matter what warped logic he might have used to come to that decision. 'That's no guarantee I would be loyal to you,' she pointed out spiritedly. 'Why should I be? You're arrogant, domineering—'

'So are you,' he mocked in reply.

'And you seem to have some sort of hold over my

father that no one will explain to me!' The last was said almost questioningly.

Patrick's mouth tightened. 'I agree with your father: business is business. Haven't I just explained that these two things are completely separate?'

'You don't "explain" things, Patrick,' she sighed. 'You simply make statements, and expect them to happen!'

He grinned. 'I think that's the first time you've called me Patrick. Plenty of other things, to my face, and otherwise, I suspect.' His grin widened to a smile. 'But never Patrick before.'

'It's your name. But you can be assured I'll never call you husband!' she said vehemently.

He seemed unconcerned. 'Never say never, Lilli. Stranger things have happened. I always said I would never marry again, but you see how wrong I was,' he reasoned patiently.

This man was so exasperating; she was going to scream in a minute! No wonder her father was having problems conducting business with him; he didn't listen to what anyone else had to say. About anything!

She gave an impatient shake of her head. 'Wasn't your first experience at marriage bad enough?' she challenged—and then wished she hadn't as his face darkened ominously. It was obviously still a sensitive subject… And it was also the reason he had no intention of marrying for love… She couldn't help wondering what the beautiful Sanchia had been like as a person, to have created such bitterness in a man as self-assured as Patrick…

'And what do you know of my first marriage?' he said softly—too softly. 'You would have been thirteen when

I married, and sixteen when I divorced—in neither case old enough to be part of that scene.'

Lilli raised her eyebrows. 'You obviously continue to have gossip value, because people are still talking about it!'

'Indeed?' Patrick's voice became frostier. 'And what are these ''people'' saying about my marriage?'

She looked at him warily; obviously, despite his comment last night about the social gossips, he didn't like the thought that his own life might have been under discussion. 'Only that it didn't work out,' she answered evasively.

He met her gaze compellingly. 'And?'

'What else is there to say?' she said quickly, feeling decidedly uncomfortable now. She wished she had never mentioned his marriage! But she wouldn't have done so if he hadn't come out with that ridiculous statement about marrying her... 'A failed marriage, for whatever reason, is surely a good enough reason not to repeat the experience?'

Patrick gave an assenting nod of his head. 'As is a failed engagement,' he rejoined pointedly.

Lilli felt the heat of resentment in her cheeks. 'Now that isn't open for discussion,' she said sharply.

'Why not?' he taunted. 'The man was a fool. Given the same choices he was, I would have opted for the money *and* you. Although, for my own sake, I'm glad that he didn't.'

Lilli stared at him in frozen fascination. What was he talking about? She and Andy had been engaged for six months when he decided he no longer wanted to marry her, and that in the circumstances he couldn't continue to work for her father, either. It had been a terrible blow at the time, happening, as it did, at the same time as her mother's death. But she had got on with her life, hadn't even seen Andy since the day he broke their engagement. In fact, she had no idea where he was now. And she wasn't interested, either.

Although the comments Patrick had just made about him were rather curious…

'Would you?' she said. 'But then, you're rich in your own right.'

'True,' Patrick conceded dryly. 'Now isn't that a better prospect in a husband than a man who's only interested in embezzling money from your father so that he can go off with his male lover?'

Lilli's stare became even more fixed. He *was* talking about Andy. She knew he was.

Could what he said possibly be true? Had Andy stolen money from her father? Before leaving with *another man*…?

Andy had joined the company as her father's assistant two years ago, a tall blond Adonis, with a charm to match—a charm Lilli, having become disenchanted with the 'let's go to bed' attitude of the men in her social set, had found very refreshing.

She had enjoyed his company too, often finding excuses to visit her father at his office, on the off chance she might bump into Andy there. More often than not, she had, although it had been a few months before he'd so much as invited her to join him for lunch. Over that lunch Lilli had found he was not only incredibly handsome, but also very intelligent, enjoying the verbal challenge of him as well as the physical one.

Looking back, she supposed she had done most of the chasing, but she'd realised it must be awkward for him as she was the boss's daughter. She had followed up that initial lunch with an invitation of her own, so that she might return the hospitality, suggesting the two of them go out to dinner this time. Again Andy had been fun, a witty conversationalist, and again he had behaved like the perfect gentleman when it came time for them to part.

Lilli had been persistent in her interest in him, and after that they'd had dinner together often. That her father approved of the relationship she hadn't doubted; in fact, he'd seemed deeply relieved she was spending so much time with his assistant and less time with her group of friends who seemed to do nothing but party.

Lilli had been thrilled when Andy had asked her to marry him, and if she had been a little disappointed in his continued lack of ardour after their engagement she had accepted that it was out of respect for her, and could ultimately only bode well for their future marriage.

But now Patrick seemed to be saying something else completely, was implying that Andy's lack of physical interest in her hadn't stemmed from respect for her at all, but from the fact that his sexual inclinations lay elsewhere!

He also seemed to be saying that Andy's engagement to her had enabled him to steal from her father's company...

Admittedly, as her father's future son-in-law, Andy had been given more responsibility in the company, and as Lilli's mother's illness had deteriorated Andy had been left more and more in charge of things while her father spent time at home.

Had Andy used that trust in him to take the opportunity to steal from Bennett Hotels?

As she looked at Patrick, the certainty in his gaze, that contemptuous twist to his lips, she knew that was exactly what Andy had done. He had used her to cheat her father…!

The blackness was only on the outer edge of her consciousness at first, and then it seemed to fill her whole being. Darkness. No light. Her legs buckled beneath her as she crumpled to the carpeted floor.

CHAPTER FIVE

LILLIE couldn't focus properly when she opened her eyes, but she did know enough to realise she was no longer on the floor of the dining-room, that someone—and that someone had to be Patrick Devlin!—had carried her through to the adjoining sitting-room and had laid her on the sofa there.

'My God, woman,' he rasped from nearby. 'Don't ever give me a scare like that again!'

He sounded angry—but then, he sounded like that a lot of the time!

What had she—? Why—?

Their conversation suddenly came flooding back in a sickening rush. Andy. Her father. The money…!

She moved to sit up, only to find herself pushed firmly back down once more.

'You aren't moving until I'm sure you aren't going to fall down again!' Patrick ordered as he bent over her, scowling darkly.

His expression alone was enough to make her want to shut her eyes and black out the world again, but even as she wished for that to happen she knew that the terrible truth would still be there when she was conscious again.

'Who else knows?' Her voice was barely audible. 'About Andy, I mean. The money. And—and the other man.' Her fiancé hadn't just walked out on her, which she had thought was bad enough—he had actually gone with another man!

Had the friends she'd spent the last two evenings with

known about that? Had they all been laughing, or pitying her, behind her back? Had they all known that Andy's only reason for being with her at all was so that he had easier access to the Bennett funds? She didn't want to face any of them ever again if that were the case!

'I believe your father has managed to keep all of it in the family.' Patrick's mouth twisted wryly as he moved away from her. 'Besides, I'm more interested in the fact that you obviously didn't know. Not until I just told you. Did you?'

She drew in a shaky breath, sitting up, feeling at too much of a disadvantage lying supine on the sofa. She was at too much of a disadvantage with this man already! 'Obviously not,' she managed coolly. 'Who told you about—about Andy?'

'Gerry,' he said quietly. 'Yesterday. In an effort to warn me off you.'

'Which obviously didn't work,' Lilli returned, their conversation giving her the time she needed to collect her thoughts together—and God knew they had fragmented after Patrick's earlier revelation.

'Obviously not.' Patrick grinned. 'You didn't seem exactly heartbroken to me about the loss of your fiancé—even before you knew the truth about him!'

Too much had happened at that time for her to dwell on Andy's sudden disappearance from her life. Since her mother's death she had got through every day as it arrived; there had been no time to cry for her broken engagement. And now that she knew the truth she felt more like punching Andy on the nose than crying for him! How dared he used her in that way? How dared he abuse her father's trust in him?

She stood up, smoothing her pencil-slim black skirt down over her thighs, straightening her emerald-green cashmere sweater, before moving to stand before the mirror over the fireplace, tidying the wispy tendrils of her hair back into the neat plait that hung down her spine.

She could sense Patrick watching her as she smoothed her hair, could have seen his reflection in the mirror if she had chosen to turn her head slightly—but she didn't.

He and his sister were not 'family', even if her father was involved in an affair with Geraldine, even if Patrick did keep insisting he was going to marry her—and she hated the fact that her father seemed to have confided all of this to his mistress. She hated Geraldine Simms more than she had before because her father had confided in the other woman about Andy's betrayal and yet he hadn't told her!

Because now Patrick Devlin knew about it too...

'I'm afraid I'm busy for lunch today, Patrick.' She turned back to him casually.

His mouth quirked as he looked at her, his gaze mocking. 'And every other day, hmm?' he said knowingly.

Lilli calmly met his eyes. 'It is Christmas,' she shrugged.

But despite the numerous invitations she had received during the last few weeks she hadn't accepted any of them. She hadn't refused them either, had been too listless to bother with them. In view of what she had learned about Andy, she had no intention of accepting them now either. But Patrick Devlin didn't need to know that.

'I'm aware of what time of year it is,' Patrick replied. 'But I didn't think you were.' He looked around at the lack of any Christmas decorations in the room.

Neither she nor her father had felt like putting up a tree or their usual decorations this year. It would be their first Christmas without her mother, and so far neither of them had the heart for seasonal celebrations.

Although now that her father was involved with Geraldine Simms he might feel differently about that; the other woman's home had certainly been highly festooned with decorations at the party two days ago!

Lilli's mouth tightened, her eyes glacially green as she looked across at Patrick. 'We're still in mourning for my mother,' she stated flatly. Although she somehow didn't think her father was any more!

'Caroline.' Patrick nodded in acknowledgement of Lilli's mother. 'I met her several times. Before her illness curtailed her social life. She was a very beautiful woman. You look a lot like her,' he added softly.

Pain flickered in the depths of Lilli's eyes. Somehow it had never occurred to her that this man could have known her mother. Although, as he'd said, until her illness had incapacitated her a year before her death, her mother had been a familiar part of the social scene. Even her illness hadn't robbed her of her incredible beauty, the two of them often able to fool people into believing they were sisters rather than mother and daughter.

'I really do have to get on now, Patrick.' She gave a pointed look at her slender gold wristwatch.

To her chagrin he grinned across at her. 'Miss Bennett has spoken,' he taunted.

Angry colour darkened her cheeks at his continued insistence that she was two people. 'At least she's polite!' she snapped.

'To the point of coldness,' he acknowledged dryly. 'Why aren't you curious to know more about your ex-fiancée, Lilli?' His eyes were narrowed thoughtfully.

Because so much made sense now—Andy's initial reluctance to ask her out, his lack of ardour during their engagement. She didn't want to dwell on those things, felt humiliated enough already!

'My father will tell me anything I need to know,' she dismissed quickly.

Patrick gave a disgusted snort. 'He doesn't seem to have told you very much so far!'

She glared at him. 'My father is very protective of me.' She was positive that was the reason her father hadn't told her about Andy. She had been devastated by her mother's death, and to have learnt of Andy's complete betrayal at the same time would have been unbearable. In fact, the more she thought about it, the more she was sure Andy had chosen his timing for that very reason...! She had felt hurt before, but what she thought of Andy now wasn't even repeatable!

'To the point of stupidity, I now realise,' Patrick countered harshly. 'You simply have no idea.'

She swallowed hard at his accusing tone. She was beginning to realise, and she only loved her father all the more for trying to spare her further pain. Although it seemed to have caused him complications he could well have done without, including, she was sure, being at loggerheads with this man.

'The love of a parent for a child is all-forgiving,' she defended chokily, aware as she said so that it was time this 'child' stopped being cocooned and began to be of some help to her father. He had carried this heavy burden on his own for too long.

Possibly it was the reason he had become involved so quickly with someone so unsuitable as Geraldine Simms...?

In recent years, with her mother so ill, her father had begun to confide in Lilli instead when it came to business matters, but she realised that for the last few months she had been too engrossed in her own pain to give him the attention he had so obviously needed. Which was why he had turned to someone outside the family for comfort.

'And the love of a child for the parent?' Patrick prompted softly.

Lilli gave him a sharp look. This man was too astute; he had guessed she was thinking of her father's involvement with his sister!

'Yes,' she answered unhesitating. She didn't like her father's involvement with Geraldine Simms, but after what she had just learnt of her father's recent worries she was no longer going to give him a hard time over it. She would just have to be around to help pick up the pieces when Geraldine tired of playing with him!

Patrick was still watching her closely. 'Do you like children, Lilli?'

She met his gaze defensively. 'Yes—did you think I wouldn't?' She and Andy had discussed the idea of having—

She and Andy…! How ridiculous the idea of them having children seemed now!

Patrick shrugged. 'You didn't seem too keen earlier when I mentioned having four—'

'I like children, would dearly like some of my own,' Lilli interrupted firmly. 'I just don't intend for them to be yours!'

He looked totally unconcerned by her vehemence. 'But think of the social coup you will have made by getting me to the altar,' he mocked. 'I've made no secret of my contempt for the institution of marriage!'

As Sally had clearly told her last night. Certainly, walking off with the much coveted prize of Patrick Devlin as a husband would more than compensate for the humiliation of having had a fiancé who had left her for another man! But once all the excitement had died down she was the one who would be married to this man, and was a lifetime of his torment really worth that? At this moment in time, she didn't think so!

'Thank you for the offer—but no,' she said crisply.

He looked at her with assessing eyes. 'It won't be open for ever, you know,' he said.

She gave a wry smile. 'I never thought that it would.' She was still dazed he had asked her at all!

His mouth twisted mockingly. 'But the answer is still no?'

'Most definitely,' she agreed forcefully.

'For now,' he said.

Lilli looked at him suspiciously. She was still reeling from the shock of Andy's betrayal, couldn't even think straight yet. But she did know she didn't want to marry this man.

'I really do have things to do, Patrick,' she told him again firmly, wishing he would just leave now so that she could think.

He studied her for several seconds, and then he gave a brief nod. 'I have no doubts our paths will cross again,' he murmured huskily.

She didn't know how he could be so sure. They hadn't met at all in the previous five years. Admittedly, Patrick seemed to have lived in America for most of that time, but he had no doubt been in London on several occasions during those years, if only to see his sister, and Lilli had managed to avoid ever meeting him. The only connection she could see between them now was the business he had with her father, and her father's relationship with his sister.

'Maybe,' she returned enigmatically.

He grinned again. 'But not if you can manage to avoid it!' he guessed.

'We've managed never to meet socially before, so perhaps it would be better if we left it that way,' she told him coolly.

'For whom?' he drawled. 'Having met you, Lilli, I'm in no hurry to lose you again.'

Was he never going to leave? She did have things to do—and going to see her father was top of that list. She intended speaking to him before his meeting with Patrick later this afternoon...

'And please don't say I've never had you to lose,' Patrick went on mockingly. 'You may have chosen to have a convenient memory lapse about the other night, but, believe me, I remember all of it!' he assured her.

She clearly, to her intense mortification, remembered waking up to the sound of him singing happily in the shower yesterday morning; he certainly hadn't sounded like a man dissatisfied with his night! But she hadn't 'chosen' to forget anything; she just didn't, apart from that brief memory flash earlier, remember what had happened between them that first night.

'I'm sure you do,' she dismissed briskly. 'But at the same time I doubt you ask every woman you go to bed with to marry you!'

He raised dark brows. 'In the last five years since my divorce?' he said thoughtfully. 'I think so—yes...' He nodded.

Lilli stared at him. Oh, Sally had said he didn't get involved, but— But Patrick couldn't really be saying she was the first woman he had been to bed with since his divorce. Could he...?

Patrick smiled at her stunned expression. 'It isn't exactly a secret, Lilli. Sanchia taught me never to trust anyone. Especially a woman,' he added hardly. 'And I never have,' he ground out harshly.

She drew in a sharp breath. 'I'm a woman,' she told him shakily.

'Undoubtedly so,' he agreed, touching her lightly on one creamy cheek. 'But I don't have to trust you to marry you. As I've already said, our marriage would be a business arrangement.'

She moved abruptly back from that caressing hand. 'No doubt with a suitable pre-nuptial agreement,' she derided scornfully.

He met her gaze steadily. 'That sort of agreement is only relevant if you intend divorcing each other at some later date. I have no wish to go through another divorce. The next time I marry it will be for life.'

She couldn't break her gaze away from his! She wanted to. Desperately wanted to. But she felt as if she was drowning in the depths of those dark grey eyes. And she knew he meant every word he said...!

She tilted her head back, flicking her plait back over her shoulder. 'No love, no divorce; is that the way it works?' she challenged, wishing she sounded a little more forceful. But she was seriously shaken by the determination of his gaze.

'Exactly.'

Lilli shook her head. 'I find that very sad, Patrick.' She frowned. 'Marriage should be for love.'

'Always?'

'Always,' she echoed firmly.

His mouth twisted. 'You can still say that, after the experience you've just gone through? With your parents' marriage as another shining example of marital bliss?' He shook his head. 'There's scepticism, and then there's stupidity, Lilli, and I'm very much afraid that you—'

'That is enough!' she cried, eyes as hard as emeralds now. 'Leave my parents out of this discussion. You know nothing about them or their marriage. All you know is that my father is now involved with your sister. But it won't last.' Her lips pursed disdainfully. 'Your sister's affairs never do.'

'And your father's affairs?' he taunted.

'My father doesn't have affairs!' Her cheeks were hot with indignation, her hands clenched angrily at her sides. 'Your sister has just caught him on the rebound from my mother's death. He wouldn't have looked at her twice while my mother was alive!' she added heatedly.

Patrick looked at her pityingly. 'Is everything this black and white for you, Lilli? No shades of grey at all?'

'My father brought me up never to accept less than the best,' she told him with passion. 'And so far I never have…!'

Patrick looked at her wordlessly for several long seconds, and then he slowly shook his head. 'And I hope— sincerely hope, Lilli—that you never do,' he murmured. 'And I mean that, Lilli. I really do.'

Somehow she believed him. 'Thank you,' she accepted.

His mouth quirked. 'Now go away?'

She gave a rueful smile. 'Yes.'

He laughed softly. 'I've enjoyed knowing you, Lilli. It's certainly never been boring. See me to the door?' he prompted throatily.

She had intended doing that anyway; as he had already said, she had been brought up to be a good hostess, and telling a guest to find his own way out, no matter who he was, was not polite! Besides, after trying to get him to leave for the last twenty minutes, she wanted to make sure he had actually gone!

'Certainly,' she agreed.

Patrick chuckled as the two of them walked down the hallway to the door, grinning as Lilli turned to him questioningly. 'You're very refreshing, Lilli; as far as I'm aware, you're the first woman who couldn't wait for me to go!' he explained self-derisively.

Not such a perfect hostess, after all! 'I—'

'Have things to do,' he finished for her. 'So you've already said.'

'Several times,' she reminded him playfully, relieved they had at last reached the door.

Patrick turned to her. 'Don't say goodbye, Lilli,' he murmured as she would have spoken. 'You may wish it were, but we both know it isn't.'

She knew no such thing! There was absolutely no reason—

There was no time for further thought as Patrick bent down and kissed her!

And it wasn't a light kiss either, as he pulled her easily into his arms and moulded her body against his.

Lilli felt as if she was drowning, couldn't breathe, was aware of nothing but the possession of this man. And it was complete possession, of the mind, body, and senses.

She could only look up at him with dazed green eyes as he released her as suddenly as he had kissed her.

'No matter what you think to the contrary, neither of us can say goodbye to that, Lilli,' he told her gruffly in parting, the door closing softly behind him as he finally left.

Lilli didn't move, could hear the thunder of her own blood as it rushed around her body. She had been out with men before Andy, quite a few of them, but none of them, including Andy, had evoked the response that Patrick did. It was incredible. Unbelievable.

Dangerous…! How could she respond to a man she didn't even like very much? For there was no denying the force of electricity that filled the air whenever they were together.

Well, despite what Patrick might have claimed to the contrary, she intended them not to be together again.

'Lilli…?' Her father stood up uncertainly from behind his desk, his eyes searching as he moved to kiss her lightly on the cheek in greeting. 'I didn't expect to see you again until this evening.' He looked at her a little warily, Lilli thought.

Which wasn't surprising, considering what she had learnt from Patrick earlier. Her father had carried that knowledge around with him for months now, and, on closer inspection, he looked grey with worry. Until today Lilli had put his gauntness down to the loss of her mother, but she now realised it was so much more than that. But she had no intention of letting him worry alone any longer.

She had been lucky when she'd arrived at his office a few minutes ago, his secretary able to happily inform her he was alone, and could see her immediately. Her father didn't look quite so pleased to see her!

Lilli looked at him with wide, unblinking eyes. 'Exactly how much money did Andy take?' she said evenly. 'And what are you doing about it?'

Her father staggered, as if she had actually hit him, sitting back down in the leather chair behind his desk, his face white now, eyes as green as her own gleaming brightly.

Her own legs felt slightly shaky, she had to admit, knowing from her father's reaction to those two simple questions that Patrick had told her the truth about Andy's disappearance. And, having told her the truth about the money, he no doubt had also told her the truth about whom Andy had gone away with…!

'Oh, Daddy!' She moved around the desk to hug him. 'You should have told me,' she said emotionally.

'No prizes for guessing exactly who did,' he muttered bitterly.

She moved back slightly to look down at him, her own eyes glittering with unshed tears. 'It's irrelevant who did the telling, Daddy. And to give Patrick his due,' she added grudgingly, 'he didn't realise I didn't already know.'

Her father's smile came out as more of a grimace. 'Did he survive the telling unbruised?'

Her mouth twisted at the memory of their conversation. 'Physically, yes. Verbally—probably not.' She shrugged. 'But I'm really not interested in Patrick Devlin's feelings just now; he isn't important.'

'I'm afraid he is, Lilli,' her father sighed. 'Very much so, in fact.'

She moved to sit on the edge of his desk. 'Tell me,' she invited.

It wasn't very pretty in the telling, and for the main part her father avoided meeting her gaze. It was more or less as Lilli had worked out in her own mind; Andy had used her father's preoccupation with his wife's illness to embezzle money from the company.

'How much?' she prompted softly.

'A lot—'

'How much Daddy?' she said forcefully.

He swallowed hard. 'Several million—'

'Several million!' Lilli repeated incredulously. 'Oh, my God…!' she groaned—this was so much worse than she had thought. Her eyes widened. 'That's why Patrick is involved in this, isn't it?' she realised weakly.

Her father scowled darkly. 'He had no right telling you that part,' he rasped harshly.

'He didn't,' she assured him shakily. 'I'm not completely stupid, Daddy; I can add two and two together and come up with the correct answer of four. Andy stole money from you, Patrick is a banker, you are now having difficult business discussions with Patrick; it isn't hard to work out that the two things are connected!'

'I wish to God they weren't!' Her father stood up abruptly, his expression grim. 'The money that Andy took was made through transactions at Cleveley Bank. It had been put in a separate account, ready to pay a loan we took out just over a year ago when we expanded into Australia. The loan was due for repayment two months ago. But when I accessed the account before that I found all the funds had been redirected out of the country,' he recalled heavily, even the memory of it, Lilli could see, bringing him out in a cold sweat.

'Into an account in Andy's name,' she easily guessed.

'Yes,' her father acknowledged dully.

'And Patrick now owns Cleveley Bank,' she said flatly. 'That's why the two of you have been locked in some sort of negotiation.'

Her father nodded. 'And Devlin won't give an inch.'

'But surely if you're prosecuting Andy Patrick can't just—'

'I'm not prosecuting Andy, Lilli,' her father told her.

'What?' she cried. 'But why on earth not? If you bring a case against Andy surely the bank can't— It's because of me, isn't it?' she suddenly realised, becoming very still. 'You haven't charged Andy because you don't want to involve me in this,' she groaned, realising this was

what Patrick had meant earlier about the extent of her
father's protectiveness of her. Well she knew now, and
she had no intention of letting this situation continue.
'Daddy, I know all about Andy, about the money,
about—about the other man.' She gave a pained grimace
as he looked at her worriedly. 'And when you have your
meeting with Patrick this afternoon I want you to tell
him you are in the process of bringing a case against
Andy. There's no way he can continue to hound you in
this way if you're involved in a court case to try and
retrieve the money.' Even as she spoke she wasn't sure
of the truth of that statement.

She wasn't really sure how her father would stand
legally even if he were prosecuting Andy over the theft
of the money. And from what she had gathered from
Patrick's comments the night she had met him—comments she now understood completely!—his sister's
pleadings on behalf of her lover hadn't moved him, so
perhaps this was going to make no difference to him
either. After all, her father was the one who owed the
money, and it probably wasn't the business of the bank
if that money had been embezzled...

Her father sighed again wearily. 'Lilli, if I bring
charges against Andy, then the whole story will come
out.'

'I'm aware of that.'

'And you will end up looking totally ridiculous,' he
continued gravely.

Her mouth twisted wryly. 'It won't be the first time!'

'I mean seriously humiliated, Lilli.' Her father shook
his head. 'Andy's sexual inclinations are of no interest
to anyone at this moment, but they will make headlines
when put together with his engagement to you and his
embezzling money from me. You would end up a laugh-

ing-stock, Lilli, and I won't have that,' he stated determinedly.

'At any price?' she prompted softly.

His mouth tightened stubbornly. 'At any price.'

Her expression softened lovingly, her smile a little shaky. 'I appreciate what you're saying Daddy. And I thank you for your loving protectiveness. But there's really no need,' she added brightly. 'You see, I won't end up a laughing-stock at all. Because I intend marrying Patrick Devlin!'

The answer to the problem was suddenly so simple. As Patrick had said, he was a good catch as a husband—and no one could possibly laugh at her, or pity her over her engagement to Andy, when she had managed to captivate such an eligible man as Patrick Devlin.

There was also the additional fact that, although Geraldine's pleadings on her lover's behalf might have fallen on stony ground, Patrick could hardly appear callous enough to the business world as to actually hound his own father-in-law.

Her marriage to Patrick was the answer to all their problems...

CHAPTER SIX

'LILLI!' Geraldine Simms looked totally stunned as her maid showed Lilli into her sitting-room. She stood, very beautiful in slim-fitting black trousers and an even more fitted black jumper, her hair a tumble of deep red onto her shoulders and down her spine, her expression of surprise turning to one of wariness. 'What can I do for you?' she asked slowly.

Lilli steadily returned the other woman's stare, seeing Geraldine as men must see her—as her own father must see her! She was a self-assured woman of thirty-two, and there was no doubting Geraldine's beauty—almost as tall as Lilli, with that gorgeous abundance of red hair, eyes of deep blue, her face perfectly sculptured.

No wonder her father was smitten!

Lilli mouth tightened as she thought of Geraldine's relationship with her father. 'You can tell me where I might find Patrick,' she said abruptly. Contacting the man seemed to be her problem at the moment, and as her father had refused to tell her where Patrick's office was Lilli had had no choice but to come to Geraldine.

In fact, her father was proving altogether difficult at the moment where Patrick was concerned. Richard Bennett had been horrified by her announcement that she intended marrying Patrick, and had flatly refused to have any part of it when Lilli had proved stubbornly decided on the matter, to the point where he wouldn't even tell her where he was meeting with Patrick this afternoon. So, much as Lilli had wanted to avoid the other woman,

Geraldine had seemed the obvious source—was sure to know, as he was a guest in her home, where her brother was.

'Patrick?' Geraldine looked even more startled. 'Why do you want to see Patrick?'

Lilli stiffened. She hadn't relished the idea of coming here at all, wished there were some other way of contacting Patrick; she certainly didn't intend to engage in a dialogue with Geraldine! 'I believe that's between Patrick and myself,' she returned coolly. The pluses of accepting Patrick's proposal far outweighed the minuses, but at the top of the minuses was definitely the fact that this woman was his sister!

Geraldine shook her head. 'Lilli—'

'I believe Lilli said it was private between the two of us, Gerry,' Patrick interjected as he strolled into the room, wearing a dark blue business suit and white shirt now, obviously dressed for the office. 'Did you decide to accept my lunch invitation, after all?' He turned enquiringly to Lilli.

'Yes,' she agreed thankfully. She hadn't actually expected him to be here, had no intention of accepting his marriage proposal in front of his sister. She had never been so pleased to see him!

'Fine.' He took a firm hold of Lilli's arm. 'See you later, Gerry,' he added dismissively, turning Lilli firmly toward the door.

'But—'

'Later, Gerry,' Patrick repeated hardly.

Lilli released her arm from Patrick's grip as soon as they were outside, silent as he unlocked his car before opening the door for her to get inside. She was silent, because at this moment she couldn't think of anything to say. Now that she was actually face to face with

Patrick again, the enormity of what she was about to do was quite mind-boggling. How could she agree to be this man's wife, bear his children? But, by the same token, how could she not?

'Save it until we get to the restaurant.' Patrick reached out and briefly clasped her clenched hands as they lay in her lap, his eyes never wavering from the road ahead. 'I booked a table for one o'clock.'

She turned to him sharply. 'You booked…? You knew I would have lunch with you all the time?' Anger sharpened her voice.

'I—hoped that you would change your mind,' he answered carefully.

He had known she would have lunch with him after all. What else did he know…?'

Lilli gave him an assessing look before turning her head to stare rigidly out of the front windscreen. She felt as a mouse must do when being tormented by a cat— and she didn't like the feeling any more than the mouse did! This man always seemed to be one step ahead of her, and in a few short minutes she was going to agree to be his wife. What on earth was her life going to be like, married to him?

Even the restaurant he had chosen had been picked with privacy in mind, each table secluded in its own booth, the service quietly discreet as they were shown to one, Patrick obviously known here as he was greeted with obsequious politeness; Lilli, as his guest, was treated with that same solicitousness.

'Is it too early to order champagne?' Patrick asked her lightly as the waiter hovered for their drinks order.

Lilli's chin rose defiantly, she might be down, but she wasn't defeated! 'As long as it's pink,' she told him haughtily. 'I never drink any other sort of champagne.'

Patrick's mouth twisted wryly. 'I'll try to remember that.' He turned to the waiter. 'A bottle of your best pink champagne,' he ordered.

'I don't think I've ever been here before.' Lilli gave a bored look round the room once they were alone again, noting how it was impossible, from the angle at which the booths were placed, to see any of the other people dining at the adjoining tables. 'It looks like the ideal place for a man to bring his mistress without fear of them being seen together,' she added scathingly.

Patrick smiled at her description. 'I wouldn't know,' he drawled, also looking casually about them. 'But you could be right.' He turned back to her. 'The food is excellent.' He indicated she should look at the menus they had been given.

Lilli looked at him for several long seconds, until she could withstand the laughter in his eyes no longer. 'The food,' she finally conceded, looking down at her menu.

'And the company,' Patrick added softly. 'Just Lilli,' he murmured huskily.

And she had been trying so hard to be Elizabeth Bennett. Damn him!

Her mouth tightened. 'Let's just get this over—'

'The champagne, Lilli,' he cut in softly, drawing her attention to the waiter waiting to pour their bubbling wine.

She drew in a ragged breath, sitting back in her seat while the champagne was poured into their glasses. She really did just want to get this over with now, and these constant interruptions weren't helping her at all.

Patrick raised his glass in a toast as soon as their glasses were full. 'To us, Lilli,' he stated firmly. 'Or am I being a little premature?' he prompted as she made no move to pick up her own glass.

'How long have you known?' she said heavily. 'That I would marry you,' she explained as he raised questioning brows.

He shrugged. 'I told you last night as we danced, but I suppose I actually realised the merits of it after I had left you yesterday afternoon—'

'I mean, how long have you known I would marry you?' she cut in impatiently, glaring at him frustratedly.

'Oh, that.' He sipped his champagne before glancing down at his menu.

'Yes—that,' she bit out tautly. 'You really are the most arrogant, infuriating—'

'I love it when you talk to me like that.' He grinned. 'No one else does, you know. Except Gerry, and— I realise you don't even like the mention of her name.' He frowned and she flinched. 'But she is my sister, and as such will become your sister-in-law once we're married.'

Lilli met his remark coldly. 'Even so, I don't see that I have to have anything to do with her.'

'Lilli—'

'I mean it, Patrick,' she told him. 'I accept your marriage proposal—but it won't all be on your terms!'

'I never for a moment thought it would—'

'Oh, yes, you did.' Her eyes flashed deeply green. 'But you chose me because of the person I am, and that means the whole person; no matter what you think to the contrary, Lilli and Elizabeth Bennett are not two divisible people—and neither of them wants anything to do with your sister!'

'Hmm, this is difficult,' Patrick murmured thoughtfully.

'Not as difficult as trying to pretend the two of us will

ever accept each other! She's your sister. I will be your wife. The two of us—'

'I wasn't referring to that situation,' Patrick dismissed with a wave of his hand. 'I simply don't know whether to have the salmon or the pheasant for lunch.' He pursed his lips thoughtfully as he studied the menu once again.

Lilli stared at him incredulously. Did nothing trouble this man? Did he make a joke out of everything?

'No, Lilli, I don't,' he murmured softly as if reading her mind, reaching out to clasp one of her hands with his as it lay on the table-top. 'Close your mouth, my darling, and stop upsetting yourself,' he teased. 'The problem between you and Gerry will sort itself out in its own good time. You're both adult women. And I have no intention of interfering.'

Lilli wasn't incredulous any more, she was stunned. 'Darling'. He had called her his 'darling'... And as her husband he would have a perfect right to call her any endearment he pleased. He would have the right to do a lot more than that!

She hastily removed her hand from beneath his. 'I want a long engagement—'

'No,' he cut in calmly, to all intents and purposes still studying his menu.

Colour heightened her cheeks. 'I told you this isn't going to be all on your terms,' she reminded him tautly.

He gave a brief nod. 'And I agreed it wouldn't,' he said. 'But a long engagement is out of the question. With a special licence we can be married before Christmas.'

Lilli gasped. 'Before—! You can't be serious,' she protested, sitting forward. 'It's only nine days away; I can't possibly be ready to marry you between now and then!'

'Of course you can,' he assured her smoothly. 'Now

I suggest we order our meal,' he added pleasantly as the waiter approached their table. 'I have a meeting at three o'clock,' he reminded her.

His meeting was with her father. They really didn't have the time before that meeting to sort this out properly. She couldn't decide on the rest of her life in an hour and a half!

'I haven't even had a chance to read the menu yet,' she told him dully; she had looked at it, but she hadn't actually read it.

'Another few minutes,' he told the waiter pleasantly.

Lilli shook her head. 'I'm really not hungry.'

Grey eyes looked compellingly into hers. 'You have to eat, Lilli.'

She swallowed hard. 'I really don't think I can—'

'Avocado salad and the salmon,' Patrick told the waiter decisively. 'For both of us.' He turned back to Lilli once they were alone again. 'I'll agree to any other terms you care to suggest, Lilli,' he offered. 'But the timing of our marriage is not for negotiation.' His mouth tightened. 'I have no intention of your father settling his problem with Andrew Brewster—and you breaking our engagement so fast you end up bruising yourself in your speed to get my ring off your finger!' His eyes glittered coldly as he looked at her between narrowed lids.

'A 'barracuda in a city suit' was how her father had described this man—and how right he was. Breaking off the engagement was exactly what she had been hoping to do! She really didn't want to be married to this man, had hoped—oh, God, she had hoped her father would be able to solve his financial problems without her actually having to go through with marriage to Patrick Devlin.

She should have known Patrick would see straight through any ideas like that!

Her head went back proudly, her eyes glittering brightly. 'I suppose you've decided what I'm to wear for this wedding, too?'

'White, of course, Lilli.' He sipped his champagne, surveying her over the rim of his glass. 'Or are you telling me you don't have the right to wear that colour?' he challenged tauntingly.

'You can ask that, after the other night?' she scoffed.

'Our night together?'

'Of course our night together! Or doesn't it count if the bridegroom was the lover?'

Patrick looked at her thoughtfully for several long seconds. 'I think I should make one thing plain, Lilli,' he finally said. 'My first marriage, after the initial honeymoon period, was a battleground. It's not an experience I care to repeat!'

'Then why choose to marry someone you don't love and who doesn't even pretend to love you?' Lilli asked sceptically.

'Respect, Lilli. I have respect for you, for the love and loyalty you've shown towards your father—'

'A love that gives you the leverage to pressurise me into marrying you!' she accused heatedly.

His facial muscles tightened. 'I believe we both said we would keep my business with your father out of this?'

'You don't honestly think I would give marrying you a second thought if it weren't for that, do you?' She shook her head scathingly.

'It wasn't mentioned in the proposal. And I don't believe it was mentioned in the acceptance?' He raised dark brows pointedly.

'It may not have been mentioned, but—'

'Let's leave it that way, hmm?' His voice was dangerously soft now.

Lilli surveyed him mutinously, silenced by the coldness in his voice. But he couldn't seriously expect her to act as if she were in love with him? That would be asking the impossible!

She drew in a ragged breath. 'Patrick—'

'Our food, Lilli.' He sat back as the avocado was placed in front of them.

This was ridiculous. They couldn't possibly discuss something as important as the rest of their lives over lunch, with the constant interruptions that entailed. How on earth did he think—?

'Try the avocado, Lilli,' Patrick encouraged gently. 'I think we might both feel a little more—comfortable, once we've eaten something.'

She very much doubted this man knew what it was like to feel uncomfortable. But he was probably right about the food settling her ragged nerves; she hadn't eaten anything at all today. The only problem with that was that her stomach was churning so much she wasn't sure she would keep the food inside her if she ate it!

'Try it, Lilli.' Patrick held a forkful of his own avocado temptingly in front of her mouth.

She gave him a startled glance, slightly alarmed by his close proximity. But the determined look in his eyes told her he wasn't about to move away until she took the avocado from the fork he held out.

'This is ridiculous,' she muttered as she moved slightly forward to take the food into her mouth. 'Anyone would think we were a couple really in love,' she added irritably before moving back from him, picking up her own fork to eat her meal.

'Better?' He nodded his satisfaction with her compliance.

She had to admit, inwardly, that the food was indeed excellent, and it wasn't choking her as she had thought it might—but Patrick treating her as a recalcitrant child was! 'Don't treat me like a six-year-old, Patrick—'

'Then don't act like one,' he came back swiftly. 'I certainly don't want a temperamental child for a wife! Think, Lilli,' he continued hardly. 'Your father—does he know you've come to accept my proposal…?'

She swallowed. 'Yes.'

'And?'

'And what?' She frowned her tension.

Patrick's mouth twisted mockingly. 'And he's ecstatic at your choice of husband?' he taunted.

She gave a snort. 'Don't be ridiculous—'

'Exactly,' Patrick acknowledged dryly. 'As Gerry is going to be overjoyed at my choice of wife!'

Lilli stiffened. 'I'm really not interested in how your sister feels about me.'

'And your father's approval is of little importance to me, either,' he returned. 'But, if I'm correct in my assumption concerning your reasons for accepting my proposal, after all, then it's primarily to help your father, but also because once your father prosecutes Brewster the man's private life is bound to become public knowledge. But you will obviously have caught a much bigger fish on your marital hook, and so have no fear of becoming the object of the scorn or gossip that could ensue. Stop me if I'm wrong—'

'You know you aren't!' she snapped resentfully; did this man know everything? 'But exactly where is all this leading to?' she prompted impatiently.

'This is leading to the fact…' he deliberately held

another morsel of avocado temptingly in front of her, leaning intimately forward as he did so '…that our engagement, and subsequent marriage, will be more believable to everyone, including your father and my sister, if it seems that we are genuinely in love with each other.'

Lilli stared at him as if he had gone insane—because at that moment it seemed he actually might be! No one could possibly believe the two of them really loved each other, least of all her father.

'Without that belief, Lilli,' Patrick continued, 'everyone will know the whole thing is a sham—and you will end up looking more foolish than if this whole thing had become public months ago!'

He was right… Once again he was right! Why hadn't she thought of that? Because she hadn't been thinking at all, only feeling, and this marriage to Patrick had seemed to solve everything.

She swallowed hard. 'What do you suggest?'

His mouth quirked. 'That you eat this avocado; it's in danger of falling off my fork!'

She was in danger of being at the centre of the biggest social farce to become public in years!

She ate the avocado, knowing as she did so exactly what she was committing herself to. The avocado, for all Patrick was making light of it, represented something so much more than a morsel of food. It took all of her will-power to chew it and actually swallow it down.

Patrick touched her cheek gently. 'I'm willing to give this a try if you are, Lilli.'

What choice did she have? She wanted her father to do something about the money that had been taken from his company, and for that to happen the whole thing had to become public. And it would only work if she and Patrick had a believable relationship.

She drew in a ragged breath. 'I'm not sure I can,' she told him honestly.

'I'll try and make it easy for you.' He leant forward and brushed his lips against hers. 'There, that wasn't so difficult, was it?'

He was so close, his breath was lightly ruffling the hair at her temples. So close she could see the dark flecks of colour in his grey eyes. So close she could smell the elusiveness of his aftershave. So close she couldn't stop the slight trembling of her knees, the tight feeling in her chest, the disruption of her breathing.

'Not so difficult,' she admitted gruffly.

'And do you agree it will be better than people thinking we hardly know each other?' he teased.

That was the last thing she wanted! 'I agree.'

'The wedding will be next week—I thought a three out of three in the agreeing department was expecting a bit much!' He grinned as she looked panicked at the suggestion. 'It will fit in with the idea of a whirlwind romance,' he explained. 'Everyone loves a romance, Lilli—especially if it appears a love-match!'

Her stomach had given a sickening lurch at the very thought of being married to this man in only a matter of days. She swallowed hard. 'That sounds—reasonable.' What difference did it make? Patrick intended them to be married, had no intention of her dragging out their engagement in the hope she might never need to tie the knot. So she might as well get on with it!

He sat back so that their plates could be taken away—and allowed Lilli to breathe again!

This man was going to be her husband. They would live together. Patrick would come to know her body more intimately than she knew it herself. He—

She was panicking again! Take each step as it comes!

she told herself. If she looked at the whole thing she would become hysterical. Yes, that was it; she just had to take each day, each step, as it arrived. She would be fine. After all—

'Make sure you have a white dress for the wedding, Lilli.' Patrick interrupted her thoughts. 'I'm aware you've been desperately trying to forget the night we spent together, but—'

'Please,' she hastily cut in. 'That night was completely out of character. I have never done anything like that before, and—'

'And you haven't done anything like that now, either, Lilli,' Patrick dismissed mockingly.

'How can you possibly say that?' She shook her head in self-disgust. 'I—'

'You were very beautiful that night, Lilli, very alluring, and I have to admit that, for the first time in years, I was physically interested. And I would probably have been only too happy to enjoy all the pleasure you were so obviously promising. Unfortunately—' he shook his head dramatically '—the champagne and wine took their toll on you, and you fell asleep on the bed in the hotel while I was in the bathroom.'

Lilli stared at him, not sure she was hearing him correctly.

He laughed softly at her stunned expression. 'I can see you're having trouble believing me. But I can assure you it's the truth.'

'But I—I was undressed,' she protested disbelievingly. She could clearly remember her embarrassment the next morning when she'd woken up to find she was only wearing her lace panties!

He nodded. 'You most certainly were. And you have a very beautiful body. But the only reason I know that, the reason you were undressed, is because I couldn't let you spoil that beautiful gown you were wearing. You looked lovely in it, and I'd like to see you in it again one day. You were asleep, so I simply took the dress off you and settled you more comfortably beneath the bed-clothes.'

'And you—where did you sleep?' She was still reeling from the shock of realising she hadn't made love with this man at all.

But that memory flashback she had had…? She couldn't have dreamt being in his arms, being kissed by him, caressed by him—could she?

Patrick smiled. 'There was only the one double bed in the bedroom, Lilli, and I have to admit I'm not that much of a gentleman; I slept beside you, of course. And very cuddly you were too. In fact, you became quite charmingly friendly at about four o'clock in the morn-ing,' he added wistfully. 'But there was no way I could make love to a woman who was too much asleep still to know where she was, let alone who she was with—'

'Stop it!' she cut in sharply. 'What you're saying is incredible.' She shook her head dazedly. 'How do I know you're telling the truth?' She frowned her uncer-tainty.

He gestured carelessly. 'What reason do I have to lie? It wouldn't do my reputation any good at all if it became public knowledge that I'd spent the whole night in bed with you and didn't even attempt to make love to you! Although, in retrospect, I can't say I'm disappointed by the fact. Unless I'm very much mistaken,' he continued at her questioning look, 'you have more right than most to wear white on your wedding day. And our wedding night will be the first time you've ever made love with any man. I feel very privileged that I'm going to be that man,' he added huskily.

This was incredible. Unbelievable…! But, as Patrick had so rightly pointed out, what reason could he possibly have for lying about it?

But until just now he had let her continue to think— Knew what she had believed had happened between them, and he hadn't disabused her of that belief.

She really had thought she had made love with this man two nights ago, had had no reason to think otherwise. And Patrick had perpetuated that belief with his remarks after that night, had known how she hated the idea of having gone to bed with him in that reckless way. He had continued to let her believe it…

Because it suited him to. Because he had enjoyed watching her discomfort over an incident she would rather forget had happened.

And she had just agreed to marry this man, to live with him, to bear his children. All four of them!

She had, she now realised, made a pact with the devil himself!

CHAPTER SEVEN

'I BELIEVE we have guests coming to dinner this evening?' Lilli's father addressed her stiffly when he came in from his office a little after six; Lilli was in the day-room pretending to be interested in a magazine.

Pretending, because she couldn't really concentrate on anything at the moment!

How she had got through the rest of the lunch with Patrick, she had no idea. She vaguely remembered him talking about trivial things through the rest of their meal, seeming unconcerned with her monosyllabic answers, putting her in a taxi at two forty-five, so that he could go to his meeting with her father. His parting comment, she now remembered, had been something about them dining together this evening, so that her father could get used to the idea of him as a son-in-law.

But, however long his meeting with her father had taken, Patrick had somehow also found the time to call a prestigious newspaper and have notice of their forth-coming marriage put in the classifieds!

Lilli knew all about this because a reporter from the newspaper had telephoned her here just over an hour ago wanting further information on their whirlwind romance. Lilli's answer to this had been, 'No comment.' But not ten minutes later Sally had also telephoned to find out if it was true; it seemed a friend of a friend also worked on the newspaper, and, knowing Sally was a friend of Lilli's, had telephoned her for information. Which Sally couldn't give, thank goodness—because she didn't know any of the details of Lilli's relationship with Patrick!

There was no doubt that Patrick was going to give her no chance for second thoughts, was making this marriage a foregone conclusion by publicly announcing it.

Not that Lilli could have had second thoughts even if she had wanted to. But, Patrick being Patrick, he had made sure that she couldn't, not without causing even more publicity for herself.

She looked up at her father with dull green eyes, noting how strained he looked, matching her own dark mood of despair. 'Guest,' she corrected flatly.

'Guests,' her father insisted as he came further into the room, moving to the tray of drinks on the side table, pouring himself a liberal amount of whisky, swallowing half of the liquid down in one needy gulp. 'Patrick is bringing Gerry with him,' he told Lilli abruptly before swallowing the remaining contents of the glass he held.

This information brought Lilli out of her mood of despondency, her eyes now sparkling angrily. 'He is not bringing that woman to this house,' she stated furiously. 'I told him earlier exactly how I felt about his sister. He knows that I—'

'Lilli, Gerry isn't only Patrick's sister, she's the woman in my life,' her father cut in carefully. 'And while you might have strong feelings about that—in fact, I'm sure you do!—I would rather not hear them.'

'But—'

'I mean it, Lilli,' he told her in a voice that brooked no further argument. 'Now, as my banker, Patrick has advised that I go ahead with bringing a case against Andy for embezzlement,' he continued without a pause. 'He also told me the two of you are to be married before Christmas!'

Lilli's anger against Geraldine Simms left her so suddenly she felt like a deflated balloon. 'If that's what Patrick says, then it must be true,' she told him dryly.

'Lilli—'

'It's what I want, Daddy.' She stood up forcefully, moving restlessly about the room, tidying objects that didn't really need tidying.

'Do you also want to go and live in New York?' he asked.

'New York…?' Lilli stopped her restless movements, staring at her father. 'Did you say New York?'

Her father nodded. 'It's where Patrick is based. His business in England is almost concluded,' he added bitterly. 'He'll be returning to New York in the New Year. And, as his wife, you will go with him.'

She had to admit, she hadn't given much thought to where they would live after their wedding; she was still having trouble coming to terms with the idea of marrying Patrick at all! But New York…! She had completely forgotten he was based in America…

'Lilli, you haven't really thought this thing through at all,' her father sighed as he saw her confused expression. 'You don't even know anyone in New York.'

Except Patrick…

'You'll be all alone over there,' her father continued quietly.

Except for Patrick…

'There will be no one there to love and take care of you,' her father added in a wavering voice.

Except Patrick…!

This was turning out to be worse than she had realised. Her father was right; she hadn't really thought it through at all, had just been looking for a solution to their immediate problems. The long term was something she hadn't really considered.

'Did Patrick tell you we would be going to New York?' she enquired.

'No, it was Gerry who thought of it—I called in to see her on my way home from the office,' he explained defensively as Lilli looked troubled.

Which explained why he was home later than usual. Geraldine had really got her claws into him, hadn't she?

'She's as worried as I am about your marriage to Patrick,' her father told her harshly.

Lilli stiffened. 'Well, thank her for her concern, but I'm quite capable of making my own decisions—and living with the consequences of them, even a move to New York.' She walked angrily to the door, wrenching it open. 'I think you underestimate my ability to adapt to living in New York. I'm sure I'll have a wonderful time. Now, if you'll excuse me, I have to go and change for dinner.' She closed the door firmly behind her.

How dared her father discuss her with that woman? How dared he?

'You look very beautiful,' Patrick told her huskily.

He had arrived at the house with his sister only minutes ago, the four of them in the sitting-room, Lilli's father busy with the dispensing of drinks, the beautiful Gerry already at his side. There was no doubt the other woman *was* beautiful, or that Lilli's father obviously thought so too—he seemed to have come quite boyishly alive in her company. Lilli hated even seeing the two of them together!

'Thank you.' She distantly accepted the compliment, very aware of the other couple in the room.

'As usual,' Patrick added softly.

Lilli turned to look at him, a contemptuous movement to her lips. 'You don't have to keep this up when it's just the two of us, Patrick!'

'But it isn't just the two of us.' He looked pointedly across the room at her father and his sister.

She drew in a ragged breath. 'My father would see straight through any effort on my part to pretend I'm in love with you.'

'Then I would advise you to try a little harder,' Patrick told her hardly. 'Unless you want to cause him even more grief! Andy Brewster was *your* fiancé, Lilli,' he callously reminded her.

As if to confirm Patrick's words, her father glanced worriedly across at the two of them, Lilli forcing a re-assuring smile before turning back to Patrick. 'You don't play fair,' she told him in a muted voice.

'I don't "play" at all, Lilli,' he corrected her harshly. 'You should have realised that by now!'

Her eyes flashed her resentment. 'Is that the reason you've already sent the announcement of our marriage to that newspaper?'

Patrick didn't seem at all surprised at her accusation. 'I'm not even going to ask how you know about that; the London gossip grapevine must be one of the busiest in the world! But talking of our marriage...I have a present for you,' he tacked on gently.

She didn't want presents from him; she wished she didn't want anything at all from him!

'Don't look so alarmed, Lilli.' He pretended to chide her. 'This is perfectly in keeping with our new relationship. Ah, Richard, perfectly on cue with the champagne,' he greeted the other man as he held out the two glasses of bubbly pink liquid. 'I was just about to give Lilli her engagement ring.'

An engagement ring! There had been no mention of
an engagement, only the wedding. She couldn't—

'We can change it if you don't like it, Lilli,' Patrick
assured her as he took the small blue ring-box from his
jacket pocket, flicking open the lid to show her the contents.

If she didn't like it! How could any woman not like
such a ring? It was beautiful, the hugest emerald Lilli
had ever seen surrounded by twelve flawless small diamonds.

Lilli had never seen a ring like it before, let alone
been offered such a beautiful piece of jewellery; the ring
Andy had given her on their engagement, a ring she had
discarded to the back of a drawer when their engagement
had ended, had been a diamond solitaire, delicate, un-
obtrusive. Patrick was intent on making a statement with
this magnificent emerald and diamond ring. Of owner-
ship. 'Oh, Patrick,' Gerry breathed in an awestruck
voice. 'It's absolutely beautiful!'

He replied ruefully, 'I believe that should be Lilli's
line.'

Maybe it would be—if she could actually speak. But
all she could do was stare at the ring. It was too much.
Just too much. It must have cost a small fortune!

She had been brought up within a well-off family,
could never remember being denied anything she had
ever wanted, but this ring, and what it must have cost,
had suddenly brought home to her exactly how wealthy
Patrick was. Such wealth was, in its own way, quite
frightening. And she was about to marry into it!

'You don't like it,' Patrick said, his gaze narrowed on
the sudden paleness of her face.

She moistened dry lips. 'It isn't that...'

'Richard, you mentioned showing me the Turner you have in the dining-room?' Geraldine prompted.

Lilli looked sharply at the other woman, her mouth tightening at the obvious ease of the relationship between this handsome woman and her own father. 'There's no need to leave Patrick and I alone, Geraldine,' she announced. 'We aren't about to have an argument.'

She had to admit, for a few minutes she had been thrown totally by the ring Patrick had bought for her, but that one glance at how close Geraldine was standing to her father was enough to shake her out of that. Yes, the ring was beautiful. Yes, it had cost a small fortune. But then, Patrick Devlin wouldn't expect his future wife to wear anything but the best. The very best. The ring wasn't actually for her, it was for Patrick Devlin's fiancée—who just happened to be her. Once she had all that sorted out in her mind, there was no problem.

'Of course I like it, Patrick,' she assured him lightly. 'Any woman would,' she added with cool dismissal.

His eyes glittered dangerously. 'I'm not interested in "any woman's" opinion, Lilli,' he rasped. 'I wanted *you* to like it. I should obviously have let you choose it yourself.' He snapped the ring-box shut. 'We'll go out tomorrow and look at some others—'

'You chose this ring, Patrick.' She grasped his wrist to stop him putting the blue velvet box back in his pocket.

He looked down at the paleness of her slender fingers against his much darker skin, before slowly bringing his gaze back to her face.

Lilli withstood his probing assessment of her unflinchingly—although she couldn't say she wasn't relieved when he finally smiled. She couldn't have held his gaze for much longer, would have had to look away. 'The ring, Patrick,' she reminded him chokily.

'Only if you're sure it's what you want.' His smile had gone again now; that harshness was back in his face.

'I'm sure.' There was a challenge in her voice, and she slowly released his wrist, leaving the next move to him.

'Well, I'm not sure I am,' her father asserted. 'This whole thing is ridiculous—'

'The ring is absolutely gorgeous, Daddy.' Lilli smoothly stopped what she was sure was going to be her father's tirade.

'Lilli, you have no idea what you're doing,' he told her exasperatedly. 'You don't have to do—'

'Daddy!' She silenced him. 'Let's drink our champagne. After all, this is supposed to be a celebration.'

'I see nothing to celebrate!' Her father slammed down the glasses he had been holding for them. 'In fact—'

'Richard, I really would like to see that Turner.' Geraldine was the one to interrupt this time, taking a determined hold of his arm.

For long moments it looked as if Lilli's father would refuse, and then he acquiesced with an abrupt nod of his head, his back rigid as he and Geraldine left the room.

'I gather he doesn't approve of your choice of husband?' Patrick drawled softly as he watched the other man depart.

Lilli looked at him with flashing green eyes. 'Did you honestly expect him to?'

Patrick shrugged. 'I think he could be a little more understanding of what you're doing—'

'Understanding!' she echoed scathingly. 'I think he's too angry and upset at the moment to understand anything!'

'I did warn you he would need convincing this marriage was something you really want.'

'And just how am I supposed to do that?' she scorned. 'You can't be trusted, Patrick. You totally deceived me about that night we spent together—'

'That really rankles, doesn't it?' he mocked.

'Of course it rankles!' She had thought of little else since parting from him this afternoon. 'You—'

'Would you rather we had spent the whole night making mad, passionate love to each other?' he taunted.

'Of course not!' Her cheeks went hot with embarrassment just at the thought of it.

'Of course not,' he mimicked softly, suddenly very close. 'Lilli, your first time should be gentle and sensitive. Special. Not a night you don't even remember!'

She swallowed hard, moved, in spite of herself, by the seduction in his voice. 'You still lied to me—'

'When I said you were a ten?' he supplied.

Her blushed deepened. 'About the whole thing! You—'

'I never lied, Lilli,' he assured her. 'I never lie. Remember that,' he added. 'Because I expect the same honesty from the people I deal with.'

Especially wives! God, Sanchia had to have been incredibly brave—or incredibly stupid!—to have deceived this man.

'You're beautiful, Lilli.' He touched her cheek gently, his fingers trailing lightly down her throat to the milky softness of her slightly exposed breasts in the close-fitting black dress she wore. 'You respond to my lightest touch,' he murmured in satisfaction as she trembled. 'I know we're going to be physically compatible.'

Her skin felt on fire where his fingers had caressed. 'A ten...' she murmured weakly.

'Perfect,' he corrected her firmly. 'I only made that remark that day because I was damned angry with you and what I thought you had done. I don't give scores on sexual performance, Lilli. I'm sure I made it plain to you there haven't been any women since I parted from Sanchia five years ago?'

'You said as much, yes…'

'If I said it, then it's the truth,' he bit out harshly.

'Patrick Devlin doesn't lie!'

'You know, Lilli,' he said with pleasant mildness, 'I'm getting a little tired of having to deal with your temper—'

'I never knew I had one until I met you!' she returned heatedly.

'You mean no one ever said no to you until me,' he derided.

He was mocking her again now. And that just made her more angry than ever!

She looked at him defiantly. 'I don't want to live in New York after we're married,' she stated—and then wondered where on earth it had come from. She hadn't meant to say that in anger at all, had intended discussing it with him calmly and reasonably. The problem with that was, she never felt calm and reasonable when she was with him!

'I don't think it's right to discuss that now, Lilli,' he dismissed predictably. 'Stop fighting me over everything, woman,' he ordered as he pulled her into his arms. 'And then maybe we can both start enjoying this!'

Enjoy being with this man? Enjoy being held by him? Enjoy being kissed by him!

Because he was kissing her. Again. And, as on those other occasions when he had kissed her, her body suddenly felt like liquid fire, her legs turning to jelly, so that she clung to his shoulders as the kiss deepened, Patrick's lips moving erotically against hers, his tongue moving lightly over the sensitivity of her inner lip. Lilli moaned low in her throat as he did so.

'Good God…!'

It was her father's shocked outburst that intruded into the complete intimacy of the moment, and it was with some reluctance that Lilli dragged her mouth away from Patrick's, turning slowly to look dazedly in her father's direction.

'Don't look so shocked, Richard.' Patrick was the one to break the awkward silence. 'I realise you have some strange ideas about the reason Lilli and I are to be married, but as you've just witnessed—only too fully!—one of those reasons is that we are very attracted to each other. Haven't you ever heard of ''love at first night''?'

Lilli ignored the pun, recovering her senses a lot slower than Patrick had. But with their return came the realisation that Patrick must have heard the other couple's impending return—and this show of passion had been all for their benefit, so that Geraldine and her father would believe the two of them were seriously in love!

If her father's nonplussed expression was anything to go by, it had succeeded! Why shouldn't it have done? Lilli was able to visualise all too easily—to her acute discomfort!—exactly the scene of intimacy her father and Geraldine had just walked in on. She had obviously been a more than willing recipient of Patrick's kisses and caresses!

'It happens this way sometimes, Richard,' Patrick continued, his arm like a steel band about Lilli's waist as he secured her to his side. 'Now that the two of you are back, we can put on Lilli's ring and drink the champagne.'

Lilli watched in a dreamlike state as Patrick slid the ring onto her finger, all the time having the feeling that, once it was on, her fate was sealed.

Who was she trying to fool? Her fate had been sealed from the moment she first met Patrick Devlin.

And as she watched the ring being put on her finger, weighed down by the emerald and diamonds, she knew it was now too late to turn back.

Too late for all of them…

CHAPTER EIGHT

'HOLD still, Lilli, or we'll never get these flowers straight in your hair,' Sally chided lightly.

Lilli stared at her own reflection in the mirror. Hardly the picture of the ecstatic bride on her wedding day!

Oh, the trappings were all there—the white dress, her hair in long curls down her spine, the veil waiting on the back of the chair to be put over the flowers Sally was now entwining in her dark curls.

Sally, the friend she had chosen as her attendant. Sally, who had been absolutely astonished to discover the 'gorgeous man', from the night of Gerry Simms' party, was in fact Lilli's father.

If Lilli had been in the mood for humour, she would have found Sally's incredulity funny. It was definitely the first time she had seen her friend lost for words!

'There.' Sally stood back now to admire her handi-work. 'You look absolutely beautiful, Lilli. Breath-taking!'

She did. The white satin dress and long veil made her look like something from a fairy tale.

Except she wasn't marrying Prince Charming.

She was marrying Patrick Devlin.

Her heart still sank just at the thought of being his wife. It had not been an easy week; Patrick had been at the house constantly as hurried arrangements were made for their wedding. Lilli had given in over everything— the timing of the wedding, the white dress, the private reception later today for family and a few close friends, even the choosing of identical wedding rings.

The one thing she hadn't agreed to—though her father was her choice of witness and Gerry was Patrick's—was Gerry helping her get ready for the wedding. Her mother should have been the one here with her, and as her father's mistress Gerry Simms did not fit the bill! Hence Sally's presence instead.

Thirty more minutes and Lilli and Patrick would be husband and wife. She would be Mrs Patrick Devlin.

As far as Sally—and most of London, it seemed!—was concerned, she should be the happiest woman in the world at this moment.

Happy! She was far from being that. She was going to be married to Patrick, his to do with whatever and whenever he wished. Tonight, they would make love.

God, how she wished she could claim the shiver that ran down her spine at the mere thought of it was caused by revulsion, but she knew in her heart of hearts that it wasn't. The thought of making love with Patrick, of the two of them naked in bed together, entwined in each other's arms, certainly made her quiver—but with anticipation!

Because something else had been happening during the last few days, with Patrick constantly teasing her, bullying her a little, kissing her—oh, yes, the kissing hadn't stopped. In fact, he seemed to take delight in kissing her and touching her whenever the opportunity arose for him to do so. And there seemed to be all too many of those!

To her dismay, Lilli found she was falling in love with him… She had made a pact with the devil—and, to her horror, had found she was falling in love with him!

'What is it, Lilli?' Sally seemed concerned.

From a very long way away, it seemed, Lilli looked up at her dazedly.

'You've gone as white as those tea-roses in your hair,' Sally explained anxiously. 'Lilli, I— Please don't think I'm intruding,' she continued hurriedly, lightly touching Lilli's arm, 'but are you sure you aren't rushing this? I mean, you and Patrick haven't known each other that long, and— Well, he was so very much in love with Sanchia.' She shook her head, looking very good herself in a sleek red suit, blonde hair loose about her slender shoulders. 'I wouldn't want you to be hurt again,' she added worriedly. 'Andy was such a swine to walk out on you the way he did, and I—'

'I don't want to talk about Andy,' Lilli interjected; without Andy's involvement in her family, today wouldn't be happening at all! 'And I appreciate your concern, Sally,' she went on with a softening of her voice, genuinely fond of the other woman, despite the penchant she had for gossiping. 'But I can assure you I do know what I'm doing.'

How could she not know? Patrick had made it more than obvious that, while they would have a full marriage, and hopefully several children, love would never come into it.

That was what bothered her about this marriage. She was falling in love with a man who had told her quite bluntly he would never feel the same way about her. Courtesy of Sanchia. Well, he might have loved her very much, but the collapse of that marriage, in the way that it had, meant he would never love again. Legacy of Sanchia.

Lilli hated Patrick's first wife, and she had never even met her!

And how was she going to survive in a marriage without love, loving her husband, but never being loved by him in return?

Somehow this was worse than the completely loveless marriage she had initially anticipated.

So very much worse!

So, yes, she knew what she was doing, but she had no choice in the matter; the wedding was mere minutes away now instead of days—days that had flown by all too swiftly!—and, more importantly, her father's lawyers had already started work on bringing a case against Andy. In fact, he might already be aware of it!

Sally sat down, leaning forward conspiratorially. 'Well, Patrick is an absolutely—'

'Gorgeous man,' Lilli finished for her, smiling teasingly. 'I never realised before, Sally, the fascination you have for gorgeous men!' She stood up to pick up her veil, placing the circle of flowers on top of her shining hair, studying her reflection in the mirror. The 'sacrificial lamb' was well and truly ready for the altar!

'You're referring to your father, of course.' Sally ruefully accepted her teasing. 'I still can't believe he's the man from the party. When I arrived here the other day to find the two of you together in the sitting-room, I must admit that my first thought was you were being unfaithful to Patrick even before the wedding!' She gave a grimace. 'Do you think he's serious about Gerry? Or do I actually stand a chance where he's concerned?' She looked questioningly at Lilli.

'He isn't serious about Gerry,' Lilli replied defensively, her eyes flashing deeply green at the mere suggestion of it.

'So would you mind if I—?'

'Be my guest,' she invited, although the fact that her own father suddenly seemed very sought after, by beautiful young women, was still a rather strange concept for her to accept. Admittedly, he was only in his mid-forties, but she had somehow never thought of him in that light before. 'But for the record, Sally,' she went on, 'I don't intend ever to be unfaithful to Patrick—before or after the wedding!'

'Fine,' Sally accepted, grimacing at Lilli's vehemence.

'Sally…' Lilli remonstrated firmly.

Her friend held her hands up defensively. 'I believe you—okay?'

Lilli laughed. 'Time will tell. In the meantime, I think we have a wedding to go to!'

'Oh, gosh, yes.' Sally stood up hurriedly. 'It may be traditional for the bride to be late, but in this case I'm not so sure the groom wouldn't come looking for you! I'll get off now, and see you at the registry office.' She gave Lilli a reassuring hug before leaving.

Amazingly Lilli's conversation with Sally had lifted her feelings somewhat, and she was smiling as she descended the wide staircase, her smile widening warmly as she saw her father standing at the bottom waiting for her, looking especially handsome today in his grey morning suit.

'Daddy, you look magnificent,' she praised glowingly as she reached him.

'*I* look—!' There were tears in his eyes as he looked down at her. 'Lilli, you look beautiful. So like your mother did at this age. I wish she could have been here to see you—'

'Not now, Daddy,' she dismissed briskly; talking about her mother was the one thing she couldn't cope with today, of all days. It was going to be difficult enough to get through anyway, without thoughts of her mother. Besides, she very much doubted this marriage was what her mother would have wished for her. It wouldn't do to dwell on that thought... 'Patrick will be becoming impatient,' she said brightly.

'Talking of Patrick...' Her father frowned, turning to the table that stood in the centre of the reception area, picking up a flat blue velvet box. 'He sent this for you earlier.' Her father snapped open the lid of the box, the two of them gasping as he revealed the most amazing necklace Lilli had ever seen. The emerald and diamond droplet in the centre of the delicate gold chain was an exact match for the engagement ring Lilli had transferred to her right hand for the marriage ceremony...

Her hand trembled slightly as she picked up the card that lay in the circle of gold, recognising the large scrawling handwriting as Patrick's before she even read the words written there. His cryptic sense of humour was all too apparent in the message.

Something new, Lilli—and if your eyes had been blue instead of green it could have been something blue too! Please wear it for me today.

Yours, Patrick.

'Lilli...!' her father breathed dazedly, still staring at the perfection of the necklace.

She swallowed hard, carefully replacing the card in the box before releasing the necklace and holding it out to her father. 'Would you help me put it on, Daddy?' She turned around, carefully lifting up her hair so that he could secure the catch. 'We'll have to hurry, Daddy,' she encouraged as he made no effort to do so. 'The car is waiting outside.'

'I still can't believe—Lilli, you're my little girl, and—'

'Please, Daddy.' Her own voice quivered with emotion. 'Put the necklace on and let's just go!' Before she totally destroyed the work of the last hour and began to cry.

He did so with slightly shaking fingers, careful not to ruffle her hair. 'Absolutely incredible,' her father said huskily as he stepped back to look at her.

Lilli gave a tight smile, not bothering to glance in the hall mirror as they walked out to the car. 'Only the best for Patrick. He would hardly give his future wife anything less.'

'I was referring to you, not the necklace,' her father gently rebuked. 'But then, you are the best; those jewels only enhance what is already perfection.'

She laughed. 'I think you may be slightly biased, Daddy!'

'I think Patrick Devlin is a very lucky man,' he stated. 'Take a deep breath before we go outside, Lilli,' he warned as he held her arm. 'I think half the world's press is gathered outside to snap a photograph of Patrick Devlin's bride!'

Which certainly wasn't an understatement!

A barrage of flashing cameras and intrusive microphones were pointed at the two of them as soon as they stepped outside into what was a crisply cold but bright, sunny December day. Questions were flung at them thick and fast, questions Lilli chose to ignore as she and her father hurried to the waiting car. The press had been hounding her continuously since the announcement of the wedding had appeared in the newspaper, and the wedding day itself had been sure to engender this excess of interest.

It was all so ridiculous to Lilli. Didn't these people have a war or something to write about and fill their newspapers with? This interest in what was, after all, just another society wedding, albeit with one of the principal players possibly being one of the richest men in England, seemed rather obscene to Lilli, and—

She was half in the car and half out of it when, her face paling, she caught sight of a familiar face amongst the crowd.

Andy…

She shook her head in denial of her imaginings. It couldn't have been Andy. Not here; this was the last place he would ever be seen. The only place she *wanted* to see him was in a courtroom, in the dock!

'Lilli…? Her father was waiting to get into the car beside her. 'What is it?' He saw her ashen cheeks.

'Nothing.' She turned to give him a glowing smile, the cameras clicking anew at what she supposed must look like the blushing bride on her way to her wedding. 'We'll be late if we don't go now,' she encouraged.

Her father looked as if he was about to add something to that, but at her determined expression he seemed to change his mind.

She had made her decision last week; there would be no last-minute nerves, no change of plan. That glimpse of someone she had thought looked a little like Andy had shaken her a little, but that was all…

'If I don't have the chance to tell you so again, you look absolutely beautiful,' Patrick whispered to her as they awaited the arrival of their guests to the private reception her father had organised at the Bennett Hotel.

Lilli barely glanced at him. She was almost afraid to. Half an hour ago she had married this man, was now his wife—and she had never been so scared of anything in her life before! In fact, she couldn't ever remember feeling scared before at all.

But Patrick had seemed like a remote stranger when they'd met at the registry office, making Lilli all too aware that that was exactly what he was!

Brides who had known their groom for years, and were secure in mutually expressed love, still had wedding-day nerves over the rightness of what they were doing; how much deeper, in the circumstances, was her own trepidation?

Just looking at the man who was now her husband was part of her panic. How on earth had she ever thought she could spend the rest of her life with this man? He was as good-looking as the devil, cool as ice, didn't love her, and had assured her he never would. God, this was—

'Gerry, when our guests arrive, greet them for us and assure them we will be with them shortly.' Patrick spoke quietly to his sister even as he grasped Lilli's arm.

Lilli's father frowned at him; the four of them had been the first to arrive at the reception room. 'Where are the two of you going?'

Patrick's hand was firm on Lilli's elbow as he led her away. 'Upstairs to our suite so that I can kiss my bride in private,' he told the other man grimly.

'But—'

'Let them go, Richard,' Gerry advised, her hand resting gently on his arm.

Lilli was shaking so badly now she could barely walk, the thought of actually being alone with Patrick sending her into a complete panic. This was real. Far, far too real, as the warmth of Patrick's guiding hand on her arm told her all too forcefully. It had seemed such a simple decision to make—the only decision she could make in the circumstances!—but the reality of it was all too much. She wanted to scream. Run away. To shout—

'Not here,' Patrick said suddenly, moving swiftly to swing her up into his arms.

Much to the interest of all the other hotel guests who stood watching them, he strode purposefully through the lobby to the lifts, several indulgent smiles directed their way as people observed their hurried departure. It didn't need two guesses to know what these people were thinking. But they were wrong! So very wrong...

Patrick, literally kicked open the door to the suite he had arranged for them to stay in tonight, setting Lilli down once they were safely inside. She looked up at him with widely apprehensive eyes.

'*Now* you can scream,' he encouraged indulgently.

Her breath left her with a shaky sigh. 'It was that obvious?'

'Only to me,' he assured her. 'I'm only surprised this didn't happen earlier. You've been too controlled this last week—'

'But I am controlled.' She swung impatiently away from him, angry with herself because she didn't seem able to stop shaking. 'I'm just being very stupid now,' she confessed self-disgustedly.

'You're being a twenty-one-year-old young lady who just made probably the biggest decision of her entire life.' Patrick's hands gently squeezed her shoulders as he turned her to face him. 'But I promise you I'll treat you well. That I'll try to curb this urge I have to dominate. I will honour and cherish you,' he added gruffly.

But he wouldn't love her; that omission was all too apparent to Lilli.

'But it isn't that, is it…?' Patrick said slowly, studying her closely. 'Tell me what it is, Lilli?'

She couldn't possibly tell him how she felt, that as she'd looked at him earlier as they'd made their wedding vows to each other she had known that she, at least, meant every word. She wasn't falling in love with him— she had already done so!

There was absolutely no doubt in her mind that she loved Patrick. It was nothing like what she had felt for Andy, was so much more intense, so— Oh, God, Andy… Had it been him she had seen earlier, or just someone that looked very like him?

Patrick shook her gently as she frowned. 'What is it, Lilli?' There was an edge of urgency to his voice now.

'I thought— You're going to think I'm imagining things now. But I—I thought I saw Andy outside the house earlier.' She frowned again up at Patrick as he released her abruptly, his expression serious now. 'I told you it was stupid—'

'Not at all,' Patrick barked. 'I have it on good authority that Brewster is back in London.'

She swallowed hard. 'He is?' She suddenly felt very sick. After what Andy had done to her father, and to her, she had no wish for him ever to come near her again. But with Patrick's confirmation that he was in London she was even more convinced that it had been Andy she'd seen outside the house…

Why? What had he been doing there? What had he hoped to achieve by being outside her father's house on her wedding day to another man?

'It's a little late for second thoughts, Lilli.' Patrick was watching her closely. 'You're my wife now.'

With all that entailed. He owned her now; it was there in every arrogant inch of his tensely held body. Minutes ago, his gentleness and understanding drawing her close to him, she had almost been tempted to tell him how stupid she had been, that she was in love with him! Thank God she hadn't. She was a Devlin possession, a beautiful trophy to display on his arm, a wife with none of the complications of love involved.

She nodded in cool agreement. 'Our guests will have arrived downstairs.'

'You feel up to meeting them now?'

'Don't worry, Patrick, I won't embarrass you. My nerves simply got the better of me for a moment. It won't happen again.'

'No,' Patrick finally said slowly. 'I don't believe it will.'

Regret…? Or perhaps she had just imagined that particular emotion in his voice; the last thing he wanted was an emotional child for a wife. Her loss of control wouldn't happen again. After all, he had just assured her he would treat her well! He couldn't possibly realise that, loving him as she did, there were cruel things he could do to her…

And he must never know!

'We made a bargain, Patrick,' she told him distantly. 'And, like you, I never break my word once it's given.'

His expression hardened. 'I'm glad to hear it. Now, as you've already pointed out, our guests will be waiting.' He indicated she should precede him out of the suite, walking this time; the two of them were physically apart as well as emotionally.

That moment of gentleness and understanding was well and truly over, and for the next three hours Lilli didn't have the time even to think, concentrating on their guests, portraying the image that she and Patrick were a golden couple. There was no doubting they succeeded;

family and friends smiled at them indulgently every time Lilli glanced around the large table where they all sat eating their meal. No doubt the few members of her family present thought she was very fortunate to have married someone as eligible as Patrick, especially after the 'Andy incident', as most of them referred to her previous engagement. Once the embezzlement story hit the headlines, perhaps some of them would draw their own conclusions, but for the moment everyone was obviously enjoying themselves.

Except, Lilli noticed, the late arrival standing in the doorway looking at the gathering with contemptuous blue eyes...

She didn't recognise the woman, so she could only assume she was a guest of Patrick's. A very beautiful guest, Lilli acknowledged with a stab of jealousy. Tall and blonde, with ice-blue eyes, she stood almost six feet tall, with the slender elegance of a model about to make an entrance onto the catwalk.

That icy blue gaze met Lilli's puzzled one, the woman's red pouting mouth twisting contemptuously as her hard eyes swept critically over Lilli—and obviously found her wanting—before passing on to Patrick. Now the blue eyes weren't so icy; in fact, they became positively heated, seeming to devour him at a glance!

Lilli felt herself bridle indignantly. How dared this woman—whoever she was—come here and look at her husband in that way? Patrick had told her, several times, that there had been no women in his life since his marriage ended, but the way this woman was looking at him seemed to tell a very different story!

Lilli's indignation rose. If she belonged to Patrick now, then he also belonged to her, and women from his past had no place at their wedding reception.

She turned to him sharply. 'Patrick—'

'My God…!' he exclaimed even as she spoke, the intensity of the blonde woman's stare somehow seeming to have made him aware of her presence in the doorway, his face set grimly, a nerve pulsing in his jaw. 'What the hell…?' he ground out disbelievingly.

Lilli blinked at him, unsure of his mood. She had seen him mocking, contemptuous, coldly angry, passionately aroused, even gently teasing, but she had no idea what emotion he was feeling as he took in the woman in the doorway. Every muscle in his body seemed to be tensed, and his fingers looked in danger of snapping the slender stem of the champagne glass he held.

'Patrick…?' Lilli prompted uncertainly now.

His glass landed with a thump on the table-top as he stood up abruptly, unseeing as he looked down at her. 'I'll be back in a few minutes,' he grated, turning to leave.

Lilli didn't need to be told he was going to the woman across the room, a woman he obviously knew very well if that blaze of awareness in the woman's eyes as she looked at him had been anything to go by! He couldn't do this to her, not at their wedding reception!

'Let him go, Lilli,' his sister advised quietly as Lilli would have reached out and stopped his departure. Gerry was looking across the room at the blond woman too now.

Lilli's mouth tightened resentfully, both at Gerry's intervention and Patrick's powerful strides across the room towards the beautiful woman. Her eyes flashed deeply green as she turned to the woman who was now her sister-in-law. 'You know that woman?' she asked.

'Oh, yes.' Gerry's mouth twisted contemptuously, although her gaze was soft as she looked at Lilli. 'I'm

hardly likely to forget the woman who made Patrick into
the hardened cynic he is today!'

Sanchia!

The beautiful woman in the doorway, the woman who
had looked at Patrick so possessively, was his ex-wife?
Here? Now?

Lilli turned sharply, just in time to see Sanchia smile
seductively up at Patrick, before he took a firm hold of
her arm and forcefully escorted her from the room.

CHAPTER NINE

'GERRY…? What the hell is she doing here?' Lilli's father hissed agitatedly.

Lilli turned to him. 'You know Patrick's ex-wife too?'

'Of course. Your mother and I were part of that crowd five years ago,' he reminded her.

Before her mother's illness became such that it was impossible for her to go anywhere…

'Where are you going, Lilli?' Her father's hand on her arm restrained her as she stood up.

Her expression was calm, a smile curving her lips—even if the green of her eyes spat fire. 'I'm going to join my bridegroom,' she told him, releasing her arm. 'Don't worry, Daddy.' Her smile was wry now at his expression of panic. 'I can assure you, I intend it to be a civilised meeting.'

Gerry grimaced. 'Sanchia isn't known for her civility!'

Lilli gave a genuinely warm smile as she bent down to answer the other woman. 'I'll let you into a secret, Gerry,' she murmured. 'Neither am I when I'm pushed into a corner!' She straightened, looking towards the door through which Patrick had left so hastily minutes earlier. 'And I've just been pushed,' she muttered as she turned to move determinedly towards that door.

Gerry touched her arm lightly as she passed her. 'Just watch out for the claws,' she warned.

Lilli nodded her thanks. 'I'll do that.'

It wasn't difficult to locate Patrick and Sanchia once

she was out in the corridor; the sound of raised voices came from a room a little further down the hallway, Patrick's icily calm, the female voice—Sanchia's— raised to the point of hysteria.

The claws Gerry had warned Lilli about were raised in the direction of Patrick's face as Lilli silently entered the room, Patrick's hands on the other woman's wrists to prevent her nails actually making contact with his cheeks.

'Dear, dear, dear,' Lilli murmured mockingly as she closed the door firmly behind her. 'Do I take it this isn't a happy reunion?'

The two people already in the room were frozen as if in a tableau. Both turned to face Lilli as she calmly stood looking at them, dark brows raised questioningly. Patrick looked far from pleased at the interruption, but Sanchia slowly lowered her hands, her icy blue eyes suddenly speculative as she looked Lilli up and down.

'The bride,' she drawled derisively.

Lilli steadily met the other woman's contemptuous glare. 'And the ex-bride,' she returned just as scathingly, knowing she had scored a direct hit as Sanchia's mouth tightened furiously. 'Patrick, our guests are waiting,' Lilli reminded him lightly.

Sanchia released her arms from Patrick's steely grip, eyes blazing. 'Unless he's changed a great deal—which I very much doubt!—Patrick doesn't respond well to orders!' The accent to her English was slightly more noticeable in this longer speech.

Green eyes met icy blue. 'Patrick hasn't changed. In any way,' Lilli added pointedly. 'Darling?' she prompted again.

He couldn't let her down now. He just couldn't! If he did, their marriage was over before it had even begun.

No matter what his feelings towards Sanchia—and Lilli really had no idea what they were, or indeed about the other woman's towards him; Sanchia had obviously felt strongly enough about something, possibly Patrick, to have turned up here today!—it was Lilli he was married to now. And she had married him. For better or for worse.

To her relief Patrick walked determinedly to her side, his expression grim as his arm moved possessively about her waist. 'As I've told you, Sanchia—' he looked at his former wife resolutely '—there's no place for you here.'

'This—this child—' Sanchia looked at Lilli scornfully '—could never take my place in your life! You need a real woman, Patrick—and I was always that.'

Lilli stiffened at this mention of intimacy between the two, although her outward expression remained calm. She didn't particularly want to hear about Patrick's marriage to Sanchia. And Patrick, his arm still about her waist, must have felt her reaction.

'Patrick likes them a little younger nowadays,' Lilli told Sanchia wryly, knowing by the angry flush that appeared in the other woman's cheeks that her barb had hit its mark. Sanchia was probably only ten years older than her, but she obviously felt those years…

'Inexperienced, you mean,' Sanchia returned bitchily. 'Patrick bores easily too,' she warned.

Lilli smiled. 'I'm sure you would know that better than I.' She felt the tightening of Patrick's hand on her waist, but chose to ignore it; she knew she was playing with fire, but at this particular moment she didn't mind getting her fingers burnt.

Sanchia gave a snort before turning to Patrick. 'I give this marriage a matter of months, darling,' she drawled, picking her bag up from the table. 'And I'll still be around when it's over. In fact, I'm thinking of moving to New York.'

'Really? I'm sure you'll enjoy the life over there.' Patrick was the one to answer her. 'Frankly—' his arm settled more comfortably about Lilli's waist '—I'm tired of it. Lilli and I will be living in London.'

That was news to Lilli! They hadn't so much as mentioned where they would live after their marriage since the night Patrick had given her the engagement ring, and she had behaved so stupidly about moving to New York. Now, it seemed, they weren't going to live there at all...

'I don't believe it,' Sanchia gasped. 'You've always loved New York.'

He gave an acknowledging nod. 'And now I love Lilli—and her family and friends are all in London.'

Two bright spots of angry colour appeared in Sanchia's cheeks. 'My family and friends were in Paris, but you refused to live there!' she accused heatedly, turning to Lilli with furious blue eyes. 'Enjoy his indulgence while you can,' she advised. 'I can assure you, it doesn't last for long!'

Considering one of this woman's indulgences had been other men, that wasn't so surprising!

Lilli met her gaze unflinchingly. 'I wouldn't hold your breath,' she said.

Sanchia gave a hard smile. 'Or you yours! Take care, Patrick.' She reached out to run a caressing hand down his cheek lightly. 'And remember, I'm still here.'

This last, Lilli knew, was said for her benefit. And while a visit from an ex-wife was enough to chill the heart of any new one—no matter what the circumstances of the divorce had been, the previous wife having an intimate knowledge of the man, of his likes and dislikes, that was totally intrusive—at that moment Lilli didn't

feel in the least threatened by the other woman, had seen
the look of absolute loathing in Patrick's face for
Sanchia when she'd entered this room a few minutes
ago. Patrick disliked his ex-wife intensely.

'Excuse us,' Patrick told Sanchia coldly. 'We have a
wedding reception to attend.' His hand was firm against
Lilli's back as he guided her to the door, neither of them
looking back as they left. '"Patrick likes them younger
nowadays"?' he repeated as soon as the two of them
were out of earshot in the hallway.

Lilli glanced up at him from beneath lowered lashes,
knowing by the curve to his mouth that he wasn't in the
least angry at her remark. 'I believe I said "a *little*
younger",' she returned, grinning up at him mischie-
vously.

Patrick looked down at her, shaking his head incredulously. 'You weren't in the least thrown by her appearance here, were you?'

She wouldn't go quite so far as to say that, but if it
was what Patrick believed...

She shrugged, the two of them standing outside the
reception room now. 'Should I have been?'

'Not at all,' he returned easily. 'The part of my life
that contained Sanchia is dead and buried as far as I'm
concerned.' His expression was grim.

'That's what I thought.' Lilli accepted—gratefully, inside!—putting her hand in the crook of his arm. 'Let's
join our guests; you still have a speech to give!'

'Oh, God, yes,' he groaned. 'I'm not quite sure what
to say about my bride any more,' he added dryly.

Lilli grinned. 'Beautiful. Intelligent. Undemanding—'

'Sometimes wise beyond her years,' he put in. 'And
full of surprises. I was sure you would give me hell over

Sanchia turning up here, today of all days. Full of surprises…'

She shook her head. 'You can't be held responsible for the actions of a vindictive woman. She wanted to cause trouble between us, unnerve you, and upset me— I vote we don't give her the satisfaction!'

'I stopped caring years ago about anything that Sanchia does,' Patrick revealed. 'I was more worried about you and how you would feel about it.'

And she could see that he had been, his concern still in the deep grey of his eyes. 'Don't be,' she told him brightly, needing no further assurances from him concerning his ex-wife. 'And as for being full of surprises— when did *we* decide to live in London?' She quirked dark brows again.

He frowned in thought. 'I believe it was the night we became engaged.'

'No.' Lilli shook her head. 'You refused to even discuss it then.'

'Because at the time I was intent on kissing you, if I remember correctly.' He grinned as she blushed at the memory. 'But your wish not to live in New York was duly noted, and—'

'Acted upon.' Lilli frowned. 'I can see I'll have to be more careful about what I say in future. Or was Sanchia right about your indulgence?' she added teasingly. 'Won't it last?'

Patrick's arms moved smoothly about her waist. 'It isn't a question of indulging you, Lilli. You said you didn't want to live in New York, and, as I have no feelings either way, it seems obvious that we live here. I want you to be happy in our marriage,' he added gruffly. 'And if living in London is going to help do that, then this is where we'll live. I thought, with your agreement, that we could go house-hunting in the new year?'

He probably couldn't see it—and, in the circumstances, Lilli had no intention of pointing it out to him, either, because living in London suited her fine!—but the fact that he had made this decision on his own, without any consultation with her, was an act of arrogance in itself.

'Fine,' she nodded.

'Do you mind staying here in the hotel until we find a house? I somehow don't think we should move in with either your father or my sister.'

Lilli grimaced. 'Certainly not!'

Patrick grinned. 'Ditto.'

She blinked up at him. 'That's amazing, Patrick; do you realise that's three things we've agreed on in the last five minutes?'

'Three things…?' He looked serious as he thought back over their conversation.

She nodded. 'To live in London. And that your ex-wife is a bitch! She even chose to wear a white suit to come here today.' Lilli had duly noted the deliberate ploy of Sanchia to upstage the bride; the beautiful silk suit obviously had a designer label, and white was usually the colour reserved for the bride on her wedding day. She didn't doubt that Sanchia had been reminding her that she had been Patrick's bride first!

He grimaced. 'But the jacket, if I remember correctly, was edged with black. And Sanchia is more black than white!'

There was so much pain behind that stark comment. Lilli could only hope that one day he would feel comfortable enough in their relationship to talk to her about the marriage that had ended so disastrously.

For the first time that she could remember in their acquaintance Lilli was the one to reach up and initiate a kiss between them.

Patrick seemed as surprised as she was to start with, and then he kissed her back.

It hadn't been premeditated on her part; Lilli could have had no idea Sanchia would choose that particular moment to storm out of the reception room further down the hallway. But that was exactly what she did, her eyes narrowing glacially as she took in the scene of intimacy. With one last furious glare in their direction, she turned on her heel and walked away.

For good, Lilli hoped.

'Good timing,' Patrick told her dryly as he grasped her elbow to take her back to their guests.

He believed she had kissed him at that moment deliberately, so that Sanchia would see them!

And perhaps it was better if he continued to think that, Lilli decided as they moved around the huge dining-room chatting to each of their guests. Patrick had clearly stated he did not want a wife who loved him, only one that would be faithful and loyal.

Loving him as she did, those two things would be quite easy to be, and it was best to leave it at that...

'Thank goodness that's over!' Patrick pulled off his bow-tie with some relief, discarding his jacket onto a chair too, unbuttoning the top button of his shirt. 'I thought your father and Gerry were never going to leave.'

Lilli smiled at the memory of her father dithering about downstairs, drinking two glasses of champagne that he really didn't want, simply because now the time had come for him to leave Lilli alone with her husband and he was reluctant to do so.

She shook her head. 'And I thought the bride was the one that was nervous; you would have thought it was Daddy's wedding night the way he kept so obviously delaying our departure upstairs!' She smiled affectionately, sitting in one of the armchairs in the sitting-room of their suite, her veil discarded hours ago, the tea-roses still entwined in the flowing darkness of her hair.

Patrick looked across at her with dark grey eyes. 'And are you?' he said gruffly. 'Nervous,' he explained softly at her frown.

She swallowed hard. 'A little,' she acknowledged huskily.

He came down on his haunches beside her chair. 'You don't have to be, you know.' He smoothed the hair back from her cheeks. 'It's been a pretty eventful day, one way or another. And now it's very late, and we're both tired, and we have the rest of our lives together. I suggest we both take a shower and then get some sleep.' He straightened. 'There are two bathrooms in this suite; you take one and I'll take the other.'

Lilli looked at him dazedly as he picked up his jacket. He didn't want her!

'Lilli?'

She focused on him with effort. He was so tall and masculine, so devastatingly attractive. And he was her husband.

Damn it, she wanted to make love with him! This was their wedding night. And a part of her—the part that wasn't nervous!—had been anticipating the two of them making love. And now he had decided they weren't going to, after all...

He gave an impatient sigh. 'Stop looking at me as if

I've just hit you! I'm not a monster, Lilli, and I can see how tired you are. A shower and then sleep will be the best thing for you at the moment.'

The exhaustion she had felt on their way up here had suddenly vanished. Patrick didn't want to make love to her! Was this the way it was when you didn't marry for love? Or was he more affected by Sanchia's visit than he had admitted? Had seeing the other woman again made him realise he had made a mistake? What—?

'You're letting your imagination run away with you now,' he rasped suddenly, looking at her assessingly. 'Asking yourself questions that, in the clear light of day, you will recognise as nonsensical. I'm trying to be a gentleman, Lilli,' he explained. 'But if it makes you feel better I could always throw you down on the carpet right now and—'

'No!' she cut in forcefully, getting to her feet, avoiding looking at him as she did so. 'I'll go and take that shower.'

He nodded abruptly. 'I'll see you shortly.'

Lilli went through to the bedroom; her clothes had been brought here the day before and unpacked into the drawers. She took out the white silk nightgown before going through to the adjoining bathroom, thankfully closing the door behind her.

She had made a fool of herself just now, and it wasn't a feeling she was comfortable with. Patrick wasn't an eager bridegroom, in love with his new wife, desperate to make love with her. There was no urgency to consummate their marriage. They had plenty of time for that…

Patrick was already in bed when she came through from the bathroom half an hour later, the sheet resting about his waist, his chest bare, the hair there dark and curling, his skin lightly tanned. His hair was still damp from his shower, and he looked—

Lilli quickly looked away as he turned towards her, knowing the flare of desire she felt at the sight of him would be evident in her eyes. 'I'm sorry I took so long.' She moved about the room, hanging up her wedding dress and veil. 'It took me ages to get the flowers out of my hair and then pull a brush through it.' She held up a hand to her long vibrant hair. 'And then I—'

'Lilli, just leave all that and get into bed,' he interrupted wearily. 'You're wearing me out just watching you! It isn't as if it matters whether or not the dress gets creased; you won't be wearing it again.'

She thrust the dress on its hanger into the back of the wardrobe, as if it had burnt her. No, she wouldn't be wearing it again. Because she would always be married to Patrick. And look how disastrous it was turning out to be!

'Don't make me come and get you, Lilli,' Patrick urged as she still made no effort to get into the bed beside him. 'I never wear anything in bed, and I have a feeling you're the one that would end up feeling embarrassed if I were to get up right now!'

She scrambled into the bed beside him so quickly that her foot became entangled in the sheet and threatened to pull the damn thing off him anyway!

How stupidly she was behaving; she inwardly sighed once she had finally settled onto her own side of the wide double bed. Not at all like the normally composed Lilli. And as for Elizabeth Bennett…!

Patrick reached out to switch off the light, lying back in the darkness.

Lilli lay stiffly on her side of the bed, her eyes adjusting to the small amount of light shining into the room through the curtains at the window. She was never going to be able to sleep, couldn't possibly—

'If it's not too much to ask—' Patrick spoke softly beside her '—*I* would like to give my wife a cuddle before we go to sleep.'

She swallowed hard as he propped himself up on one elbow to look down at her, his individual features not discernible to her, although she could make out the shadows of his face. And he looked as if he was smiling!

'*Is* it too much to ask?' he prompted huskily.

'Of course not.' She moved in the darkness, putting her head on his shoulder as he lay back against the pillow, his arm curved around her, his hand resting possessively on her hip, the warmth of his body—his naked body!—instantly warming her too.

He gave a sigh of contentment, turning to kiss her temple lightly. 'This is worth all of the hectic circus today has been.' He relaxed against her.

Lilli still felt unsure of herself. Through the ridiculousness of his marriage proposal, her reluctant acceptance of it, the hectic activity during the week that followed, she had never doubted that Patrick desired her. In fact, he had seemed to have great difficulty keeping his hands off her! But now they were married, alone together at last, he didn't seem—

'You're letting your imagination run away with you again. Lilli, has it ever occurred to you that maybe *I'm* a little nervous?'

'You?' She turned to him, raising her head in surprise.

'Yes. Me,' he confirmed, pushing her head back down onto his shoulder. 'I told you, it's a long time since I did this. Maybe I've forgotten how to do it. Maybe I won't be able to please you.' He gave a deep sigh. 'God knows, the last time I attempted to make love to a woman, she fell asleep before we even got started! I'm talking about *you*, Lilli,' he explained as he felt her stiffen defensively in his arms. 'Five minutes earlier you had been full of sensual promise, and then—nothing.'

She buried her face in his shoulder at the memory. 'I had too much to drink. It had nothing to do with—with—'

'Well, it did absolutely nothing for my ego,' he assured her. 'Now will you accept that and just leave this for tonight?'

When he put it that way—of course she would! She had never imagined that Patrick had moments of uncertainty too. He was so damned arrogant most of the time, it was difficult to imagine him being nervous about anything. Certainly not about making love to her!

'Of course I will.' She snuggled closer to him in the darkness, her hand resting lightly on his chest. 'Mm, this is nice,' she murmured contentedly.

'Go to sleep, Lilli,' he muttered.

She slept. Not because Patrick had ordered her to, but because, as he'd said, she was truly exhausted.

Quite what woke her she had no idea, but as she slowly came awake she realised it was probably because she had subconsciously registered that she was alone in the bed, the lean length of Patrick no longer beside her.

She looked sleepily around the bedroom, realising by the fact that it was still dark in the room that it must be quite early. She finally located Patrick sitting in the chair by the window, a dark robe pulled on over his nakedness.

She moved up onto her elbows, blinking sleepily across at him. 'Patrick…?'

'Who the hell is Robbie?' he returned harshly.

CHAPTER TEN

LILLIE was dazed, not really awake yet, totally thrown by the savagely accusing question.

Patrick surged forcefully to his feet, crossing the room to sit down on the side of the bed, instantly tightening the bedclothes above her, holding her pinned to the mattress. He placed his hands on the pillow at either side of her head, glaring down at her in the semi-darkness. 'I want to know who Robbie is,' he repeated in a harsh, controlled voice.

Lilli pushed her tousled hair back from her forehead. 'I don't— What—?'

'Imagine my surprise,' Patrick ground out, 'when my bride of a few hours starts calling for another man—a man I've never heard of!—in her sleep!'

She swallowed hard, moistening her lips. She didn't remember dreaming at all, certainly not of Robbie. But Patrick said she had called out his name…? 'I did that?' She frowned her confusion.

Patrick's mouth twisted. 'It's hardly something I'm likely to have made up, is it?' he grated.

No, of course it wasn't. She just couldn't imagine why she had done such a thing…

'Lilli, I'm not going to ask you again.' He grasped her shoulders. 'Who the hell is he?'

She turned away from the livid anger in his face. 'Was he,' she corrected him chokily. 'He's dead.'

Patrick released her abruptly, sitting back now, no

longer leaning over her so oppressively. 'You loved him,' he stated flatly.

'Very much,' she confirmed shakily.

He stood up to pace the room. 'I don't believe this! Now I have a damned ghost to contend with as well as an ex-fiancé…!' He shook his head disgustedly. 'No one has ever mentioned someone in your life called Robbie.' He glared at her.

'There was no need for them to do so,' she said heavily, painful memories assailing her anew. 'He's been dead a long time.' She sighed. 'Patrick, Robbie was—'

'I can guess,' he cut in savagely. 'He was the reason you settled for someone like Andy Brewster. The reason you're now married to me. He was—'

'The person that gave me the name Lilli,' she told him, her voice very small. 'Remember you once asked me about my name? Actually, it was Lillibet originally,' she recalled sadly. 'But over the years it's been shortened to Lilli.'

'Lillibet?' Patrick repeated. 'It sounds like something a child might say. What sort of—?'

'It *was* something a child might say—a very young child,' she told him slowly, no longer looking at him, her vision all inwards, on the past, on memories of Robbie. 'Robbie couldn't get his tongue around the name Elizabeth, and so his version came out as Lillibet.' She smiled at the memory, that smile fading as quickly as it appeared. 'He was only two when he died of meningitis.' She looked at Patrick with dull eyes. 'He was my brother.'

Patrick paled. 'He— But— I—'

Patrick at a loss for words would have been funny

under any other circumstances. But at the moment it was lost on her.

'I was eleven when he died. One day he was here, giggling and fun, and the next he had— I—I—' She fought the control she always lost when talking of her brother. 'I loved him from the day he was born. Perhaps the difference in our ages helped with that; I don't know.' She shook her head. 'But I could never accept— I didn't understand. In some ways I still don't. He was beautiful.' She looked at Patrick with tear-wet eyes. 'I loved him so much,' she added brokenly. 'I have no idea why I called for him last night. I don't remember. I just—'

'Hey, it's all right.' Patrick sank down beside her on the bed, his arms moving about her as he held her close against him. 'I had no idea, Lilli. I'm so sorry. I do vaguely remember something—God, I'm just making this worse.' He angrily berated himself. 'I shouldn't ''vaguely remember'' anything! Robbie was your brother—'

'But you didn't know him. You didn't know us.' Her voice was muffled against his chest. 'Robbie was special to me; I still can't think of him without crying. I'm sorry.' She began to cry in earnest now.

'Lilli, please don't cry,' Patrick groaned. 'I do know what it's like to lose someone you love. I was seven when my mother gave birth to Gerry. Gerry was born, and my mother died. I was left with that same bewilderment you obviously were. And my father and I were left with the onerous task of bringing up a new-born baby. For fifteen years we managed to do exactly that, and then my father died, and it was left completely to me.'

As he spoke of his mother and father, his childhood

with Gerry, his voice somehow lost its smoothness, acquiring a slightly Irish lilt to it. And Lilli could only guess, from the emotion in his voice, just how difficult it had been for him to lose his mother—and be presented with a totally helpless baby.

His statements had been starkly made, telling her about none of the trauma he and his father must have felt in surviving such sorrow. Or how difficult it must have been for him, at only twenty-two, to have the sole charge of a fifteen-year-old girl. And yet he had done it and, from the success he had made of his business life and the closeness between himself and Gerry, all too capably.

Lilli shook her head. 'I didn't know—'

'Why should you?' He lightly touched her hair. 'We have the rest of our lives to get to know about each other, both past and present.'

Lilli hoped that would include speaking about his marriage to Sanchia. As she looked up into the gentleness of his face, she thought it would...

'I didn't mean to make you cry just now,' he continued. 'I only—I just— I was jealous,' he admitted. 'I thought he was a man you had cared for.'

She looked up at him with puzzled, tear-wet eyes. If he had felt jealousy, did that mean he cared for her, after all? Even as her heart leapt at the thought, she realised it wasn't that at all; what Patrick possessed, he possessed exclusively. Didn't he despise Sanchia because she hadn't been exclusively his?

She shook her head. 'You need have no worries like that concerning me. Andy was my one and only venture into commitment—and look how disastrously that turned out!'

Patrick settled himself on the bed beside her. 'Well,

you're totally committed now,' he told her with satisfaction. 'How does it feel?'

'Not a lot different than before.'

He looked at her with teasing eyes. 'Do I detect a note of disappointment in your voice?'

Did he? Possibly. There couldn't be too many virgin brides who had built themselves up to being made love to on their wedding night—only to be told by their bridegroom that he was too tired! Although that wasn't strictly true... He had said they were both too tired. And the proof of her own tiredness was that she couldn't even remember falling asleep, although she must have done so almost immediately she shut her eyes.

But she wasn't sleepy now; in fact, she was wide awake...and suddenly very aware of Patrick as he lay beside her wearing only a robe to hide his nakedness.

Patrick gently raised her chin, smoky grey eyes looking straight into candid green. 'I know what you were thinking last night, Lilli,' he said gruffly. 'Oh, yes, I do,' he insisted as she would have protested. 'But the truth of the matter is, I want you too much, want us to enjoy each other too much, to have it spoilt in any way.'

She swallowed hard, the desire he spoke of evident in the burning intensity of his gaze. 'We're not tired now,' she pointed out shyly.

He laughed. 'No, we're not. And we are going to make love, Lilli.' He bent his head, his mouth claiming hers, lips moving erotically against hers, the tip of his tongue lightly caressing the inner moisture of her mouth.

Her arms curved up about his neck as she held him close to her, heart pounding, his hair feeling soft and silky beneath her fingertips, shoulders and back firmly muscled.

Lilli relaxed against the pillows, pulling Patrick with

her, his robe and her nightgown easily disposed of as flesh met flesh, Lilli's softness against Patrick's hardness, the dark hair on his chest tickling the sensitive tips of her breasts now.

And then Patrick's lips were teasing those sensitive tips, Lilli's head back as she gasped at the liquid fire that coursed through her body, groaning low in her throat as she felt the moist warmth of his tongue flicking over her hardened nipples.

His lips and hands caressed every part of her body during the timeless hours before dawn, encouraging her to touch him in return, to discover how he liked to be caressed too, to be kissed. But she seemed to know that instinctively, revelling in the response her lips and hands evoked, until his tender ministrations reached the most intimate part of her body and she could no longer think straight as heat such as she had never known before consumed her in flames.

And then Patrick was once more kissing her on the lips, his hands on her breasts as he slowly raised her to fulfilment once again. And again. And again.

And when his body finally joined with hers there was no pain, only pleasure of another kind, his slow, caressing movements deep inside her taking her to another plateau completely. A plateau Patrick joined her on, his own groans of pleasure merging with hers, before they lay damply together, their bodies merged, their breathing deep and ragged.

'I don't think you could have forgotten a thing,' Lilli finally said when she at last found the strength to talk.

Patrick laughed. 'I hope not—any more than that and I could die of a heart attack!'

She lay on top of him, moving slightly so that she could look into his face, unconcerned with her nakedness now; there wasn't an inch of her body that Patrick didn't now know intimately. 'You weren't nervous at all last night, were you?' she realised shakily.

'You needed time to get used to me.'

'Used to' him; she was totally possessed by him at this moment! 'But you weren't really nervous, were you?' she persisted.

'Lilli.' He smoothed the tangled hair back over her shoulders, revealing the pertness of her breasts. 'If you only knew the ways I've imagined making love to you!'

He still hadn't answered her question. Or perhaps he had... He had been thinking of her last night, giving her time to become accustomed to their new relationship.

'I think I just experienced them,' she recalled breathlessly.

'Oh, no, Lilli. We've barely touched the surface,' he assured her with promise.

She quivered in anticipation, only able to imagine the delights yet to come.

'But not right now,' Patrick soothed, settling her head comfortably against his shoulder. 'Now we're going to have a nap.'

She swallowed hard. 'Like this?'

'Exactly like this,' he said with satisfaction. 'I like having you as part of me. And vice versa, I hope.' He quirked dark eyebrows.

'Oh, yes,' she admitted shyly, very much aware of the way in which he was still 'part of' her! 'But it must be late.' Daylight was visible now through the curtains at the window. 'Shouldn't we—?'

'This is the morning after our wedding, Lilli,' he teased. 'No one, least of all the hotel staff, will expect to hear from us for hours yet. At which time we will order breakfast—even if it's two o'clock in the afternoon. This is a Bennett hotel; I'm sure they will accommodate us!'

Lilli was sure they would too. But whether or not she would ever, as the owner's daughter, be able to face any of the hotel staff again after her honeymoon was another matter!

But for the moment she didn't care, was content in Patrick's arms, being with him like this. And as she drifted off into sleep she had a feeling she always would be...

'What the hell—?'

Lilli woke suddenly, to the sound of Patrick's swearing, and the reason for it—a loud knocking on the outer door of their hotel suite.

She sat up groggily, just in time to see Patrick pulling on his robe and tying the belt tightly about his waist. 'I thought you said no one would disturb us today?' she giggled, pulling the sheet up to her chin as she watched him.

'I didn't think anyone would dare to!' He scowled darkly, glaring in the direction of the loud banging. 'It had better be for a good reason!'

As he strode out of the bedroom to the suite door Lilli couldn't help but feel sorry for the person who was standing on the other side of it, although she had to admit she was a little annoyed at the intrusion herself. Patrick's words, before they'd both fallen asleep, had promised so much more...

He didn't return immediately, as she had expected he would, and finally her lethargy turned to curiosity; it must be something important to keep Patrick away this long. She could hear the murmur of male voices in the sitting-room...

She pulled on her white silk robe over her nakedness, belting it securely before running a brush lightly through her hair; she might have just spent several hours of pleasure in her husband's arms, but she didn't want everyone to realise that just by looking at her!

'Daddy!' She gasped her surprise as she saw he was the man talking to Patrick. 'Good grief, Daddy, what on earth are you doing here?' She shook her head dazedly.

'Would you believe he came to make sure I hadn't strangled you on our wedding night?' Patrick drawled derisively. 'Or you hadn't stuck that knife in my back that he once suggested!'

Lilli looked at the two men, her father flushed and agitated, Patrick calm and controlled. 'Actually—no,' she answered firmly. 'So, why are you really here, Daddy?' she prompted.

'You certainly didn't raise a fool, Richard,' Patrick said appreciatively.

The older man gave him an exasperated glare before turning back to Lilli. 'Good afternoon, Lilli,' he greeted her. 'I'm sorry to interrupt—I mean, I realise I shouldn't have—' He broke off awkwardly, the way they were both dressed—or undressed!—telling its own story. 'Gerry told me I shouldn't come here…'

'You should have listened to her,' Patrick bit out tersely. 'I, for one, do not appreciate the interruption.'

Lilli had stilled at the mention of the other woman's name. Then she remembered how kind Gerry had been to her yesterday when Sanchia had appeared so inappropriately at the wedding. Although she still resented the other woman's place in her father's life, some of what Patrick had told her earlier about his sister made her realise that, as her own father was to her, Gerry was all the family Patrick had. And, as such, Lilli couldn't continue to alienate her.

'Perhaps you *should* have listened to her,' she told her father quietly.

Her father's eyes widened, but he didn't comment on the lack of the usual resentment in her voice when she spoke of the other woman. 'Maybe I should,' he agreed. 'But I thought this was important.'

Lilli returned his gaze frowningly; he must have done to risk Patrick's wrath by intruding on their honeymoon in this way. And he had obviously got more than he bargained for by finding them so obviously still in bed! 'How important?' she said slowly.

'Very,' he insisted firmly.

'I disagree,' Patrick put in hardly.

Lilli's father shot him a questioning glance. 'I think that's for Lilli to decide, don't you...?'

Patrick's head went back arrogantly. 'As it happens, no. I don't think this concerns Lilli at all. Not any more.'

She was intrigued by the mystery of her father's visit. Obviously, whatever it was about, Patrick didn't want her involved in it.

She moved to sit on one of the armchairs. 'Tell me,' she prompted her father.

He glanced uncertainly at the younger man, obviously far from reassured by Patrick's stony expression.

'Daddy!' Lilli encouraged impatiently.

He no longer met her gaze. 'Perhaps Patrick is right; this can wait until after your honeymoon—'

'We've had our honeymoon,' she assured him firmly. 'Have you forgotten we're joining you tomorrow for Christmas.' She didn't even look at Patrick now, knowing she would see disapproval in his face. But she was not a child, and she refused to be treated like one, by either man.

Her father slumped down into another of the armchairs. 'I'd completely forgotten it's Christmas…!' he groaned.

'Don't let Gerry hear you say that,' Patrick warned mockingly. 'She loves Christmas. I suggest you make sure you have something suitable for her by tomorrow!'

'Stop trying to change the subject, Patrick.' Again Lilli didn't so much as look at him. 'I'm not so easily deterred.'

'Does that mean you've already bought my Christmas present?' he returned tauntingly.

She had, as a matter of fact—a beautiful watch, already wrapped and ready to give him on Christmas morning. But that wasn't important just now.

'It means,' she said with slow determination, 'that I'm not going to be sidetracked. Daddy!' She was even more forceful this time.

'She gets her stubbornness from me, I'm afraid,' he told the younger man ruefully.

'It's irrelevant where she gets it from,' Patrick dismissed tersely. 'This is none of her business.'

'I'll be the judge of that,' she snapped. She had been kept in the dark too much already by these two men; it wasn't going to continue.

'You aren't Elizabeth Bennett any more, Lilli,' Patrick rasped. 'You're Mrs Lilli Devlin. And *Mr* Devlin has already decided this does not concern you!'

She stood up angrily. '*Mr* Devlin doesn't own me,' she returned furiously. 'Maybe someone should have told you: women aren't chattels any more! Now, either one of you tells me what's going on, or I'll go and ask someone who will tell me,' she added challengingly.

Patrick looked at her scathingly. 'Such as who?'

'Such as Gerry!' she announced triumphantly, know-ing by the stunned look on both the men's faces that this hadn't even occurred to them as a possibility. Lilli wasn't so sure it was either; she might feel less antago-nistic towards the other woman, but she wasn't sure she would be able to go to her about this! But hopefully neither of these two men would realise that... 'Well?' she prompted hardly when her announcement didn't pro-duce the result she wanted, looking from one man to the other, her father looking decidedly uncomfortable, Patrick stubbornly unmoved. 'Fine,' she finally snapped, walking towards the bedroom, her clear intention to go and dress before leaving. 'Gerry it is!'

'Lilli, I forbid you to go anywhere near Gerry!' Patrick thundered autocratically.

She halted in her tracks, turning slowly, looking at him with cool incredulity.

'Uh-oh,' her father muttered warily. 'You've done it now, Patrick. The last time I forbade Lilli from going near someone she ended up *marrying* you!'

Patrick's mouth quirked. 'That hardly applies in this case, does it? Besides, it's because Lilli is married to me that I—'

'Think you can tell me what to do,' she finished scath-ingly, shaking her head. 'I don't think so,' she bit out coldly. 'Daddy?' she prompted in a voice that brooked no further argument.

He sighed, giving a regretful glance in Patrick's di-rection before turning back to Lilli. 'Andy telephoned me this morning,' he stated without flourish.

She gasped in shock. Whatever she had been expect-ing, it wasn't this!

She froze momentarily. 'Andy did...?'

Her father nodded. 'He wants to see you, Lilli,' he told her softly.

She hadn't been mistaken yesterday; it had been Andy standing outside in the crowd as she went to the wedding. But why did he want to see her…?

CHAPTER ELEVEN

'YOU just aren't thinking this through at all, Lilli,' Patrick said as he sat watching her dress. 'Brewster believes that by talking to you, appealing to your softer nature, he may be able to stop your father's legal proceedings against him!'

She didn't look at him, hadn't done so since he'd followed her into the bedroom a few minutes ago. They had made love in this room, knew each other intimately, and yet she still felt slightly self-conscious at having Patrick watch her, thankfully pulling up the side zip to olive-green trousers before pulling on a matching sweater.

She was still stunned by Andy's contact with her father, couldn't imagine what had made him do such a thing. She certainly didn't agree with Patrick's last comment; she had every reason to hate Andy, and he must be well aware of that fact. Where Andy was concerned, she had no 'softer nature' to appeal to!

'And just how do you think he hopes to achieve that?' she replied, still smarting from Patrick's earlier attempt to tell her what she could and couldn't do. Marriage was a partnership—particularly this marriage!—and she was not about to be told whom she could or couldn't see.

'You were engaged to the man—'

'And he used that engagement to cheat my father,' she reminded him forcefully.

'You loved him—'

'I thought I did,' she corrected him; loving Patrick as

153

she now did, she knew damn well she had never really loved Andy at all!

'You were going to marry him—'

'And now I'm married to you.' She looked at him challengingly. 'A fact I'm unlikely to forget!'

Patrick returned her gaze. 'We made a bargain, Lilli—'

'And I won't renege on that,' she returned sharply. 'But being married to you does not make me your prisoner. I have no idea why Andy wants to talk to me,' she added as his face darkened ominously, 'but I honestly don't see that it can cause any harm.' Her father was right; telling her not to do something was a sure way of ensuring that she did!

Patrick stood up, throwing off his robe, completely unconcerned by his own nakedness as he took underwear from a drawer. 'I'm coming with you,' he informed her as he dressed.

'No!'

He halted in the action of buttoning up his shirt. 'What do you mean…no?' he said slowly.

'I mean no, Patrick,' she repeated firmly, outwardly undaunted by his fury—inwardly quaking. Patrick was again the coldly resilient man who had come to her home the day after their initial night together, a man who seemed like a stranger to her. But she wouldn't allow Patrick to see any of her inner apprehension. 'Andy asked to see me—'

'And I'm now your husband—'

'We aren't joined at the hip, Patrick!' she snapped impatiently. 'And I really don't have the time for this,' she added after glancing at her wristwatch. 'The sooner I see Andy, the sooner we'll all know what's going on.'

'I've already told you what's going on: the man believes he can use emotional pressure, or possibly black-mail—'

'Strangely, I would rather hear all this from Andy himself.' Her eyes flashed deeply green.

Patrick looked at her between narrowed lids. 'You still care for the man…!'

'Rubbish!' Her cheeks were flushed with anger at the very suggestion of it.

In truth, she had come to realise in the last week exactly how shallow her feelings for Andy had been… And it was because she loved Patrick, loved him in a totally different way, completely, intensely, in every way there was to love a man—even his anger!

Andy had been a challenge to her, she had realised, a man who didn't respond to the way she looked as other men always had—for reasons she understood only too well now! But his lack of interest had only piqued her own interest in him a year ago, and it was only since loving Patrick, when every nerve-ending, every part of her, was live to his presence, that she had realised how lukewarm her desire for Andy had been.

To have married him, she now knew, would have been a complete disaster. But she couldn't explain that to Patrick without admitting how she had come to realise that fact. And she couldn't, at this moment, admit to Patrick that he was the very reason she could now see Andy without fear of emotional pressure, of any kind, having any effect whatsoever. Loving Patrick consumed all of her emotions; there was no room for anyone else.

But it was almost as if Patrick's tenderness last night, and again this morning, might never have happened as he continued to glare at her accusingly. Lilli didn't have time to deal with his temper just now, wanted to get this meeting with Andy over and done with.

'Daddy's waiting,' she told Patrick briskly. 'We can talk when I get back—'

'I won't be here, Lilli,' Patrick said flatly.

She gave him a startled look. 'What do you mean…?'

He shrugged. 'By your own words, our honeymoon is over. In which case, I may as well go to my office for a couple of hours.'

For a moment she had thought—! Ridiculous—she and Patrick were married, for life, by his own decree. And, both being determined people, she didn't doubt they would have many disagreements in the future, but that didn't mean either of them intended giving up on their marriage. As Patrick had said earlier, they had made a bargain. For all they knew, she could already have conceived the first of those four children…

Patrick nodded abruptly. 'I'll see you later, Lilli.' He strode out of the room.

No parting kiss, not even a second glance; he just went. And it was with a heavy heart that Lilli joined her father in the suite lounge where he had sat waiting for her.

He looked up, frowning at her. 'Patrick looks—' He hesitated over his choice of description.

'Furious,' she finished for him. 'That's probably because he is.' She slipped on her jacket.

'Actually, I was going to use a much more basic word to describe how he looked,' her father returned ruefully.

She gave a warn smile. 'He doesn't want me to see Andy.'

'I think he made that more than obvious earlier.' Her father grimaced. 'And for once I have to agree with him.'

Her eyes widened accusingly. 'I wouldn't even know

Andy wanted to talk to me if you hadn't come here and told me!'

'I know,' he said wearily. 'And I think now I was probably wrong to do so.'

She laughed dismissively. 'Let's go, Daddy—before you start proving as stubborn as Patrick!' She took a firm hold of his arm and led him out of the suite, locking the door behind them; Patrick had his own key if he returned before them. 'I believe you said Andy wants me to meet him at—' She named a very exclusive hotel as they entered the lift. 'He's staying there on your money, I suppose!' she added scornfully.

Her father raised his eyebrows. 'Who knows? I'm at a complete loss as to what's going on. All he would say when he telephoned earlier was that he had to talk to you—'

'I thought you said he telephoned *you*?' she reminded him.

'I had to say that.' He grimaced. 'How do you think Patrick would have reacted to being told it was you your ex-fiancé wanted—insisted!—on talking to all the time?'

Exactly as he had reacted now—he had walked away!

But she still didn't understand; why did Andy want to talk to her? He had to know how she felt about him now, had to realise that what they had once shared had been over the moment he decided to cheat her father. And used her to do it!

She gave a heavy sigh. 'Maybe we had better not speculate any of this until we see Andy—'

'*You* see him,' her father corrected her. 'He had the damned nerve to tell me he doesn't want to speak to me. Although, to be honest, now that I'm involved in legal proceedings against him, I don't want to speak to him either. I think if I saw him, after the heartache he's caused, I would probably just hit him and think about the consequences of that action later—which wouldn't help anyone! I'll wait outside the hotel for you. But make sure he realises, exactly as I told him on the telephone this morning, that whatever he has to say to you will make no difference to the legal proceedings being brought against him.'

Now she was even more puzzled by this meeting between Andy and herself. He didn't want to see her father... She didn't know what she had been expecting— perhaps a plea from Andy, or even the blackmail that Patrick had suggested. Now she wasn't so sure...

Andy sat alone at one of the tables in the huge reception area, a pot of coffee in front of him. Lilli had time to study him before he was aware of her presence. The last three months hadn't been kind to him either; his handsome face was ravaged and tired-looking, his suit fitting him loosely, as if he had lost weight too.

Lilli hardened her heart to the way he looked; he was the cause of everyone's unhappiness, including his own, from the look of him!

She walked to the table, standing beside it looking down at him wordlessly as she waited for him to say something.

He stood up. 'At least sit down, Lilli,' he said, holding back the chair for her. 'You're looking well,' he told her as he resumed his own seat opposite her.

'What do you want, Andy?'

'I suppose it is a little late for social politeness between us,' he conceded. 'Could I just say, I never meant to hurt you, Lilli—?'

'Didn't you?' she interrupted.

He gave a sad sigh. 'No...'

'You hurt me because of what you did to my father, but on a more personal level…?' She shook her head, her eyes flashing her pain. If she had been hurt in any way by the end of their engagement then it had been her pride that had taken the blow—and, as Patrick had already assured her all too clearly, she had more than enough of that!

Andy looked at her closely for several seconds, and then he slowly nodded. 'I'm glad about that. I thought by the announcement of your marriage to Devlin that I couldn't have done you too much harm—'

'I haven't come here to discuss the harm—or otherwise!—that you did to me,' Lilli cut in. 'My father is the one— What on earth is that?' She stopped as Andy produced a small flat package from his jacket pocket, the paper brightly coloured, decorated with a silver bow and ribbon. 'I realise it's Christmas tomorrow, Andy—' her mouth twisted contemptuously as she looked at the present '—but I—'

'It isn't a Christmas present, Lilli, it's a wedding gift,' Andy told her, holding out the small present to her.

Her eyes widened, her hands tightly locked together in her lap. 'I don't want anything from you!' And she knew, without even consulting him, that Patrick wouldn't want it either!

'You'll want this.' Andy continued to hold out the gaily wrapped gift, but when she still didn't take it he put it down on the table between them, standing up. 'Please tell your father I'm sorry.'

'Where are you going?' she said incredulously as he would have walked away; she still had so much to say to him!

He gave a little smile. 'I'm not going anywhere, Lilli;

I'm staying exactly where I am. The last three months have been a nightmare—'

'You think they've been a nightmare for *you*?' she demanded disbelievingly. 'What do you think it's been like for my father? He—'

'I know,' Andy acknowledged heavily, coming down on his haunches beside her chair, reaching out to clasp both her hands in his. 'I do know, Lilli. That's why I'll understand if, after opening your present, your father still wants to prosecute me.' He shook his head sadly. 'It was all so tempting, Lilli, too much so in the circumstances.' He looked at her pleadingly. 'I was involved in a relationship that—well, I was in over my head. I thought if I had some money of my own—'

'I know about your—relationship, Andy,' she told him hardly. 'It's the reason I know you could never really have cared for me!'

He closed his eyes briefly, those eyes slightly over-bright when he raised his lids to look at her once again. 'I did—do—care for you, Lilli. You're a wonderful woman—'

'Please, Andy.' She instantly shook her head. 'Don't take me for a complete fool!'

He let out a deep breath. 'I know how it must seem to you, but I— If things had been different—'

'Don't you mean, if *you* had been different?' she countered, pulling her hands away from his.

'Yes,' he acknowledged. 'But you really are an exceptional woman, Lilli—a caring, beautiful woman. And you deserved so much better than me—'

'She got it!' interrupted a harsh voice.

Lilli and Andy turned sharply in the direction of that voice, Lilli troubled, Andy guarded, slowly straightening to face the other man. Lilli couldn't even begin to imagine what Andy thought of Patrick's presence here—she was too busy wondering about that herself!

Patrick's mouth showed his contempt as he looked at the younger man. The two were in such stark contrast to each other, Patrick so dark where Andy was golden, Patrick's face masculine, Andy's, seen against such stark masculinity, appearing much softer, his features so regular and handsome he appeared almost beautiful.

As the two men continued to stare at each other, Lilli couldn't help wondering if Patrick had entered the hotel in time to see Andy holding her hands…!

Whatever he had or hadn't seen, his cold anger of earlier this afternoon certainly hadn't diminished; he still looked furious!

'Lilli and I were married yesterday,' he informed Andy icily, pulling Lilli to her feet so that she stood at his side, holding her there firmly, his arm like a steel band about her waist.

Andy nodded. 'I realise that.'

'Then you must also realise that you have intruded on our honeymoon,' Patrick barked. 'An unwelcome intrusion.'

'I realise that too,' Andy acknowledged ruefully. 'But I had something I had to give to Lilli.' He bent down and picked up the gaily wrapped present before handing it to Lilli. 'I hope the two of you will be very happy together,' he added lightly, although he seemed to frown as he glanced at Patrick's harshly set face, his expression softening as he turned to Lilli. 'You're a very lucky man to have Lilli for your wife.' Even as he spoke to Patrick he bent forward and lightly kissed Lilli on the cheek. 'Take care, love. And be happy.' He turned and walked away.

There was complete silence as Andy left the hotel,

Lilli still clutching the small present he had given her, Patrick silent at her side. She didn't need two guesses as to why; he was absolutely furious—at her for seeing Andy at all, but also at the fact that the man had dared to kiss her, albeit on the cheek!

'For goodness' sake, stop brooding, Patrick!' she told him spiritedly as she moved out of his grasp. 'I don't recall that I behaved this way yesterday when your ex-wife decided to turn up at our wedding!' In fact, that subject hadn't been mentioned, by either of them, since.

He looked blank, as if the memory was something he had completely forgotten about. And perhaps it was; Sanchia didn't appear to be someone he wanted to remember. But that didn't change the fact that his reaction to Andy now was completely unfair to her.

Patrick relaxed suddenly. 'Let's sit down for a while. Your father has gone home, so he isn't going to be waiting outside. I spoke to him on my way in,' he supplied at her questioning look. 'I couldn't see the point in both of us waiting for you.' The two of them sat at the table Andy had recently vacated.

Of course not. And, of course, her father would also have seen the sense of that—with a little help from Patrick...!

'Open the damned present,' Patrick instructed tersely. 'Although I still think, given the circumstances, that Brewster had a damned nerve wanting to see you at all, let alone give you a present!'

Lilli wasn't really listening to him, was staring down at the gift she had just unwrapped, the silver ribbon and bow hanging limply from her hand now.

'What is it?' Patrick prompted sharply. 'Lilli!'

She looked across at him, her eyes unfocusing, her face pale. She couldn't think, let alone speak!

'For God's sake…!' Patrick stood up to come round the table and take the package roughly out of her hand, looking quickly at the contents. 'My God…!' he finally breathed dazedly.

Lilli knew exactly what had caused his astonishment. The same thing that had caused her own… Andy's gift to her was a bank account, made out in her name. For the amount of five million pounds!

The amount he had taken from her father…?

She looked up at Patrick. 'Is that what he owed?'

His expression was grim now. 'More or less,' he grated.

She frowned. 'How much less?'

He shrugged. 'Probably the interest that should have been earned in the last three to four months. Brewster has probably needed that for his living expenses. I doubt your father will mind that, as long as he gets the capital returned to him.'

Lilli was still totally fazed, couldn't believe what had just happened. 'Why do you think Andy did it? Gave it back, I mean.' It was almost like a dream, and if it weren't for that bank account—for five million!—Lilli would have had trouble believing Andy had been here at all.

Patrick threw the bank book and account statement down onto the table, sitting in the chair opposite hers once again. 'I did some checking during the short time I had before coming here. Brewster's relationship has apparently foundered, probably because of the pending court case; his lover is apparently the type who doesn't care to be associated with criminals! So maybe Brewster just decided to try and salvage at least part of his life and try to walk away. I have a feeling your father will let him do that.'

So did she, once she had spoken to her father. 'He's certainly going to be ecstatic at the return of this.' She touched the statement as if she still couldn't believe the money was actually there, within her father's grasp.

Patrick said, 'He's gone back to Gerry's house, if you want to take it to him.'

This time Lilli didn't feel that sickening lurch in her stomach at the mention of the relationship between his sister and her father. Maybe she was getting used to the idea…

'And you?' Patrick suddenly asked her. 'How do you feel about it?'

She gave a glowing smile. 'Wonderful! Daddy has his money back, and it looks as if all the publicity a court case would have engendered can be avoided as well. It's— But you don't look too pleased, Patrick.' She suddenly realised he looked grimmer than ever. 'Do you think there's something wrong with the return of the money?' She looked down at the bank statement. 'Is Andy playing some sort of cruel joke on us all? Do you—?'

'Relax,' Patrick advised. 'The money is in a bank account in your name. It's yours. But it means the two of us have some serious talking to do once you've seen your father,' he added firmly.

Lilli looked startled. 'We do…?'

'One day, Lilli,' he bit out. 'Do you realise that if Brewster had returned that money to you just one day earlier you wouldn't now be my wife?' He looked at her intently. 'Would you?'

All the colour drained from her face as the force of his words hit her. One day… If Andy had come to see her the day before her marriage to Patrick, then he was right—there would have been no wedding. She wouldn't now be Patrick's wife. Never would have been!

She couldn't speak as this sickening realisation hit her.

'Exactly,' he grated, standing up. 'I really do have some things to do at the moment, Lilli. But we'll talk about this later at the hotel.'

Lilli sat and watched him go, her eyes dark green pools. Exactly what were they going to talk about? Not divorce? Did Patrick realise, with the return of this money, that they should never have been married at all? Did none of last night and this morning matter to him? Did he want to end their marriage before it had even begun?

CHAPTER TWELVE

'But this is wonderful!' Her father's delight was obvious as he smiled broadly. 'Absolutely marvellous!'

'But is it?' Gerry said slowly, looking at Lilli. 'Lilli doesn't look too happy.'

Her father turned to her too now, noticing the paleness of her face. 'Lilli?' he said warily. 'Brewster didn't say or do anything to upset you, did he?'

'No,' she dismissed with a shaky laugh.

'There aren't any hidden conditions attached to the return of this money, are there?'

She had come in a taxi straight to Gerry's house, knew she had to put her father's mind at rest as soon as possible. But inside she was still in shock from Patrick's enigmatic comments before he'd left her, couldn't actually remember the taxi journey here.

'No hidden conditions,' she assured her father wryly. 'I think Andy was quite relieved to get rid of it; a life of crime doesn't seem to have brought him too much happiness!'

'Then—'

'Where is Patrick, Lilli?' Gerry interjected. 'Richard said he came to join you at the hotel…?'

'He did.' She avoided the other woman's gaze: Gerry saw far too much! 'But he had some business to attend to,' she added brightly.

'Did he?' Gerry returned sceptically.

Lilli still didn't meet her sister-in-law's eyes. 'He said he did, yes.'

'But…?'

'Really, Gerry.' Lilli gave a light laugh, although no humour reached the dull pain in her eyes. 'You know Patrick—if he says he has something else to do, then he has something else to do.'

'I do know Patrick,' his sister acknowledged softly. 'We've always been very close. He more or less brought me up, you know.'

'Yes, he told me about that,' Lilli replied, those moments of intimacy between them seeming a lifetime away.

'Did he?' Gerry nodded her satisfaction with that. 'Then you must realise that the two of us know each other rather better than most brothers and sisters, that we've always had an emotional closeness?'

Lilli gave the other woman a puzzled glance. 'I don't understand where all this is leading to—'

'It's leading to the fact that Patrick is in love with you,' Gerry told her impatiently. 'And I have a feeling— a terrible feeling!—that because of this—' she held up the bank book and statement '—Patrick is going to do something incredibly stupid!'

Lilli was quick to protest, 'Patrick isn't in love with me, and—'

'Oh, yes, he is,' the other woman assured her with certainty.

'—he never does anything "incredibly stupid",' Lilli finished determinedly. 'Unless you count marrying me in the first place,' she added bitterly.

'Lilli, exactly what has Patrick said to you?' Gerry probed.

Lilli stood up and turned away from both her father and the other woman. 'Apart from more or less saying

we should start talking about a divorce?' she said
fiercely. 'Not a lot!'

'A divorce?' her father echoed incredulously. 'But
you were only married yesterday! He can't be serious—'

'They were married yesterday, Richard,' Gerry cut in
gently. 'But today the reason for Lilli marrying
Patrick—that money—' she gestured in the direction of
the bank book '—was made null and void. That is the
reason Patrick believes you married him, isn't it, Lilli?'

She was starting to resent Gerry again; this was none
of her business, even if she was Patrick's sister! 'It is
the reason I married him,' Lilli came back; she didn't
believe either of these two could seriously have ever
been fooled into believing otherwise!

'So you're going to agree to a divorce?' Gerry
watched her shrewdly.

Lilli felt ill just at the thought of it, knowing she must
have once again gone pale. 'If that's what Patrick's
wants, yes.'

'And what do *you* want?' the other woman persisted.

'You know Patrick; I don't think I'll have a lot of say
in this one way or the other!'

'Lilli, your father told me Patrick said he hadn't raised
a fool.' Gerry spoke plainly. 'But at this moment you're
being extremely foolish!' she added caustically.

'I don't think I asked for your opinion!' Lilli felt deep
resentment.

'And now you're being very rude,' her father said
sternly, moving forward to put his arms about Gerry's
shoulders. 'Gerry is trying to help you—'

'I don't need—or want!—her help,' Lilli told him
forcefully, her hands clenched at her sides at this show
of solidarity from the couple. The last thing she needed
at this moment was to have their relationship pushed in

her face. She felt as if her whole world was falling apart already, without that!

'Calm down, Richard.' Gerry put a soothing hand against his chest as he would have exploded angrily. 'Lilli is hurt and upset—and God knows we all do stupid things when we feel like that! I think it's time, Richard,' she opined slowly, 'that Lilli heard about some of the stupid things I did in the past—don't you?'

He looked down at her uncertainly. 'I—'

'It's time, Richard,' Gerry repeated firmly. 'Unless you want Lilli to make the same mistake I did? Because, believe me, these two are even more stubborn than we are, and at this moment, basically because she's here and Patrick isn't, I think Lilli is more open to reason.'

Lilli's father glanced across at his daughter uncertainly, Lilli steadily returning his gaze. She had no idea what all this was about, and she wasn't sure she wanted to know either. But she did know that when she got back to the hotel Patrick was going to talk about their future— or lack of it!—and anything that delayed that happening was acceptable!

'Very well.' Her father finally gave his agreement. 'But listen carefully, Lilli. And try not to judge,' he added almost pleadingly.

'Do I need to sit down for this?'

'Yes,' her father confirmed, going to the drinks tray on the side dresser. 'You're also going to need this.' He handed her a glass of brandy. 'We all are!' He handed another glass to Gerry, and kept one for himself.

Lilli sat, although she made no move to drink the brandy, putting the glass down on the table beside her chair, looking up expectantly at Gerry.

The other woman looked apprehensive at her sceptical expression. 'Your father is right, Lilli—you aren't going to like what you hear,' she said. 'But please try to understand; this isn't being done to hurt; I'm doing this for an altogether different reason.'

'I'll try,' Lilli conceded dryly.

'Lilli—'

'Leave it, Richard,' the other woman told him lightly. 'Lilli makes no pretence of doing anything other than disliking me, and at least it's honest. It isn't what I would like, but it's honest.' She walked over to the blazing fire, suddenly seeming to need its warmth. 'Six years ago I met a man I fell very much in love with,' she began. 'Unfortunately, the man was married— We haven't all led neatly packaged lives, Lilli,' she added at Lilli's derisive expression. 'The man was married. Unhappily—I know, aren't they all?' she acknowledged self-deprecatingly. 'But in this case it was true. I had seen the two of them together, knew that the wife was involved with someone else. And I—I fell in love with the husband. And he loved me in return.'

'But your marriage only lasted a couple of months,' Lilli pointed out. 'Hardly the love of a lifetime!' she said scathingly, wondering why she was being told all this.

'Because I didn't marry the man I loved!' Gerry returned curtly. 'There were complications. The man had a child. At fifteen, not a very young child, I'll admit, but a child the father loved very much. And there were reasons why—why this man couldn't leave his wife and child.'

'Once again, there always are,' Lilli returned without interest, this was an all-too-familiar story, surely…?

Gerry drew in a harsh breath. 'But in this case the wife threatened to completely alienate the child from the father if he dared to leave her—'

'But I thought you said she was involved in an affair, too?'

'She was,' Gerry rasped. 'And if things had been—different she had intended leaving her husband! But the woman became ill, seriously so, and her—lover decided he didn't want to tie himself to a woman dying of cancer.'

Lilli had become suddenly still, her eyes wide now as she stared at Gerry. 'Go on…'

'Your father and I were deeply in love, Lilli,' Gerry told her emotionally. 'We had intended being together. But he—he left it too late to agree to giving your mother a divorce. She had been diagnosed as terminally ill, her lover left her, and suddenly all she was left with was a broken marriage. And her daughter.' Gerry swallowed hard. 'She was determined to hang onto both of them—at any cost.'

Lilli could hardly breathe, felt suddenly numb.

'Your parents' marriage began to deteriorate after your brother died, Lilli,' the other woman continued huskily. 'Your father buried himself in his work—and loving you. And your mother went from one affair to another. And the love they had once felt for each other turned to a tolerant contempt. By the time I met your father four years later they were living completely separate lives, with you as their only common ground.'

Lilli looked at her father with pained eyes, couldn't believe she could have been so blind to her parents' loveless marriage. Or perhaps she hadn't… She had known they spent little time together, that her mother could be verbally vicious to her father when she chose to be, but she had always put that down to the pain of her illness. Now she could see that perhaps it had been that they simply didn't love each other any more…

'Daddy…?' She looked at him emotionally now.

'I'm sorry, Lilli. So sorry.' He gripped her hands tightly. 'But it's all true. In fact, there's so much more. Your mother had asked me for a divorce before she found out about her illness, was going off with this other man—'

'Richard…!' Gerry looked at him uncertainly.

He shook his head, his gaze still on Lilli. 'It's time it all came out, Gerry. Your mother was leaving us, Lilli. She had told me she was going, asked me for a divorce—on her terms, of course. She wanted a huge settlement of money, and in return she would leave you with me. The man she was involved with was ten years younger than her, and he didn't want Caroline's fifteen-year-old daughter cluttering up their lives.'

'Mummy was leaving me behind,' Lilli said dazedly.

'Yes,' he replied. 'And I was happy to give her the money if I could keep you. Then she found out she had cancer…' His expression darkened. 'And everything changed!'

'Lilli!' Gerry came to her side as she swayed where she sat. 'No more of that, Richard,' she said briskly. 'I only wanted to try to explain a little…'

'I've misjudged you,' Lilli realised flatly, reaching out blindly to clasp the other woman's hand—blindly because her eyes were full of tears. 'Patrick knows all of this, doesn't he?' She realised only too well now what he had meant when he'd said her father had been protective of her to the point of stupidity! She looked up at her father now. 'You gave up your chance of happiness because you didn't want to lose me,' she said brokenly.

'You had already been through so much when we lost Robbie—'

'You gave up the woman you loved—Gerry—' she

looked at the other woman as the tears began to fall down her cheeks '—so that Mummy wouldn't destroy all our lives. And you…' She tightly squeezed Gerry's hand. 'You married someone else on the rebound.' She recalled her father's words… 'An angry and upset Gerry is a force to be reckoned with!'

'Oh, Lilli!' Gerry moved to hug her. 'Don't make the same mistake. Please!'

She pulled back slightly. 'You mean Patrick?'

'I mean my stubborn, arrogant brother,' Gerry confirmed. 'It runs in the family, I'm afraid. Your father went out of my life five years ago because I was too stubborn to listen to him. I married—disastrously—to spite him. I loved him, wanted to be with him, and although I understood what he was doing it was impossible for me to stay in his life. My marriage was a mess, and within a couple of months I had to admit I had made a terrible mistake.' She grimaced at the memory. 'Don't do something stupid like I did, Lilli. I know Patrick; he would never have married you if he didn't love you.'

'When he asked me to marry him it was because he said I had the qualities he wanted in his wife, in the mother of his children—'

'He probably believed it when he said it too.' Gerry shook her head with affectionate exasperation. 'But it's all nonsense. Patrick is in love with you— Yes, he is, Lilli,' she insisted firmly even as Lilli opened her mouth to deny it. 'Do you love him? The truth, Lilli. It's the day for the truth,' she went on throatily.

Lilli took a deep breath. 'I— Yes!' The word was virtually forced out of her. It was one thing to admit to herself how she felt, quite another thing to admit it to someone else. Even someone she realised she had completely misjudged… God, Gerry should have been the one resenting her all this time, not the other way around. So many years wasted… And what Gerry was saying to her now was, did she want to waste as many by giving up on Patrick without a fight? But Gerry had known Richard loved her, whereas Patrick didn't love Lilli at all…

'Then what do you have to lose by telling him so?' Gerry sat back, her expression encouraging. 'Your pride? Oh, Lilli!' She held her hand out towards the man she loved, straightening to stand at his side. 'My pride, after I made such a mess of things, cost me years I could have spent with your father. Long, lonely years, when I went out with lots of men who meant nothing to me, men who, because of their own male pride, would never admit to anyone that those relationships were never physical. I've been so lonely, for so long, without your father, Lilli; but thank God he came back and claimed me once he was free to do so!'

'And—thank God—she let me!' Lilli's father added with feeling.

Lilli smiled shakily up at the two of them. 'So when are the two of you getting married?'

'As soon as you and Patrick agree to be our witnesses,' her father told her.

Patrick… A shadow passed over her face, her smile, emotional as it was, fading.

'I'm ordering you to stay away from him, Lilli,' her father told her expectantly.

Her smile returned, a little wanly, but it did return. 'That won't work this time, Daddy. I—' She broke off as the telephone began to ring, Gerry going to answer it.

'Good afternoon, Patrick,' she greeted once he had identified himself as the caller. 'Richard is ecstatic over the news, and— Yes, Lilli is still here.' She glanced across the room at a now tense Lilli. 'Well, we're all just about to sit down and enjoy a celebratory glass of champagne— Yes, I know it's your honeymoon,' she answered him smoothly. 'But it's Christmas too. And we all have something to celebrate—why don't you come and join us—?' Gerry suddenly held the receiver away from her ear, wincing as the loudness of Patrick's voice down the receiver could now be heard by all of them, although the words themselves were indistinct. 'Well, it's your choice, of course. Lilli will be back later.' Gerry looked down at the receiver, shrugging before placing it back on its cradle. 'I'll give him twenty minutes.' She grinned.

'For what?' Lilli frowned, having been frozen in her seat since she realised it was Patrick on the telephone, her hands still shaking slightly.

'For him to get here.' Gerry grinned her satisfaction. 'And you doubted he loves you! Patrick never shouts, Lilli. He's never needed to. The softer he talks, the more anxious people are to do what he wants. But he's shouting now, Lilli—and it's because I deliberately gave him the impression you wouldn't be going back to the hotel until later this evening.' She laughed, glancing at her wristwatch. 'Eighteen minutes, and counting!'

Lilli was sure the other woman was wrong. As his sister, she might know Patrick very well, but she had no knowledge of him as a husband. There was no way Patrick would come to her...

And she wasn't going to him yet either, wasn't ready for that, readily falling in with her father's suggestion that they have the champagne after all. Anything to delay going back to the hotel. And discussing their divorce...

'To the two of you.' She toasted her father and Gerry with pink champagne. 'May you be happy together at last.' She owed them this much, owed them so much more than she had ever realised.

Her marriage to Patrick meant she was no longer a child, and she was learning all too forcefully what Patrick had said all along: things were never just black and white. No one was to blame for the triangle that had evolved six years ago, not even her mother. Maybe it wasn't emotionally fair, but, faced with a sure slow death, her mother had clung to the things that she still could, and that included her husband and daughter. Given the same circumstances, Lilli wasn't sure she would have done the same thing, but it was what had happened, and it was over now. It was time to shut the door on that, and start again.

For all of them, it seemed…

She swallowed down her feelings of apprehension with the champagne. Time enough to face all that later; right now was the time to let her father celebrate. And for him and Gerry to be allowed to be happy with each other at long last.

'Hmm, three minutes early,' Gerry suddenly murmured after another glance at her watch. 'He must have broken several speed limits to get here this fast at this time of the day—and on Christmas Eve!' She smiled across at Lilli. 'I just heard Patrick's car in the driveway.' She listened again. 'Patrick entering the house,' she added ruefully as the front door could be heard slamming loudly shut. 'Patrick entering the room,' she announced before turning to face him, a glowing smile lighting up her face. 'Patrick, what a surprise!' she greeted warmly. 'You decided to join us, after all.'

He didn't even glance at his sister, all his attention

focused on Lilli as she stood near the fire. 'I thought you were coming back to the hotel once you had spoken to your father,' he grated accusingly.

Her hand trembled slightly as she held onto her champagne glass. 'We were celebrating,' she said with soft dismissal.

'Richard and I were just going off in search of another bottle of champagne,' Gerry said lightly. 'Weren't we, darling?' she prompted pointedly.

'Er—yes. We were,' he agreed somewhat disjointedly, frowning at Lilli and Patrick.

Patrick returned his gaze coldly. 'Pink, of course,' he said. 'It's Lilli's favourite.'

'How well you know your wife,' Gerry drawled, lightly touching his cheek as she passed him on her way to the door. 'We shouldn't be too long,' she assured Lilli gently in passing.

The room suddenly seemed very quiet once the other couple had left, closing the door softly behind them, even the ticking of the clock on the fireplace suddenly audible.

Lilli could only stare at Patrick. Dear God, he looked grim. Her hands began to shake again as she tightly gripped the glass.

'But not for much longer, hmm, Lilli?' he suddenly exclaimed as he strode further into the room, dark and overpowering in black denims and a black sweater. 'Will I know you as my wife?' he added at her puzzled frown.

Something seemed to snap inside her at that moment, a return of the old Lilli through the fog of uncertainty, pain, truth—so much truth, it was still difficult to take it all in!—and she faced Patrick unflinchingly as she carefully placed her glass down on the table behind her. 'I thought we had an agreement that our marriage was

for life,' she reminded him haughtily—every inch
Elizabeth Bennett at that moment. But she was neither
Just Lilli nor Elizabeth Bennett any more, she was Lilli
Devlin—and she was about to fight for what she wanted!
'The agreement—verbal though it might have been—
was binding on both sides. You can't just opt out of it
when it suits you, Patrick.' She still didn't believe that
Patrick loved her—it would be too much to hope for!—
but if she could remain his wife, who knew what might
happen in the future...?

'When it suits me—!' he exploded furiously, a nerve
pulsing erratically in the hardness of his cheek. 'It
doesn't *suit* me at all to have my wife walk out on me
the day after our wedding! Even Sanchia waited a little
longer than that.'

'Forget Sanchia,' Lilli returned. 'I am not her, am
nothing like her. And I'm not walking out on you.'

'I have just spent most of the day, the day following
our wedding, at the hotel on my own,' he bit out. 'I
would say that's walking out!'

'Rubbish,' she snapped back. 'I spent all of the morning and part of the afternoon, at the hotel with you,' she
reminded him, a blush to her cheeks as she remembered
those hours of intimacy. 'We've been apart maybe three
hours at the most—'

'And look what happened in those three hours!' he
said disgustedly.

'What, Patrick? What happened during that time?' she
challenged. 'My father had his money returned to him.
What does that have to do with us, with our marriage?
You told me last week that it wasn't mentioned during
the proposal or the acceptance; so what bearing does this
afternoon's events have on our marriage? Well?' she
pressed after several seconds of tense silence.

He gave a snort. 'Everything!'

She became suddenly still, looking at him carefully. 'Why?'

'Oh, for God's sake, Lilli.' He paced about the room. 'It may not have been mentioned, but we both know how relevant Brewster giving the money back is to us; you admitted as much yourself earlier this afternoon when I asked you!'

She thought back to their conversation after Andy had left, to what Patrick had said, because she hadn't said anything! 'And just how did I admit it, Patrick?' she asked softly. 'I don't believe *I* said anything.'

'You didn't have to,' he groaned. 'The look on your face when you realised how close you had come to not marrying me spoke for itself; you went white!'

She drew in a deep breath. Pride, Gerry had told her, had cost her six years of happiness with the man she loved…

'Are you interested in why I went white, Patrick?' she said.

'I know why you went white,' he ground out, glaring at her. 'You missed keeping your freedom by twenty-four hours!'

Lilli steadily met his tempestuous gaze, unmoved by the fierceness of his expression. 'You're partly right—' She ignored his second snort of disgust in as many minutes, choosing her words carefully. 'I realised,' she said slowly, 'how narrowing I had avoided not marrying you—'

'Then we don't have a problem, do we, because—?'

'Be quiet, Patrick, and let me finish what I'm saying!' She glared at him. 'And listen, damn it! I said "how narrowly I had avoided *not* marrying you" —because if Andy had come back into our lives two days ago *you* would have been the one to call off the wedding. Wouldn't you?' she persisted.

'I—'

'Not me, Patrick,' she continued unwaveringly. 'I wouldn't have called it off, because I *wanted* to marry you!' The last came out in a rush, Lilli holding her breath now as she waited for his reaction.

He continued to look at her, but some of the fierceness went out of his expression, uncertainty taking its place.

And uncertainty wasn't an emotion Lilli had ever associated with Patrick before...

'Why?' he said bluntly.

She swallowed hard. Could she really just tell him—? Pride, Gerry had called it. And look what it had cost the other woman in terms of real happiness...!

She drew in a deeply controlling breath. 'Because I love you!' Once again the words came out in a rush, and it was her turn to look uncertain now. 'I know you don't love me,' she continued hurriedly at Patrick's stunned expression. 'That you decided never to love again after Sanchia—'

'As you said earlier—forget Sanchia,' he dismissed harshly. 'As far as I'm concerned she ceased to exist the day she decided to destroy our child because she believed pregnancy would ruin her figure—'

'Patrick, no!' Lilli gasped disbelievingly. How could anyone destroy another human life for such selfish reasons? The life of Patrick's child... Which was why he had asked her if she wanted children... Why he had made such a point of telling her she would look beautiful when she was pregnant...! 'Oh, Patrick...!' Her voice broke emotionally as she went to him, her arms going about his waist as she rested her head against his chest.

'You said you loved me...?' he said quietly.

He stood a little apart from her, his own arms loose at his sides, his expression distant as she looked up at him. 'Not the past tense, Patrick.' She shook her head firmly. 'I do love you. Very much. And I do not want a divorce,' she added determinedly. 'I told you before, you aren't going to have everything your own way—'

'I don't want a divorce either!' His voice rose agitatedly, moving at last, his arms coming tightly about her waist. 'I thought you did. I thought— Lilli, I know what I said to you when I asked you to marry me.' He looked intently down at her. 'I was trying to protect myself, trying—' He shook his head in self-disgust. 'I lied, Lilli. I—'

'You don't tell lies, Patrick,' she reminded him softly, hope starting to blossom somewhere deep inside her, too deep down yet to actually flower, but it was there nonetheless...

'Lilli. Just Lilli. *My* Lilli.' His hands cupped either side of her face as he raised it to his. 'That first night at the hotel, as you lay sleeping in the bed— Don't look like that, Lilli,' he admonished gently. 'You were beautiful that night. I lay beside you for hours just watching you.' He smiled as she looked startled. 'You were— are—so beautiful, and yet as you slept you looked so vulnerable. By the time morning came I had decided I wanted to spend the rest of my life waking up with you beside me. I didn't recognise those feelings as love then, but—'

'Love?' she echoed huskily, that hope starting to flower now, to grow and grow, until it filled her.

'Love, Lilli. I fell in love with you that night. Although I certainly didn't recognise it as such.' He grimaced. 'Only that I wanted you with me for the rest of my life. But when I came out of the bathroom that morning you had gone…'

'I felt so embarrassed by what I had done.'

'I realise that,' he nodded. 'It was the shock of my life, only a matter of hours after that, to discover you were actually Richard Bennett's daughter. With all the complications that entailed—'

'I know about my mother, Patrick,' she interrupted. 'And about Gerry and my father. I— We've all made our peace.'

'Have you? I'm glad. Gerry's life was such a mess five years ago, and for years I harboured very strong feelings against your father for causing that unhappiness. And then two months ago Gerry took him back into her life, and I— I didn't take the news too well initially. Maybe I was a bit over-zealous—businesswise—where your father was concerned, because of that. Part of me wanted him destroyed in the way he had destroyed my sister's life,' he admitted heavily.

'And you hated me because I was his daughter,' Lilli said knowingly.

'I didn't hate you.' His arms tightened about her once again. 'I could never hate you. I was not—pleased to discover you were his daughter.'

'You believed I had slept with you deliberately,' she reminded him teasingly.

'Only for a matter of a few hours. I was so damned angry when I found out who you really were that it seemed the only explanation for the way you had left the party with me—'

'I had just seen my father with Gerry,' she told him. 'I was angry and upset, and although I didn't know you were Gerry's brother the two of you seemed close, and so I—I decided to go with you to spite her. Not very nice, I'll grant you, but at the time I just wasn't thinking straight. I got the shock of my life when I woke up that morning in a hotel bedroom and heard you singing in the adjoining bathroom!'

'Well, of course I was singing,' he grinned. 'I had just found the woman I wanted to spend the rest of my life with!'

'And I thought I had spent the night making love with you and couldn't even remember it!' she recalled with a groan.

'I know, love,' he said. 'That was obvious when I came to your house later that day.'

'And you let me carry on believing it!' she reproved exasperatedly.

'Don't be too angry with me, Lilli.' He kissed her gently on the lips. 'It was the fact that we hadn't made love that made me realise I had made a mistake about that. When I sat and thought about it later, if you really had set out to trick me that night, you would never have allowed yourself to go to sleep in the way that you did, and you certainly wouldn't have left the hotel so abruptly. I also realised, as I sat angrily churning all this through my mind, that our night together actually made things less complicated rather than more so. It enabled me to ask you to marry me,' he explained at her questioning look, 'to point out all the advantages of such a marriage, without ever having to admit how I felt about you. I didn't want to love anyone, Lilli, but— What I feel for you is like nothing I have ever known before. I want to be with you all the time. To make love with you. To argue with you—we do them both so well!' He smiled. 'I've never felt like this before, Lilli,' he told her intently. 'I love you so very much.'

She believed him! Patrick loved her. And she loved him.

And if either of them needed any further proof of that then the kiss they shared was enough, full of love and aching passion—enough to last a lifetime.

Lilli's eyes glowed, her cheeks were flushed, her lips bare of gloss, when she looked up at him some time later. 'Would you really have let me go?' she prompted huskily.

He frowned. 'If it was what you wanted,' he said slowly.

No, he wouldn't. She knew him too well already to actually believe that. 'Without a fight?' she teased.

'No,' he admitted dryly.

She laughed softly, hugging him tightly. 'I'm so glad you said that—because I wouldn't have gone without kicking and screaming either!'

His answering laugh was full of indulgent joy. 'We're never going to part, Lilli. I'll do everything in my power to make you happy.'

'Just continue to love me,' she told him. 'It will be enough. I—'

'Can we come back in yet?' Gerry looked cautiously around the door she had just opened. 'Only the champagne is getting warm!'

'Do come in.' Lilli held her hand out towards the other woman. 'Let's drink the champagne and make a toast.' She smiled glowingly at her father as he came in carrying the tray with the champagne bottle—pink, of course!—and another glass. 'To a wonderful Christmas and New Year for all of us,' she announced as they all held up their glasses, sure in her heart that every year was going to be a happy one from now on. For all of them.

'How could you do this to me?' Patrick groaned tragically. 'I'll never survive!'

Lilli laughed at his comical expression, very tired, but filled with a glow that shone from deep inside her. 'You'll survive only too well,' she said knowingly. 'Now there will be three of us to love and spoil you.'

'Twins!' Patrick looked down into the cribs that stood next to the hospital bed, gazing in wonder at the identical beauty of the babies that slept within them. 'And both girls,' he added achingly. 'I'm going to end up spoiling all of *you*!'

Lilli smiled at him indulgently. Their daughters had been born fifty-five and fifty-one minutes ago, respectively, and Patrick had been at her side the whole time she had been in labour. As he had been at her side during the whole of the last year...

Lilli had been right; this past year had been the happiest of her life. And she knew it had been the same for Patrick, that the birth of their beautiful daughters on New Year's Eve had made it all complete.

'Think how poor Daddy felt.' She gave a happy laugh. 'James Robert was born on Christmas Day!' No one, it seemed, could have been more surprised than her father when Gerry had presented him with a son a week ago.

It was probably the celebrating that had been going on ever since the birth that had brought on Lilli's own slightly premature labour. But it hadn't been a difficult birth, and their darling little girls were worth any pain she might have felt.

'Now all we have to do is think of names for them both,' Patrick said a little dazedly.

He was right. They hadn't even known she was expecting twins, and because they had been absolutely convinced the baby she carried was a boy they hadn't chosen any girls' names at all.

'Is there room for three more in there?' Her father stood in the doorway, his baby son in his arms, Gerry at his side. 'Or are the Devlins taking over?' he added teasingly.

Lilli's family was complete as her father, Gerry and her new little brother came into the room.

Since she and Patrick had admitted their love for each other, Lilli had been convinced that every new day was the happiest of her life. But as she looked at all her family gathered there together, all so happy, she knew this was definitely their happiest day. Yet…

Rebecca Winters, an American writer and mother of four, is excited to be in this new millennium because it means another new beginning. Having said goodbye to the classroom where she taught French and Spanish, she is now free to spend more time with her family, to travel and to write the Mills & Boon Tender Romance® novels she loves so dearly. Rebecca loves to hear from readers. If you wish to e-mail her, please visit her website at: www.rebeccawinters-author.com

THE NUTCRACKER PRINCE
by
Rebecca Winters

CHAPTER ONE

"Shh, Anna, honey. Remember, we can only sing to the music at home, not during the ballet." Meg Roberts quietly admonished her six-year-old daughter, who was sitting on her lap and blithely singing the words to the "Waltz of the Flowers" a little off-key.

Even though the Saturday matinee performance of the St. Louis ballet company's *Nutcracker* catered to families with younger children, Meg noticed a good number of adults in the audience, as well.

"I'm sorry, Mommy. When will the prince come out?" Anna whispered so loudly it drew a quelling look from an older woman seated in front of them.

Before Meg could caution her again, Anna put a finger to her own lips and flashed her mother a mischievous smile—a smile that never failed to swell Meg's heart with love and pride. Anna's exuberant personality shone through her sparkling eyes, which fastened in rapt attention on the dancers once more.

In the near darkness Meg studied her daughter. Anna's cheeks were flushed with the excitement of attending her first ballet. Though Christmas was only eight days away, Anna had talked of nothing but this day for more than a month; even now, she

hugged the picture book of the *Nutcracker* to the
bodice of the red velvet dress Meg had made for
her.

The well-worn treasure brought from Russia went
everywhere her daughter did. With its Russian print-
ing Anna couldn't read the words, but it was the
illustrations that captured her heart—particularly the
ones of handsome Prince Marzipan fighting the
Mouse King. From the very first instant she'd caught
sight of his tall, uniformed physique, Anna had remarked on the dark hair and blue eyes similar to her
own. Even more poignant, from Meg's point of
view, was the fact that her daughter had endowed
Prince Marzipan with all the qualities she attributed
to the father she'd never seen or known.

The fact that the Prince did bear a striking resem-
blance to Anna's father made it impossible for Meg
to put her own bittersweet memories away, especially since he'd given Meg the book in the first
place. It was a constant reminder of the man who,
with practiced ease, had made love to a foolish, vulnerable, starry-eyed Meg—the man who'd left her
pregnant. But even without it, there was no forgetting Konstantin Rudenko. Not when Anna was the
very image of him.

With each passing day Meg grew more troubled
as she identified yet another similarity in their coloring and features. Every day she was beset by disturbing flashes of recall that refused to die. Certain
facial expressions, the way Anna's head swiveled
around when she heard something that interested
her, all would trigger long-suppressed memories fol-

lowed by waves of shame and humiliation. Especially now that Meg knew she'd been set up, lied to, used....

"Look, Mommy!"

The Russian cossack dancers came out to perform their gymnastic feats, and once again Anna forgot where she was and broke into more off-key singing about balalaikas and clicking feet.

"Quiet!" the older woman snapped over her shoulder, and this time several other people turned around, as well.

Mortified, Meg hugged her daughter tighter. "You mustn't talk or sing," she whispered into Anna's short dark curls. "You're disturbing other people. If you make another sound, we'll have to leave."

"No, Mommy," she begged with tears in her eyes. "I haven't seen the prince yet. I promise to be good."

"You always say that, and then you forget."

"I won't forget," Anna asserted so earnestly Meg had to smile. Still, she knew it would be a sheer impossibility for her daughter to remain quiet throughout the rest of the performance.

"You'll have to stay on my lap."

"I will." She wrapped her arms around Meg's neck and gave her a kiss on the cheek before settling down. For a little while, Anna's model behavior lulled Meg into a false sense of security, and they both watched spellbound as the delightful story unfolded.

Then the symphony's brass section announced the

arrival of the toy soldiers. Without warning, Anna slid off Meg's lap. "There's Prince Marzipan, Mommy. See?" she cried in ecstasy, pointing to the male dancer who led the march. Her absorption with the Prince made her oblivious to everything else around her, but Meg hadn't missed the furious glare of the woman in front of them.

Luckily by now, other enchanted children throughout the audience had gotten to their feet and were contributing to the heightened noise. Their cheers and clapping made Anna's outburst seem less noticeable. From the glow in her eyes, Meg knew what this moment meant to her daughter, who stood entranced until the Prince leapt offstage after defeating the Mouse King.

The second he disappeared Anna whirled around and climbed onto Meg's lap again. "Mommy," she said in a loud whisper, "I have to *you know what.*"

Meg shouldn't have been surprised. The excitement had been too much, and she knew Anna wouldn't be able to wait until the performance was over. "All right. Don't forget your book." Throwing their coats over one arm, she reached for Anna's hand with the other and they made their way past several people to the center aisle.

"Slow down, honey," Meg cautioned, struggling to keep up with Anna who practically ran to the ladies' lounge off the nearly empty foyer. She was still chattering about the Prince when they emerged a few minutes later.

"Can I go see him when it's over, Mommy?" Anna blurted while they stood in the short lineup at the drinking fountain before going back into the concert hall.

"I don't think that's allowed."

"Mrs. Beezley said I could."

"We'll see," Meg murmured, wishing Anna's first-grade teacher hadn't put the idea in her head. Mrs. Beezley's opinions often carried more weight than Meg's.

"Our precocious daughter appears to be enjoying herself," Meg heard a male voice say from behind her. She assumed the man must be talking to his wife and didn't give it further thought as she waited for Anna to finish drinking from the fountain.

"Do you remember that lowly woodcutter's cottage outside St. Petersburg, *mayah labof?*"

Meg let out a gasp and the world came to a sudden standstill.

Konstantin. No. It couldn't be.

But his question, whispered with that quiet, unmistakable sensuality she remembered so well, spoke to the very depths of her soul. She hadn't imagined his voice.

Her body broke out in a cold sweat and she felt herself swaying. She closed her eyes in shock.

He was supposed to be living on the other side of the world, leading a life she would never want or be able to comprehend. Yet her heart beating frantically in her chest told her something vastly different.

He wasn't in St. Petersburg. He was *here,* in *this* theater, and he had just called her *my darling*. If Meg turned around, she'd be able to touch him.

Dear God.

But even as she recognized the reality of his presence, her body trembled in anger and panic. She was furious with herself for the weakness that brought the memories flooding back. The still-sensual memories of his lovemaking seven years ago—when she'd only been part of a night's work for him.

Her intellectual side had always known he was the enemy, but there was a time she'd been so in love with him her heart had refused to listen or care, had most of all refused to believe.

He knew about Anna.

The knowledge shouldn't have shaken her like this. Of course he knew about Anna. He knew things about people no human being had a right to know, because that was his business. His *only* business.

Which meant he'd been following them, waiting for the perfect moment to seize his property, to seize his daughter....

What better spot than someplace public, where he knew Meg couldn't or wouldn't make a scene because it would alarm Anna? Sick with fear, Meg felt her heart race out of control.

With startling clarity she remembered those terrifying hours she'd spent in the dark—alone—on the dank floor of a Moscow jail, her guards devoid of compassion or pity.

"Meg?" His voice interrupted her thoughts. She didn't know how much time had passed—only seconds, she supposed, but that was long enough to relive the years of heartache. She did not turn around as he began to speak.

"I don't know what you've told her about her father, but now that I'm here, we'll tell her the truth together. Forget any ideas of running away from me, or I will most assuredly cause a scene. Since I know how much you would hate to upset Anna, I expect your full cooperation."

His English was as perfect as ever, formal, precise. The training he'd received in the KGB left nothing to chance. Anyone listening would assume he was from the United States, perhaps the East Coast.

A moan escaped her lips, and the sound caught Anna's attention. She gave up her place at the fountain for the next child. "Mommy? What's wrong?" Apprehension gripped Meg so tightly she couldn't move or breathe; it prevented her from doing any of a dozen things her survival instincts screamed for her to do. No trap ever devised worked as well as the threat to one's own flesh and blood. "N-nothing, honey. Let's hurry back inside."

She grabbed Anna's hand and almost dragged her toward the doors of the concert hall. Meg knew she didn't have a prayer of eluding *him,* but she refused to remain there like a paralyzed animal while he gloated over another easy victory.

"Mommy, you're hurrying too fast," Anna complained, but Meg, whose fear escalated with every passing second, increased her speed.

It didn't matter that there had been drastic changes in Russia since detente. He might no longer be KGB, but he could still be working for the present powers in a classified capacity. Secret police still existed in the former USSR.

As far as she was concerned, he was a dangerous man she'd never wanted to see again—a man who could pass himself off as an American, with no one the wiser—a man who now walked within whispering distance of them and had obviously been monitoring the events of her life for years.

He was a man who would stop at nothing to achieve his objective. And she had an idea his objective now was Anna.

But this time there was one difference. She was no longer that naive twenty-three-year-old who had credited him with a set of values similar to her own. Time and experience had worked their damage, and that vulnerable young creature no longer existed. All that remained of their long-ago nights of passion was Meg's bitterness—and her daughter.

If she and Anna could make it inside before he caught up with them, she could buy a little time to work out what to do. By now she was half-pulling, half-carrying Anna, her own heart pumping hard and fast.

"Meg? Anna?"

At the sound of their names being called, Anna yanked free of her mother and turned around. "Who are you?" she asked, her face bright with curiosity.

Defeated by his cunning, Meg was forced to come to a stop and face the man she'd once, briefly, loved. The man who had fathered Anna. She didn't want to look at him, didn't want to acknowledge him. But Anna was watching them with avid interest, and

Meg was afraid to upset her or force his hand too soon.

When she finally dared a glimpse, the intense blue of his heavily lashed eyes almost made her reel. He'd always been the most attractive man she'd ever known, yet he looked different, somehow, from the way she remembered him.

The first time she'd met him, his brown-black hair had brushed the collar of his drab gray suit and trench coat, typical KGB garb. Now he wore his hair shorter and dressed like a successful American businessman in a navy suit and pale blue shirt that enhanced his six-foot height and lean, muscled frame. But the difference she perceived was subtler than that.

Unlike the married middle-aged men at the European-auto dealership where she worked as a secretary/cashier, he'd grown even handsomer, if that was possible, over the past seven years. In his late thirties now, he possessed a virile appeal that her body recognized and responded to without any volition on her part.

"I'm someone who loves you and your mommy very much," he said in answer to his daughter. Anna resembled him in so many attractive ways, Meg was afraid she'd see the similarities right off.

"You do?" Anna sounded amazed and, worse, intrigued.

Meg's eyes closed in growing fury. He meant business. Damn him for his matchless ability to charm his victims. As always, he resorted to ways that had nothing to do with brute force.

With an overwhelming sense of helplessness she waited to hear his response, part of her still denying he had sprung out of nowhere like one of those disturbing dreams that haunts you for years afterward.

"What's your name?" Anna asked softly.

"Konstantin Rudenko."

"K-Konsta... What did you say?"

He chuckled. "Your mommy calls me Kon."

The audacity, the cruel, calculating arrogance of the man, filled Meg with rage.

"It's Russian, like yours."

"You mean I have a Russian name, too?"

"That's right." He pronounced it with his native accent, his voice tender. Then his eyes sought Meg's as if to say, "You've never forgotten me."

"No!" Meg cried out against this threat to her fragile emotions and hard-won independence, but it was too late. In a quick, protective move she placed both hands on her daughter's shoulders.

Anna's young, inquiring mind seized upon the information she'd just learned and carefully imitated his pronunciation of her name. She tried to pull away from her mother. "My mommy told me my daddy lives in Russia, so he can't ever come to visit me," she said in a loud whisper, remembering too late that it was a secret between the two of them. Her mother had told her over and over that no one else must ever know.

"Anna!" Meg chastised her, but the effort was fruitless.

"Well, your mommy is wrong, Anochka," he asserted, using the diminutive of her name.

This time Anna wriggled loose from Meg's grip and moved closer to inspect him. "You look just like Prince Marzipan!"

Quick as lightning she peered over her shoulder at Meg, who was shaken by the stars in her daughter's eyes. "Mommy! He looks like the Prince!" And she immediately opened her book to the page whose edges were worn from constant use. "See?" She pointed out the similarities to him.

In a lithe move he got down on his haunches, making it easier for Anna to show him her proof. A satisfied smile lifted the corners of his mouth, and he fingered one of the curls bouncing over her forehead. "Did you know I gave your mommy this book when she left Russia after her first visit, more than twelve years ago?"

For the second time in a couple of minutes, Meg gasped out loud. Anna's eyes grew huge. "You did?"

"Yes. It's my favorite book, too. That's because we're father and daughter, and we think alike."

His eyes flashed Meg another meaningful glance. "Your mommy was sad because your grandfather died while she was on her trip. So when she went home, I put this book in her suitcase to comfort her because she had admired it. I hoped it would make her feel better and bring her back to Russia one day, because I cared for her even then."

Tears stung Meg's eyes. *Liar,* her heart cried. But she couldn't dispute the fact that this beautiful, over-priced book, which she'd admired at the House of Books in Moscow and couldn't afford, had ended up in her luggage. It was all thanks to the dark, attractive KGB agent, assigned to the foreign-student sector, who had hustled her from jail to the airport.

Meg, along with other seventeen-year-olds on her bus, had been detained because they'd given away blue jeans, T-shirts and other personal articles to friendly Russian teenagers. Unsuspecting, Meg had given her Guess? sunglasses to a young girl—and ended up in prison. She still shuddered when she thought of that nightmarish incident.

During her confinement, one of the guards told her the tour director had just learned that Meg's father had died back in the States. Because of Meg's unwise decision to break the law and consort with black marketers, he informed her, she might not be able to go home for the funeral, maybe not be able to go home at all.

He'd seemed inhuman to Meg, incapable of emotion. He'd left her alone to ''think about'' what she'd done, and Meg had collapsed on the floor in despair. For hours she'd sobbed out her grief for the loss of her mother a year earlier and now her beloved father. William Roberts was dead, thousands of miles away, and she would never see him again.

But before morning, Kon had come to get her, and she was escorted through hallways to a back door, where a car waited to take her to the airport. She never saw her traveling companions again, and returned to the United States in time to bury her father, the book her only memento.

After her cruel treatment at the hands of other

agents under his command, Kon's authority and subsequent intervention had been the only reason she
was allowed to return to the States without further
repercussions. His gift, totally unsolicited, had
caused her to rethink her opinion that all KGB
agents were monsters.

Six years later, when she qualified for a new opportunity, arranged through the State Department, to
travel to Russia as a cultural-exchange teacher, she
looked forward to the experience. Meg had hoped
to locate him and thank him in person for his kindness.

She'd seen him again, all right. Naively she'd believed that their meeting was accidental, never realizing that Kon had kept track of her back in the
States. The knowledge was almost unbearable. It
meant his feelings had never been real. And it meant
that on her second trip to the USSR, after the invalid
aunt she'd lived with and taken care of had passed
away, Meg was targeted. She'd learned about this
from the CIA on her return. Kon's every move had
been calculated to make her fall in love with him,
for reasons best known to the KGB. It had happened
before, to equally naive, usually young American
men and women—tourists, diplomatic employees
and others. What had occurred between Meg and
Kon was, as it turned out, not all that rare. Kon's
"love" had been politically motivated; he'd been in
control.

And now he'd come for Anna.

"Are you really my daddy?"

Anna's simple question broke the silence. The

hope in her earnest young voice had Meg practically in tears. She realized they'd come to the moment of truth. Kon would show no mercy.

"Yes, I'm your daddy, and I can tell you're my little girl. We have the same blue eyes, the same dark brown hair, and the same straight noses." He tweaked hers gently, and Anna giggled. "But you smile just like your mommy. See?"

He whipped some pictures out of his suit-coat pocket. "That's your mommy and I eating ice cream and champagne. I'd just told her I loved her. Look at her mouth. It curves right there—" he touched Anna's lower lip "—exactly like yours."

Anna giggled again before putting the precious storybook on the floor so she could look at the black-and-white snapshot. For once in her life she was struck dumb. So was Meg, who could remember him touching her mouth like that. Then he'd kissed her until she'd never wanted him to stop....

At the time she'd been blissfully unaware that someone was taking pictures of them.

There had to be many more photographs where those came from. Meg had little doubt that a camera had recorded their days and nights together, and she felt a deep, searing pain that the most wonderful experience of her life—loving Kon—could have ended up in the KGB microfilm files.

"Mommy, look! This is a picture of you."

"That's right," he murmured, "and here are some other photos of your beautiful mother and me in front of her hotel and at a nearby museum."

Kon couldn't have come up with a more cunning

plan to win over his daughter than this—offering her hungry eyes absolute proof of her parents' relationship.

On both of Meg's trips to Russia, picture-taking had been strictly forbidden, except for the shots taken at Red Square, the military pride of the nation. Which explained why she didn't have even one photograph of Kon to keep in remembrance.

"And here," he said when Anna had finished inspecting the others, "is a picture of your mommy and me at the airport. I begged her to stay in Russia and marry me, but she got on that plane, anyway." His voice sounded desolate, and Meg thought cynically that it was a mark of his consummate acting ability.

By now his arm had gone around Anna's tiny waist and she leaned against his chest without even realizing it. Watching her daughter, Meg felt her heart shatter into tiny pieces.

Anna raised troubled eyes to her mother. "Why did you do that, Mommy?" Tears threatened. "Why did you leave my daddy alone?"

Meg fought for a stabilizing breath, despising Kon for doing this to her. To them. "Because I couldn't have come back to America if I had stayed any longer, and I had responsibilities at home. Classes to teach, commitments to my students."

"You're a teacher?"

After a brief pause she said, "Not anymore, honey. But I was—once."

"Like Mrs. Beezley?" Anna sounded totally puzzled by her mother's admission.

"Yes. I taught high school." But having a baby on her own had forced her to grow up in a hurry, and when she realized the truth of what had gone on while she was in Russia, she gave up teaching Russian and wanted nothing more to do with the country, the language or her memories. Anna was too young to understand, so Meg had never told her about that aspect of her life.

Unfortunately Anna had found the *Nutcracker* book in a box in the storage room where Meg had hidden it. The little girl had fallen in love with it on sight and commandeered it for her own. Meg had never had the heart to take it away from her, but she'd never explained its origins, either.

"Is it true, Daddy?"

With that one question, Meg knew it was all over. Not only had Anna accepted Kon as her father without reservation, but now she was questioning Meg's veracity.

What an ironic fact of life that a mother could give her all to her child for six years, and then a man, whose only contribution had been biological, could come along and in a heartbeat win that child's unquestioned devotion and adoration.

"Yes, it's true. Your mother speaks excellent Russian, and when she wasn't teaching English to some Russian students, we spent every moment of her four months in St. Petersburg together."

Meg's breathing had grown shallow. "Anna...why don't you ask your father why he didn't come to America with me?" She knew her voice sounded brittle.

"But I did come," he countered with a swiftness that took her breath. "You see, in order to leave my country, I had many things to do first, many responsibilities. But I've always known about you, Anochka. I've always loved you, even when I was far away. Now I'm finally here, and I'm going to stay."

For as long as it took to win over Anna. Then he would disappear with her. Meg was sure of it. She wondered when this latent fatherhood instinct had taken over to bring him halfway around the world to claim his child.

"You can sleep in my room," Anna declared, tying up all the loose ends with the simple reasoning of an innocent child. She could have no comprehension of the scattered debris of their separate lives.

"I'd like that," he murmured softly. "That's why I've come—to live with you and your mommy. I want us to be a family. Can I ride home in your car? I didn't bring mine to the ballet."

"We have a red Toy-yoda. You can sit in the back with me and read me my book while Mommy drives us."

"We'll take turns reading. Do you like where you live?"

"Yes. But I wish we had a dog. The mean apartment man won't let us have one."

"Then you'll love Gandy and Thor." He bundled her in her winter coat while they chatted.

"Gandy and To—what?"

"Thor. They're my German shepherds, and I've told them all about you. They can't wait to get acquainted. And once they do, they'll play with you and be your friends forever.'' At his words, Anna squealed in delight.

Impotent rage welled up inside Meg. Nothing was beneath him, certainly not the wholesale bribery of his vulnerable daughter. Meg was close to screaming, but the *Nutcracker* had ended and people were pouring into the lobby. For Anna's sake, she had to keep tight control on her emotions until she could be alone with him out of her daughter's hearing.

Konstantin Rudenko was used to being an absolute, unquestioned authority in his own country, but there was no way she would allow him to strongarm her here, in *her* home.

Meg marched over to her daughter and put a firm hand on her shoulder to separate her from her father. ''Let's go, Anna.''

But Anna wasn't listening. Her hands had reached out to explore the texture and hard coutours of Kon's face. For a traitorous moment Meg relived the sensation, the slight raspy feel of those cheeks against hers after she spent the night in his arms. Making love...

''Will you let me carry you to the car, Anochka? I've dreamed of holding my own little girl for a long, long time.''

Anna, who up to this point hadn't liked any man who paid too much attention to Meg, was obviously mesmerized by his husky voice and the loving look in his eyes. She slid her arms around his neck and let him pick her up, her expression one of sublime joy.

''What does that *noska* word mean?''

"My little baby Anna. That's what the daddies in Russia call their darling daughters."

"I'm not a baby. You're funny, Daddy." She gave him his first kiss on the cheek.

"And you are adorable, just like your mother." He crushed her in his arms, as if he'd been waiting his whole life for this moment.

Meg looked away, pierced to her soul to see Anna's enchantment with a man who wasn't beyond manipulating a child's deepest and most tender emotions to get what he wanted.

She would never forgive him for this. *Never.*

CHAPTER TWO

"WHICH WAY to your car, *mayah labof?*" he asked, repeating the calculated endearment that still had the power to touch her emotionally, though she fought against it. "Anna and I are ready."

Meg was on the verge of shouting that since he'd followed them to the theater, he no doubt knew exactly where her car was parked. But when she saw how perfect father and daughter looked together, with Anna's arm placed trustingly around his neck, Meg's throat choked up and no words would come.

Anna had wanted her own daddy from the time she'd watched her best friend, Melanie, with *her* father. It always made Anna feel left out. Within the last few minutes, though, bonds had been forged that no power on earth could break.

Other people leaving the theater would see at once that they were father and daughter, and Meg noticed how several women's eyes lingered on Kon's striking features.

If anything, it was Meg's relationship to the dark-haired little girl in his arms people might question. Meg's shoulder-length ash-blond hair and gray eyes suggested a different ancestry altogether—yet another irony Meg was forced to swallow. She fastened her coat against the cold, wintry afternoon and headed for her car, parked on a side street around the corner.

She walked several paces from Kon so she wouldn't accidentally brush against him. She felt relieved when he got into the back seat of the car with Anna, keeping some space between them.

He might think he had the upper hand now, especially while Anna clung to him and bombarded him with questions. But once they were home, they'd be in Meg's territory. *She'd* set the rules. They'd have dinner immediately, she decided, and as soon as Anna had eaten, it would be her bedtime.

With her daughter asleep, Meg would be able to have it out with Kon and get rid of him before Anna awakened. As soon as possible, Meg would contact the attorney who had helped settle her father's and aunt's affairs: she would get a court order forcing Kon to stay away from her and Anna.

Since no marriage had taken place and he wasn't an American citizen, she wondered what rights he had where their daughter was concerned. Certainly when her attorney learned the truth of Kon's KGB background, he would do everything in his power to protect Anna from being alone with her father—not to mention being taken out of the country. How she wished her Uncle Lloyd was still alive. He'd worked in navel intelligence and could have counseled her on the best way to proceed.

Meg had no idea how high up in the KGB Kon had risen, but she couldn't imagine him renouncing a system that had dominated his entire life. Of course, political ideologies weren't something she and Kon had discussed when they were together.

He'd always managed to find them a place where they could be alone because they were so hungry for each other, could never get enough of each other. Their conversation had been that of lovers.

Evidently when his tactics had failed to get her to marry him—which would have meant turning her back on her own country—he'd had to devise another scheme. He'd decided to come after Anna. But he'd waited until she was old enough to respond to his machinations and his charms.

Maybe he genuinely wanted a relationship with his daughter, but Meg also knew how much he loved his country, how deeply immersed he'd been in its ideology. Naturally he would want Anna to feel the same way, and that meant taking her back there with him.

"Where are my dogs, Daddy?"

"At the house I bought for you and your mother."

"Oh, Mommy!" Anna cried joyfully and clapped her hands. "Daddy has a *house* for us! Where is it, Daddy? Can we go see it now?"

"I think your mommy has other plans for tonight," he told her.

Meg bit her tongue in an effort to keep quiet. She almost ran into a van standing next to the driveway that led to the parking garage of her apartment complex. Kon had deliberately brought up subjects guaranteed to delight a little girl starving for a father's love and attention. If Meg fought with him in front of Anna, it would only alienate her daughter and cause more grief.

And there would be grief.

But by the time Anna awakened the next morning, she would discover her father permanently gone from their lives. Meg wouldn't rest until she had some kind of injunction placed against Kon. Back at the apartment, she would manufacture a reason to run to one of her neighbors so she could phone Ben Avery in private. She didn't care if she had to keep her attorney and a judge up all night!

The second Meg pulled in her parking space and turned off the engine, Anna scrambled from the car, too involved with Kon to be thinking about her mother. "Come on, Daddy. I want you to see my aquarum." She couldn't quite manage the *i*. "You can feed my fish if you want to."

"I'd like that, but first we have to help your mommy," Meg heard him say in a low voice before he shut the rear door and opened the driver's side. She shouldn't have been surprised by his solicitude. Nothing was done without a motive, and she suspected he wasn't about to let her out of his sight.

Avoiding his gaze, she got out of the car, pulled away from the hand that gripped her elbow and walked ahead of them on trembling legs. She headed blindly toward the door leading into the modern, three-story complex.

It would have done no good to reach for Anna, who still clutched her book in one hand and her father's hand in the other, impatiently waiting to show him her world.

"Melanie lives right here!" she exclaimed as they passed a door on their way down the second-floor hall.

"Is she your friend?"

"Yes, my best friend. But sometimes we fight. You know—" Anna leaned toward him confidingly "—she says I don't have a daddy."

"Then you'll have to introduce us later and we'll prove to her she's wrong."

Anna skipped along beside her father, her face illuminated with joy by his words. "She says my mommy had a *luvver*." This was news to Meg, who could feel her world falling apart so fast she didn't know how to begin gathering up the pieces. "What's a luvver, Daddy?"

While Meg cringed, Kon slowed his pace and picked Anna up in his arms once more. "I'm going to tell you something very important. When a man and a woman love each other more than anyone else in the world, they get married and become lovers. That's why you were born, and we both love you more than our own lives."

"But you and my mommy didn't get married."

"That's because we lived in different countries, which complicated everything. But now that I'm here, we'll get married and live happily ever after."

Meg could hardly breathe.

"Can you get married tomorrow?"

Kon laughed low in his throat. "How about next week at my house? We'll need to help your mommy pack everything and move out of the apartment first."

Terrified of creating a scene that would traumatize Anna and arouse even more interest from her neighbors—many of whom were just coming home from Christmas shopping with packages in their arms and had already noticed Kon holding Anna—Meg practically ran down the hall to her apartment. She'd hung a large holly wreath tied with a red ribbon on her door, but hardly noticed it now.

She fumbled with the key, trying to get it in the lock, Kon's mesmerising power over Anna frightened and enraged her. He'd learned his seductive techniques through years of KGB training. He'd learned to consider human feelings expendable.

"Take me to my bedroom, Daddy. My aquarium's in there," Anna dictated her wishes, pointing the way as he carried her across the small, modestly furnished living room Meg had cleaned earlier that day. The unlit Christmas tree stood in the corner, a slightly lopsided Scotch pine, but Meg couldn't afford anything better. Still, the gold and silver balls among the tiny colored lights looked festive when Kon stopped long enough for Anna to flip the wall switch so he could see the effect.

Meg closed the front door, ignoring the triumphant glance he cast her. He'd made it this far without her interference. As soon as they disappeared down the hall, she unbuttoned her coat and threw it over a chair, realizing this might be the only time she'd be free to talk to her attorney.

Mrs. Rosen, the widow across the hall, was a retired musician. She could usually be found at home this time of the evening giving violin lessons. Anna was her youngest student and had made significant progress in the past year. But Anna's musical ability was the last thing on Meg's mind as she let herself out of the apartment, praying the older woman was in so she could use her phone and ask her to keep an eye on Meg's door while she made the call. Just in case Kon had thoughts of an immediate escape....

"Ms. Roberts?"

Meg jumped, surprised to be met in the hall by a man and woman dressed in casual sports clothes and parkas. They stood in front of her, blocking her path.

The van that had been parked next to the driveway flashed into her mind, and a feeling of inevitability swept over her. Naturally Kon wouldn't have made his move without accomplices. More KGB? Since detente, they were officially known as the MB, but Meg knew very well that despite the chaos in Russia, they could still be dangerous. It was possible some of their operatives continued to function in the U.S. for counterintelligence purposes.

As if reading her mind, they both pulled identification from their pockets.

CIA. Meg swayed on her feet, and the dark-haired, fortyish woman put a hand on her arm to steady her. "We know the appearance of Mr. Rudenko has come as a shock to you, Ms. Roberts. We'd like to talk to you about it. Inside."

Infuriated, Meg jerked her arm free. "Do you actually expect me to believe you're from the CIA?" she hissed. "I know how the MB works. Just like the KGB! You pass yourselves off as anything you like, and you'd double-cross, triple-cross your own families if necessary."

The man, who wore horn rims and looked around fifty, gave her a patronizing smile. "Please cooperate, Ms. Roberts. What we have to tell you should abate your fears," he said with an exaggerated sincerity that nauseated her.

Meg stiffened. "And of course if I refuse, you'll force me back into my apartment at gunpoint. But since you know I'd never do anything to upset my daughter, you're confident I'll do whatever you ask." She turned and reentered her apartment, the two agents close behind.

Just then a door down the short hallway opened and a grim-faced Kon appeared, checking up on her, no doubt, to make sure she was cooperating. Just like old times. Of course back then she'd thought it was because he couldn't stay away from her. In the background she could hear water running and assumed he had talked Anna into taking a bath to distract her.

Meg stared into those damnably blue eyes. "You make me sick," she snapped. "The whole bunch of you! And—" she pointed at Kon "—as far as I'm concerned, if you've forsaken your own country, you're a traitor to all! Now why don't you leave unsuspecting people and children alone? Go find some uninhabited part of the world where you can play absurd war games to your hearts' content. If you battle each other long enough, none of you will be left alive—thank God."

With a nonchalance that stunned her, Kon loosened his tie and removed his jacket. Without taking his eyes off her he tossed it on top of her coat, drawing her unwilling attention to the play of hard muscle in his arms and shoulders. He behaved as if this was an everyday occurrence in his own home.

"Anna's bath will be through in a few minutes, and then she expects to come out and eat dinner with us. She'll be alarmed if she hears you shouting like

a fishwife, instead of being cordial to Walt and Lacey Bowman from the auto dealership where you
work. Is that what you want?'' He pressed the advantage. ''Or shall I tell her that you've had to go
back to the office on an emergency? There's a va-
cant apartment down the hall and I have the key.
It's entirely up to you where this conversation takes
place.''

''Mommy? Daddy?'' Anna burst into the room
unexpectedly, dressed in pajamas dotted with kan-
garoos, her curls bobbing. But when she saw the
strangers, her smile faded, and to Meg's intense relief she ran past Kon straight to her mother. Meg
picked her up and held her tightly in her arms. If
she had her way, she'd never let go of Anna again.

''Honey?'' She strived to keep her voice from
shaking. ''These are the Bowmans. They work in
the sales department at Strong Motors every day after I come home from the office.'' She was impro-
vising, because they'd left her no choice. ''You've
never met them before.''

The older woman smiled. ''That's right, Anna.
But Walt and I have heard a lot about you.''

''You're a mighty cute little girl,'' the man
chimed in. ''You look a lot like your mommy and
daddy.''

''Daddy looks like Prince Marzipan.''

The woman nodded. ''I heard you went to the
Nutcracker today. It's my favorite ballet. Did you
like it?''

''Yes. 'Specially the Prince!''

Kon's eyes actually seemed to moisten as he lovingly fastened his gaze on his daughter. Meg turned

her head away, astounded once again by his incredible acting ability.

"We need to talk to your mommy for a minute," the man continued. "Is that all right with you?"

"Yes. Daddy and I can fix dinner. We're going to have macaroni. Daddy says they don't eat macaroni in Russia. It's a…an Amercan invenshun."

"That's right, Anochka." He chuckled in delight. "I can hardly wait to try it. Come with me." In the next breath Kon plucked his daughter from Meg's arms and carried her to the kitchen and out of earshot, leaving Meg alone with the two agents. She'd probably never know who they really were or who they worked for. It could be either government—or both.

The older woman ventured a smile. "Do you mind if we sit down?"

Meg's hands tightened into fists. "Yes, I mind. Say what you have to say and go."

She knew her voice sounded shrill, but she'd been suppressing all that pent-up fear and rage since Kon had first ambushed them in the theater foyer. Right now she was on the verge of hysteria; she was ready to scream the apartment complex down, Anna or no Anna.

Everyone remained standing. The man spoke first. "Mr. Rudenko defected from the Soviet Union more than five years ago, Ms. Roberts."

Meg shook her head and let out a caustic laugh. "He's KGB. They don't defect."

His brows lifted. "This one did."

"If such a thing happened, then it was mere pretense so he could kidnap Anna at some point and take her back to Russia with him!''

"No," the woman interjected. "He became an American citizen this October. After the secrets he exchanged for asylum, he can never go back."

"Why should I believe you?" Meg exploded, the adrenaline pumping through her body so furiously she couldn't stand still. "In the first place, our government no longer needs to make deals with Russian defectors to get information. Not since detente. Now I want you out of here. Out of Anna's and my life!''

"We do make deals when it's a top-ranking KGB official,'' the man persisted. "One, I might add, who belonged to an elite inner circle and could shed light on highly sensitive issues—give us valuable information about the kidnappings of American citizens, both civilian and military, within and outside the Soviet Union."

The other woman nodded. "He never approved of those tactics in the old regime, nor the cruelty to Russians and non-Russians alike. That's one of the reasons he defected."

Grudgingly, Meg had to admit they were right about one thing. If Kon hadn't intervened, she might still be in that Moscow jail.

"The information he provided has answered questions our government never dreamed would be cleared up,'' the woman went on. "In some cases, the facts Mr. Rudenko obtained have relieved the speculation and suffering of families who've never learned what became of their loved ones."

"Mr. Rudenko has done a great service to our country and caused a good deal of embarrassment to his own,'' the man asserted in a firm voice. ''Do you remember that news item several years ago about the missing airforce pilot—the son of an elderly woman living in Nebraska? His plane had disappeared over Russia almost fifteen years ago.''

Meg's thoughts flashed back to the heart-wrenching story, which had been the main topic of the media at the time. She could still hear the woman sobbing with relief as much as sorrow—relief because the Pentagon had finally received positive proof of her son's death. She remembered the woman saying that now she could die in peace.

''That was thanks to Mr. Rudenko, who was able to provide detailed information about the pilot's incarceration in Lublianka prison and his subsequent death.''

Meg's eyes narrowed on the two of them. She simply couldn't trust anything to do with Kon, who never made a move without a motive. She'd discovered, to her cost, that all his apparently generous actions—such as purchasing that book on the *Nutcracker* and putting it in her luggage—had a hidden purpose.

''Even if what you tell me is true,'' she said, ''it changes nothing. There's something strange about a man who would defect as far back as five years ago, then wait until today to show up and declare that he wants a relationship with his daughter.''

Her face twisted in pain. ''As far as I'm concerned,'' she continued, her voice rising, ''it's a lie, and you're part of it! I don't give a damn which side you're working for. It has nothing to do with me.

Now get out of my apartment and don't ever come back!''

"Because of his defection, he had to go under-cover at once and assume a new identity,'' the woman explained calmly, ignoring Meg's outburst. "Out of fear of placing you and your daughter in danger, he has been living apart from you for the past five years and has avoided making contact un-til—''

"Until he could trap us in a public place where I didn't dare upset my daughter. Who's just old enough to be seduced by the attention of a long-lost father,'' Meg said bitterly.

The man shook his head. "Not until the threat of danger had passed and he'd established himself fully in his new life.'' He paused. "Now Mr. Rudenko has done exactly that. He's written several books on Russia already, including an exposé of the KGB and its methods. That one's coming out in the spring, under an assumed name, of course. The publisher's expecting it to make the *Times* list. So he's doing well financially, and he'll be able to support you and Anna.''

"I don't want to hear any more. Just get out. Now!''

"When you've cooled off enough to ask ques-tions, phone Senator Strickland's office and he'll tell you everything you want to know.''

Senator Strickland? The face of the aging Mis-souri senator came to mind. He was a politician whose integrity had never been questioned, at least as far as Meg knew. Which didn't mean much. Senator Strickland could probably be bought as easily as the next man.

"Perhaps you don't realize he's on the Senate Foreign Relations Committee and has been cooperating with us since 1988. He knows all about your love affair with Mr. Rudenko and the daughter you conceived during your stay in the Soviet Union. We can assure you that he's your friend and that he's sympathetic to your situation. He expects to hear from you in the near future."

Meg felt the blood drain from her face. If by the most remote chance they were telling the truth, then not only the KGB but the CIA and her own state senator knew the most intimate details of her private life! The idea was so appalling Meg couldn't think, couldn't speak.

The woman eyed her for a long moment. "Ms. Roberts, your fear and distrust are entirely understandable, which is why Mr. Rudenko asked us to speak to you—to help you accept that he's a citizen now and wants a relationship with his daughter."

"You've spoken to me," Meg muttered through stiff lips. "Consider your mission accomplished."

In a few swift strides she reached the door and flung it open, anxious to be rid of the pair and desperate to get Anna to bed before Kon could exert any more influence over her. But the happy sounds of Anna's excited chatter and her father's deep laughter coming from the kitchen mocked Meg's determination to bring this cozy situation to an immediate and permanent end.

She watched till the two agents were out of sight, then quietly shut the door and slipped across the hall to ring Mrs. Rosen's bell. She prayed Kon wouldn't choose that moment to check up on her.

When there was no answer, Meg panicked. She would have started for the Garretts' apartment down the corridor, but didn't dare leave her own apartment unguarded. Besides, the sound of her daughter's tearful voice checked her movements.

Through the closed door she could hear Anna asking Kon if "those people" had made her mommy go to work. Meg didn't wait to hear his response and hurried back into the apartment, her only thought to comfort her daughter.

"Mommy!" Anna cried when she saw Meg. She ran over to her, her distress vanishing instantly. "Where did you go? We got dinner all ready!"

"I think your mother was just saying goodbye to the Bowmans at the elevator. Isn't that right?" He supplied the plausible excuse faster than Meg could think. In an unguarded moment her troubled gaze flew to his. The triumphant expression in those blue depths said he understood exactly what she'd been up to, but that she'd never be rid of him, so why not accept her fate gracefully.

"Come on, Mommy. We're hungry."

Anna tugged at Meg's hand, forcing her to break eye contact with Kon. He followed them into the kitchen at a leisurely pace. Her plan to talk to her attorney would have to be put off until dinner was over.

Whether intentionally or not, Kon's hands brushed against her shoulders as he pulled out a chair for her. She despised the tremor that shook her body when he touched her, afraid he could feel it.

But to her relief his attention was focused on Anna. He helped her sit down at the small dinette table, where a plate of cheesy macaroni and broccoli and a glass of milk had been placed for each of them.

"We have to have a blessing first," Anna insisted as soon as her father sat down on her other side. "It's your turn to say it, Daddy. Please?"

"I'd be honored," he murmured in a husky voice, squeezing her small hand in his large one.

Meg forgot to close her eyes as she watched the two identical dark heads bow while he offered a prayer in Russian—a beautiful, very personal prayer that thanked God for preserving the lives of the woman and child he loved, for uniting them at last, for giving him the opportunity to start a new life, for providing food when so many people in Russia and the rest of the world had none. And finally for bringing the three of them this first Christmas together. Amen.

"What did you say, Daddy?" Anna asked, picking up her spoon and scooping up the macaroni.

He lifted his head and stared at his daughter. "I told God how happy I was finally to be with you and your mommy."

Her mouth full of macaroni, Anna declared, "Melanie says it's stupid to believe in God. Wait till I tell her that God let you come to Amerca to be with Mommy and me. I love you, Daddy."

Anna's comments and sweet smile—even more endearing because of the cheese sauce clinging to her lips—combined with the eloquent emotion darkening his eyes was too much for Meg. She found it difficult to maintain the same degree of anger she'd felt before they'd sat down to eat.

His unexpected display of reverence had sounded amazingly sincere. For a brief moment, Meg had been in danger of forgetting that everything Kon did was part of an act. An act that over the years had become second nature to him.

Was it possible he *did* have religious convictions which he'd been forced to hide until now? Could he fake something like that? She didn't know.

His glance switched to Meg. "Did we do the macaroni right?" he asked quietly. "Anna helped me make it. Our little girl is a good cook."

"And a tired one," Meg remarked without answering his question. Tearing her gaze from his, she brushed a stray curl from her daughter's flushed cheek. "I think we'll skip dessert and go straight to bed. You've had a big day, honey."

Anna nodded, surprising Meg who'd been prepared for an argument. "Daddy said I had to go to bed early and get a good sleep so I'd be ready for our trip in the morning."

Trip? What trip? Dear Lord!

Adrenaline set Meg's heart pounding like waves crashing against the shore. Her eyes darted wildly to Kon. He had just finished his milk and eyed her over the rim of the glass, registering her fear with a calm that roused her emotions to a violent pitch.

"Since tomorrow is Sunday, it will be the perfect opportunity for you and Anna to see where I live. It's a two-hour drive from here."

Meg sucked in a breath and pushed away from the table like an automaton. Refusing to let him bait her any further, she turned to Anna and said, "If you're finished, let's run to the bathroom and brush your teeth."

"But I want Daddy to help me. He promised to tuck me in bed. He's going to teach me how to read my *Nutcracker* book in Russian, and I'm going to read him my Dr. Seuss stories."

"Then I'll do the dishes," she said, forcing her voice to remain level. She refused to give Kon the satisfaction of knowing his unexpected appearance had knocked out her underpinnings.

She ignored his curious stare, kissed Anna's forehead and started clearing the table. Acting as if she didn't have a care in the world, she set about loading the dishwasher while they got up from the table and left the kitchen.

By the time she'd wiped off the counters and watered the large red poinsettia her boss had sent her, the apartment was quiet. Removing her high heels, she turned out the kitchen light, then stole across the living room and down the hall, listening for voices.

Meg caught snatches of Anna reading Dr. Seuss's *Inside, Outside, Upside Down.* Occasionally Kon would stop her and make her pronounce the Russian equivalent of the words. Her accent appeared to entertain him no end, and he taught her some more, sometimes laughing deep in his throat at her efforts, but more often than not praising her, calling her his darling Anochka. Eventually there were no more sounds.

Meg shivered as she remembered the times she'd lain in his arms, unable to get enough of his lovemaking, never wanting him to stop calling her his beloved. But it had all been a lie, and the pain of his betrayal was more real than ever. Sweat beaded her hairline.

She entered Anna's bedroom on tiptoe and moved past the aquarium and dresser toward the twin bed. Kon was stretched out on top of the covers, his eyes closed, his arm around the child. She lay under her Winnie the Pooh quilt and had fallen asleep against his broad shoulder, several books, including the *Nutcracker,* still scattered on the bed.

The reading light fastened to the white headboard outlined Kon's features. They looked more chiseled in repose and revealed new lines of experience around his eyes and mouth. She leaned over to study him more closely.

He looked tired, she thought, then berated herself for feeling any compassion or noticing the small physical changes in him since they'd last been together—changes that made him look more appealing than ever. She couldn't allow herself to respond to that appeal or to soften in any way.

Because he was planning to steal Anna.

She couldn't forget that for a second. Right now, with Kon asleep, was the perfect time to alert Ben Avery. He could start proceedings to have Kon legally removed from the apartment. No matter how much it would upset Anna, Meg needed to do this, and she needed to do it immediately. There was no way she would allow Kon to step one foot outside the door with her daughter.

Quietly she retraced her steps to the kitchen and lifted the receiver of the wall phone to call her attorney.

She gasped when she heard a sudden movement behind her. She swung around to face Kon, who stood between the living room and the kitchen, far too close for her peace of mind.

He hadn't been asleep at all!

Heat seemed to pour from her body when she realized what that meant—he'd been watching her the whole time she'd been in Anna's room. No doubt when she'd leaned close to study him while he lay there on the bed exhausted, he'd been aware of her conflicting emotions, and the knowledge compounded her anger.

Anna might think of him as Prince Marzipan, but to Meg he was a devil prince, painfully handsome in a dark, saturnine way. The faint glow from the Christmas tree lights seemed only to emphasize it.

''Whomever you're calling to come and take me away will have to kill me first. I'm here to be with my daughter. But you're Anna's mother, which gives you the ultimate power.'' His voice trailed off.

Like someone in a trance, Meg hung up the receiver and stared at him, her fear and pain so acute she couldn't swallow. ''Maybe that was true, once. But this afternoon you presented Anna with a fait accompli.'' She spoke haltingly, the tears welling up in her eyes. ''How could you have been so…rash? So insensitive? What you told Anna—your declaration of fatherhood—has changed our lives forever!''

''I hope so,'' he said in a hoarse whisper.

Her hands knotted into fists. ''I won't let you take her back to Russia!'' she cried. ''I'll do whatever I have to do to prevent that from happening. *Whatever I have to do,*'' she warned him a second time.

''Your imagination is as predictable as your paranoia, but I have no intention of kidnapping her. Our daughter would despise me forever if I took her away from you. That is hardly the emotion I want to evoke in my one and only child. Besides, I'm very much afraid that Konstantin Rudenko is persona non grata in the former Soviet Union these days.

''If I were to touch the trees of Mother Russia just one more time,'' he murmured in a faraway voice, ''it would be my last act as a free man.'' A mirthless smile broke the corner of his mouth. ''I have no desire to deprive my daughter of her father. Not when I've spent the last six years in near isolation making plans and preparations—so we can live the rest of our lives together, Meggie.''

CHAPTER THREE

MEGGIE. The name he called her the first time he'd kissed her…

Suddenly she was that naive, starry-eyed twenty-three-year-old, sitting in the front seat of Kon's black Mercedes as he drove her from the Moscow airport to the hotel in St. Petersburg where she'd be living for the next four months.

Already infatuated with Konstantin Rudenko long before she'd arrived in Russia the second time, she knew she was in love the minute she set eyes on him again. The austere, heart-stoppingly attractive KGB agent had been assigned to guard her and escort her to and from school. Her feelings for him had been growing ever since he'd rescued her from prison on her first trip, giving her that beautiful book.…

As before, his word was law and everyone jumped at his slightest dictate. He'd dealt with all the red tape and smoothed her way, making her feel safe and looked after rather than policed. To add to her happiness, she'd learned that part of his duty was to phone her room every morning between three and four o'clock to make sure she hadn't slipped away from the hotel unnoticed.

Being a foreigner on the loose in a Russian city

constituted a crime punishable by imprisonment, something she had no desire to repeat.

Once installed at the hotel, Meg couldn't wait for his nightly phone calls to begin. But a problem arose when she discovered she'd been given a middle-aged roommate, a Mrs. Procter who had a master's in Russian from a university in Illinois. Meg was crushed because it meant that any phone conversations with Mr. Rudenko could be overheard by her roommate.

He, like the agent assigned to Mrs. Procter, would phone and ask her, very formally, if all was well, then start to hang up. But Meg couldn't let him end the calls there, and for the first few nights had tried to engage him in conversation by discussing her students' papers with him—anything she could think of to prolong the contact.

After a few days she'd managed to keep him on the phone as long as fifteen or twenty minutes, occasionally touching on the personal, learning that his first name was Konstantin. But Meg wanted much more from Kon, as she'd secretly nicknamed him, than a nightly phone call. But for that, she needed privacy, which Mrs. Procter's presence made impossible.

The older woman was scandalized by Meg's behavior and expressed her disapproval of what she referred to as Meg's ''promiscuous'' character. It didn't take long for Meg to realize she couldn't take much more of the unpleasant woman's attitude or presence.

Most important, she couldn't bear it when Kon just drove off at the end of each day after depositing her at the hotel, never lingering to chat for even a few more minutes.

By the end of the second week, Meg had craved his company to the point that she started plotting ways to get him to spend more time with her. That Friday, when he'd pulled up in the parking spot designated for KGB by the hotel, she didn't immediately get out of the car.

With her heart in her throat, she turned to him. Her gaze feasted on his slightly-too-long hair and the searing blue of his eyes, eyes that never revealed his innermost thoughts or feelings.

"If you don't mind, t-there's something important I need to discuss with you. Since the hotel frowns on my being late for dinner, I was hoping you'd join me. Or better yet," she continued in a slightly breathless voice, "I was hoping you might take me to a restaurant, where we could talk in private. So far I've only eaten at the hotel, and I'm eager to see more of the city while I'm here."

A frown marred his handsome features. "What is the problem?" he asked in a businesslike tone, which was hardly encouraging.

"I-it's about my accommodations."

"They are not up to your American standards?"

"No. It's nothing like that. Maybe it's because I've never had to live with a roommate before. But I'm afraid Mrs. Procter and I don't get along too well. We're such different ages and…I was wondering if I could be given a room by myself. I don't care if it's small, and I'd be willing to pay extra for it. All I'd re- ally like is my privacy." *And the op-*

portunity to talk to you all night long, if you'll let me.

He cocked his head and studied her gravely. She would have given anything to know what he was really thinking. "Come," he said unexpectedly. "Let's go inside. While you eat your dinner, I'll see what can be done."

Her heart leapt. At least he hadn't said no. Elated by that much progress, Meg alighted from the car and entered the hotel with Kon at her heels. While he approached the clerk at the front desk, she hurried to her room on the second floor to deposit her briefcase and freshen up.

So excited she was trembling, Meg applied fresh lipstick and dabbed on some French perfume, then slipped into a coffee-toned silk dress that had a tailored elegance. She brushed her ash-blond hair till it gleamed and fell softly about her shoulders, all the while praying he would find her attractive enough to join her in the dining room for a meal. Their first together…

But her heart plummeted to her feet when she went downstairs to the lobby and was greeted instead by the desk clerk. He informed her that a new room on the third floor had been arranged for her, that she should eat her dinner, then transfer her personal belongings.

Though grateful for Kon's swift help and intervention, she couldn't hide her disappointment; he'd left without saying goodbye. No longer interested in dinner, she went back upstairs ahead of Mrs. Procter, who was at one of the tables in the dining room talking to another teacher from England. No doubt they were gossiping about Meg.

Thankful to be free of that woman, Meg moved everything out of the room before Mrs. Procter learned what had happened and asked a lot of probing questions.

The interior of the tacky, modern hotel was drab and uninteresting, but her new room turned out to be considerably larger than the first one. It contained a good-sized desk with a lamp where she could do her schoolwork. Once again, she was touched by Kon's thoughtfulness and consideration. She could hardly wait until he phoned her that night to thank him.

When she heard a rap on the door, she whirled around, assuming it was one of the hotel staff. But before she had time to reach for the handle, the door opened.

She gasped softly when she saw Kon standing there. He'd never come to her room before. Her heart started to race. Their eyes met and she saw something flicker in his gaze as it swept over her face and body, something that made her go hot and liquefied her bones.

He wasn't indifferent to her. She could see it, feel it.

"Will the room do?" he asked in a husky voice.

She had difficulty finding words. "Yes," she finally managed. "It's perfect. Thank you."

He stared at her through half-closed lids. "There's a club not far from here where we can go for a drink and you can see something of the nightlife. I could spare an hour if you wish."

She swallowed hard. "I do."

"The nights are cold now. Wear something warm."

Scarcely able to breathe with the emotions running rampant inside her, she turned toward the closet for her raincoat.

"I'll wait for you at the car."

She glanced back in time to see him disappear down the dimly lit hallway. A club meant there might be dancing. The need to touch him, to be held in his arms, was fast growing into a permanent ache.

Within seconds she was ready and practically flew down the two flights of stairs and through the lobby, not wanting to waste one precious moment. As she emerged, her eyes went straight to his. She knew her cheeks were flushed with a feverish excitement she couldn't hide.

He was standing next to his car, his hands in his coat pockets—a remote, solitary figure. Evidently he'd been keeping an eye on the entrance, because as soon as he saw her, he stepped forward and opened the passenger door.

Without saying a word, he started the engine and they pulled away from the curb into moderate evening traffic, driving alongside bikes and trolley cars. Meg loved St. Petersburg, called the "Venice of the North" because of its waterways and bridges. Maybe the city looked so beautiful that night because she'd been fantasizing about the man who sat an arm's length away from her. She could hardly believe they were going out together. If she had her way, it would be longer than one hour. Far longer…

He obviously knew the city well. He took them

through several narrow, winding alleyways before pulling to a stop behind some expensive-looking cars parked next to a cluster of old buildings.

Her pulse racing, she watched him come around to help her from the car, something he'd always done. But this time there was a subtle difference. This time she felt his hand go to the back of her waist as he guided her through the first set of doors. She could hear sixties' music, of all things, being played inside the building.

His lips twitched in a half smile, transforming the austere-looking KGB agent into the devastatingly attractive man she'd been dreaming about. "You're surprised."

"You knew I would be." She smiled back, so enamored of him, she felt giddy.

"We're not quite as stodgy as propaganda would have you believe."

After helping her remove her coat, which he checked with an attendent, he ushered her through an ornate bar area to another room, where couples were dancing to a live band. The talented musicians and singer made her feel as if they'd just walked into a New York nightclub.

Out of the corner of her eye she saw Kon give the waiter a signal. The man rushed over and within seconds, they were escorted to a free table. Kon said something privately to the waiter, who then left them alone.

Kon seated her, then pulled out the chair opposite. He eyed her with a hint of speculation. "Do you trust me to have ordered something I believe you'll like?"

She lifted solemn eyes to him. "Because of you, I was freed from that awful jail and able to get home in time for my father's funeral. I'd trust you with my life." She spoke with complete and heartfelt sincerity.

For once, something she said managed to penetrate that outer KGB shell and reach the man beneath. She could tell by the way his eyes darkened in color, and the sudden stillness that came over him.

The band started playing an old Beatles tune.

"Let's dance," he murmured in a low voice.

Meg had been waiting for those words. She followed him onto the floor on shaky legs, so eager to be in his arms, she was almost afraid of the moment he'd touch her, afraid he'd know the powerful effect he had on her.

Perhaps he did know how she felt, because to her chagrin he kept her at a correct distance, never taking advantage of their closeness in any way, or letting her think her nearness disturbed him.

Like many of his compatriots in the room, he was a wonderful dancer, and their bodies seemed perfectly attuned. After three dances they returned to their table, where she discovered champagne cocktails and goblets of ice cream that tasted more like lime sherbet.

"What a delicious combination," she marveled, realizing that the entire evening felt enchanted because she was in love with him.

Thirsty from the dancing, Meg drank her cocktail quickly. Then she looked across at him, wondering what he could be thinking to produce such a sober expression. Anxious to lighten his mood, she leaned toward him. "Shall we dance again?" She hoped her question didn't sound too much like begging.

"There's no more time," he told her with a cool, disappointing finality. "I'll get your coat while you finish your ice cream."

She didn't want the evening to end, but had little choice in the matter. He was in charge. Meg supposed it was something of a miracle that he'd taken even an hour from his rigid routine to accommodate her wishes.

"Shall we go?"

She nodded and pushed herself away from the table. They made their way through the crowd to the entrance. This time he didn't touch her as they stepped outside to walk the short distance to his car. In fact, there was a distinct difference between the way Kon treated her now—almost as if he were angry—and the way he'd responded to her earlier in the evening. Was it because he'd revealed something of the man beneath the KGB persona? Maybe now he wanted to show her that it had only been a momentary aberration, that she shouldn't expect it to happen again.

Once they were in the car, driving back to her hotel, Meg didn't speak. The forbidding aura surrounding him prevented her from initiating further conversation. She stared out the side window, dreading the moment he'd say good-night and walk away.

They were almost at their destination when he suddenly made a right turn out of the city, away from lighted streets into darkness.

"Kon? W-where are we going? This isn't the way

back to the hotel.'' But he refused to answer her and pressed forward until they were well into the woods. She started to feel nervous. "I thought you had to get back to…to whatever it is you do.''

Still he ignored her and kept driving until they came to a deserted lay-by. He turned off the road and pulled to a stop, cutting the engine. The only sound she could hear was the fierce hammering of her own heart.

Glancing outside, she noticed trees lining the road and saw the stars twinkling overhead. The beauty of the night did not escape her, but she couldn't concentrate on that now. The man at the wheel had become an enigmatic stranger, and she was very much at his mercy.

When she couldn't stand the silence any longer, she turned toward him. The shadowy light from the dashboard revealed the look in his eyes, an unmistakable longing that changed the rhythm of her heart.

"Are you afraid of me?"

"No," she answered in a tremulous voice. And it was the truth.

He let out a smothered curse. "You should be. In the last six years, you've changed from a lovely, spirited teenager into an exciting woman. My comrades envy me because I chose to guard you myself."

She moistened her lips, gratified to hear the unmistakably possessive ring in his voice. "I-I'm glad you did. It saved me the trouble of looking for you."

"Explain that remark."

Meg stared down at her hands. "Just that I've

never forgotten your kindness to me. I intended to look you up and thank you. And—I hoped—get to know you better.''

She heard his sharp intake of breath. ''Your honesty is as shocking now as it was six years ago.''

She lifted her head, half turning to face him. ''You said that as if it offends you.''

''On the contrary, I find it refreshing beyond belief. Will it shock you senseless if I tell you how much I want to make love to you, go to bed with you? How much I want to kiss every inch of your face and hair, your beautiful body?''

At those words, she couldn't control the trembling. ''No,'' she murmured, looking into his eyes, ''because I've wanted the same thing since I got off the plane in Moscow.''

Groaning, he said, ''Come here to me.'' He reached out to pull her into his arms, but she was already there.

''Meggie.'' She heard him whisper her name before his mouth fastened on hers. He kissed her with a hunger that obliterated any fears she might have entertained that he wasn't as attracted to her as she was to him.

Overjoyed by the knowledge, she clung to his warmth, kissing him with total abandon, letting sensation after sensation carry her to unexplored dimensions of wanting and need. She'd craved this physical closeness for so long, she was afraid they were both part of a dream. She never wanted to wake up.

In her bemused state she wasn't aware of time passing. Nor did she notice the eventual glare of headlights coming in their direction—until they flashed inside the car.

With a speed and strength she could scarcely grasp, Kon thrust her back to her side of the car, her lipstick nonexistent, her face hot, her body throbbing.

By the time the other vehicle had driven past them, Kon started the engine and pulled onto the road, maneuvering the car with the same finesse and precision that he did everything else, his features schooled to show no emotion.

"Kon— I—I don't want to go back. I don't want the night to end. Please don't take me home yet."

"I have to, Meggie."

"Because of your job?"

"Yes."

"When can we be together again? Really together, for more than an hour?"

"I'll work something out."

"Please let it be soon."

"Don't say anything else, Meggie, and don't touch me again tonight."

His emotions were as explosive as hers. For once, she didn't mind that he was taking her back to the hotel, not when she knew his passion for her was as profound as hers was for him. His unnatural silence after what they'd just shared proved there was no going back to their former relationship.

When they reached the hotel, he remained at the wheel and let her get out on her own. The moment she was safely inside, he sped away, as if in pursuit of another car.

Meg dashed through the foyer and up the stairs,

thankful to be going to an empty room. At least she could relive the rapture of the night in total privacy.

But long after she'd showered, brushed her teeth and gone to bed, she lay wide-awake. The adrenaline seemed to pulse through her bloodsteam; she couldn't sleep. The phone was right by the bed and she turned on her side, waiting for his call.

When it came, she'd grabbed the receiver before the second ring.

"Kon?" she cried out joyously.

"Never answer the phone that way again."

Chastened, she whispered, "I'm sorry. I didn't think."

"It's already Saturday. Be ready at ten and pack some warm clothes for the weekend." The line went dead.

Meg put back the receiver and hugged her pillow, delirious with love and longing. Sleep would be impossible now.

To keep from watching the clock, she got out her homework and made up her lesson plans for the following week. When she'd finished that task, she graded her students' poetry, writing notes at the bottom of each paper.

Work was a godsend; it kept her busy until nine, when she put everything away and packed the things she'd need for their trip. At nine-thirty, she left her room and went downstairs to breakfast, nodding to the few teachers she knew. She breathed a sigh of relief that Mrs. Procter wasn't among them.

Promptly at ten, Kon entered the foyer. She felt his powerful presence even before she saw him— like a gravitational pull. She hurried toward him, carrying her overnight bag in one hand, her purse in the other.

To any passerby, he would have looked like the same KGB agent who'd been ferrying her back and forth since her arrival in St. Petersburg. The difference was apparent only to Meg. When Kon gazed at her in that special way, she felt an emotional and physical awareness she couldn't hide. She felt a sensation of falling helplessly toward him, unable to stop.

He couldn't have had much sleep, either, but the relaxed mouth and the darkness beneath his eyes gave him a slightly dissipated air that only added to his attractiveness. Meekly, she followed him to his car and got in while he stowed her bag in the trunk.

They headed out of the city in much the same direction they'd taken the night before. The traffic lightened, and soon after, they reached the forest road.

Meg turned in her seat, admiring his striking profile, and his tautly muscled body. He was as formally dressed as always. In fact, she'd never seen him in anything but a white shirt and dark suit—his uniform, she supposed. He wore it well. Too well. She couldn't keep her eyes off him. "I've never gone away with a man before," she confessed. "H-have you? Gone away with a woman, I mean."

He flashed her a brief but piercing glance. "Yes."

"I should never have asked that question, but this is all new to me."

Naturally he'd had affairs. She knew from their nightly conversations that he was in his early thirties. An unattached male as attractive as Kon would never be without female companionship.

''There haven't been as many women as your fertile imagination is conjuring up,'' he said in a gently mocking voice. ''My work makes it virtually impossible to sustain any kind of lasting relationship. The few women I've known also worked for the Party.

''If it means anything, Meggie, I've never been attracted to a non-Russian woman before. What surprises me is the strength of my feelings for you, how far I've been willing to go to get you alone.''

She shivered with excitement. ''Th-thank you for being honest with me. If we can have that, I won't ask for anything else.''

His long fingers tightened on the steering wheel. ''You've never made love with a man, have you.'' It was a statement, not a question.

''No. Does that make a difference to you?''

''Yes.''

She blinked to fight the sudden sting of tears. ''I see.''

He muttered something in Russian she couldn't quite catch. ''We're here, Meggie.''

She'd been so caught up in their conversation, she hadn't noticed anything else. Now when she turned her head, she could see they were in the middle of a dense wood, parked outside what could only be described as a lowly woodcutter's cottage.

The reality of the situation came to her with full force. She'd hoped her candor would be enough to make up for her inexperience, but now she knew differently. Kon was a tough, sophisticated, worldly man—and he was probably ready to turn around and take her back to the city.

She couldn't bear that. She bolted suddenly from the car, taking off into the woods.

"Meggie? Where do you think you're going?" he called after her, sounding exasperated.

"I-I'll be right back."

"Don't go too far. It's easy to get lost."

"I won't." *Just give me a moment to pull myself together,* she cried inwardly and kept on running until she was out of breath.

She flung herself against a tree trunk to rest. She felt a rush of embarrassment because she was behaving like anything but a mature woman. She wouldn't blame him if he'd lost complete interest.

That was when she heard him calling her. He sounded angry, upset. Maybe he believed the woman he'd assigned himself to guard had managed to give him the slip. If only he knew the truth—that she *never* wanted to be apart from him. Never.

From the sound of his voice, he was getting closer. If she wasn't mistaken, his tone conveyed real anxiety. Did she dare believe he was actually concerned for her? Could he possibly have feelings for her as deep and as real as those she had for him?

The answer came when he caught up with her as she hurried back toward the hut. "I'm sorry if I worried you," she said when she saw his chest heaving and heard a torrent of unintelligible Russian escape lips narrowed to a taut, uncompromising line.

In the next instant he reached for her, drawing her against his hard body, his eyes a scorching flame of blue.

"Meggie..."

The fierceness, the unexpected raw passion in his outcry, robbed her of breath, telling her what she needed to know. He still wanted to be with her. Nothing had changed.

Blindly she lifted her mouth for his kiss—and was lost. He picked her up in his arms and carried her into the hut, shoving the door closed with his boot.

Her heart streamed into his, and what happened next felt completely natural and inevitable. Drunk on her desire for him, she forgot they were anything but a man and a woman, aching to know the taste and feel of each other.

From that moment on, the barriers imposed by their roles as foreign visitor and KGB agent were cast aside. Their all-consuming need for each other had dictated their relationship. A need that found release and marked the beginning of the rest of their days and nights together. The only thing they'd wanted was to love each other into oblivion....

To think it had all been part of a game plan.

Meg shook off the memories. She thought she'd put that pain behind her forever. But Kon's takeover since his reappearance in her life and Anna's had reopened wounds that would never heal now. She stared at him with accusing eyes.

"Tell me something," she said, not bothering to hide her reaction to the bittersweet memories. "How did you manage to keep a straight face when you asked me to be your wife?"

"Which time was that, Meggie?" he asked quietly. "As I recall, I begged you to marry me every time we made love. Perhaps I should ask *you* a question. Whatever possessed me to keep asking you when I knew what your answer would be?'' He managed to sound as desolate as he had earlier, when he'd told Anna about his parting scene at the airport before Meg flew away from him.

He was good at this! He was so good, it terrified her.

''Spare me the deceit, Kon!'' She spoke scornfully to mask her uncertainty. ''You're a man who did a job for your country. Throughout your career, I'm sure you've managed to infatuate other unsuspecting female visitors like myself. Perhaps you've even fathered other children in the line of duty—'' She stopped suddenly, breathless with anger.

''Why seek out Anna when there are thousands of single women in Russia who would love to marry you and bear your child? From what I understand, women there far outnumber men. You could choose anyone you wanted and have a family if—''

Calmly he interrupted. ''The woman I've chosen is standing right in front of me, and the child I already have fell asleep in my arms only moments ago.''

She clenched her teeth. ''You *did* choose me, I'll grant you that. My uncle was in naval intelligence, remember? And after he died my aunt told me about the KGB and the way they tried to convert specially chosen foreign visitors. Like me—the niece of an American military officer. Especially since I was obviously interested in Russia and even came back a second time.

''You did everything by the book, Kon. And with all your charm, you came close to succeeding. You

tried to woo me away from my country by first be-
friending me, then seducing me. But in the end, it
didn't work. I still went back to the States, and you
were probably reprimanded for your failure. So you
had me watched, and when you found out I was
pregnant, you waited and plotted until the time was
right to claim your daughter and return to Russia.''

She could tell her voice was getting louder, but
she was fast losing control. ''Well, I'm not going to
let you do it! We're not married, and if you try to
take her anywhere, I'll have you brought up on kidnap—''

''Mommy!'' Anna's frightened cry shocked Meg
into silence. Stunned by the interruption, she looked
past Kon to see her daughter hovering near the
Christmas tree, hugging her favorite doll. The glint
of tears on her pale cheeks devastated Meg. ''Why
are you mad at my daddy?''

Kon moved so fast Meg didn't have time to blink.
In one lithe move he gathered Anna in his arms and
kissed her nose. ''She's not mad at me, Anochka,''
he assured her while he rocked her back and forth.
''Your mommy is upset, with good reason. I used
to live in Russia, and she's afraid that one day I'll
want to go back and take you with me.''

''Without *mommy?*'' Anna asked, as if the idea
was unthinkable. Meg was moved to tears.

''No one is going anywhere without Mommy,''
he stated with unmistakable authority, his eyes never
leaving Meg. She wondered how he could carry
playacting this far and still sound so convincing. She
watched him kiss the top of Anna's head.

''Now it's time for you to go back to bed, because

we've got a big day planned for tomorrow, and your mommy and I haven't finished talking yet. You know we've been apart a long time. There are things I need to tell her. Can you understand that? Are you old enough to run to your room and crawl under the covers by yourself?''

"Yes." Anna nodded, making the dark curls dance on her forehead. Her head swiveled around and her eyes, full of pleading, fastened on Meg. "Daddy loves us, Mommy. Can we go see our house tomorrow? The dogs are waiting for me."

Meg stared at her daughter in wonder. How simple it all appeared to Anna's trusting mind. How pure her faith. She didn't know the meaning of real fear or betrayal. Those emotions weren't within her experience—how could she comprehend them? Now that her beloved prince, her daddy, had actually materialized, her child's world was complete.

"I live in Hannibal." He offered the surprising revelation so quietly it was as if his mind had spoken to Meg's.

"It's in the state of Missouri," he added dryly. "It's famous as the home of Mark Twain."

That provoked her to say, "Next you'll be telling me Mark Twain is still alive and entertaining friends at his house on Hill Street."

He gave Anna another hug. "Interesting you'd mention Hill Street. I live farther up the hill on the same side of the street."

It seemed the fairy tale was never ending. A KGB agent in the land of Becky Thatcher and Huck Finn.

Meg let out an angry laugh and folded her arms

to prevent herself from flinging something at him. "Anna, it's long past your bedtime."

"She's right," Kon agreed. "Kiss me good-night, Anochka."

Meg refused to watch their display of affection and turned on her heel, heading for Anna's room. She was unable to credit the fact that less than eight hours ago Anna hadn't known her father's name, let alone imagined seeing him in the flesh.

She stood by the side of the bed until her daughter scrambled beneath the quilt, but she couldn't avoid the innocent blue eyes staring into her soul. "God sent Daddy to us. Aren't you happy, Mommy? Please be happy."

Meg sagged onto the mattress and buried her face in Anna's neck, hugging her daughter close. "Oh, honey—" she began to sob quietly "—if only it was that simple." Convulsion after convulsion racked Meg's body, and Anna's comforting pats only contributed to her debilitating weakness.

"It *is* that simple," a deep, masculine voice said from the doorway. "And we're *all* going to be happy."

CHAPTER FOUR

THE NEXT THING Meg knew, his hand was sliding into her hair and caressing her scalp. It sent a shock wave through her system. Her breath caught, and she released Anna. She was so shaken by his touch she got to her feet and fled from the room in fresh panic.

Kon followed more slowly. "You're tired, Meggie. Go to bed. I'll sleep on the couch. If Anna wakes up during the night, I'll take care of her."

Meg spun around, the cathartic release of pent-up emotion making her feel reckless. But her desire to get everything out in the open diminished when she faced him in her stocking feet. Next to him she felt small and physically weak, emotionally overwhelmed. He seemed even taller, darker and infinitely more dangerous than before.

"Why, Kon?" she blurted, fighting the attraction that was still there in all the old insidious ways. "Why have you really come? Don't tell me it's because you're in love with me. We both know that's a lie. You used me!" she accused him. "I-I'll admit I was the aggressor. In fact, I threw myself at you and made your job pathetically easy. Because of my naïveté, I'll go on paying for that for the rest of my life.

"But why make up stories that will only devastate

a vulnerable little girl? If you're really telling the truth and you *have* defected, then the only reason I can imagine for any of this is that you hope to get joint custody—to keep Anna to yourself for six months every year. I couldn't bear that. Do you hear me?''

Her question rang in the air, but for once he didn't have a ready response. While she waited, he lowered himself to the couch and ran his hands through his hair, a gesture she remembered from countless occasions in the past. It drew her attention to his fit, lithe body, which at one time had known hers so intimately....

She shook her head, furious that she could entertain such primitive thoughts when he was more her enemy now than ever before.

Deep in contemplation, she scarcely noticed that he'd pulled a pocket-size tape recorder out of his suit jacket. He placed it on the round marble-topped coffee table, one of the few pieces of furniture she'd kept after her parents had died—one of the few good pieces they'd owned. Her father's schoolteacher salary hadn't supplied much more than the necessities of life. Without winning scholarships, Meg would never have been able to go abroad in the first place.

Suddenly the sound of hysterical sobbing filled the living room. Meg blinked in shock when she recognized her own teenage voice. Her eyes flew to Kon, whose head was bent over the recorder, listening.

Immediately Meg was transported back to that dank Moscow jail cell. She remembered beating the stone floor with her fists in abject despair. The agony

of that black moment came rushing in, overwhelming her with its intensity, and she couldn't stop the
tears from streaming down her face.

*Oh, Daddy. You're gone...my daddy's gone....
I've got to get home to you! They've got to let me
out of here! Let me out of here, you monsters....
Daddy...!*

To be confronted by her own screams, her own
sorrow, was too much to bear. Without conscious
thought she flew at Kon, but he'd already pressed
the stop button. "Why would you have kept that
tape?" She clutched at his arm, shaking him, forcing
him to look at her. "What are you trying to do to
me? How could you be so cruel?" she lashed out,
uncaring that her tears were wetting his shirt.

Catching her off guard, he pulled her onto his lap.
He gripped her face in his hands, preventing her
from thrashing about by trapping her legs between
his. With a gentle stroke of his thumbs, he smoothed
the moisture from her lashes. "When I instructed
the guard to play back the tape for me and I heard
your relentless sobbing, it released a memory buried
so deep in my psyche I didn't know it was there
until that moment."

His breath warmed her face, but she was too distraught to realize the danger of being this close to
him again.

"What memory?"

His body tautened. "Of an icy-cold morning
when two men came to my schoolroom in Siberia
and told me I was to go with them, that my mother
needed me at home. I was eight years old. I remember that very distinctly because my father, who

worked with his hands, had made me a sled for my birthday. I loved my father and was very proud of it. In fact, I pulled it to school so I could play with it on the way home and show my friends.

"When I told the men I needed to get my sled, which the teacher had told me to put around the back of the one-room building, they said there was no time, that it would be there tomorrow. I was upset about it, but my fear that something bad had happened to my mother was foremost in my mind.

"They put me in a horse-drawn sleigh and set off in the opposite direction from my house. When I told them we were going the wrong way, one of the men slapped me and told me to be quiet. He said that the state was my family now. That I wasn't to speak about my family again or they would kill my sister and my parents."

Meg's involuntary cry went ignored by Kon. He kept on talking in the same low, steady voice. "But if I was good, they would tell my family I had gone out on the ice over the lake with my sled and had fallen through before anyone could save me."

She shook her head in disbelief. "You're making this up. You have to be," she whispered, unable to conceive of anything so horrifying. But when she dared to look into his eyes, she glimpsed an unspeakable kind of bleakness, a pain that made her heart lurch.

"I said the same thing to myself while they drove me farther and farther away from the only security I'd ever known. Then came night. They must have put me in a barn, because I was pushed into some straw and told that if I cried, they would kill me.

But if I showed I was a man, then it would prove I was worthy of the great honor they had bestowed upon me, the honor of serving the state.''

''Oh, Kon!'' She broke down, overcome by the enormity of what he'd told her. For the moment the enmity between them was forgotten. She became mother, sister, lover, wanting only to give comfort to the child in him who could not be comforted. It seemed the most natural thing in the world to press her head into his neck and murmur incoherent endearments, much the same way she did when Anna needed consolation.

''I've heard stories of such things happening.'' She spoke against the side of his neck. ''But I never wanted to believe them.''

''I'd forgotten all of it,'' he said, brushing the silvery-blond strands of hair from her face while he rocked her in his arms, ''until you were detained. Then your pain became my pain and I couldn't distinguish between them, couldn't tell the difference. It was in my power to keep you incarcerated as long as I desired, regardless of your grief. You'd broken the law and deserved to be punished. That was what I believed. That was part of the KGB's bullying tactics.'' He gave a deep, shuddering sigh. ''But when I heard you call out for your daddy, something inside me snapped. I had to let you go.''

The rocking stopped and his haunted eyes met hers. ''No child, young or old, should be made to suffer the kind of night I was forced to endure in that barn, knowing I'd never see my family again. Knowing I'd never hear my mother tell me another story. Knowing I couldn't even keep the sled my father had just made for me. Not allowed even the smallest memento of the family I'd loved.''

He was telling her the truth, Meg knew. A strangled sound escaped her throat. He'd wanted to console her during that terrible night. There'd been nothing he could do then, so he'd given her the book, secretly putting it in her suitcase. During her second visit, Meg had asked him about it and he'd been noncommittal. ''Just a gift,'' he'd said. Now she understood.

''You wouldn't explain when I asked you before,'' she said. ''But it was because you knew how devastated I felt. How alone.''

''Yes. I wanted you to leave with something you treasured, one good memory of my country. And of me...''

Meg lowered her head. ''When the customs official in New York opened my suitcase, I saw it lying on top of my things. I couldn't believe it. I knew you had to have put it there, but I didn't understand why, and I couldn't figure out how you knew I wanted that particular book.''

''All the staff at your hotel were KGB, Meggie. That's why the teachers and students from America were put there. It was easier for your guide to monitor your group's activities and report to me. He was careful to make notations on the kinds of things that interested you in the shops, particularly any reading material. Part of an agent's work was to seek out those visitors who might be sympathetic to Soviet communism and win them over.''

Meg shuddered to think that from the time they'd arrived in Moscow until the moment Kon had rushed her to the plane, she and her friends had been collected and examined like insects under a microscope.

"He must have been disappointed when I passed up the free propaganda for a book on the *Nutcracker*. I wanted it badly but couldn't afford it."

"If anything, he was surprised. Normally American students grab at whatever is given away. Even if it's not free, they have their parents' money to squander. But you were different."

She took a steadying breath and wiped more tears from her face. "How was I different?"

"You were a lovely teenager, independent and spoiled like all of your crowd, but incredibly brave in front of the guards. So free in spirit. Young as you were, you never cowered. A part of me was intrigued by that remarkable quality in you."

She raised her head and their gazes held for a long moment until Meg stirred restlessly in his arms. She felt amazed by his confession, but more troubled and confused than ever. There could be no doubt about the nightmare he'd lived through as a child. But since the age of eight, the KGB had been his family.

Some of what he'd said today, tonight, was the truth. But which part was the lie? *And what was she doing on his lap with her body practically molded to his, their mouths only inches apart?*

Alarmed that her perspective had been clouded by compassion, she pushed her hands against his chest and struggled to her feet. She needed to separate herself from him—to fight off the sensual appeal he'd always had for her.

Something must be fundamentally wrong with

her, letting him penetrate her defenses like this! It was all because he'd been able to arouse feelings that were in direct conflict with her fears.

"Your new family did a remarkable job of training you," she said coldly, attempting to put emotional distance between them. "Accosting Anna and me at the theater the way you did was a perfect example of the typical KGB takeover. It comes as naturally to you as breathing, doesn't it, Kon?

"But there's one thing you didn't know. If you try to take Anna from me, I will fight you in court. She's known only me since she was born. It would be cruel to separate us. I won't let you!"

"I've already told you that's not my intention. I want all three of us to live together." A complacent smile curved his lips. "In any event, it's too late for ultimatums, isn't it, Meggie? My daughter and I have already bonded, and I promised her I'd be here when she wakes up in the morning. Surely after spending four months in my company, you learned that I never break a promise."

"You broke *one*," she said icily. When his eyebrows rose she went on, "You'd promised I wouldn't get pregnant. I was foolish enough to believe you."

His eyes narrowed. "You and I both know I used protection. Every single time. But it appears we underestimated our little girl's determination to be born."

"No, Kon. All it means is that I underestimated how far you'd go to make it look like an accident."

His mouth thinned ominously. "Let's get something straight. The second time you came to Russia, it was not my intention to make you pregnant. If that *had* been the plan, I would have taken you to bed the day you stepped on Russian soil.''

He didn't need to add that she'd been his for the asking. The humiliation she felt produced a blush she couldn't hide.

''For your information,'' he continued, ''I had many responsibilities, of which you were only one, a quite insignificant one. I should have assigned you to a guard at the lowest echelon. In fact, it was such a routine job that one of my colleagues actually made a comment wondering why I would bother myself with anything so trivial as the surveillance of an unimportant American schoolteacher.

''I won't insult your intelligence by denying that some of the agents did sleep with their targets to obtain secrets. One of the reasons I assigned myself to you was to protect you from just such a situation.''

''Why would you do that?''

He sat back against the cushions. ''Because there was a refreshing innocence about you when you left Russia the first time. An honesty. Six years later, when I saw your name on a list of foreign teachers coming for a short-term stay, I wanted to see if that innocence was still there.'' He paused for one breathless moment.

''The only change I could see was that the teenage girl had grown into a beautiful woman. More than ever I wanted to make sure no man took advantage of you while you were in my country.''

''I don't believe you, Kon.''

He cocked his head to the side and studied her

briefly. "Did I ever once force myself on you, Meggie? Have you forgotten that you were the one who rejected me?"

Somehow their arguments always ended with his turning things around so she appeared to be the culprit. Until she met Kon, she'd never been in love. There had been no serious boyfriends in Meg's teens, no prior physical experiences to give her insight or prepare her for the full-blown emotional and sexual feelings she'd had for the man who was Anna's father.

Meg was an only child, born to a mother in her forties and a father in his fifties, both of whom were overjoyed to have a child at last. Being devout Christians who lived on a modest income, they'd sheltered her, pressured her to make the most of her studies, insisted she take advantage of every academic opportunity.

They'd been pacifists who had strongly believed in understanding as the key to world peace. In keeping with their beliefs, they'd enrolled her in a special Russian program from grade school through college. Neither of them lived long enough to realize that this well-intentioned idea would lead her down a path of forbidden passion to the life-and-death situation she faced now, in her own apartment.

"I couldn't give up my citizenship and walk away from my whole life!"

"Certainly not for me," he said beneath his breath, but she heard him and became angry all over again at his power to make her feel guilty. "So I took whatever you were willing to offer, which was as many days and nights in your arms as we could manage. I'm a man, Meggie. You know how it was with us.''

"You mean you know how I thought it was with us,'' she said acidly. "Obviously everything was a lie! You set out to manipulate me and...seduce me. And you succeeded.''

His gaze swept over her face and body. Oddly, it reminded her of the way he'd looked at her when she'd been detained by the airport guards.

"You're right. I did set out to win you over. But I've already told you—my success was hardly complete.''

Meg, prepared for any excuse except his cold-blooded admission, felt she'd just been slapped.

"Before detente, part of my job was to keep track of foreign visitors, most of whom were tourists. Your uncle's information was correct. If any of them made a second visit, they were kept on a special list and targeted as either possible recruits or possible subversives. Special agents were assigned to scrutinize their behavior. If the same visitor came a third time, he or she was detained indefinitely.''

His gaze bore into hers. "Evidently your bad experience in our jail didn't prevent you from returning, which proved what I'd thought about you—that you had an indomitable will. Intrigued by that, I made certain you were placed under my personal supervision.''

Meg's head flew back. "And I was naive enough to suppose our meeting again was pure coincidence,'' she said angrily. "I couldn't believe my luck. Here I thought it might be impossible to track you down so I could thank you for letting me go home to my father's funeral, for giving me that book. Instead, there you were. Right at the Moscow airport!'' She struggled to keep her voice steady.

"What was even more astonishing was realizing I'd been put in your charge,'' she went on after a moment. "In the midst of all that red tape and the endless questions, you once again whisked me away to St. Petersburg. I felt like a princess who'd been rescued by a knight in shining armor. I put you on a pedestal. Imagine putting a KGB agent on a pedestal!'' she exclaimed savagely.

He heaved a deep sigh. "Can this keep till morning? I'm tired. Good night, Meggie.''

Before she could say another word, he'd removed his shoes and stretched out on her couch, turning on his side so his back was toward her. The sight of him made her shake with rage.

"What do you think you're doing?''

"Shh. You'll wake Anna. I thought it was clear what I'm doing. I'm going to sleep.''

Aghast, she cried, "But you can't! Not here!''

He half turned and looked over his shoulder at her, his dark hair attractively disheveled. "If you're inviting me to join you in your bed, I won't say no.''

She refused to dignify that remark with an answer. "I'm calling my attorney, Kon.''

"It's awfully late, isn't it? But you can try,'' he said in a bored voice. Then he lay back down and punched the bolster a couple of times to get into a more comfortable position.

Meg whirled around and dashed into the kitchen.

The receiver was missing. He must have detached

and hidden it while she was putting Anna back to bed.

"Relax. You're perfectly safe with me here. If by morning you still want to call your attorney, go ahead. All it means is that you'll end up meeting Senator Strickland sooner rather than later. Sweet dreams, Meggie."

She made a noise that sounded like something between a cry and a groan, impotently staring at Kon's back. Within minutes, she heard his breathing change. He'd actually fallen asleep!

What was she going to do? Kidnap Anna from her own apartment?

A mirthless laugh escaped. Short of rendering her daughter unconscious, she'd never manage. Anna wouldn't stand to be dragged away from Kon when they'd only just been united. And where could Meg take her without being followed?

Physically and emotionally drained, she reflected on comments one of her divorced friends at work had made. Cheryl had talked about how hard it was dealing with an ex-husband who still acted as if he was part of the family. She'd described her feelings of oppression and claustrophobia, and her frequent sense of fear.

For the first time Meg thought she understood a little of what Cheryl had meant. But Meg suspected that if she was to tell her friend about her past association with Kon, about what had happened to her and Anna during the ballet, the other woman wouldn't believe her. Meg could hardly believe it herself.

Yet one of her deepest fears had already been

realized. Kon had taken Anna's heart by storm. As for Meg's other fear—that he would insist on taking Anna to live with him for part of the year—only time would reveal Kon's true intentions.

Instead of being relieved by the insight he'd provided about his forced recruitment to the KGB at such a tender age, Meg found that it only deepened her anxiety. After all, Kon had been brutally torn from his own family, with everyone lost to him. Then he'd learned of Anna's existence. What could be more natural than to claim his own flesh and blood to fill that void?

Today's episode at the ballet provided Meg with absolute proof that from now on, wherever he went, whatever he did, he'd make sure his adoring daughter was by his side. And he'd let no one stand in the way, least of all Meg.

Kon was an expert at manipulation and intrigue. What would be the point of contacting her attorney or Senator Strickland, or the CIA for that matter? None of them was capable of giving her the reassurance she needed.

This was a crisis without precedent, one she'd have to work through by herself. Kon's first step would be to lull her into a false sense of security— then he'd strike. Eventually they'd have to battle it out in court. Perhaps the best thing for now would be to play along until she saw her way clear to thwart him.

A shiver passed through her body. She turned off the Christmas-tree lights, and Kon was no longer visible. But somehow the darkness tended to magnify his presence.

The irony of the situation wasn't lost on Meg. At one time she would have given everything she possessed to see him lying there on her couch. After learning she was pregnant, her ultimate fantasy had been to see Kon walk through the front door straight into her arms.

I was out of my mind, she berated herself, wishing with all her soul that she'd had the wisdom to listen to her aunt.

After Meg had lost both parents, she'd lived with her aunt, Margaret, who'd been crippled with arthritis and suffered from a bad heart. Margaret had been horrified when Meg finally found the courage to tell her about the incident in Moscow, which had resulted in her being arrested and jailed.

Margaret was the widow of Meg's uncle Lloyd, her father's brother and a man with a distinguished career in naval intelligence. He'd died tragically from a slip on the ice when Meg was in her early twenties. Lloyd had been the most vocal in questioning the wisdom of Meg's Russian studies, let alone her traveling to the USSR. Margaret had seconded his opinions.

The brothers had had opposing viewpoints about Russia's threat to the world. Meg's father was not only a pacifist but a political scientist who'd believed language was the basis of understanding other people. He'd argued that there would come a time when the two nations could coexist peacefully. The U.S. would need teachers and ambassadors who understood and spoke Russian, people like Meg.

Uncle Lloyd, on the other hand, had remained adamant that the kind of situation his brother described was a pipe dream. He'd used all the cold hard facts at his command to support his arguments. When Meg told her aunt about the incident, Margaret had reiterated those facts, saying that if Uncle Lloyd had still been alive, he would have made an international incident of his niece's incarceration.

Meg hadn't been able to understand why her aunt was so upset. After all, she'd told her how the attractive KGB agent had intervened and gotten her to the airport in time to make it home for the funeral, how he'd given her a farewell gift.

But the more she defended him, the more her aunt argued. Margaret had finally confided inside information she'd gleaned from her husband about the mission of the KGB, not the sort of thing made public to the American people, details learned from several important Soviet defectors.

When Meg looked back, she felt remorse for having treated her aunt with scorn and disbelief. It seemed that Meg was her father's daughter, and she'd brushed off Margaret's advice, never dreaming that one day the older woman's warnings would come back to haunt her.

About the time Anna was born, Meg's aunt had passed away. Right after that, detente occurred. Stories began to trickle out of Russia about the inner workings of the KGB. To Meg's horror, it appeared that everything her aunt had tried to tell her was true.

And now Kon was here, a new threat to her peace of mind.

Suddenly Meg felt limp with exhaustion. She made her way to the bedroom, where she changed into a loose-fitting T-shirt and sweatpants. Taking the pillow from her bed, she went into Anna's room, needing comfort.

She climbed under the quilt and pulled Anna close, wrapping her arms around her. She caught her breath—the faint scent of Kon's soap lingered on Anna's cheek and hair. With a groan she turned sharply away and smothered her face in the pillow.

The clean fragrance brought back poignant memories of Kon on the last night they were together. She remembered the smoldering blue of his eyes before he made love to her, his insatiable desire for her and the Russian endearments that poured from his soul. Once again, he'd begged her to be his wife, to stay with him forever.

Meg never tired of hearing those words, and she'd told him there was nothing she wanted more—as long as they could arrange to spend half the year in Russia and the other half in the States. Through her uncle's contacts at the Pentagon and Kon's position in his government, surely something could be arranged. Since both of them loved their countries, it seemed the only solution if they were to have a life together.

He'd shaken his head. "What you want is an impossibility, Meggie. The only way we can be together is for you to give up your citizenship and live with me. You have no family now. If you love me enough, you'll do it."

"I think you must know how much I love you, Kon. But what if you grow tired of me? I couldn't bear that," she'd whispered into his hair, clinging to him. "What would happen if you decided you didn't want me anymore and asked for a divorce? I'd be alone, unable to return to the States.''

Kon had responded with an anger that was all the more terrible because it was so quiet and controlled. He'd disentangled himself from her body and climbed out of bed to get dressed. Devastated by his reaction, Meg drew the covers to her chin and sat up.

He'd trained accusing eyes on her. ''You don't know the meaning of love if you can lie in my arms and talk about marriage and divorce in the same breath. One of the problems in your country—''

''Not just my country, Kon—'' she interrupted him, then fell silent. The last magical night they'd shared began to disintegrate.

In a few long strides he was out the bedroom door while she sponge-bathed as best she could, then dressed for the trip to the airport. Kon took her cases to the car and helped her inside, all the while ignoring her questions and overtures. His frozen silence broke her heart.

Once more he was the forbidding and unapproachable KGB agent. He'd rushed her to the airport in record time, instructed a guard to deal with her bags, then walked her to the plane. The way he'd helped her find her seat reminded Meg of the first time she'd left Russia.

Déjà vu except for one thing. She and Kon were alone inside the huge body of the jet. No other passengers had been allowed to board yet. Meg felt torn, and she wondered if a human being could endure this much pain and still survive.

''Meggie...''

She remembered the tortured sound of his voice and how she'd let out a gasp and looked at him. Perhaps it was the shadowy interior that had made his eyes glisten.

"Don't go. Stay with me. I love you, *mayah la-bof*. We'll be married right away. I have plenty of money. You can have your choice of the finest apartments. We'll live very well. I'll always take care of you," he'd vowed in an almost savage voice before crushing her in his arms.

More than anything in the world, she'd wanted to say yes. She'd molded herself to him, kissing him with all the intensity that was in her. But she was too much a product of her Western upbringing. Fear of what might happen in the future kept her from accepting his proposal.

Consumed by tears and frantic because their time had run out, she'd cried, "Do you think I want to leave you? My life is never going to be the same without you!"

At her words an expressionless mask had come down over his face and he'd held her at a distance.

"Kon, don't look at me like that! I can't bear it. I-I'll save my money and try to come back next year."

"No." He'd ground the word out with a strange finality she didn't understand. "Don't come back. Do you hear me?" He shook her hard. "Don't ever come back."

"But—"

"It's now or not at all."

His implacability had defeated her and she'd slumped against him, sobbing. "With you, I'm not afraid. But if something happened to you, I'd have nowhere to turn.''

She heard his sharp intake of breath. ''Goodbye, Meggie.'' He'd let her go and started down the aisle. Any second, and he would disappear from her life forever.

She'd cried his name in panic, but it was like shouting into the wind.

He was gone.

CHAPTER FIVE

"MOMMY! MOMMY!" Meg felt a pat on her face. "Why are you crying?"

Meg awoke from her half sleep with a start and stared at her daughter through bleary eyes, completely disoriented. *It was morning.* "I—I must have had a bad dream."

"Is that why you slept with me?"

After a brief hesitation Meg said, "Yes."

"You should have slept with Daddy. Then you wouldn't have been scared. Melanie says her mommy and daddy sleep together except when they have fights. Then he sleeps at her grandma's. Did you and Daddy have a fight?"

Was there any subject of a delicate nature Anna and Melanie *hadn't* discussed?

Meg expelled an exasperated sigh and threw back the covers to get out of bed, deciding not to comment. Anna must have been up for some time because she'd dressed in her favorite blue velour top with the pink hearts and matching pants. And Meg hadn't even been aware of it.

Anxiety made her reach out and cling to her daughter for an extra-long moment. Anna hugged her back, then struggled to be free.

"We had pancakes for our breakfast but I told

him you like toast so he fixed that and said I should come and get you.''

Now that Anna mentioned it, Meg could smell coffee. Since Anna didn't know how to prepare coffee, that meant Kon had taken over. As he always did, commandeering the apartment, her daughter, her life—

But could she really expect him to act in any other way, know any other method—an eight-year-old boy stolen by the state and taught to be the complete authority figure?

Furious to find herself thinking of *any* excuse for him, Meg vented her feelings on the bed, which she'd started to make. Anything to put off the moment she had to face him again.

"Hurry, Mommy. I want to go see our house and the dogs.''

"But we'll miss your Sunday-school class," Meg reminded her, already knowing how Anna would react. She couldn't help saying it, anyway.

"Daddy says there's a church by our house. I can go to Sunday school there next week. He says there are six kids in my class.''

Meg's movements became so jerky she actually ripped the top sheet, which had caught on the end of the metal frame.

Anna's eyes rounded. "Uh-oh, Mommy. Something tore.''

"So it did," Meg mumbled and threw on the comforter before she headed to the bathroom.

"I'll tell Daddy you're up!''

After Anna darted off, Meg glanced at herself in the mirror. A pale, haggard face stared back, but that

was just fine with her. She took care of the necessities, then pulled her hair back, securing it with an
elastic. She decided against makeup or perfume. For
that matter, she'd leave on her sweats. The vivacious
young woman who used to do everything possible
to make herself beautiful for Kon had died.

"Mommy? Telephone!"

Meg's head jerked sideways. She hadn't even
heard it ring. Kon must have reattached the receiver
earlier that morning and picked it up the instant it
rang.

"Coming."

She hated it that the second she saw Kon standing
by the wall with the receiver in one hand, a cup of
coffee in the other, her heart thumped crazily in her
chest. She avoided his disquieting gaze as she took
the phone from him, then turned her back. It should
be a sin for a man to be so attractive that her senses
couldn't help responding to him. Even her palms
had moistened.

"Hello?" She strove to sound calm and normal.

"Am I speaking to Ms. Meg Roberts?"

Meg blinked at the sound of an officious-sounding
female voice.

"Yes?"

"Please stay on the line. Senator Strickland would
like to speak to you."

She leaned against the doorjamb for support and
concentrated on Anna. At Kon's urging the child
began to clean up the mess she'd made on the table
with her nail polish. She'd obviously been getting
ready for their trip.

"Ms. Roberts? Senator Strickland."

She instantly recognized that aging, raspy voice with the sustained pauses. "Yes, Senator."

"I'm calling to offer you my support and assure you that I couldn't be happier about the reunion with that young man of yours."

Reunion? Young man?

"I'd say that any man who would go through this kind of pain, danger and suffering must truly be in love. You realize your young man was one of the Soviets' most important defectors? And then there were the six years of semi-isolation while he waited to claim his American sweetheart and child.... I understand you're having some difficulty with the situation. But Mr. Rudenko deserves a hearing and I damn well hope you're giving him one."

Meg surmised that the two CIA agents had already filled him in on last night's meeting with her and he wasn't happy about it. But she was incapable of making more than a noncommittal sound in reply.

"My wife and I would consider it an honor if you would plan to join us for dinner soon. I'll have my secretary arrange it with you after the Christmas holidays. You two need time alone to renew the romance and make plans. I envy you that." He chuckled amicably.

Meg felt she was going to suffocate. "Th-thank you, Senator," she whispered.

"If there's anything I can do for you in the meantime, you call my secretary and she'll let me know. I'm sure this will be a very merry Christmas."

The line went dead. In a daze she put the phone back on the hook only to hear it ring again. She could feel Kon's penetrating gaze as she lifted the receiver once more. Clearing her throat she said, "Hello?"

"Hi."

Her eyes closed tightly. "Hi, Ted."

"Hey? What's wrong? You don't sound like yourself."

She rubbed the back of her neck with her free hand and walked as far into the living room as the cord would allow, away from prying eyes and ears.

"I—I guess I've come down with something." Even if Kon hadn't turned her world inside out, she still would have proffered an excuse not to go out with Ted. She didn't mind lunch with him once in a while, but that was it. He didn't interest her. No man did.

"I'm sorry to hear that. I was about to ask if you and Anna wanted to go sledding with me at the park this afternoon. Afterward I figured we'd get dinner someplace."

Now he was trying to appeal to her by including Anna. "That sounds very nice. Maybe another time when I'm feeling better," she lied.

"Right." The disappointment in his voice was palpable. "Then I'll see you at the office."

"Yes. I should be there tomorrow. I'm sure all I need is a good night's sleep. Thanks for calling."

Aware she sounded nervous, she said goodbye, dreading the short walk to the kitchen to hang up the phone.

"Ted Jenkins, salesman of the year at Strong Motors," Kon said, clearly baiting her. "Thirty years old. Divorced. Frustrated because he doesn't have a relationship with you and never will. Why don't you eat your breakfast while I help Anna on with her snowsuit? Then we can be off.''

''How do you know about him?''

''Like any man in love, I made it my business to find out if I had serious competition. Walter Bowman was willing to go in there on the pretext of buying a sports car. Ted Jenkins ended up taking him for a test run, and by the end of the ride, he'd learned enough to give me the information I wanted.''

Under normal circumstances, any woman would be thrilled to know that the man she loved cared that much. But nothing about their relationship was normal.

Still, part of her *was* thrilled. And that meant it was starting to happen all over again.... Ignoring the plate of cold toast sitting on the counter, Meg fled from the room. She felt a desperate need to avoid Kon's probing gaze.

He didn't play fair! And she was terrified he would discover the kind of power he still had over her. The wisest thing would be to pretend to go along with his plan for Anna's sake.

Their daughter was determined to see where he lived. Once her curiosity had been satisfied, Meg would tell Kon he'd have to work through her attorney if he hoped to spend time with Anna after today. Any future visits would have to be in Meg's presence.

No matter that he'd somehow gained the confidence of Senator Strickland, Kon wasn't above the law. Her anger made her motions clumsy and she broke a shoelace. She groaned in frustration. Now she'd have to wear loafers instead of running shoes.

"Here's your coat, Mommy. Daddy's outside warming up the car for us."

"Well, wasn't that thoughtful of him," she muttered sarcastically beneath her breath. She was bristling with indignation at the thought that he'd taken her keys off the counter without even asking.

"Daddy says you need a rest, so he's going to drive. He says you've been working too hard, so he's going to take good care of you."

Meg couldn't let this go on any longer. After buttoning her coat, she crouched down to talk to her daughter, who was clutching her doll. "Honey—" she smoothed the dark curls, which bounced right back over Anna's forehead "—I know you're happy about meeting your daddy, but that doesn't mean we're all going to live together."

"Yes, it does," Anna said with complete assurance. "I told Daddy I wanted a baby sister like Melanie's. And you know what?" Her eyes grew rounder. "He said he could give me a sister just as soon as you get married next week. He wants a big family."

Meg gasped out loud and buried her face against Anna's small shoulder. "Anna! Mommy isn't going to marry your daddy."

"Yes, you are," she stated confidently. "Daddy said so. He promised he's going to stay home with us all the time. Don't be scared, Mommy." She stroked Meg's hair.

Meg clung to her daughter for a full minute before

getting control of herself. "Sometimes grown-ups can't keep their promises, Anna."

"Daddy will 'cause he's my daddy and he loves me," she argued, sounding close to tears. "Let's hurry, Mommy. He's waiting for us."

She broke free of Meg's grasp and scuttled out of the apartment before Meg could stop her. Afraid of what was already happening to Anna, Meg grabbed her purse from the kitchen counter, locked the door and dashed after her.

Luckily, Sunday mornings were quiet around the complex, especially during the winter. Most of her neighbors were still inside their apartment, and Meg was spared answering difficult questions like, *Why do you look so pale, Meg? Who's the attractive stranger who stayed over at your apartment last night? Why is he driving your Toyota with Anna seated up front next to him?*

Kon got out of the car at her approach, his eyes narrowed on her face. More than ever, she was glad she hadn't dressed up or bothered with makeup. Most likely he was comparing the tired, anxiety-ridden mother to the passionate, love-besotted young woman she used to be.

"If you'd rather drive, I'll sit in back," he offered.

He sounded so reasonable her temper flared. "Why break your record and give me a choice now?" She kept on walking around the other side of the car and climbed into the back before he could help her.

He followed her and shut the door. After a searching glance, which she refused to meet, he went around to the driver's side and got in. Seconds later, they were off.

He turned on a radio station playing Christmas carols and Anna began singing, much to Kon's delight. Meg could see his face through the rearview mirror as he sang with her. She couldn't help but be touched by the adoring expression he cast Anna every so often.

As the Toyota covered the miles, it dawned on Meg that she'd never been chauffeured around in her own car before. It was a novel experience to ride in the back seat and let Kon do the work, all the while keeping their loquacious daughter entertained. Grudgingly Meg admitted that not having to be in charge made a nice change, especially now, with the roads growing icy and wind buffeting the car.

But of course if Kon wasn't in the picture, she would never have gone driving with Anna on a wintry day like today in the first place. Their normal routine was to walk to the church a few blocks away, then come home and fix lunch. Afterward, Meg usually encouraged Anna to practice her violin. Then her daughter would either play at Melanie's apartment, or vice versa, while Meg caught up on some reading or sewing.

Lately Anna had been spending more time at Melanie's because of her fascination with the new baby. This was why she'd become so obsessed with the idea of having a brother or sister of her own and had divulged her fantasies to Kon. So far he'd proved he could grant her every desire. Was it any wonder that Anna adored him? Just the way *Meg* had once adored him?

Unable to help herself, she found her eyes straying to the back of his dark head, the broad set of his shoulders, his incredibly handsome profile. *There ought to be a law!* she cried inside. Abruptly she turned away to stare out the window, but not before his smoldering glance had intercepted hers for an instant. It sent a shock wave through her body, disrupting the rhythm of her breathing.

The force of her own reaction upset her so much she didn't realize that they'd pulled into a rest area and come to a stop.

"I don't have to go to the bathroom yet, Daddy."

Despite Kon's low chuckle, Meg felt nervous, wondering why they'd stopped. He turned in the seat so he could eye both of them.

"We're almost at Hannibal. But before we get there, I have a secret to tell you." His grave tone increased Meg's apprehension. "I know your mother can keep it, but what about you, Anochka? If I tell you something very, very important, will you remember that it is our family secret, no one else's?"

Our family. Meg's breath caught while Anna's eyes grew solemn and she slowly nodded her head.

"When I left Russia, I had to change my name."

"Why, Daddy?"

Meg felt a strange tension radiating from him, as if there was a surfeit of dark emotion he had difficulty suppressing.

"Some people got mad because I left my country," he said in a hollow voice, "and some people in America were mad because I came here. They didn't like my Russian name. They didn't like me."

Something in his tone led Meg to believe he'd suffered. Anna was equally affected.

"We like you, Daddy!" She rushed to her father's defense, her child's heart ready to forgive him anything. "We *love* you, don't we, Mommy?"

"And I love both of you," he said in a husky voice, preventing Meg from refuting him. "So to keep us all safe, I took a different name."

With such important news to consider, Anna forgot to sing along with the carol that had just started playing on the radio, even though "Deck the Halls" was one of her favorites. "What's your new name?"

"Gary Johnson."

Gary Johnson? Meg fought to keep from bursting out laughing. No man in the world ever looked or acted less like a Gary Johnson than KGB agent Konstantin Rudenko. It was ludicrous.

"That's the name of a boy in my class!" Anna cried excitedly. "He's got blond hair and a pet c-coca-too. Mrs. Beezley let us bring our pets to class and Mommy helped me bring my fish."

Kon nodded, seemingly pleased with her response. "Thousands of boys and men in the United States have the name Gary Johnson. That's why I picked it."

"And now nobody's mad at you anymore?"

"That's right. I have lots of new friends and neighbors, and they all call me Gary or Mr. Johnson."

"Can't I keep calling you Daddy?"

Kon undid her seat belt and pulled her onto his lap so he could kiss her. "You're the only person in the whole wide world who gets to call me Daddy, Anochka.''

'''Cept when I get a new sister.''

"That's right," he murmured, hugging her tight.

Anna finally lifted her head so she could see over the seat, her blue eyes glowing like jewels. "Mommy, you have to call Daddy Gary from now on. Don't forget,'' she said in a hushed voice.

Anna's remark was so touching, Meg's heart turned over and she averted her eyes. As far as Kon went, though, it would be impossibile for her to call him Gary. In fact, the whole situation was too fantastic: she just couldn't do it. But that really didn't matter, because she wouldn't be seeing him except at visitation times, and then they wouldn't be around other people.

She felt Kon's glance sweep over her. "Your mommy has always called me 'darling,' so I don't anticipate any problem.''

Meg couldn't take much more of this farce. She felt as though she'd aged a hundred years since the ballet yesterday.

"I think another snowstorm's coming, *Gary*," she mocked. "If we're going to see your house, then I suggest we get moving.''

His brilliant smile twisted her insides. "It sounds as if you're as excited as I am.''

After he'd put Anna back in her seat and fastened the belt, he started the car and they reentered the freeway. Hannibal was only six miles farther. "I can hardly wait until we get home,'' he confided to his daughter, tousling her curls with his free hand. "I've been lonely for my little girl.''

"I'm here now, Daddy, and you won't ever be lonely again, will he, Clara?" she said to the doll she'd named after the girl in the *Nutcracker*. "Clara loves you, too, Daddy."

"I'm glad to hear it."

Hard as she tried, Meg couldn't blot out the sound of his deep, attractive voice or the loving look he exchanged with their daughter. Anna's sweet, generous spirit brought a lump to Meg's throat, and it seemed to have affected Kon in a similar manner, because he whispered the Russian word for sweetheart and reached for Anna's hand.

The takeover was complete. Anna would never be wholly hers again. Meg couldn't bear it and she put a hand over her heart, as if she could stop the pain. *What was she going to do?*

They left the freeway and entered the small town of Hannibal, made famous by Sam Clemens, who had written about his boyhood on the Mississippi in the mid-nineteenth century.

Meg didn't know what Kon had in mind, but supposed that for Anna's sake he would drive them past the riverboat landing in the downtown area, where the Mark Twain Home and Museum were located.

Instead, he took a route that led past all the historic homes decorated for Christmas until they came to the famous Rockcliffe Mansion. They drove another block, then he turned a corner and entered a driveway that needed to be shoveled after last night's snow. They wound around the back of a quaint, white, two-story clapboard house with green trim; it reminded her of the restored Becky Thatcher Bookshop in the historic district.

"We're home, Anochka." He pulled to a stop in front of a detached two-car garage and undid Anna's seat belt.

Anna couldn't keep still, her bright eyes missing nothing. "Where are my dogs, Daddy?"

"On the back porch, waiting for us."

Meg stared at the house in disbelief, then switched her gaze to Kon. He was helping Anna from the car, her doll forgotten. Meg couldn't equate this doting father and family man with the all-powerful KGB agent who, at one time, had inspired fear in the hearts of Soviet citizens and foreigners alike.

She got out of the car, then watched spellbound as Kon told both of them to wait right there while he mounted the steps and unlocked the door.

Anna let out a shriek of delight as a handsome German shepherd came running down the stairs and circled her in the snow, sniffing at her hands and swishing his tail. No doubt Kon had experience with dogs trained in pursuit. This one had been handled so expertly he didn't bare his teeth or growl or jump up on her, relieving Meg of any initial worry in that department.

At Kon's command, the dog came to a standstill and let Anna pet him. It didn't surprise Meg that her daughter showed no fear. An elderly couple across the street from the apartment complex had a friendly golden retriever Anna and Melanie loved to play with.

"Meggie, come over and meet Thor," Kon urged, his voice alive and inviting. It conjured up memories of another place, another time, when she'd lived for nothing but him and whenever they were apart counted the hours till they were together again.

For the next few minutes Meg let go of her anxieties about Kon's motives long enough to become acquainted with the dog. Thor appeared as ecstatic as Anna to make friends. He showed his affection with licks and whimpers and a few exuberant barks that made Anna giggle and her father laugh out loud.

Meg had never heard such a happy sound from him. Forgetting to be on her guard, she raised her head, smiling, and discovered he was looking at her in the old way, his eyes fiercely blue and possessive. She felt her body tremble and turned away.

"Where's the other dog?" Anna wanted to know.

"Gandy's busy inside," came the cryptic reply. "Shall we go see what she is doing?"

"Follow me, Thor," Anna cried excitedly as she scrambled up the back steps behind her father. Before Meg had even reached the door she heard Anna's awestruck voice. Curious to see what had produced such reverence, Meg hurried into the warm, closed-in porch, where she caught a glimpse of a female German shepherd lying on a makeshift bed in the corner, with three tiny suckling pups. The new mother lifted her proud head at their approach.

Thor crept next to Kon, who hunkered down and put his arm around Anna while they gazed at the beautiful sight. "This is the early Christmas present I told you about, Anochka," he whispered.

"Oh, Daddy!" she squealed in rapture. "Look at the littlest one. She could fit in my hands."

"She's a he." His voice was tender, gently mocking.

Anna absorbed that bit of information and said, "Can I hold him? Please?"

"In a little while, when he's through eating. We musn't disturb them right now."

"What's his name?" she whispered loudly. With Anna, there was no such thing as a quiet whisper.

"I thought I'd leave that up to you since he'll be your dog. The other two we'll find a new home for as soon as they're ready to leave their mommy. But this puppy's just for you."

Once again Anna's eyes looked like exploding stars as she turned to Meg. "Mommy, I'm going to call him Prince Marzipan Johnson."

Meg started to laugh—she couldn't help it—and Kon joined her.

"Why don't we call him Prince for short?" Kon finally managed to say. He got to his feet. "I think we've tried Gandy's patience long enough. Why don't you go inside with Thor and start exploring." He opened another door that led into the house. "See if you can pick out your bedroom."

"*My own bedroom?* Come on, Thor." She put a hand on the dog's collar and they squeezed through the opening together. Meg couldn't tell which one of them was the most excited. But the moment they disappeared, the reality of the situation pressed in on Meg until she could hardly breathe.

"Kon—"

"Later, Meggie. Unless you want to join me in the shower."

She jammed her hands in her coat pockets and fastened her attention on Gandy, who'd returned her attention to the pups. Long after Kon had gone into the house, Meg stood there, willing the image of his hard, fit body, which had once known and claimed hers, to leave her mind.

The bittersweet torture of those memories held her unmoving, and though Anna was calling her, Meg couldn't bring herself to step one foot inside Kon's house. A house she suspected he'd bought with money he'd been paid for selling secrets.

CHAPTER SIX

MEG WAS AFRAID.

Afraid she'd like his home too much. Afraid he'd break down her resolve a little more, until the edges blurred and she didn't know what was phony and what was real. Afraid she'd be like Anna, totally vulnerable and accepting, until—until what? Meg didn't know anymore.

Even if he *had* defected, he was still a son of Russia, a man who loved his country. Now that a detente had been reached, she wouldn't blame him for wanting to return to his birthplace, that isolated village in Siberia for a visit. A place where he'd played with his sled as a little boy, where he'd been happy in the bosom of his family.

He had money and he could travel under an American passport. And he could take Anna with him. What could be more natural than to want to recapture his own stunted childhood through his daughter's eyes, to instill in her his love of Mother Russia? If he had joint custody, he could take Anna wherever he wanted and Meg would never need to know.

Ages ago, she'd turned down his marriage proposal because she hadn't wanted to live in Russia on a permanent basis. That would never change.

Kon knew how she felt. She was sure there'd be no warning if he uprooted Anna temporarily.

It was time to have a talk with him.

An excess of nervous energy propelled her into the house. But halfway through the kitchen Meg came to a halt, arrested by the white ceiling-to-counter cabinets in the traditional British pantry style. Wide cherry floorboards gleamed with a golden patina against white moldings and pale yellow walls, creating a sense of mellow warmth and beauty. It was a classic look that was continued throughout the rest of the downstairs.

The moderately sized house with its old-fashioned, small-paned windows reflected a spare traditionalism. The use of a few period pieces in the living and dining rooms, combined with comfortable, overstuffed furniture covered in a predominantly green chintz, gave it a timeless appeal.

Her eye followed the graceful sweep of the staircase with its hand-carved railing. Slowly she wandered into a study set off by French doors. Two pilastered bookcases on either side of a brick fireplace contained an impressive library of classical literature, with books in several languages, including, of course, Russian.

File cabinets and a desk complete with lamp, computer, keyboard and monitor supplied the only modern touch.

Did the decor reflect Kon's personal taste or had he purchased this charming home as is?

How could she possibly know the real man beneath his KGB-created persona when her only contact with him had been inside a police car, or a hotel or restaurant staffed by KGB?

Or a woodcutter's cottage?

Meg shivered as she contemplated the enormity of what she'd done. Anna had been conceived in a stranger's bed, by a stranger, in a strange land....

Certainly Kon couldn't have taken his lover home with him in those days, wherever and whatever "home" might have been. The normal human experience of a man and woman meeting and getting to know each other had eluded her completely where he was concerned.

According to Walt and Lacey Bowman, Kon had lived here in Hannibal for five years. Had the American government provided him with this house, along with a ready-made identity to hide the fact that he was a Russian defector?

Who was the real Kon?

Was Konstantin Rudenko the name his parents had given him at birth, or had the Soviet government supplied him a new one when they'd kidnapped him for service?

Meg thought she'd go mad trying to answer those questions, and she buried her face in her hands.

Another pair of hands settled on her shoulders. Strong, warm, masculine hands that felt achingly familiar. She should have tried to move away, but her body was being controlled by a force more powerful than her will to fight it. A low, husky voice whispered, "Don't try to solve all the world's riddles right now." It was as though he'd read her mind.

Her breath caught as she felt questing fingers encircle the nape of her neck and gently massage the tense muscles. "You and I haven't had a moment alone until now," he murmured, grazing her earlobe with his teeth. "Much as I adore Anna, I thought I'd lose my mind if she didn't find a way to entertain herself so I could kiss her mother. Dear God, it's been six endless, excruciating years, *mayah labof.*"

The heat from his body radiated to Meg's, and those old, familiar longings took over, trapping her despite everything she knew and feared about him. His mouth traveled along her hot cheek, his smooth, freshly shaved skin scented from the soap he'd used in the shower.

"There's been no one else for me since you left me, and I have the strongest impression there's been no one else for you, either. What we shared could never be repeated with anyone else. Help me," he groaned against her lips before drawing her fully into his arms.

Meg tried not to respond, but she felt as if some drug had dulled her power to think, to remember that he was the enemy. His mouth started to work its magic, and before she knew how it had happened, her mouth opened to his. Her passion flared out of control. Just like before…

It was happening again, just as she'd feared. The mindless rapture, this explosion of sensual feeling that left her weak and clinging to him. It had been so long since the last time he'd aroused these sensations that her desire leapt to pulsating life.

Somehow, without her being aware of it, he'd undone her coat and now he was urging her body closer, running his hands over her back, insinuating his fingers beneath the waistband of her skirt to touch her sensitized skin.

With a helpless moan she slid her arms around his neck, and her body arched against his solid warmth, knowing where this was leading, wanting it so badly, she was barely conscious of footsteps running down the stairs and an excited young voice chatting with Thor.

Anna.

Meg couldn't let her daughter see them like this. She shoved her hands against his chest, but Kon must not have heard Anna, because he deepened their kiss, effectively suffocating her cry of panic.

His mouth craved hers with the relentless hunger of a man who'd been deprived too long. To her shame, Meg offered herself in wanton abandon even as Anna came bouncing into the study with an exuberant Thor at her heels.

Mortified to have been caught out like this, Meg tried to pull away from Kon and waited for the inevitable comment from their curious, precocious daughter. But for once, Anna failed to say anything at all.

The unnatural silence must have alerted Kon, who with a low groan reluctantly lifted his mouth from hers. His eyes burned a hot blue as they studied her trembling mouth.

Since he seemed as incapable of speech as his daughter, Meg realized it was up to her to divert Anna's attention.

She took advantage of Kon's temporary weakness to separate herself from him. But she wasn't prepared for the sense of loss she felt as soon as she'd moved out of his arms. Nor was she prepared for the speculative look in Anna's eyes; it reminded her of Kon—the same penetrating gaze. Thor rubbed against Anna's side, waiting.

Heavens, Anna made Meg feel like a lovestruck teenager whose parents had found her in a compromising position with her boyfriend! Before she could think of something to say to defuse the situation, Anna took the initiative.

"Have you and Daddy been making a baby?"

She should have been ready for that one. Her breathing grew shallow as she felt Kon's hands slide to her shoulders. He kneaded them with gentle insistence.

"Not yet, Anochka," he answered calmly. "First your mother has to agree to marry me. Shall I ask her now?"

"No! Please…" Meg begged him, but Anna was nodding solemnly, and Meg knew she herself would have fainted if Kon hadn't been standing behind her, holding her in his firm grip.

"Meggie." He ignored her plea and murmured into her hair, caressing the top of her head with his chin. "With Senator Strickland's help, special arrangements have been made for us to have a private wedding here at the house on Wednesday. A friend of mine who's a judge on the state's Supreme Court will marry us, and Lacey and Walt will serve as witnesses. The only detail left is for you to say yes."

Yesterday he'd placed the noose around her neck. Now he'd drawn it tight.

"I want us to be a family. Anna shouldn't have to grow up without her father the way I did, and I certainly don't want anyone else raising her. Obviously you don't, either, or you would have married before now.''

Which was true, but she'd rather die than admit it to him.

''You can quit your job at Strong Motors and be a full-time mother to Anna. This house needs a mother and father, husband and wife. I didn't even want to put up a Christmas tree or decorations until we could do it together.''

There was a long silence while Meg tried to absorb what he was saying.

''Anna,'' she finally said in a shaky voice, ''I need to talk to your father alone. Why don't you and Thor go out on the porch and see how the new puppies are doing? But don't touch them.''

''Are you going to marry my daddy?'' the child persisted stubbornly.

''Anna,'' Meg said as sternly as she could, ''do as I say, please.''

But her daughter refused to mind her, and the hint of tears shimmering in her eyes was almost more than Meg could bear. ''I want to live with Daddy. I have a pink room and a bed with a tent over it, and a mirror and a little table and…and everything!''

''Anochka…'' her father warned quietly. That was all it took for their daughter to grab Thor by the collar and leave the room.

How did Kon do that?

Meg wheeled around in exasperation, noting all at once how incredibly attractive he looked in American jeans and a dark turtleneck. She was determined to ignore her own powerful response to him. ''I have no intention of marrying you and we certainly don't need to get married for you to see Anna." Her chest heaved as though she was out of breath. "If you'll tell me what days you want to be with her, I'll drive her here and let you spend time together before I take her home again."

"This is your home now," came the implacable response. "I want both of you here every day and every night for the rest of our lives."

"That isn't possible, Kon. But I'm willing to work out a visitation schedule."

"I'm not."

He was impossible! "It's that or nothing, I'm afraid. You've had your reunion with your daughter. Now I'm taking Anna home. Please give me my car keys."

It shocked her when he reached into his pocket and handed them to her without a word, a strange smile on that darkly handsome face.

It shocked her even more that he did nothing to prevent her from leaving the house. He stood on the steps and kept Thor at bay while Meg dragged an hysterical Anna through the snow to the car.

"Daddy! Daddy!" she screamed at the top of her lungs as Kon went back inside and closed the door. Her daughter's cries reminded Meg of the tape he had played for her the night before. They had to be tearing him apart, yet he didn't lift a finger to help her. Even though that was what Meg wanted, the pain of the whole thing was almost beyond endurance.

"Don't let Mommy take me away, Daddy!" Anna's heartbreaking plea could be heard for miles,

Meg was sure, and the tears didn't stop even when she'd driven away.

Meg found it terrifying that no matter how hard she tried to reason with her daughter, no matter how hard she tried to explain that she could see her father again very soon, Anna cried hysterically all the way home.

"I hate you, Mommy," she said in a hoarse voice when they pulled into their parking spot. "Clara hates you, too, and we're never going to love you again."

Anna's face was flushed and she looked feverish. Guilt almost had Meg restarting the car and returning to Hannibal. But she had to remain firm now or everything would be lost.

Damn you, Kon, she muttered under her breath, fighting back scalding tears of pain and frustration. Before now, there'd never been a discordant note between her and her daughter.

Oh, he was good at his job. Good at creating subversion and chaos! The tears would not be halted now.

Damn you for making me want you, Kon—as badly as Anna wants you. Damn. Damn. Damn!

"MEG? IT'S AN OFFICE aide calling from Anna's school. Line two."

Meg closed her eyes. Anna was probably sick. She'd refused to eat any food after they'd gotten home from Hannibal yesterday, and this morning she wouldn't touch her breakfast before Meg drove her to school.

"Thanks, Cheryl."

With a trembling hand Meg picked up the receiver and pressed the button, her headache so fierce she didn't know how she was going to make it through the rest of the day. Four aspirin still hadn't done the trick, and now she was starting to feel nauseated. If this kept up, she'd have to go home.

"Yes? This is Meg Roberts."

"Hi. This is Carla Morley. I'm helping out today because Mrs. Hixon is home with the flu. I'm just checking with you to see if it's all right if Anna's father drives her home. Anna didn't feel well when she got to school this morning and had me phone him in Hannibal when we couldn't reach you at lunchtime. He drove here as fast as he could."

How did Anna know his phone number unless he gave it to her when Meg was unaware?

"The problem is, you haven't put Mr. Johnson's name on the emergency card, but he said that was because he was out of the country until recently. But as I explained to him, I can't give him permission to take Anna off school grounds unless you give your consent."

Dear God. "Just keep Anna there. I'll be right over. And thank you for being so conscientious." Meg's voice shook. It was entirely possible that without Carla Morley's intervention, Kon could be halfway back to Hannibal with Anna—who was so upset with Meg right now she would have willingly accompanied him anywhere.

Cheryl flashed Meg a look of concern as she hung up the phone. "Is something wrong with Anna? You're as white as a sheet."

"Sh-she's sick." It was the truth. And there was

no way she could tell anyone about Kon right now, not even Cheryl. "I'm going to have to take her home. Would you mind covering for me?"

"Of course not. You shouldn't have come to work this morning, anyway. Go home and stay there until you're both better."

"Thanks, Cheryl. I'll cover for you next time."

On her way out of the car showroom, Ted tried to engage her in conversation, but Meg told him Anna was sick and she couldn't stop to talk. He went out to the back lot with her and helped her into the car, telling her he'd call later to see if there was anything he could do.

Meg thanked him for his concern but told him it wasn't necessary. Then she didn't give him another thought as she drove the seven miles to Anna's school. Fortunately for her, the storm predicted the day before had failed to materialize. The streets were relatively free of snow, and she broke the speed limit getting to her destination. She parked in the school-bus zone to save time and leapt from the car.

With pounding heart she dashed into the main office, where she discovered Anna sitting on Kon's lap, her curly head resting against his chest. The sight of father and daughter never failed to jolt Meg; they looked so *alike*—and so right together.

Kon's enigmatic gaze rested on Meg. Her sigh of relief at finding her daughter safe quickly changed to one of consternation when she saw Anna's flushed face. "Honey, Ms. Morley said you were sick."

"I don't feel good." The small, weak voice

sounded odd to Meg's ears. Caught up in a welter of emotions, she ran directly to Anna, who surprisingly offered no resistance when Meg reached for her. There was no more "I hate you, Mommy," to make her feel worse than she already did.

Ms. Morley flashed her a commiserating smile. "There's a bad flu bug going around. Quite a few of the students are out with it this morning."

"That's probably it," Meg murmured indistinctly. Kon had risen to his full, intimidating height and she could feel his eyes on her, challenging her to make a scene in front of the other woman.

"Luckily today's the last day before Christmas vacation," the aide said amiably. "She'll have the whole holiday to recuperate."

Meg couldn't get out of there fast enough. "Thank you, Ms. Morley."

"Think nothing of it. As soon as Mr. Johnson got here, he was able to calm her down. Seeing her daddy made all the difference, didn't it, Anna?" The woman smiled at Anna, then Kon, obviously charmed by him. "Merry Christmas."

Meg silently blessed the woman for not bringing up the authorization issue. No doubt Ms. Morley dealt with many divorced parents throughout the school year and had learned to be discreet.

"Merry Christmas," Anna called back in a voice that sounded much more cheerful than before.

"How did you know your father's telephone number?" Meg asked Anna the minute they were out of the office. She was acutely conscious of Kon at her elbow opening doors for them.

"I told Ms. Morley that Daddy lives in Hannibal

and I said his name was Gary Johnson—like he told us. She called him for me.''

To Meg's chagrin, Kon sent her a withering glance. ''Our daughter is very bright and resource-ful,'' he began in Russian. ''If you're not careful, your paranoia is going to alienate her.''

His rebuke made Meg feel small and mean. And guilty, of course, because she was always prepared to think the very worst of him. She realized that, ironically enough, the incident verified at least part of his story, which put him at a moral advantage. That call had proved he was in the phone book, that he had been established for some time.

''Can we go home now? I didn't get to hold Prince yesterday and he misses me.''

''I'll take care of him for you, Anochka.'' Kon had spoken before Meg could manage a word. She felt her world disintegrating a little more—Anna no longer considered their apartment home.

Perhaps Kon noticed that the blood had drained from her face. When he opened the passenger door of Meg's car for Anna, he said, ''Right now both you and your mother need to get to bed.''

Anna stared up at her with concern. ''Are you sick, Mommy?''

''No,'' Meg hastened to reassure her as Kon fas-tened the seat belt. ''I'm just a little tired.''

''Is Daddy coming with us?''

''That's up to your mother,'' he inserted smoothly, throwing the onus on Meg, who continued to be the villain in this cleverly orchestrated piece.

''Don't go away, Daddy!'' Anna started to cry again, deep, heaving sobs that poured from her soul and washed her cheeks in tears. Meg felt suddenly, completely, helpless.

She slumped against the car door, all the fight gone out of her. She didn't have the strength to battle Kon and her daughter, too. In a dull voice she said, ''Your father can follow us home in his car if he wants.''

Like magic Anna's tears subsided.

Meg expected to see a triumphant expression on Kon's face as he walked her around to the driver's side of the car.

But as he opened the door for her, a brief glint of what looked like pain darkened the blue of his eyes. It fragmented her emotions even more because she had to wonder if he could summon emotion like that at will—just for effect.

''I'll be right behind you, Anochka.''

''D-do you p-promise?'' Anna's halting question ended on something between a cough and a hiccup.

Meg's hands curled tightly around the steering wheel. She didn't recognize her daughter when Anna behaved like this, when she became this anxiety-ridden child who constantly feared her father would disappear from her life. Her normally trusting and vivacious personality had undergone a complete change.

Apparently Kon was not immune to Anna's fragile condition, either; he unexpectly opened the back door and got into the car. ''I'll ride with you and pick up my car later.''

Before Meg could fathom it, Anna had unfastened her seat belt and climbed into the back with Kon, flinging her arms around his neck. Meg could see them through the rearview mirror, and her heart seemed to expand with something that felt like pain as she watched the tender way Kon was comforting their daughter. He rocked her back and forth in his strong arms, whispering endearments.

And that was when it came to her. He *loved* Anna.

Emotion like that *couldn't* be faked. Some sixth sense told her that in his own way he adored his little Anochka as much as Meg did. And Anna loved him back just as fiercely. If Meg had held on to the vain hope that this was a passing phase from which Anna would recover once Kon was out of sight, she'd better let go of it now.

The drive back to the apartment was silent, with Meg deep in her own thoughts. When she pulled into her parking spot and got out of the car, she saw that Anna had fallen asleep with her tearstained face half-buried in Kon's neck. The night before, Anna had cried for hours before she'd passed out from exhaustion.

He maneuvered himself and Anna from the back seat without disturbing her and followed Meg into the building.

There were few people around this time of day, for which Meg was thankful. She opened the door of the apartment, and Kon carried Anna to her bedroom. Meg trailed behind them and stood in the doorway, watching the deft way he discarded Anna's parka and shoes and tucked her into bed. He lightly caressed her cheek with the knuckles of one hand. Then abruptly, he straightened and started toward Meg, his expression inscrutable.

A little frightened of the tension between them,

she hurried into the living room, feeling far too susceptible to his presence. She wondered if she was on the verge of an emotional breakdown.

"We can be married the day after tomorrow and never have a recurrence of what happened today. But if you're too selfish to think of Anna's best interests, then be warned that I do intend to have a relationship with her."

"What about *my* best interests?" She jerked around, her ash-blond hair and pleated black wool skirt swinging.

He studied her features, the hectic color in her cheeks, her glittering gray eyes, the curves beneath her oyster-colored silk blouse. "You're not in love with anyone else."

"That's beside the point," she lashed out.

"It *is* the point, Meggie. If you'd stayed in Russia, we'd be married today and Anna could easily have a sister or brother by now."

"You're talking about a period of time that's come and gone. I was a totally different human being then! We couldn't possibly have worked anything out because you were already married—to your country. And…and I was afraid." Her breath quickened with the force of her emotions.

"I defected," came the swift rejoinder. "Surely that should tell you something."

"Why?" she cried. "*Why* did you defect? It doesn't make sense for a man in your position. And please don't insult my intelligence by telling me you were overcome with love for me!"

His dark brows furrowed. "I may have been a government agent, but I'm still a man, Meggie. One, moreover, who became enamored of a young American woman to the point that I took many dangerous chances, many risks, to spend time with you. When you left, I…contracted a disease.''

CHAPTER SEVEN

A DISEASE?

Meg's anxious gaze darted to his. "D-did you become ill?" she whispered, her hand going to her throat, where she was positive he could see the hammering of her pulse.

He shifted his weight. "It's a term used by agents to refer to burnout. I'd never had a sick day in my life, and suddenly I went into a depression that left me emotionally ill for months. I lost weight, suffered from insomnia and battled a restlessness I'd never known before.

"As I once told you, there'd been a few other women in the past, mostly other agents working on assignments under me. One relationship lasted a little longer than the rest, but I was always able to move on without becoming emotionally involved."

She hadn't known about the relationship that had gone on longer. How *much* longer? Had he asked that woman to marry him, too? A shaft of pure, unadulterated jealousy left her feeling weak and vulnerable. Until he added, "For some inexplicable reason, it wasn't that easy to walk away from you.

"A comrade suggested I take a leave of absence and go on vacation. So I went to the Urals to do some climbing and fishing. But what should have been a two-week retreat lasted all of two days, and I returned to my post because this restlessness was eating me alive.

"I plunged into my work with such ferocity even my peers tended to stay away from me. But by then I was diagnosed as suffering from severe clinical depression and, oddly enough, the only pleasure I found in life was to follow your movements— through another agent living in the United States."

Meg rubbed her arms, suddenly chilled to the bone, though in reality the apartment was pleasantly warm.

"On one particularly bleak day, the agent telephoned me to say that the beautiful Meg Roberts was pregnant."

He said nothing further for a long moment, apparently lost in recollection. Then he resumed, speaking in a low, rapid voice.

"No one could have been more surprised than I, because I'd taken precautions against that happening." His eyes narrowed on her mouth. "Since I gave you no opportunity to be with another man while in Russia, and since I had irrefutable proof that you hadn't been with another man after leaving the country, I knew you were pregnant with *my* child."

She bowed her head to avoid the possessiveness in his eyes.

"The knowledge that a baby we'd made together was growing inside you took hold of me. It was as if I were there with you, sharing this miraculous experience, and it brought me out of the wretched blackness that had been engulfing me daily.

"When the agent supplied me with a picture of Anna taken while she was still in the hospital nursery, I almost lost my mind. I couldn't be there to hold her, to inspect her fingers and toes, to kiss her soft skin and watch her nurse at your breast. That was the moment I decided to defect."

"Kon…"

"At that point the government was in turmoil, and detente was looking like a real possibility. The changes reshaping my country made me take a long, hard look at my personal life, at my future. All those years I'd served the KGB and that was the only life I'd known.

"But Anna's birth forced me to ask questions about what I wanted for myself." He paced the floor, then came to an abrupt halt. "Don't be deceived by what I'm telling you, Meggie. Russia will always have a claim on my soul. I've been given the finest education in the world, the best lodgings, exceptional pay, diversion when I needed it. And above all, Russia is my homeland. But I found myself wishing that I *belonged* to someone and that someone belonged to me."

He picked up her family photographs from an end table by the couch and studied them for a while. "I don't even know if my parents and sister are still alive. I know nothing about them. They believe I'm dead because this is what they were told thirty years ago. That part is finished."

He put the pictures back and flicked her an indecipherable glance. "I need my daughter. Being with her for the last two days has already filled part of that void in my life."

She sucked in her breath. "If that's how you felt, why didn't you approach me as soon as you arrived in the States? We could have worked out visitation." When she thought of the years that had already gone by…

"When I got out of Russia, I gave your government classified information. The normal procedure was for me to go into hiding. Eventually I was set up with a new identity.

"Since then, the international picture has changed, and the threat isn't the same anymore. But because I know how certain factions of the old guard still think, how the Party mind still works, and because I wanted to make absolutely certain that you and Anna remained unharmed, I waited until now to approach you."

He eyed her steadily. "It was a risk to stay away so long knowing that at any time you could become involved with another man and get married, providing Anna with a stepfather. But it was a risk I had to take because I knew that one day, one way or another, I'd eventually have a relationship with her—and, I hoped, with you."

He gazed at her, a dark, brooding look on his face. "That day is here," he said quietly. "But the choice is yours—do we work out a visitation system, when Anna's already traumatized by everything that's happened? Or do we get married and give her her rightful father and mother?

"In a world where the traditional family unit seems to be disappearing, we're in a position to give her the stability millions of children are denied. The stability I was denied," he added hoarsely.

Maybe she was a gullible fool, but Meg suddenly had the intense conviction that he'd been speaking the truth. Probably because he was so open about telling her that his bond to Russia would never be broken....

"I won't, you know," he murmured, voicing her fears about kidnapping aloud. "Perhaps marrying me is the only way to erase this irrational idea you have that I'm going to take Anna away."

"But you love Russia. I know you do!"

"Yes, but I can't go back, Meggie. My life is here with you. I earn my living at home and I keep a low profile. As my wife, you won't have to work unless you choose. We'll be together twenty-four hours a day. It's what we both wanted before you left Russia." In a low voice he added, "But whether or not you sleep in my bed will be up to you. How does that sound?"

How *did* it sound?

Terrifying, her heart cried. How could she live in the same house with him, year in and year out, wanting him in all the ways a woman wanted a man, yet always feeling afraid he would miss his country, his old life? He said *now* that he couldn't go back, that it was over, but what if he changed his mind? It was all too easy to see how that might happen.

"It's a little matter called trust, Meggie. A rare quality our daughter seems to have in abundance. Apparently she didn't inherit it from you."

Meg reeled from his bitter words. Ignoring her, he took a few strides to the kitchen and reached for the phone.

"Who are you calling?" Meg asked in confusion.

In even tones he said, "I'm simply phoning for a taxi. I need to be driven to my car. The school called me before I could feed and water the dogs. I need to get back to them."

"But if you're not here when Anna w—"

"As I said," he broke in with that arrogant hauteur left over from his KGB days, "visitation has its flaws when we try to function as parents from two separate households." He started punching the buttons.

When she thought of the state Anna would be in when she found him gone, Meg realized she couldn't go through that kind of emotional turmoil again. In a panic she cried, "Wait!"

A tense silence stretched between them. Kon still held the receiver in his hand. "If you're offering to drive me over to Anna's school, it isn't necessary. She needs the sleep and there's no one to mind her." He finished punching the last two numbers.

Her head reared back. "Damn you! You know that isn't what I meant!"

She watched him hang up the receiver, and even from a distance, she could see the glimmer of satisfaction on his face. She despised him for it.

"From the moment you hijacked us at the ballet, you knew you'd win. It was just a matter of time. An agent never accepts losing."

He frowned. "This isn't about agents or ideologies. This is no game, Meggie. I'm fighting for my life, for you and Anna. Without you, I have no future."

His voice throbbed with naked emotion, and it tore her apart. His words rang with undeniable conviction, bypassing logic to speak to her soul, successfully destroying the last fragile barrier she'd raised between them.

"AND SO, BY THE POWER vested in me, I now pronounce you husband and wife, legally and lawfully wedded from this moment on. What God has joined together, let no man put asunder. You may now kiss the bride."

Had it been only two days since she'd agreed to marry him?

From the time Kon had slipped the solitaire diamond ring and wedding band on Meg's finger, he'd kept hold of her hand. As the final words of the ceremony were pronounced, his grip tightened possessively.

The soft, pale pink chiffon of her calf-length wedding dress flattered her coloring, but she was positive Kon could detect every fluttering heartbeat through the thin material. Meg refrained from looking at him, fearing that she'd see a gloating look in his eyes, a look of victory.

In fact, from the time she'd entered Kon's living room with Anna for the late-afternoon ceremony and had acknowledged Judge Lundquist and the Bowmans—whom she'd learned were not husband and wife, having adopted the fictitious name as part of their cover—she had ignored her husband-to-be. Now she closed her eyes as she turned to him for the ritual kiss.

But when she felt his warm mouth unexpectedly brush the backs of both her hands instead of her lips, her eyes flew open in astonishment. She'd never heard of a groom kissing the bride's hands before and wondered if it could be some kind of Russian wedding custom.

Until he suddenly lifted his dark head and his scorching blue eyes trapped her confused gaze. "Finally!" His triumphant whisper told her he'd been aware of her refusal to look at him until now. Before she could react to his subterfuge, his mouth captured hers and he took full advantage, deepening their kiss, demanding a response that stirred her senses in spite of her attempt to remain unmoved.

"It's time for my kiss, Daddy," Anna demanded, pulling at his sleeve. The others chuckled quietly.

Meg was shocked back to reality for an instant when Kon broke their kiss. He scooped Anna from the floor and embraced them both, first kissing his daughter's cheeks, then returning to Meg's unsuspecting mouth, which he kissed so thoroughly she was in danger of forgetting there were other people in the room. Not only that, it seemed Walter Bowman had been filming the proceedings with a camcorder, a revelation that made her flush with embarrassment.

The ringing of the telephone, followed by Lacey Bowman's announcement that Senator Strickland was calling to congratulate them, brought Meg's senses under some semblance of control. She pulled away from Kon on unsteady legs, then bowed her head for a moment, ostensibly to rearrange Anna's crushed nosegay, but actually to take a few steadying breaths. After that, she straightened the collar of her daughter's taffeta dress. Finally she followed Kon into the study to speak to the senator.

The older man did most of the talking, which was just as well, because Meg was so bemused by her new status as Kon's wife she couldn't talk with any coherence. Especially not when Kon's arm slipped around her waist and he held her pressed against his side as if she belonged there.

Anna's voice calling them gave her the excuse to break away from Kon's grip while he finished the conversation with the senator. He seemed reluctant to release her, though, and she felt his gaze on her retreating back as she escaped.

"What is it, honey?" she asked as she hurried into the living room, trying to steady her breathing.

"Look!" Anna squealed happily. "It's Prince Marzipan!"

At first Meg thought she was talking about the puppy. Then her attention was drawn to a large nut-cracker—almost two feet high—that her daughter had lifted from a box sitting on the coffee table, the red and green wrapping paper in shambles.

"An early Christmas present from Walt and me," Lacey Bowman murmured in an aside. "Since she loved the ballet, we thought she might like one as a memento."

"See, Mommy?" Anna rushed over to show it to Meg, her face glowing with joy. "He looks like Daddy! And his mouth opens and closes! Watch!" She took hold of the handle and worked the jaw of the beautifully hand-crafted nutcracker. Meg suspected it had been carved and painted in Russia, rather than Germany. The detailing of the soldier's cossack hat and uniform was unmistakable.

By now Kon had reentered the living room and

come to stand behind his daughter, placing his hands on her shoulders. When Meg sensed his nearness, she raised her head and gasped softly at the similarity between the dark hair and blue eyes of the toy soldier and Kon's own striking coloring. The contrast of his olive complexion against the midnight blue suit and white shirt was almost dazzling.

He stood tall like the nutcracker, the personification of a dark and dashing Russian prince. Meg's heart took up its crazy thumping and she could easily imagine him in a cossack uniform and sable hat, a handsome, impossibly romantic male figure astride his horse.

Her husband.

She swallowed hard and turned a flushed face to the judge, who winked at her, then proposed a toast to the happy family. Meg drank the champagne Lacey served each of them. Kon declined his drink to pick up Anna—nosegay, nutcracker and all. Teasingly, he helped her to a champagne glass of cranberry juice so she could feel part of the celebration.

Despite Meg's attempt to harden her heart against Kon, his devotion to their daughter pierced her armor. She couldn't deny that, though Anna had always been a happy child, Kon's appearance in their lives had added another dimension of loving; even in the short time that had elapsed, his presence had boosted Anna's confidence and made her feel that much more secure.

On Monday evening, when she'd awakened from a much-needed sleep to learn that her mommy had decided to marry her daddy after all, Anna's almost hysterical reaction to everything Meg did or didn't do immediately disappeared.

Instead, an inner glow seemed to radiate from her, and she was at peace again. She cooperated willingly with all the packing and work involved in moving an entire household to a new town. Meg noticed that their impending marriage had produced such a calming effect on Anna the difference in her behavior was like night and day.

Everyone at the wedding could see how delighted she was with her daddy, and Walt kept the camcorder on Anna. Right now she was discussing the merits of her new nutcracker with Kon, both of them hamming it up a bit for the video. Lacey finally told Walter to stop taping and join them in a final congratulatory drink. Meg felt too nervous to swallow more than a few mouthfuls of champagne.

Before the ceremony, she'd dreaded the arrival of Walt and Lacey, who'd been in league with Kon from the beginning. But now that they'd finished their toast and were making plans to leave, Meg found she'd actually enjoyed their undemanding company and special kindness to Anna, and she didn't want them to go—for once they did she'd be alone with Kon. Her husband—who posed more of a personal danger to her peace of mind than ever before.

Anna hugged Lacey and thanked her for the nutcracker before she and Walt left the house in a flurry of goodbyes and Christmas wishes.

Kon shut the door behind them, then turned around, his glance sweeping over Meg's face and body. It reminded her of the many times in Russia when his gaze had said he could hardly wait to get her alone. That look had always left her shaken and trembling, and she felt no different now. Finally, to her relief, he turned to his daughter.

"Now that the wedding is over and we are an official family, I thought we'd celebrate someplace exciting."

Anna's eyes worshiped him. "Where are we going, Daddy?"

"With your mother's approval, I'd like to take us to dinner at the Molly Brown Theater to watch the Christmas show. There'll be singing and dancing and all your favorite Mark Twain characters. How does that sound?"

While Anna pleaded for her mother's acquiescence, he waited for Meg's reaction. The show catered to families with small children, and there would be other people around to act as a buffer, so Meg couldn't think of a better way to fill the next few hours. "I—I think that sounds lovely."

Kon appeared pleased by her agreement and glanced quickly at his watch. "We need to leave now if we're going to be on time."

"I'll find my coat." Anna dashed from the room and Meg hurried into the hall to catch up with her. She couldn't tolerate being alone in the same room with Kon while she was still trying to forget the taste and feel of his mouth, the passion he evoked whenever he touched her.

Over the past few days she'd managed to cope with his presence, not only because there'd been so much to do—dresses to buy and arrangements to make for the move—but because Anna and Melanie were constantly around, acting as unofficial chaperons.

And, of course, Anna had told everybody in the apartment complex about the wedding, which had prompted a number of people, including Melanie's family, the Garretts and Mrs. Rosen, to drop by with fruitcake and cookies and offer their congratulations.

Kon, who looked upon his daughter with fatherly pride whenever she played her violin for him, had taken an instant liking to Anna's teacher. He'd assured Mrs. Rosen that he'd drive Anna into St. Louis every week so she wouldn't miss her lessons. He'd also promised Anna they'd go early enough for her to spend time with Melanie. Naturally that won Melanie's overwhelming approval and devotion.

In fact, she'd spent most of Tuesday staring at Kon, following him around, plying him with questions. He answered them with infinite tolerance and good-natured humor while he dismantled the aquarium, taking care to put the fish in jars Anna had filled with water for the transfer to Hannibal.

Meg knew Anna would miss her friend, but she could tell it was going to be much more of a wrench for Melanie. The movers would be coming after Christmas to load their belongings; by New Year's, Meg and Anna would have left the complex for good.

In an effort to smooth the transition for both girls, she'd invited Melanie to come the following weekend for a sleep-over. That had naturally initiated a whole new series of conversations and plans and made the move less upsetting.

Persuaded by both Kon and Anna, Meg had resigned from her job without giving the usual two-week notice; she hoped that because business was slow during the Christmas holidays, her boss wasn't too angry with her.

Inevitably Ted had heard about Meg's impending marriage to Anna's natural father, and he called her to find out what was going on. Unfortunately Kon happened to answer the phone first, telling Ted she was too busy to talk and would call him back after they'd returned from their honeymoon.

Meg had no intention of going on a honeymoon with Kon and could just imagine Ted's reaction to that inflammatory piece of news. She decided that in a few days she'd write him a note explaining the situation. He was a nice person, and Kon had no right to intentionally offend him.

"Cold?" his deep voice murmured near her ear, startling her out of her reverie. She hadn't realized Kon had followed her and Anna into the hall. "Maybe this will warm you." His nearness made her knees go weak. Meg turned around to see Kon holding up an elegant black cashmere coat lined in black satin. "Try it on, Meggie."

As if in a trance, she put her arms into the sleeves and tied the belt around her slender waist.

"Mommy, you look *beautiful.*"

"She does, doesn't she, Anochka," Kon murmured as he shrugged into a formal, dark blue top-coat. He gazed openly at Meg's ash-blond hair gleaming silvery gold against the soft black of the coat. At the question in her eyes, he smiled. "Consider it an early Christmas present."

"Thank you," she whispered, and averted her

head, filled with a strange, terrible pain. Kon had decided to defect because of the many problems relating to his work in the KGB, but mostly because of Anna. And in order to have his daughter, he had to take Meg, too.

Meg didn't deceive herself. After all these years, Kon *couldn't* still be in love with her. Love had to be nurtured, and they'd been apart too many years. She had no doubt he'd told her that he hadn't been involved with another woman to spare her feelings.

He could shower her with gifts and convincingly act the lover, but it was for one reason only—she was the mother of his child. Anna was the key. He would never have come to Missouri to marry her otherwise.

Because of the way they'd once felt about each other, it was all too easy for Kon to claim that his love for her had never died, that it was too powerful and intense to die.

The unpalatable truth was that any woman who happened to be his child's mother would be the recipient of Kon's generosity. He'd waited six years before making his appearance; he'd even confessed that he'd taken the risk that she'd be married by the time he deemed it safe to present himself. That hardly sounded like a man deeply and passionately in love.

She thought back on his admissions about the other women in his life, agents working under him. Apparently none of them had gotten pregnant, and she supposed that was why he'd felt nothing lasting, why he hadn't married during all those years in the KGB.

Little did she realize when she first went to bed with him in that cottage seven years ago, her life would be irrevocably changed, that her chance to find love with a typical American man—the kind of love her mother had found with her father—would pass her by.

"Pretend to have a good time for Anna's sake, will you? It is our wedding day, after all." He spoke in a low, brusque tone meant for her ears alone as they left the dogs guarding the house and went out through the back door.

The change in his demeanor shocked her into realizing that her thoughts had been visible enough for him to read. For Anna's sake she made a mental note to avoid alienating him further.

She could tell he was still attempting to suppress his anger as he opened the front passenger door of his car. It was a Buick, the kind of car an American man named Gary Johnson might drive. Meg couldn't help but wonder what kind of car Kon would have chosen if he hadn't been forced to exist as this invented persona.

Anna's happy chatter coming from the back seat made the uncomfortable silence between the two of them even more marked. Thankfully, Meg noted that their daughter seemed oblivious to any undercurrents as they drove on streets relatively free of snow to the dinner theater situated near the riverboat landing. Kon let them out in front, then found a parking spot and joined them.

After the numbing cold outside, the building felt warm and inviting. It also looked filled to capacity, but the hostess, dressed in an 1850s' period costume, showed them to a table Kon had reserved. Located on the first level, it allowed Anna an unimpeded view of the stage show.

The next few hours flew by as they ate a delicious dinner and sat entertained by one of the actors, who did a wonderful impersonation of Mark Twain. A professionally staged musical production presented songs of the '20s through the '50s and ended with some renditions of Mississippi river music that enchanted Anna.

Meg would have loved it if she'd been here with anyone but her husband, on any day but her wedding day. Kon lounged, apparently relaxed in his seat at her side and appeared to be enjoying the performance. But when the house lights dimmed for the final act and she dared a glance at him, she saw a haunted, faraway look that hardened his features and told her he was seeing something else, thinking of another time, another place.

Perhaps for the first time since the ballet, Meg truly understood how much he must miss his country, how much he'd given up to be with his daughter.

Six years was probably an eternity to a man deprived of Russia's beautiful language and age-old cul- ture. How lonely he must be for people like himself, his compatriots. How could he stand to live here when he was a product of a fabulous and colorful history that had produced the czars and contributed so much to world culture—to literature, music, dance and theater?

Meg had fallen in love with his country. She knew better than most how much he must be yearning for the woods and mountains of his homeland. Seven years ago he'd spent many, many hours driving Meg through rural villages and long mountain roads. Unless she specifically asked that he take her to a café or a museum, he had always headed for the countryside.

It was probably natural, since his first recollections of childhood were of Siberia, of frozen tundra in winter and wildflower meadows in summer. His home had probably been little more than a mountain hut, where life had been hard, maybe even primitive, but where there had been love....

"Tears, Meggie?" Kon mocked in quiet menace as he unexpectedly turned his head and caught her staring. "Have you suddenly realized how much of a prisoner you are now that you're legally tied to me? Are you thinking that the walls of your new home are no different from the walls of that jail cell in Moscow?"

Kon was so far off the mark she was stunned. She lowered her head to search for a clean napkin so she could wipe her eyes before Anna noticed anything was wrong.

"Gary?" A vibrant female voice spoke up just as the houselights went back on. Both Meg's and Anna's heads swiveled around as a tall, curvaceous brunette still in costume put her arms around Kon's neck and lowered her face to his. "I thought it was you. No other man that gorgeous has ever sat in this audience before."

"Sammi."

Meg was shocked that the beautiful woman's name came so easily to Kon's lips. Not only that, the two of them were so familiar with each other he actually caressed her cheek with his lips before getting to his feet.

With his arm around the actress's waist, he gazed down at Meg. She was so shattered by feelings of jealousy she could hardly move—and Kon knew it! She could tell by the way his eyes glittered. "Sammi Raynes, meet my wife, Meg, and our daughter, Anna."

Meg could tell the woman was sizing them up, trying to figure out how Kon could have a daughter this old.

"You mean you went and got married on me while I was on tour?" she cried, extending a friendly hand. "You heartbreaker!" Then she turned to Meg once more. "How do you like that? This character told me he'd be waiting for me when I got back. Your marriage happened awfully fast, didn't it?"

"Actually, K—Gary and I have known each other for a long time." Meg caught herself barely in time.

The woman's eyes flicked back to Kon. "You're a deep one, you know that?"

She was probably much closer to Kon's age than Meg was. She'd clearly had more than a casual interest in him and was putting up a heroic front. But Meg had no doubt that the actress's face had paled beneath all her stage makeup.

Had Kon been sleeping with her? And for how long?

Meg had been so focused on her own problems and fears she hadn't given any real thought to the women Kon might have met *after* defecting. Just as she'd surmised earlier, his statement that there'd been no other women since Meg had been another little fabrication, another part of his strategy. Kon wasn't the celibate type and had never pretended to be. Naturally he would indulge himself when the opportunity arose. Few women could remain immune to his virile looks and charm, as no one knew better than Meg.

Dear God, she was still in love with him. She always would be.

The woman called Sammi walked around to Anna's side. "Did you like the show, honey?"

Anna nodded. "We came here 'cause my mommy and daddy got married today."

"Today? Is that why you're wearing such a pretty dress?" When Anna nodded again, she looked at Kon for confirmation.

"That's right."

"Well, congratulations. If I'd known that before the show started, I would have asked the director to announce it. Here. Have a lollipop." She pulled one from her pocket and handed it to Anna, who asked her parents if it was all right before she accepted it.

A warm, genuine smile lit Kon's features as he smiled at the actress, and something unpleasant twisted inside Meg. She'd never seen Kon smile at *her* in quite that way, not even during those carefree days in St. Petersburg when they were alone and away from prying eyes, where he could be himself.

"Thanks, Sammi. It's always good to see you," he murmured.

"The feeling is entirely mutual."

She broke eye contact with Kon, then cast a speculative glance at Meg. "You're a lucky woman.

Take good care of this marvelous man. There's no one to compare to him.''

She was right, Meg acknowledged, and her pain deepened. How did Sammi know so much about him? It seemed that Kon had allowed this particular woman to see a side of him he'd never shown Meg.

Kon gave her a final hug. "One day soon we'll invite you for dinner."

"I have a new puppy you can hold," Anna offered, easily managing to talk around the lollipop still in her mouth.

"A new puppy, too? There's so much excitement at your house, I bet you can hardly get to sleep at night."

Anna giggled and Meg warmed to the woman in spite of her own distress. "I enjoyed the show very much, Ms. Raynes. We all did."

The actress smiled her thanks and moved away. Kon walked some distance with her while they talked in private. As Meg stared at their dark heads bent toward each other, a horrible envy rose up in her. Needing to expend her nervous energy, she jumped up from the table and helped Anna with her coat before slipping on her own. Ready to face the cold, they had started making their way through the crowd when Kon intercepted them.

Meg felt his eyes on her, trying to draw her gaze, but she couldn't look at him. She waited as he picked up Anna, then followed them out of the theater to the car. She made sure she didn't walk close enough for him to touch her.

"Are we going to get our Christmas tree now?" Anna asked cheerfully.

"I think we've done enough for one day, An-ochka. How about tomorrow morning, after you've had a good night's sleep and a hot breakfast?"

"Okay. Who was that lady, Daddy? I saw you kiss her."

"She's a good friend."

"Do you love her, too?"

Unconsciously Meg held her breath, waiting for his answer.

"If you mean, do I love her the way I love you and your mommy, no."

"Does she love you?"

Kon crushed her in his arms. "There are all kinds of love, Anna. I met her several years ago when her little boy got lost during a family picnic. The whole town ended up looking for him. I happened to be the one who finally found him, asleep under some bushes near the Mark Twain Cave."

Meg's heart lurched in her chest.

"What's his name?" Anna persisted.

"Brad."

"How old is he?"

"Eight."

"Doesn't he have a daddy?"

"Yes, although his daddy doesn't live with them."

"How come *you* found him?"

"I was lucky."

Anna's arms tightened around Kon's neck. "I'm glad you're my daddy."

"So am I," he whispered.

So am I, Meg's heart echoed wildly.

CHAPTER EIGHT

WHEN THEY REACHED the house, Anna cuddled her puppy, then climbed the stairs to get ready for bed. Kon said that as soon as he'd taken care of the dogs and turned out the lights, he'd be up to kiss her good-night.

But the minute her curly head touched the pillow, Anna's eyes closed and she fell sound asleep, hugging the nutcracker in her arms.

Meg hung the beautiful party dress in the closet and tidied the room. When she felt it was safe, she carefully removed the nutcracker from Anna's now-slack grip and put it on the white French-provincial dresser. It matched the canopied bed and night table. The room was a fairyland of pink and white eyelet, everything a little girl's heart could desire.

After Christmas, when the movers delivered the belongings from the apartment to Kon's house, the room would be filled with all of Anna's things, including the rest of her dolls. So far, the only large item they'd brought with them was the aquarium, which Kon had immediately set up under Anna's supervision.

Meg wandered over to the tank and watched the fish, remembering the day she'd purchased the aquarium, never dreaming where it would finally end up. Since she knew Anna needed some kind of pet and animals were forbidden in the apartment building, fish had seemed a good solution.

Now her daughter had three dogs to love. And a father who returned all the love she gave him, yet could be firm with her when the occasion warranted. At first Meg had been afraid he would spoil Anna, but time was proving her wrong. He was very much in charge of their daughter, not the other way around.

Was it all a sham? Or could she dare believe that Kon would never have taken Anna away from her, even if they *hadn't* married?

"Meggie?"

There was a husky timbre in his voice that made her tremble. She lifted her head to see Kon's dark shape in the doorway.

"Yes?"

"Now that Anna's asleep, I'd like some attention."

Her fingers clung to the edge of the tank. "I—I'm coming."

Her mouth went completely dry as she followed him out to the hallway and shut the door. She noticed with alarm that he'd changed out of his clothes and was dressed in a blue-and-black-striped velour robe. She wondered, aroused yet half-ashamed, if he wore anything underneath.

It didn't matter that this same man had made love to her seven years ago. He was still an enigma to her, more now than ever. A virtual stranger. She wanted to trust him, but it was so hard....

"Before the wedding I told you the choice was yours to sleep in my bed or not."

Her nails cut into her palms. "But now that we're married, you've decided to do what you want, forget the promise you made."

"In a manner of speaking, yes. I want you in my bed, Meggie. I won't make love to you if you don't want me to, but I need you lying there next to me. Don't deny me that, *mayah labof.*"

"I'm not your darling," she gasped, so breathless she felt dizzy.

"You are. You always will be."

"No more lies, Kon. Please God, no more lies," she begged, the tears streaming from her eyes. "You said you wanted a relationship with Anna, and now you have it. Isn't that enough?"

"I wish I could say it was. But it isn't." His voice trailed off.

"And if I refuse?"

"Don't. I've waited too long."

"So now that you have me where you want me, you're flinging the mask away. Is that it?"

"There was never any mask," he said calmly, his hands in his pockets. "I begged you to marry me before you left Russia. I asked you to marry me as soon as I saw you at the ballet. You're my wife now. There's nothing to keep us apart."

"Nothing except the fact that I don't even know who you are," she half sobbed. "I don't know the first thing about you. I've never met your family. In Russia you were a highly placed, feared KGB agent, and I'll never know if our affair was part of a secret plan or not. You said your name was Konstantin

Rudenko. Is that the name your parents gave you or one the KGB made up?''

Her hysteria had reached a momentum, and she couldn't stop herself. ''In my country you pretend to be an ordinary American citizen named Gary Johnson. He lives in a dream house, drives a Buick and behaves like Mr. Niceguy to his unsuspecting community. How can I know the real you? Have I ever met him? Where did the child, the teenager, the young man go? Or were they ever allowed to exist? *Who are you?*'' Her frantic voice broke.

His face darkened and he shook his head. ''I don't know, Meggie. It's why I came for you. To find out.''

The admission seemed to come from someplace deep within him, and it was the last answer she'd expected. It threw her into such confusion she didn't know how to react or what to say. It drove her to the guest room, between his bedroom and Anna's. She'd slept there the night before, tossing and turning as she anticipated her wedding day with alternating feelings of excitement and dread.

Kon stood in the doorway. ''Can we start finding our answers in bed? That's where we once communicated without any problems—one man and one woman. Can we go from there?'' He grasped the doorjamb as if for support. ''I swear I won't touch you, Meggie, if that's the way it has to be. Only lie with me tonight.'' His voice throbbed with raw longing.

''After this many years' separation—'' he switched to Russian so easily Meg was scarcely aware of it ''—let me have the satisfaction of at least looking at you throughout the night, smelling the flowery scent of your hair, knowing you're within arm's reach. I'm begging you, Meggie.''

Speaking to her in his native tongue, in that particular tone of voice, tore down her last, pathetic defense. It brought back too many memories, memories that suffocated her with their sweetness.

Meg grabbed a nightgown from the dresser and hurried into the bathroom to change. Her heart pounded at every pulse point until she thought it might explode. This vulnerable, pleading side of Kon had left her utterly vulnerable, too.

He was still standing in the doorway when she came back into the room. He followed her with his eyes as she hung her wedding dress in the closet.

The short walk to the bed felt like a hundred miles. When she got under the covers, Kon turned off the light and moved toward her.

"Meggie?" he whispered.

"I—I don't think—"

"If I stay with you tonight," he interrupted her, "then you don't have to be afraid I'll kidnap Anna. That is what you're terrified of, isn't it?"

No, her heart cried. *I'm afraid of something much worse. I'm afraid you'll never love me the way I love you.*

The mattress dipped as he slid beneath the covers, and though their bodies didn't touch, she could feel his warmth and smell the soap that lingered on his skin. She had no idea if he'd disrobed and wished her mind couldn't see what the darkness blotted out.

"Talk to me, *mayah labof.*" His low, velvety voice reached out to her like a soft night wind. "Tell

me how long it took you to forget me after you left
Russian soil. Had some other man fallen in love with
you by the time your plane landed?''

Oh, Kon. She smothered her groan in the pillow
and hugged the side of the bed.

''I watched your plane until it disappeared in the
clouds, then drove back to the cottage like a demon
possessed and drank enough vodka to send myself
into oblivion. Or so I thought. But nothing was
strong enough to wipe out your fragrance on the
sheets and pillows. Dear God, Meggie—the emptiness after everything we'd shared… I didn't particularly care if I lived or died.''

''Do you think I felt any different?'' she blurted.
Whether he was still acting a part or not, his words
unlocked memories and they came flooding back
with an intensity so fresh she felt as if she were
reliving the nightmare. ''I kept thinking that if the
plane crashed, it didn't matter, which shows you the
instability of my state of mind, considering that
there were hundreds of other people on that flight.

''I had no one to go home to, and I'd left my
heart behind. At one point during the trip home, I
even found myself wishing I was dead because I
couldn't bear to imagine you with another lover,
particularly one of your beautiful, dark-haired Russian women. I always saw them staring at you with
hungry eyes whenever we went out in public.''

''Meggie!''

''They did, Kon, and you know it, so don't try to
deny it. I had no idea I could be that jealous.''

A heavy sigh escaped. ''Think what you will, but
I had eyes only for the exquisite blond creature who

got off that plane in Moscow and caused complete havoc with my comrades as she passed through control. Every agent there would have given six months' pay for the privilege of being assigned to you. When they found out you were under my supervision, I acquired enemies.''

If any other man had said that to her, Meg would have scoffed. Instead, she shuddered. He was probably exaggerating but…how would she ever know?

"Thank God your plane didn't crash," he murmured. "Tell me what exactly happened when you arrived back in the States. What you did. How you felt.''

Why did he ask these questions when he already knew the answers?

Her eyes closed tightly as if to ward off the pain. By the time she'd passed through customs and the CIA had finished with her, allowing her to go free, she'd walked away feeling as if she'd been skinned alive and her heart torn from her body.

"When the plane landed in New York, I was singled out from the others and taken to a place for a grueling, two-day debriefing.''

She heard his sharp intake of breath. "Because of me,'' he said. "Because they knew of our association.''

"Yes.''

"And that's when you were warned off for good.''

"Yes.'' Frantically wiping tears from her cheeks, she said, "Up until they told me that I'd been targeted specifically by you, I had every intention of saving my money and returning to Moscow the following summer to be with you.''

"Now you know why I told you never to come back," he muttered fiercely.

"It...it was a good thing I had so much to do after they released me, or I would have gone mad remembering my aunt's warnings. As it was, I had trouble sleeping and lost weight. I suppose what saved me was the necessity of finding an apartment and getting things out of storage. And, of course, looking for a job.''

"You didn't go back to teaching."

"No. I wanted nothing to do with anything that could remind me of you. So I took the first job that offered decent pay.''

"Strong Motors?"

"Yes.''

"Tell me about the pregnancy. When did you first discover our baby was growing inside you?''

Taking a steadying breath, she said, "As I told you, food didn't interest me and I slept poorly. When a month passed and my condition seemed to get worse because I felt tired all the time, my friend at work urged me to see a doctor.

"I fought against taking her advice, but then I started to be sick to my stomach in the mornings and realized something was wrong. So I consulted my family doctor over the phone. When he heard the symptoms, he sent me to see an obstetrician.

"I was furious when he suggested I could be pregnant, because I knew you'd taken precautions. That was when he gave me a lecture about no contraceptive method being one hundred percent reliable. After the examination the obstetrician told me I was definitely pregnant. I didn't want to believe her."

A heavy silence hung in the air. "Did you…"

"No, Kon. I never considered an abortion, if that's what you're asking. Whatever happened between us, our baby was an innocent victim. I would never have done anything to harm it. In fact, I experienced a miraculous sense of responsibility when I learned I was pregnant. I had a reason to go on living. I followed the doctor's advice so the baby would be born strong and healthy."

"Thank you for telling me that." His whisper reached her ears. "Don't you know I'd have given my life to have been there for you?"

Could he sound that sincere and still be lying? She didn't know anymore.

"When I saw Anna's baby picture," he began, "I started working on a plan to defect, one that would expose the fewest people to danger. That had to be my first priority. Of necessity it was elaborate and had to be timed to the split second."

"How did you finally get away?" She couldn't help wanting to know the answer to that question.

"I can't tell you."

Rage welled up in her all over again, and she shot straight up in bed, pushing the hair out of her eyes. "And you still expect me to trust you?"

Kon raised himself on one elbow, as calm as a panther at rest, but capable of springing at the slightest provocation. "Don't you think I'd like to be able to tell you what I went through to join you and Anna?"

"I don't understand why you can't. I thought a husband and wife were supposed to share everything."

"So did I," came his mocking reply. "But the matter of my defection falls into another category altogether. I have to keep quiet to protect others who put their lives at risk to help me."

There was too much to absorb. "Do you think you're still under surveillance by your government?"

"Actively, no. But I'm on a list."

She had difficulty swallowing. "Does that mean you could still be in danger?"

"From which government?"

His question chilled her. "Don't tease me, Kon."

"Maybe it's better we skip the subject altogether."

"Why would you be in danger from my government?" she persisted.

"Perhaps because they don't trust me any more than you do." He reached out for her pillow and pulled it to him, burying his face for a moment.

The vulnerability and despair in that gesture made her avert her eyes. "Even after you gave them information?"

He lifted his head. "You once said it yourself. A man who could turn his back on his country is a traitor to all."

The words she'd thrown at him. They sounded cruel. If no one ever trusted him, how lonely his life must have been for the past six years. How lonely it would continue to be for the rest of his life.

He slid from the bed, still dressed in his robe. The

tie had come loose, though, allowing her a glimpse of his well-defined chest with its dusting of dark hair. "I knew it was too much to hope that we could start over. But fool that I am, I had to try. Good night, Meggie."

He strode to the door, then paused. "I'll give you an early Christmas present now—by promising that I'll never ask you to sleep with me again."

"WHERE ARE WE GOING to put the tree, Daddy?"

"Wherever your mother thinks is best."

They'd gone shopping that morning. Meg had left it to Anna to entertain Kon while they'd gone into store after store, looking for more tree decorations. The lights and ornaments from the small Scotch pine they'd dismantled at the apartment would only cover part of the eight-foot tree they'd purchased.

But now that they were home, Meg couldn't go on ignoring Kon. Anna listened to every word and nuance of meaning, observed everything that passed between her parents. So Meg stated that the best spot might be in front of the living-room window. Everyone driving by would see their tree. All they had to do was move the table and lamp to a different place.

The suggestion met with wholehearted approval, and Kon, dressed in jeans and sweater, set up the perfectly shaped blue spruce in a matter of minutes. As soon as Meg untangled a set of lights, Anna, with Thor at her heels, handed them to her father and he strung them on the tree. The three of them worked in complete harmony. Anyone peeking in the window would see the ideal family happily at work.

No one could know of the brooding blackness in

Kon or suspect that after he'd left her room last night, Meg had lain awake in agony, part of her wanting, aching, to go to him and crawl into his arms.

But something intangible had occurred during their conversation. The man who had devastated her by promising he'd never ask her to sleep with him again was not the same man who earlier that night had begged her to lie next to him, just to know she was there.

Lacking the confidence to face him in case he rejected her attempt at reconciliation, she remained in her bed, alone. She spent the rest of the night trying to sort out her own confused thoughts and feelings.

Every time she attempted to put herself in his place, she felt physically ill. She could imagine his sense of isolation, the inevitable gloom and depression that must have weighed him down after leaving Russia to settle in a country as foreign and unfamiliar as the United States.

The CIA had given her some things to read, articles about defectors years before; she remembered that one theme had dominated the rest. They lived with the consequences of displacement for the rest of their lives.

Perhaps that explained why Kon had become the exemplary father, throwing himself into the role so completely. Perhaps that way he could forget for a short period what he'd left behind. It would also explain why he'd wanted Meg in his bed last night, to blot out for a brief time the pain of his actions.

In all honesty, she had to admit she couldn't

blame him for those very human needs and drives. If their positions were reversed and she could never return to the United States, it would be a horrifying experience, one she'd have to sublimate somehow, just as he was doing.

"Mommy, you forgot to open the last box."

Startled out of her tortured thoughts, Meg tore off the cellophane and handed the lights to Anna. In an unguarded moment, her glance darted to Kon, who seemed to stare right through her, as if his thoughts were far removed from the scene in front of him. Cold fear spread through her body—there was such unhappiness in his look, and a kind of bleak resignation. Meg couldn't stand it. She excused herself to start dinner.

During the next few days a feeling of domestic tranquillity existed, on the surface, at least. But Kon had withdrawn emotionally from Meg, and she was paying a bitter price. Upset and confused by this remote stranger who'd never treated her with such indifference before, she needed to do something, anything, to relieve the tension between them.

It was on one of her trips with Anna back to the apartment to finish cleaning that Meg scanned a batch of Christmas cards sent to her and came across one from Tatiana Smirnov, her old Russian teacher. The woman's newsy letter triggered an idea for a special Christmas present for Kon, one she hoped would let him know she understood the loneliness of his self-imposed exile and wanted to make up for it in some small way.

When Kon came to pick them up, Meg told him that as long as they were in St. Louis, she and Anna had a few more presents to buy. He dropped them off at a local mall, indicating that he needed to take care of some business and would be back for them in a couple of hours.

The minute he was out of sight, Meg explained her secret to Anna. Then she hailed a taxi and gave the driver an address that took them across town to an art gallery Tatiana had mentioned in her letter. A shipment of arts and crafts from Russia was up for sale. Meg and Anna spent a good hour studying the paintings, icons, dolls, hats, scarves, eggs—all kinds of memorabilia from bygone eras.

As many times as Meg went over everything, her eye kept going back to one particular oil painting. It depicted a mountain scene with a meadow of wildflowers in the foreground. Her gaze followed the dirt road that ran past an old barn, then disappeared. The painting's title, printed in Russian, convinced her. *Urals in springtime.*

Anna was taken with several of the icons but preferred the one of the Madonna and child. The combination of colors—gold and royal blue against the black of the shiny wood—drew the eye, and Meg told the saleswoman to wrap it up along with the painting.

Out of Anna's hearing she also whispered to the clerk to include the nesting doll sitting on the display table. The pink-and-black stylized figure of a Russian peasant woman hid seven versions of the same woman, each one smaller than the one before. They all fit together, and Anna would be delighted when she discovered the surprise.

The clerk put it in a sack, and when Anna wasn't

looking, Meg stuffed it into her tote bag. The purchases cost more than a thousand dollars and took most of Meg's meager savings. But the situation between her and Kon had grown so precarious she would have done anything to extend the olive branch.

They took another taxi back to the mall, where they stopped to get their gifts boxed and wrapped in beautiful Christmas paper at a gift-wrapping booth. Then they window-shopped until Kon came for them.

Though Anna was bursting to tell her father what they'd done and wanted to give him his presents right then and there, she managed to contain herself. But her eyes sparkled like blue topaz, and Kon's gaze slid to Meg's several times in silent query. The amused glimmer in his eyes made her heart turn over, their enmity temporarily forgotten in the face of their daughter's excitement.

On Christmas Eve another winter storm blanketed the area with snow, delighting Anna. Along with the dogs, she followed her father outside, watching while he shoveled the driveway and then built her a snowman. As Meg gazed out at them from the dining room window where she was setting the table for their Christmas dinner, she saw that a couple of children close to Anna's age had come by to help.

There were joyous shouts mingled with the dogs' barking, and Kon seemed to be having as much fun as the children who hovered around him.

Seeing him like this, Meg had to ask herself again—what if he was exactly what he seemed? A man who'd willingly made certain choices. A loving father. A new American citizen who embraced the land he'd chosen. A man who still loved a woman, although seven years had passed. What if there were no ulterior motives and everything he'd been telling her all this time was the absolute truth? Tears stung her eyes....

Meg couldn't sleep that night. Long after she'd slipped downstairs at midnight to put her presents under the tree, she lay wide awake in the large bed, staring into the darkness as the tears ran down her face.

Early Christmas morning Anna ran into Meg's room with both dogs at her heels, bubbling with excitement. Daddy was already up fixing breakfast, she said. According to him, Santa had come, and as soon as they'd eaten, they could go into the living room and see what he'd brought.

A feeling not unlike morning sickness assailed Meg as she got out of bed and staggered to the bathroom. After spending most of the night crying until she wondered how there could be any more tears, she was sure that facing Kon, let alone Christmas day, was almost beyond her. But she had to, for Anna's sake.

The shower revived her a little. She brushed her hair and secured it with combs at both sides, then added blusher to her pale cheeks, followed by an application of lipstick. She pulled on a cherry-red sweater dress she'd had for a couple of years. Her low black patent pumps would be comfortable to walk around in and still look dressy.

"Just keep coming toward me," Kon murmured

as she started down the stairs, the camcorder in his hands. "Merry Christmas, Meggie."

"Merry Christmas," she said when she could find the words. The sight of his dark, handsome features, his snug-fitting forest-green sweater and charcoal pants, his lithe movements left her breathless.

Anna stood next to her father in a new dress of red-and-blue plaid, a glowing look of anticipation on her face. "You have to kiss Daddy, Mommy, 'cause Daddy says it's a tradition."

"Only if she wants to, Anochka."

Meg needed no urging to close the distance between them and rise on tiptoe to brush her mouth against his. Kon would never be able to guess at the depth of her hunger for him, the kind of iron control it took not to devour him in front of their daughter. It was no use pretending that she didn't remember every second of those months when he'd been her lover.

His passion had electrified her, bringing them both a fullness of joy she hadn't known was possible.

Heaven help her. She wanted to know that joy again.

CHAPTER NINE

"CAN WE GO IN NOW, Daddy? I've eaten my eggs and drunk all my milk."

"What do you say, Meggie? Are we ready?"

She lifted her eyes to surprise a bleak look in his. It was only there for a moment, but she couldn't have been mistaken and it only added to her torment.

With a nod she put her coffee cup back on the saucer. "Why don't I get the two of you on tape first?"

Not waiting for a reply, she jumped up from the table and grabbed the camcorder from the counter, preceding them into the living room.

The next hour flew by. The dogs crouched close to Anna, who squealed in ecstasy over the new dollhouse and tea set Kon had set up for her. Meg had hidden the nesting doll in Anna's stocking, along with a candy cane and an inexpensive Little Mermaid watch.

Anna shook everything out, then examined the strange-looking toy first. "What is it, Mommy? An old lady?"

Meg laughed because her daughter didn't know what to make of it. Kon's delighted chuckle joined hers, and he threw Meg a quizzical glance, as if to ask her where she'd found the Russian treasure. The sound of lazy amusement in his voice as he talked to his daughter reminded her sharply of other times and places. A time, seven years ago, when she'd been madly in love with him and free to express that love. A night at her hotel in St. Petersburg, when he'd been lounging on the floor at her feet, just like this. Only now it was Anna's face he caressed, her bouncing curls he tousled.

"Watch this, Anochka."

In a deft movement that fascinated Meg, as well, Kon pulled the two halves of the doll apart. Anna saw a smaller version of the same doll inside and cried out in wonder.

"Open it like I did," Kon urged.

Within a few minutes fourteen halves lay spread out on the carpet, and Anna sat there with a frown of concentration on her face, trying to put everything back together again.

Meg decided now was the time to give Kon her present. "I hope you'll like this," she said in a nervous voice, wondering too late if it was the wrong thing to give him. Maybe he wouldn't want a reminder of everything he'd left behind.

He took the package from her hands and sat up to remove the paper. Anna was too aborbed with the dolls to notice how quiet the room had become, but Meg felt uncomfortably aware of the unnatural stillness. She held her breath while Kon studied the canvas. What was he thinking?

"I-it's a scene in the Urals. You must be missing Russia, and since you said you liked to hike there, I thought—"

"Meggie…" Where he gripped the edge of the canvas, his knuckles stood out white.

"I have a present for you, too, Daddy."

Anna dropped the doll parts she was having problems fitting together and scurried around the far side of the tree to fetch the package.

When she handed it to him, he put it to his ear and shook it, making Anna giggle. "I wonder what my little Anochka has given me."

Anna couldn't wait any longer. "It's an…an icon, isn't it, Mommy?"

Kon's grin slowly faded to be replaced by a sober expression as he carefully lifted the wooden plaque from the tissue and reverently traced the halos of gold with his index finger, his head bent in solemn concentration.

Anna squeezed past the dogs and knelt down next to her father. "That's the baby Jesus with his mommy," she pointed out. "I liked this one the best. Mommy said it came from Russia. Do you think it's pretty, Daddy?"

He drew Anna roughly into his arms and buried his face in her dark curls. "I love it," came the husky reply. "I love it almost as much as I love you."

Several Russian endearments whispered in hushed tones brought tears to Meg's eyes, and she covered her emotions by busying herself opening a box of candy from her boss, and another from Ted.

"Where's Mommy's present?" Anna finally asked.

"Your father already gave it to me," she said

before he could reply. "Remember the beautiful black coat I wore to the theater the other night?"

Anna nodded.

In a quick movement Kon got to his feet. "Actually, I do have another gift for your mother, but it didn't arrive in time for Christmas."

"No, please." She gathered a basket of fruit—from Mrs. Rosen—in the crook of her arm and headed for the kitchen to check on the turkey, avoiding the intensity of his gaze. "I don't want anything else. You've done too much for us already."

Relieved that he didn't follow her, she was able to get preparations under way for Christmas dinner. Anna brought her dollhouse into the kitchen and, chattering away, put a different nesting doll in each room. She gave the dolls exacting instructions on how to behave. If they didn't, she said, the nutcracker, who stood guard on one of the kitchen chairs, would have to punish them.

Eventually her new friends from across the street traipsed through the house to see her presents and look at the puppies still confined to the porch. They were all fascinated by the nesting doll, and at one point Kon had to intervene so everyone could take turns assembling the various parts.

Finally the children grew tired of even that game, and at Kon's suggestion they decided to play outside in the snow, leaving Meg in peace.

Once everything was cooking, she went to the living room to clean up the mess, but Kon had gotten there before her and the room looked immaculate. He'd put the painting and the icon on the mantel and had started a fire in the grate. She felt compelled to find him and thank him.

When he wasn't in his study she called to him from the foot of the stairs, but there was no answer. Nor was there any sign of Prince, or Thor and Gandy, whose other two pups had been given to a family across the street. Whirling around, she ran out the back of the house, but no one responded when she called and both cars were still in the garage.

Maybe everyone was in the front yard. She ran down the driveway, almost losing her balance in her heels while she shouted for Anna. Whichever direction she looked, there was no one in sight. Nothing but snow. Freezing air lodged in her lungs as she beheld the lone snowman with one of Kon's ties around its neck.

Silent testimony to a kidnapping?

A growing dread gnawed at her insides, and she raced across the street without thought of boots or coat, praying she was wrong, praying Anna was at the neighbor's house. But when the children answered the door, they said Anna had gone off with her daddy and the dogs.

By the time Meg reached the house to get her car keys, she was hysterical with fear. She backed slowly out of the driveway and drove up and down the icy streets, past the local parks, asking people if they'd seen a man and a little girl walking a pair of German shepherds and a puppy. No one had.

Realizing there wasn't another second to lose, she sped home as fast as she could and dashed into the house, her only thought to contact the police and prevent Kon from leaving the country with their daughter. He could be anywhere by now, following another elaborate plan of escape.

With tears gushing down her cheeks, she clutched the receiver and punched in 911. When she explained that her daughter was missing, the dispatcher asked for her address and said a couple of officers would be arriving shortly.

To Meg, the next few minutes felt like centuries. Though she knew it was hopeless, something made her go out to the street and call Anna's name at the top of her lungs.

Soon the two neighbor children and their parents joined her and volunteered to start a door-to-door search. Meg thanked them, but didn't tell them she suspected Kon was behind her daughter's disappearance. That was a matter for the police. A cruiser finally drove up in front and two officers followed her into the hallway to get a statement.

"Just calm down, ma'am, and tell us why you think your family is missing. How long have they been gone?"

"I don't know. An hour or so. I was busy in the kitchen before I realized I couldn't hear voices. Even the dogs are missing."

"Maybe they went for a walk."

"Naturally I thought of that, but I've been driving around the neighborhood and there's no sign of them. No one has seen them. Our other car is still in the garage."

"Maybe they stopped at a neighbor's home. It is Christmas Day, you know."

She took a shuddering breath. "You don't understand. My husband—"

"—is right here." A chilling male voice that could only be Kon's cut her off abruptly.

"We've been at Fred's house showing him the new puppy, Mommy. He has a bottle with a ship in it and a marmalade cat who's so fat she just sleeps." Anna rushed through the hall to explain and gave her mother a huge hug while the dogs circled them, whining a little. Meg couldn't speak. She simply clutched her daughter closer.

One of the officers nodded to Kon. "Your wife here got a little nervous because you and your daughter had been gone a while."

She'd seen pain in Kon's eyes before, but nothing could compare to the look of raw anguish she saw there now. The inner light faded completely, as if something in him had just died.

Another kind of fear tore at her heart. *What had she done?*

He glanced at the officer. "You know how it is when you've only been married five days. We don't like to be out of each other's sight."

Once again, Kon's superb playacting was in evidence and he handled the awkward situation like a master. But Meg knew nothing would ever be the same between them again.

He slid his arm around her shoulders and pulled her close, pressing a fervent kiss to her temple. "Fred Dykstra was on his front porch and he called to us. His house is two doors down. He's a retired widower from the railroad and he lives alone. When he saw Anna, he invited her in to give her a chocolate Santa.''

''I'm sorry,'' Meg whispered in agony. ''I—I didn't realize…''

He rubbed her arm. ''When he helped me move in, he had to put up with my talking about you and Anna all the time, and he wants to meet you. So I was coming back to the house to ask if we could invite him for dinner. That's when Anna and I saw the police car and bumped into Mrs. Dunlop, who said you were looking for us. I'm sorry if you were worried.''

This time he lowered his mouth to hers in a gesture the officers would interpret as a lover's salute. In reality Kon pressed a hard, soulless kiss against her lips, a kiss that made a mockery of the passion they'd once shared. ''I make you a solemn vow that I'll never be that thoughtless again, Mrs. Johnson.''

Meg knew he was saying one thing while he meant another. She couldn't seem to stop shaking. No amount of sorrow or remorse for her actions would put them back on the same footing they'd achieved that morning. Before she'd called the police.

''We'll be going, then.'' The officer smiled. ''Merry Christmas.''

''Sorry to have troubled you. Merry Christmas.'' Kon's fingers bit into her upper arm before he released her to see them to the door.

''Anna, run out to the porch and take off your boots, honey. You're getting water on the floor.''

''Okay, Mommy. Here, Thor. Here, Gandy.''

Meg was halfway up the stairs when she heard

Kon's footsteps and realized there was no hope of escape. He followed her into the bedroom and shut the door too quietly. He didn't say anything, merely watched her through narrowed eyes.

"I-I'm sorry," she began haltingly. "I know that sounds inadequate but—"

"Just tell me one thing," he demanded coldly. "Did you give away my cover?"

She shook her head in denial, staring at the floor. "No."

"The truth, Meggie. If you even hinted that I might have abducted her, we'll have to move and I'll be forced to take on a new identity. As it is, I'll have to get hold of…certain people to report the incident. The decision might well be out of my hands already."

His words made her more frantic than ever. "No, Kon. When I phoned 911, I only said Anna was missing. I told the Dunlops the same thing."

"But you were on the verge of telling them all about me when I walked in the hall. Don't deny it."

She struggled for the words that might placate him. There were none. "I won't," she finally murmured.

"You've missed your calling, Meggie."

She lifted tearful eyes to him and shrank from his cold, hard face.

"No Mata Hari of my acquaintance could have pulled off a more convincing act than you did this morning when you tried to give me back a little piece of my Russian soul. To include our innocent little Anna in the subterfuge was pure genius. My compliments, *beloved.*" He said the endearment with a particularly cruel twist that brought a moan to her lips. "You actually had me convinced there was hope."

Unspeakable emotion—anger and something else she couldn't define—tautened every muscle and sinew of his body before he strode swiftly from the room.

When she thought about what she'd done and the possible consequences to Kon's safety after the years it had taken him to establish his new identity, Meg collapsed on the bed.

"Mommy?"

Meg could hear Anna's footsteps on the stairs. She jumped up from the bed and hurried into the bathroom to wash her face so her daughter wouldn't suspect anything.

"Can Fred come to our house for dinner? He's nice."

As far as Meg was concerned, a guest would provide the diversion she needed to get through the rest of the day. Kon had extended the initial invitation and would have to be on his best behavior.

"Of course he can, honey. Why don't you take the dogs and go back to his house and bring him over? He can spend the day with us and sit by the fire. You can show him your toys."

"Can I go right now?"

"Yes. Don't forget your hat and boots."

"I won't."

Meg followed her down the stairs and busied herself in the kitchen until she heard Anna and the dogs leaving.

Realizing Kon needed to be told about Fred, she

hurried to his study. But the glacial look he shot her when she appeared in the doorway froze her into stillness.

"Where's Anna?"

Meg tried to swallow, but her throat felt swollen. "I sent her over to Mr. Dykstra's to bring him back for dinner. That's what I was coming in here to tell you."

He leaned back in his chair and watched her through shuttered eyes. "I'm glad she's out of the house for a few minutes. What I have to say won't take long, but I don't want her privy to it."

"D-did you pho—"

"I don't intend to answer any of your questions," he cut in brutally. "All you have to do is listen."

"I'm your wife!" she cried, aghast. "You have no right to speak to me like that, no matter what's happened."

"I forgot." He smiled with cold disdain. "Yes, you're my wife—who five days ago in this very house swore before God to love and honor me, be my comfort, my haven, my refuge—"

"Stop it!" she shouted. "I can't take any more."

He sucked in a breath and got to his feet. "You won't have to. I'm leaving."

"*What?*"

"Your name is on my bank account. You can draw out funds any time you need to. There's enough to keep you indefinitely. The house is in your name, as well."

"What do you mean?" she asked, panicking. "What are you talking about? Where are you going?"

His mouth thinned. "If I told you, you wouldn't believe me, so there's no point."

"H-how long will you be gone?"

"If it were up to you, I'd never come back, so it really doesn't matter."

She let out a groan. "Don't say that. It *does* matter. You can't do this to Anna."

"She'll recover. I was torn from my family when I was young, and I turned out all right. The Party has given me several commendations. Besides, she has *you.*"

"Kon...don't do this." She suddenly felt afraid for him. "Have I put you in danger?" When he didn't reply, she asked, "Do you hate me so much for what I did that you can't bear the sight of me any longer? Is that what this is all about?"

"I'll leave tonight after Anna has gone to sleep." He went on talking as if she hadn't spoken. "As far as she has to know, I've gone to New York on business."

"What business?" Her voice shook.

"Have you finally decided to show a little interest in my writing career?" The contempt in his question devastated her. "Did you think that was made up? That I defected to a life of luxury, living off the proceeds of the information I brought your government?"

Before they were married, she'd assumed exactly that. But too late she knew it wasn't the truth.

In a dull voice she asked, "What is it exactly that you write? Walt Bowman, or whoever he is, said something about the KGB and..." Her voice faded.

One dark brow lifted. "When I'm gone, you can

search through my study to your heart's content and figure it out for yourself. At least when we part this time, Anna will have some videos to help her remember her father. It's more than I was given when I was taken away.''

Meg could feel him slipping beyond her reach and didn't have the faintest idea how to hold on to him. In desperation she said, ''I thought you loved Anna. I thought you defected because of her, for her.''

''Does it really matter what either of us thought when it's abundantly clear I got here six years too late?'' His eyes bored holes into her.

''Now, if I'm not mistaken, I can hear Thor and Gandy, which means Anna and Fred are almost at our front door. Shall we greet our guest together, *mayah labof?*''

''MRS. JOHNSON? Senator Strickland here.''

Thank God. Meg's hand tightened on the receiver and she sat up in bed, praying Anna had finally gone to sleep and hadn't heard the phone ring. Today— the day after Christmas—had been a waking nightmare, one she never wanted to live through again.

''Thank you for returning my call. Thank you,'' she murmured. ''I'd almost given up hope that you'd even get your messages before you went back to your office next week.''

''I have a secretary who monitors my calls in case of an emergency. She phoned me at home when she heard your name.''

''Please forgive me for bothering you this late, but I'm desperate.'' Her voice wobbled despite herself. ''I need your help.''

"This sounds serious. By a strange coincidence, my wife and I were just talking about you newly-weds on our way home from a concert tonight. We were trying to decide on a date for that dinner I promised you."

Meg groaned with renewed pain. "Senator—my husband left me last night."

There was a prolonged silence on the other end of the phone. "A domestic quarrel?"

"No. It was something that goes much deeper. I don't even know where to begin. I've been out of my mind with grief, and my daughter is inconsolable. I've got to find him and tell him I love him." She broke down sobbing and it took her a minute to get control of her emotions and her voice. "He has to come back to us. *He has to.*"

"Tell me what happened."

More hot tears streamed down her face. "I drove him away with my paranoia. I accused him of planning to kidnap Anna and take her back to Russia." In a few words she explained why she'd called the police. "All this time I've refused to believe what was before my very eyes. I have to go to him and beg his forgiveness."

"Did he leave in his own car?"

"Yes."

"I'll get on it as soon as we hang up, and when I have any information, I'll contact you, but I doubt it will be before morning."

"Thank you. I'm in your debt," she said fervently.

"If I can effect a reunion between the two of you,

then I'll hold you to that at campaign time. Meanwhile, don't give up.''

''I'll never do that,'' she vowed. ''I fell in love with him when I was seventeen. I'll always love him.''

''That's the most painful kind of love, first love,'' he said kindly. ''Your husband told me he was similarly affected when he met you for the first time.''

Meg blinked. ''Kon told you that?''

''Mmm. Tell me, are you familiar with the story in the Bible about Jacob who loved Rachel?''

Her heart began hammering. ''Yes.''

''When your husband and I talked, I told him his plight struck me as being very much like Jacob's. He loved Rachel on sight and worked seven years for her. And even though he was tricked into marrying Leah because of the laws of the land, he loved Rachel so much he worked another seven years for her. Few women will ever know that kind of devotion from a man.''

After a slight pause he went on, ''Despite the laws of his former country, your husband has worked close to seven years for you, putting himself in grave danger. It hardly stands to reason that you've lost him now, no matter how dark things look at the moment.''

''Thank you,'' she whispered tearfully. ''I needed to hear that. Good night, Senator.''

The minute she hung up the phone, she got out of bed and crept down the stairs to Kon's study in search of a Bible. If memory served her correctly, she'd seen one with his collection of books when she'd gone in there earlier to go through his papers.

Naturally his work was stored on disk, but she found enough correspondence in the file cabinets to realize he wrote not only about the KGB but about the beauty, the culture, of Russia.

When she found the Bible, she sat down at his desk and opened it to Genesis 29. Verse 20 had been underlined in black ink and she skipped to it immediately.

> And Jacob served seven years for Rachel; and they seemed unto him but a few days, for the love he had to her.
>
> Suddenly the letters blurred together. She laid her head down on the table and wept.

CHAPTER TEN

"I DON'T WANT to go to my new school, Mommy. Prince will cry, and what if Daddy comes home and can't find me?"

It was going on three weeks since the Christmas holidays. Every single one of those days, Meg had been listening to Anna's tearful arguments repeated over and over again like a litany.

If Meg hadn't gone to Anna's new school with her every day and stayed in the building to work as a volunteer aide—so Anna could check throughout the day to make sure her mommy was still there—Anna would never have gone at all.

In truth, Meg wouldn't have let Anna go if she hadn't been able to spend the better part of the day with her at school. The yawning emptiness of the home Kon had created for them was unbearable without him. His absence affected everything and everyone, especially the dogs. They kept returning to Kon's study and whining, the sound eerily human, when they couldn't find him.

From the first night after his disappearance, Anna had crept into Meg's bed with her nutcracker and she'd been sleeping there ever since. Meg knew it would create more problems down the road, but she drew comfort from Anna's warm little body next to hers and didn't try to make her sleep on her own. It wouldn't have worked, anyway; Anna couldn't tolerate even a brief separation from her right now. Kon had been too wonderful a husband and father in the short week they'd lived together as a family. It was no wonder that Meg and Anna had gone into mourning and refused to be consoled.

Meg had no doubts that Senator Strickland had done everything in his power to discover Kon's whereabouts. Lacey Bowman had phoned Meg the morning after the senator's call. The only information the CIA would give Meg was that Kon was no longer in the country.

Because of Anna, Meg couldn't give in to the pain of that excruciating revelation. She had to go on pretending he was away on an extended business trip with his publisher and would come home just as soon as he could.

Every time the phone rang, Anna ran to get it and cried, "Daddy?" This happened so many times Meg thought her heart would break. She had to admonish her daughter to say hello first or she wouldn't be allowed to answer the phone at all.

So far, there'd been two disastrous sleep-overs with Melanie, who was so taken with Prince she never wanted to go home. But Anna was no longer the vivacious friend she used to be and refused to share her puppy. This, in turn, created fighting and unpleasantness. After Melanie left, Anna confided to Meg that she didn't want Melanie to come to her house anymore. Jason and Abby across the street were her friends now. Meg decided to let it go for the moment. She'd arrange something with Melanie in a few months' time.

Violin lessons were out, after Anna cried all day and night over having to leave the house to drive to St. Louis. It was too far away and her daddy might come home.

By the end of January, there was still no sign of him, and Meg had to face the dreadful truth that he might never come home. The more she thought about it, the more she believed he hadn't gone back to Russia at all but was looking for another place to live.

Kon spoke several European languages and could easily have relocated in Germany or Austria or even France. The American government would have co-operated with the country he'd chosen, giving him the proper papers and credentials to start over again.

And it was Meg's fault. She felt as though her heart had died.

Since Anna's inability to deal with her loss seemed to be growing worse, Meg's family doctor advised her to consult a good child psychologist and referred her to a colleague who practiced in Hannibal. Their first appointment would be the next Saturday at eleven. Meg recognized that she was in need of help herself and decided they could both benefit. She prayed counseling would help them; she could think of no other alternatives.

On Friday night after dinner, Meg broached the subject with Anna, who didn't like the fact that her mother had a doctor's appointment. Yet she had no choice but to go along, since she wouldn't let Meg out of her sight. Meg was in the process of explaining why they had to see this doctor when the door-bell rang.

"Daddy!" Anna shrieked, and toppled her chair in her haste to get to the front door. The dogs got there even faster, barking more loudly than usual.

Meg's adrenaline kicked in the way it always did— because there was a part of her that never gave up hope, either. But there was no point in telling Anna that if her father *had* come home, he would enter through the back porch from the garage. He wouldn't ring the front doorbell.

In all probability, it was Jason or Abby. Meg expected them to come running through the kitchen to play with Prince, who needed Kon's firm hand to learn obedience. Or it might be Fred, who'd become a welcome visitor and friend and had more influence with Anna than anyone else these days.

Meg was halfway to the front hall when she heard a woman's voice speaking a torrent of Russian. *"mayah malyenkyah muishka,"* she repeated. "My darling little mouse," she said over and over again.

What on earth?

Meg emerged from the dining room in time to see an elderly, heavyset woman dressed in black envelop Anna in her arms. The stranger's long gray hair was fastened in a bun, and she wore amber around her neck and wrist. Tears streamed down her ruddy cheeks, and she held on to Anna as if she'd never let her go.

"Anochka." A deep, commanding, familiar voice sounded from the front porch. "This is your ba-bushka, but you can call her Grandma Anyah."

"Her name is just like mine!"

"That's right, Anochka. It must be fate. She's come all the way from Siberia to live with us."

Kon.

As Meg mouthed his name, he stepped into the hallway. The sight of his tall, lean body and striking face was so wonderful she could only stare and go on staring. His dazzling blue eyes were trained on her now, but there was a humble look in them she'd never seen before.

"Meggie, may I present my *matz,*" he said in a tremulous voice.

His mother.

"She's my belated Christmas present to you. She doesn't speak any English, but we'll help her learn it, won't we?"

Meg didn't answer the unspoken plea in his unshed tears, because love had lent her feet wings. She threw herself into Kon's arms so hard it might have knocked the wind out of a less solid man. Like a powerful waterfall, her avowals of love, her pleas for forgiveness, cascaded down on him, submerging him so completely he could be in no doubt that she belonged to him heart and soul.

Meg could tell the exact moment Kon knew that trust had come to stay. He groaned his satisfaction and, in full view of his mother and Anna, found Meg's questing mouth and kissed her with all the fiery passion of those halcyon days in Russia long ago. Once again they were free to give in to their hunger, their longings. Meg forgot everything but the feel of his arms and mouth, the warmth of his hard body melding to hers.

"Are you and Daddy making a baby?"

Anna!

Kon had the presence of mind to break off their kiss faster than Meg did, but he refused to let her go. He rocked her in his arms as he rested his chin on her shoulder and spoke to his daughter.

"Tomorrow, your mommy and I are going to sit down with you and explain about babies. Right now I want her to meet *my* mommy."

In a lightning move he turned Meg around, sliding his hands down her arms before wrapping his own around her waist from behind and squeezing her so every part of their bodies touched.

"Mama, this is Meggie. My wife." His voice broke as he introduced them in Russian.

Kon's mother was still holding Anna as she lifted her head from her granddaughter's curls.

Meg gasped softly when the brilliant blue eyes so like Kon's wandered over her face and hair in a friendly yet searching perusal.

It wasn't just the eyes. Her bone structure was similar to Kon's, and Meg could see flecks of dark among her gray eyebrows that testified where he'd received his black-brown hair.

Slowly the older woman put Anna down and cupped Meg's face with her hands.

"*Mayah Doch,*" she said like a benediction.

My daughter.

Meg nodded before returning the greeting. "*Mayah Matz.*"

Then they embraced. Meg formally kissed both cheeks, feeling an overwhelming tide of love and happiness. She held her mother-in-law in her arms for a long, long time. This wonderful woman who'd given birth to Kon, who'd thought he was dead all these years. This woman Meg had always wanted to meet…

Who knew the hardships, the deprivation, she'd lived through? How Meg would have loved to witness the reunion of mother and son!

There were too many questions she wanted answered, but now wasn't the time, not when everyone's emotions were spilling over. The dogs were no less thrilled as they rubbed their heads against Kon's legs in joyous homecoming.

"I'm glad you're home, Daddy. I've been waiting and *waiting* for you."

"So have I, Anochka, so have I."

By now Anna was in her father's arms, the healing after separation already begun. He whispered the special endearments he reserved for his daughter.

Anna was exactly where Meg longed to be. He was their safety, their rock, the light of their lives. Their love.

Slowly, over one gray and one dark head, Meg felt the burning heat of Kon's desire reach out to her, and she read the unspoken message in those smoldering eyes. Like her, he was barely holding on to his control until they could be alone.

But there were his mother and Anna to consider. By tacit agreement they decided to see to their comforts first. Meg's time with her husband would have to come later. Like Jacob and Rachel, they'd waited this long and could wait a little longer. But only just a little.

She answered his unasked question in a husky voice. "We'll put your mother in the room I was using before you left. It's all made up and ready for her. She'll enjoy the privacy of her own bathroom, and Anna will love having her grandmother next door.''

He lowered Anna to the floor, his chest heaving with the strength of emotions he was having difficulty holding in check. ''Where are your things?''

She could hardly breathe. ''Where do you think?''

''They're in your room.'' Anna giggled. ''You're silly, Daddy.''

He tousled her dark curls and muttered in Russian, ''Our little pitcher has awfully big ears.''

Meg replied in kind with a straight face. ''She takes after her father.''

''And my Dimitri takes after *his* father,'' Anyah added. Kon grinned at Meg's astonishment.

The moment also gave Meg a glimpse of the older woman's sense of humor. It warmed her heart as nothing else could have done, and she hugged her mother-in-law once more before fastening loving eyes on her husband. ''Is that your real name? Dimitri?''

''Da,'' his mother answered for him. ''Dimitri Leudonovitch.''

''How do you like it, *mayah labof?*''

''Enough to give it to our son when he's born.''

She watched him swallow several times, and he looked at her with fierce longing.

Meg smiled into his eyes. ''You've been gone forever, so you'd better plan to make up for lost time.''

Anyah patted Meg's arm. ''I can see you are good

for my Dimitri. He needs to be loved by a woman like you, a woman to match his passion."

Her blunt, outspoken manner brought a blush to Meg's cheeks. To cover her embarrassment she said, "Did you know he was your son when you first saw him?"

"*Da.*" She nodded, eyeing him with motherly pride. "No child in Shuryshkary had such a face and blue eyes like my little Deema's. And you see the way his hair grows into that widow's peak, and the shape of his ears, like a seashell?"

Her weatherworn hand reached out to touch his left eyebrow, as if she, too, couldn't get enough of him. "See the little scar covered by the hair? He got that scar and the one on his left shoulder when he fell out of a tree. I think he was four. He always loved the trees and begged his papa to take him up into the mountains we could see from our house."

Kon still loved the trees and the mountains, Meg thought, reacting with a shaky breath. She'd noted all those physical characteristics of Kon's when they'd made love. Particularly the scar on his shoulder, the one he couldn't remember getting, the one she'd kissed again and again because she loved everything about his magnificent body.

Right then Kon's eyes captured hers—hot, glowing, blue coals that let her know he was remembering the same thing she was.

Meg cleared her throat. Switching to English, she asked, "Where is Shuryshkary?"

"In northern Siberia at the foot of the Urals."

"That explains so much," she whispered.

Kon nodded his dark head and they communed in

silence. But not for long, because Anna inserted herself between her parents and grandmother. "What's that sure-scary word mean?"

Kon chuckled. "It's the town where I was born, Anochka."

Unable to contain her curiosity any longer, Meg cried, "How did you ever find your mother?"

"When the idea first came to defect, I managed—with the help of another agent who owed me some favors—to get into my file. Once I read the details, I found out my mother was still alive, and I negotiated her escape with the help of your government. But like the situation with you and Anna, I had to wait all this time before I felt it was safe to bring her here. Un- fortunately there were problems that prevented her from arriving on Christmas Day as we'd originally planned."

"Oh, Kon…" Her voice shook. Now that she had answers, his behavior on Christmas Day and his subsequent disappearance made complete sense. She lifted pleading eyes to him. "Can you ever forgi—"

"All that's over, Meggie," he broke in. "Today is the beginning of the rest of our lives."

"Yes," she whispered, and linking her arm through her mother-in-law's, she said in Russian, "Are you tired? Would you like to go upstairs, or would you like to freshen up for dinner first, then take a tour of your son's house?"

The older woman looked thoughtful. "We flew all the way from San Francisco today and ate a big meal on the plane. I think I would like to get acquainted with my little granddaughter, then go to bed."

As they started for the stairs, with Anna and the dogs running ahead of them and Kon trailing with the luggage, his mother said, "Anna is very much like Deema's sister, Nadia, used to be. Bright, inquisitive, full of life."

"Nadia died of a lung disease before her fourteenth birthday," Kon explained under his breath in English.

Meg's chest constricted. "And your father?"

"One day he went logging and his heart gave out. That was five years ago."

"How has she survived all these years alone?"

"Scrubbing floors and toilets in civic buildings."

"How old is she?"

"Sixty-five."

"She's wonderful, Kon."

"She is. So are you."

Much later that night, when the house had finally fallen quiet and the lights were turned off, Kon entered their bedroom, where Meg had been impatiently waiting for him.

"The last time I looked, Mama was reading the *Nutcracker* to Anna. She's actually picked up quite a few words from our bedtime stories."

"What could be more natural, my darling?" Meg whispered. She reached eagerly for him as he shrugged out of his robe and slid into the bed. "Mrs. Beezley told me she was exceptionally intelligent for her age. Mrs. Rosen said the same thing about her talent for the violin. She inherited those qualities from her father."

"And from her mother. She's also inherited the sweetness of her spirit from you," he murmured against her mouth, kissing her breathless. "When I left them, they were communicating with amazing facility."

Meg couldn't contain her emotions. "That book has been like a magical link between all of us, my darling."

He smoothed the hair from her forehead, staring into her very soul. "That's because the *Nutcracker* is magical. When Mama embraced me and started talking to me about the past, dozens of memories came flooding back. One of my strongest impressions was of her reading the *Nutcracker* to me when I was a child. That's why it made such an impact on me—and why I wanted you to have that particular book when you left Russia. It symbolized hope and love for me, Meggie. *Our* love. Now it has all come together in a living reality." His voice broke before he claimed her mouth once more and drew her fully into his arms.

"I've yearned for you, Meggie. I love you with such a terrible hunger it frightens me."

"I'm frightened to think I almost lost you again."

"I won't lie to you, Meggie. After I left the house at Christmas, I'd pretty well lost hope for us. But I had to try again."

"Thank God you did! I love you so much! Kon—" She gasped in ecstasy at the first touch of his hand against her flesh. The pleasure was almost unbearable. "I can't believe this is happening. Am I dreaming?"

"Does it matter?" he asked in a husky voice. "We're together at last. Any more questions or explanations will have to wait, because nothing else is—or ever will be—as important as you here with me.

"Love me, Meggie," he begged, the pain of longing in his voice and body echoing hers. She gave herself up to the only man who would ever be all things to her—guardian, friend, lover, husband, father of her children.

Not many other women had traveled so far from home, on so strange and precarious a path to their ultimate destiny and fulfillment.

But she'd do it again for the love of one Konstantin Rudenko, the prince of her heart and, most assuredly, of Anna's.

Jennifer Taylor lives in the north-west of England with her husband Bill. She had been writing Mills & Boon® romances for some years, but when she discovered Medical Romance™, she was so captivated by these heart-warming stories that she set out to write them herself! When not writing or doing research for her latest book, Jennifer's hobbies include reading, travel, walking her dog and retail therapy (shopping!). Jennifer claims all that bending and stretching to reach the shelves is the best exercise possible.

A REAL FAMILY
CHRISTMAS
by
Jennifer Taylor

CHAPTER ONE

'I KNOW what I'm going to ask Santa for!'

Emma Graham, staff nurse on the Obs and Gynae Ward of St Luke's Hospital, put down her coffee-cup and looked expectantly at her friend, Linda Wood. It was two weeks before Christmas and the canteen where they were having their morning break was strewn with garishly coloured tinsel and baubles.

The whole hospital seemed to be gearing itself up for the festivities, in fact. There was much talk of Christmas parties and family visits, shopping and suchlike. Emma had remained aloof from it all as her situation was rather different to that of her friends. With no family of her own, Christmas Day was usually spent by herself if she wasn't working. It was rarely a time for celebration. However, she was as eager as everyone else was to hear what the irrepressible Linda had to say so she prompted her friend to continue.

'What? I can see you're dying to tell us, Linda, so what would you like to find in your Christmas stocking this year, then?'

'Daniel Hutton!' Linda's face broke into a mischievous grin. 'I mean, come on, girls, who wouldn't want to wake up on Christmas morning and find dishy Daniel at the bottom of your bed?'

'I'd rather find him in it, thank you. Then I'd really believe in Father Christmas!'

Everyone roared with laughter as Eileen Pierce, the oldest member of staff on their ward, added her own pithy comments. Emma joined in, although she couldn't help feeling a bit uncomfortable. Daniel Hutton was sitting at a

5

table not far from where they were sitting and he could
have overheard what they'd said.

She glanced round and felt her face heat when she found
that he was looking their way. His hazel eyes held a hint
of amusement as they met hers before he stood up.
Gathering together the papers he'd been reading, he left the
canteen without a backward glance.

'I think he heard you,' Emma said with a grimace, turning back to her friend.

'Did he? Good. Maybe it will make him get his act together.' Linda wasn't in the least abashed. 'I mean, it isn't
normal for a man who looks like he does to pay such little
attention to the opposite sex! And before anyone states the
obvious, I have it on good authority that Daniel showed a
healthy interest in the female of the species before he came
to work here. An *extremely* healthy interest, according to
my friend Sonia, who worked with him!'

'Hmmm, curiouser and curiouser. I wonder what happened? Do you think it was a relationship that went sour
and put him off women?' Jane Goodyear, their second-year
student, looked thoughtful as she stared at the door through
which Daniel had disappeared.

'Could be.' Linda chuckled. 'Maybe he needs counsel-
ling. Now, there's a thought!'

Emma shook her head in despair. 'I thought you were
crazy about your Gary? Didn't you say that you were getting engaged this Christmas?'

'So? Just because I'll soon have a ring on my finger
doesn't mean that I have to give up *all* life's little plea-
sures!'

There was a lot of laughter as they finished their break
and went back to the ward. It was busy as usual, with two
new cases having been admitted that morning. However,
several times Emma found her thoughts straying to Daniel
Hutton.

He had started work at St Luke's in the summer and there

had been a lot of speculation about the handsome senior registrar ever since. The fact that Daniel had kept himself very much to himself for the past six months had only heightened the interest in him. Nobody knew much about him, apart from the fact that he was good at his job and marvellous with the patients who came under his care.

Emma couldn't help wondering if Jane had been right about him having been put off women because of a relationship that had gone wrong. It seemed the most logical explanation. With those classically handsome looks and lean, six-foot frame, Daniel wouldn't have had a problem persuading any number of willing volunteers to go out with him!

'Can you get Mrs Horrocks ready to go down to Theatre, please, Staff?' Sister Carter popped her head round the office door as she spied Emma passing. 'Dr Hutton phoned to say that he would be up in a few minutes to have a word with her about her operation.'

'Certainly, Sister.' Emma replied. 'I was just going to check how Mrs Rogers is doing. It's the first time she's tried taking a shower on her own.'

'Fine. Do that first and then sort out Mrs Horrocks. And try to calm her down, will you?' Sister Carter rolled her eyes. 'I've never seen anyone worry as much as that poor woman does!'

Emma laughed. 'I know! The night staff said that she'd hardly slept a wink.'

'Why doesn't that surprise me? Still, she should get a bit of a nap once they give her the anaesthetic.'

Emma laughed as Sister Carter went back to her paperwork. Despite being a martinet when it came to work, the ward sister had a particularly droll sense of humour and Emma enjoyed working with her. She tapped on the bathroom door then went in to see how Mrs Rogers was faring. She found her sitting on a stool, looking extremely shaky.

'Not feeling so good, Mrs Rogers?' Emma asked solic-itously as she went to help her.

'Just a bit giddy in the head, that's all,' Shirley Rogers replied, summoning a smile.

It was so typical of her, Emma thought as she helped the woman into her dressing-gown and took her back to the ward. Shirley Rogers had been admitted for a total hyster-ectomy to remove a severely prolapsed uterus. The opera-tion had gone very well but it had still been a major one. However, despite being in some discomfort, Shirley hadn't complained once.

She was a farmer's wife with three strapping sons who all worked on the family farm. Emma knew that Shirley's main concern was that she would be well enough to return home for Christmas. However, she made a note to mention to Shirley's husband that he must make sure his wife didn't do too much when she returned home. Shirley needed a few weeks' rest to get over the operation before she started rushing around.

Once Shirley Rogers was comfortably settled, Emma went to Mrs Horrocks's bed. She was just about to draw the curtains around it when Daniel Hutton arrived.

'Thanks.' He treated her to one of his wonderful and far too rare smiles as she paused to let him pass, and Emma felt her heart suddenly knock against her ribs in the most peculiar fashion. A touch of colour warmed her cheeks and she saw one of his elegant brows rise as though he was wondering what had caused her to blush like that.

'You're welcome.' She swished the curtains around the bed and took a deep breath. She hadn't believed herself susceptible to Daniel Hutton's undoubted charms but maybe she had been a bit over-confident! However, all it took was the sight of Jean Horrocks's woebegone face to focus her mind firmly on work once again. The poor woman was obviously scared stiff by the thought of the operation she was about to undergo and Emma's tender heart went out to her.

'Now, come along, Mrs Horrocks, there's no need to worry.' Emma patted the woman's hand. 'It really is a very simple operation, as Dr Hutton will explain.'

Emma looked expectantly at Daniel who, on cue, began to add his reassurances. Carefully, he explained what would happen when Jean Horrocks went down to Theatre, taking her through each step of the procedure. Mrs Horrocks had suffered for a number of years from menorrhagia, prolonged and heavy menstrual bleeding. She was to undergo a dilatation and curettage that day, commonly referred to as a D and C.

It was a simple operation which involved removing the thickened lining of the uterus under general anaesthetic. Although there were other means of removing the endometrium, the lining of the womb, their consultant, Max Dennison, was of the old school and still preferred a D and C over more modern methods.

'So you see, Mrs Horrocks, it's all very simple, as Staff Nurse Graham told you it was.' Daniel treated the woman to his wonderful smile as he came to the end of his explanation. Emma barely managed to conceal her amazement when the older woman smiled back.

'I understand that now you've explained it to me, Dr Hutton.' Jean Horrocks settled back against the pillows, a distinctly coquettish smile curving her lips. 'I won't worry any more now that I know I'm in your capable hands.'

'I'm pleased to hear it.' One last megawatt smile then Daniel turned to Emma. 'Mrs Horrocks is scheduled for twelve o'clock, I believe, Staff. If you would page me when she leaves the ward I'll make sure I'm there to meet her when she arrives at Theatre.'

'Of course, Doctor,' Emma replied smoothly, hiding a grin as he treated her to a conspiratorial wink under cover of leaving. Obviously, Daniel had no qualms about laying on the charm if it meant that he wouldn't have an agitated and possibly disruptive patient arriving at Theatre to deal with!

'Ooh, isn't he lovely? So understanding as well. I just wish that I'd seen him when I first arrived instead of that other doctor…what was his name now?'

'Mr Dennison,' Emma supplied helpfully, checking the tags on Mrs Horrocks's wrist and ankle. They both matched, giving details of her name, date of birth and the operation she was scheduled for, so Emma initialled the notes which would accompany the patient to Theatre, confirming that the check had been done.

'That's right…Dennison.' Mrs Horrocks sniffed. 'I didn't take to him, to be honest. Told me that there was nothing to fuss about. Well, it might be nothing to him because he's a man, but it's something to me. It's my insides they're playing around with when all's said and done!'

'Which is why Dr Hutton will take such good care of you,' Emma soothed as she heard the panic creeping into Mrs Horrocks's voice once more. It seemed to do the trick because the woman relaxed again.

'Of course he will.'

Mercifully, the porters arrived at that moment to take her down to Theatre. Emma only just managed to contain her amusement as Mrs Horrocks waved to the rest of the patients as she was wheeled out of the ward. Linda stopped what she was doing and stared, open-mouthed, after the departing trolley.

'Are my eyes deceiving me or was that really Jean Horrocks on her way for her op?'

'Nope, there's nothing wrong with your eyesight.' Emma laughed ruefully. 'Hard to believe it's the same woman who's been worrying herself into an early grave for the past twenty-four hours, isn't it?'

'What did you do to her? Give her laughing gas or something?' Linda demanded.

'Something far more effective than that—ten minutes of quality time with our Dr Hutton, Emma explained. 'Worked wonders, hasn't it?'

'Too right it has! Mind you, ten minutes of dishy Daniel's time would work wonders for me, too!' Linda rolled her eyes lasciviously. Emma knew that Linda was joking but she couldn't help feeling a little irritated at her friend's insistence on calling Daniel Hutton by that ridiculous name. However, it seemed wiser not to say anything so she passed it off and carried on with her work.

There was always plenty to be done, with patients coming and going to Theatre plus the ones who were in for observation or tests. Emma had been on the ward for almost a year now and she loved her job. There was always something different to deal with.

The ward was divided into two by folding screens which were rarely closed. One side was for gynae cases and the other for obstetric patients. The only time she felt a bit down about her work was when they had a patient who had suffered a miscarriage. It was always hard to be comforting and give hope when a much-wanted baby had been lost.

They had admitted such a case that morning, a young woman in her early twenties who had miscarried the previous evening. Her name was Alison Banks and she was going to need a D and C as part of the placenta had been retained inside her womb. She was still in a state of shock so Emma had made a point of checking on her as often as she could. When she went to the bed, she found Alison crying.

'Are you OK?' she asked softly, drawing the curtain closed behind her before she approached the bed. Alison's husband was in the army and had been sent on a peace-keeping mission a month earlier. With no other family in the area to turn to, Alison was very much on her own.

'Yes. No. I don't know how I feel...' Alison ran a hand over her face and sighed. 'I keep wondering why it happened. Was it something I did? Was there something wrong with the baby? My head is spinning with it all.'

'Has Dr Hutton seen you?' Emma asked quietly, passing her a tissue.

'Yes.' Alison blew her nose but tears were still welling in her eyes.

'And what did he say?' Emma prompted. Sometimes the only way to help was to make a woman talk about what had happened.

'That it was just something that wasn't meant to be. He said that it wasn't anything I'd done and that I wasn't to blame myself. He wouldn't have told me that if it wasn't true, would he?' Alison looked beseechingly at her and Emma shook her head.

'No, he wouldn't. Dr Hutton has told you the truth, Alison. I know how hard it must be but you mustn't blame yourself.'

Emma stayed a few minutes longer then left when she was sure that Alison was a little calmer. Sister had contacted Alison's husband's regiment so that they could pass a message to him. Emma wasn't sure if he would be allowed to return home but she was hoping that he would be. Alison needed him here beside her at a time like this.

The day flew past. Before she knew it, it was time to go home. Linda offered her a lift but Emma regretfully refused. She was a bit like Old Mother Hubbard, she thought as she left the hospital, because her cupboards were completely bare! It was definitely time to visit the supermarket and stock up on essentials.

The town centre was bustling when she stepped off the bus. There was late-night shopping, with it being the run-up to Christmas, and it looked as though most of Clearsea's inhabitants had decided to make the most of the opportunity.

Emma got caught up in a crowd coming out of the chemist's and had to fight free of the crush. People were laden down with parcels and boxes, even Christmas trees. She couldn't help feeling a little left out as she felt the buzz that was in the air that night. She wasn't rostered to work that Christmas Day and she couldn't help thinking how lonely it was going to be in her flat all by herself...

'Oof!' Emma gasped as someone cannoned into her. She put out a steadying hand and just saved the little girl from a nasty fall as the child teetered on the edge of the pavement.

'That was quite a bump, wasn't it?' she said, bending down to smile at the child. She looked to be about six years old, with long dark curls and heavily lashed hazel eyes. Funnily enough, the child reminded her of someone she knew, although for the life of her Emma couldn't think who it was.

'I'm sorry.' The child looked uncertainly at her then shot a glance at the crowd milling around them. Emma looked up as well, expecting to see an anxious mother or father rushing towards them. However, nobody seemed to be taking any notice of them. It made her wonder where the little girl's parents could be. Surely she hadn't been allowed to come shopping on her own on a busy night like this?

'Isn't there anyone with you?' she asked the child, taking hold of her hand as they were jostled about.

'Uncle Daniel. We're doing our Christmas shopping tonight 'cos it will be too busy on Saturday, you see.' Two fat tears started to slither down the child's cheeks as she stared at the crowd of people. 'I was holding his hand and then this lady pushed me and now I can't see him!'

'Shh! It's all right, poppet. Don't cry. I'm sure your Uncle Daniel will be here in a moment.' Emma picked up the child. It was so busy that she was afraid that the little girl would get trampled in the crush. Where on earth was her uncle? she thought angrily. And why hadn't he had the sense to keep tight hold of his niece's hand?

'There he is! Over there! See. Uncle Daniel...Uncle Daniel!' The child's shout of joy made Emma smile. She turned to look where the little girl was pointing and was completely taken aback to see Daniel Hutton hurriedly making his way towards them.

His face broke into a relieved smile as he lifted the little girl out of Emma's arms. 'Thank heavens for that! I was having kittens when you disappeared like that, you little horror!'

The little girl chuckled. 'You can't have kittens, Uncle Daniel. Only mummy cats have kittens!'

'Well, it felt like it!' Daniel's tone was rueful but there was no doubting that he had been extremely worried. He turned to Emma and smiled gratefully at her. 'I don't know how to thank you. One minute I had hold of Amy's hand and the next she'd disappeared. I must have aged ten years in the past few minutes when I couldn't find her!'

'I can imagine!' Emma laughed softly, not finding it in her heart to scold him for having let go of his niece when it was obvious that it had been an accident and not care-lessness.

She pushed back a strand of her short blond hair with a gloved hand as she searched for something to say. Although Daniel was never less than courteous whenever he visited the ward, she hadn't held a conversation with him in the whole six months he'd been at St Luke's. She wasn't sure whether she should just say goodbye or swop a few pleas-antries first.

She decided that the first option would be best. 'Well, I'd better let you—'

'Would you like a cup—?'

They both spoke together then stopped. Daniel smiled; his hazel eyes were full of amusement as he looked at her.

'Snap! Anyway, you go first. Mine wasn't anything important.'

Emma hesitated, wishing that she knew what he'd been going to say. Had he been about to invite her for a cup of coffee, perhaps? She sighed, realising that she might have missed her chance now. Funnily enough, she would have welcomed the opportunity to get to know him better, she realised.

'I was just going to say that I'd better not keep you. Amy—is it?' She carried on when Daniel nodded. 'Amy told me that you'd brought her into town to do some Christmas shopping.'

'That's right, although I'm beginning to regret it. I never imagined it would be such a scrum!' His tone was so wry that Emma laughed.

'I'm afraid it tends to get like this round Christmas time. Anyway, so long as Amy is all right I'd better be off.' She edged away, half hoping that he would stop her. She quickened her pace as it struck her how foolish that was. Why should Daniel want to detain her now that he had his niece back safe and sound?

'Emma, hold on a second!'

She stopped as she heard him calling her. It took a moment for him to reach her and she couldn't help noticing how uncomfortable he looked. It made her wonder what on earth he wanted to say to her. Well, there was one easy way to find out!

'Yes?'

'I…um, well, I…er…just wanted to ask you something,' he stumbled in obvious embarrassment.

It was so out of character for him to behave that way that Emma gaped at him. Daniel had exuded an aura of calm professionalism whenever she'd had occasion to speak to him in the past, although the conversation had always centred on work before. Obviously, he wanted to ask her something of a personal nature now and her heart leapt as she tried to work out what it might be.

'Yes?' she prompted, her mind racing. Was…was Daniel about to ask her out on a date perhaps? It was a tantalising idea, even though she had never thought about him in that context before. Oh, she'd been aware of Daniel ever since he had started work at St. Luke's—who hadn't? But when had her interest shifted from objective to subjective?

'Have you ever had the feeling that you could be making a complete idiot of yourself?' His tone was rueful now. Emma laughed softly and—she hoped—encouragingly.

'Frequently! But I try not to let it deter me. Look, Daniel, if there's something you want to ask me then just fire away. I promise you that I don't bite!'

'All right, then.' He took a deep breath then rushed on. 'Can you sew, Emma?'

CHAPTER TWO

'PARDON? D-did you say what I think you did?' Emma stared at Daniel in confusion and saw him grimace.

'Yes. Look, I knew it was a bad idea. Forget I said anything, will you?'

He turned to leave, his face a mixture of embarrassment and chagrin. However, there was no way that Emma could let him go without finding out why he had asked her such a peculiar question.

'Daniel, wait!' She caught hold of his sleeve and stopped him as he started to walk away. He turned to face her and she saw the indecision that darkened his hazel eyes. Obviously, he was torn between a desire to get himself out of an embarrassing situation and some other pressing need. It was what that need could be which piqued Emma's curiosity.

'You must have had a good reason for asking me that, so what was it?' She held up her hand when he opened his mouth because she could tell that he was going to deny it. 'Come on, why make such a big deal of this? I mean, it's not as though you'd asked me to do something *criminal!*'

His face broke into a wry smile. 'No. Not that I could imagine you being easily persuaded into a life of crime, Emma! You're far too nice for that. Which is probably why I managed to pluck up my courage in the first place.'

'Mmm, I see,' Emma murmured, aware that her heart had zinged at the compliment. So Daniel thought she was nice, did he? It was good to know that…very good indeed!

'Look, it's crazy, trying to have a conversation in the middle of this crush,' he continued. 'There's a café not far from here. Amy and I were going to have our tea there, so how about joining us? Then I can make a clean breast of everything.'

It was impossible to resist the entreaty in his voice and Emma didn't try. She smiled back at him. 'OK. I'm starving *and* dying of curiosity so how could I possibly refuse?'

'Great!' Daniel laughed as he set Amy on her feet and took tight hold of her hand. 'Emma is going to come and have tea with us, Amy. Won't that be nice?'

The little girl nodded happily. She took hold of Emma's hand as well as they crossed the road. Emma held on tightly to the child, smiling as she felt the cold little fingers gripping hers so trustingly. She loved children and Amy was so appealing with her dark curls and Daniel's beautiful eyes. He was obviously a very caring uncle to have offered to bring the child shopping after a hard day at work. It made Emma wonder where Amy's mother was and why she had delegated the task to Daniel.

'Right, what will you have?' Daniel handed her a menu as soon as they had sat down. The café was busy but they had managed to find a table in the corner. Emma glanced at the menu and quickly made up her mind.

'Sausage and chips, please. And a pot of tea,' she added.

Daniel shook his head. 'You nurses and your tea! I wonder if anyone has ever totted up how many gallons of the stuff is drunk each day in the average hospital?'

'I've never noticed any of the doctors refusing a cup when it's offered,' she replied tartly. 'You included!'

'All right, I hold up my hands and admit it—I am a tea-aholic!' Daniel laughed softly. A smile lightened his normally serious expression. 'You'll be telling me next to stand up and declare that my name is Daniel and I'm a tea addict!'

'What's an addict, Uncle Daniel?' Amy piped up curiously.

'It's someone who likes something very much even when it isn't really good for them,' he explained simply.

'Like when I ask you if I can have some chocolate and you tell me that it isn't good for me?' Amy frowned thoughtfully. 'But you drink lots and lots of cups of tea. Aren't they good for you?'

'Probably not, poppet. I'll have to be more careful in future, won't I?'

Daniel's tone was rueful as he exchanged a speaking look with Emma. She hid her smile, thinking how good he was with the little girl. The waitress arrived to take their order then Amy asked if she could go and look at the Christmas tree that had been set up in the window of the café.

Daniel sighed as he watched his niece run over to stand in front of it. 'She's so excited about it being Christmas. It makes me more determined that it's going to be special for her this year, despite what's happened.'

Emma frowned. 'What do you mean?'

Daniel picked up his knife and toyed with it. 'Amy's mother was killed in May. She was driving home from work when a lorry went out of control and ran into her car.'

'Oh, how dreadful!' Emma's soft grey eyes darkened with pain.

'It was.' Daniel sighed as he put the knife back on the table. 'Claire was only twenty-six and I still can't believe that she's gone. She was my sister, you see, and we were very close. Our parents were quite old when they married and they had us rather late in life. When they died it brought Claire and me even closer because we were all the family we had.'

'I can imagine,' Emma said softly, although maybe that wasn't quite true. She'd never had a family of her own— no brothers, sisters or parents—so she couldn't *really* know how it felt to form such a bond. However, she didn't want to discuss her situation right then.

'So what happened to Amy afterwards? I take it that she's living with her father?'

'No.' Daniel's tone was flat yet she heard the undercurrent of anger it held. It surprised her because he always seemed so in control. However, there was no denying the depth of his feelings as he looked over to where Amy was standing, entranced, before the shimmering silver Christmas tree.

'Claire wasn't married and she never told me who Amy's father was. They split up before Amy was born and he's never seen her.' Daniel's tone was harsh. 'It appears that he was married, only he forgot to mention that fact to Claire. The truth only emerged after she'd told him that she was pregnant. He didn't want anything to do with her or the baby after that.'

'No! Oh, how awful for her,' Emma exclaimed sadly.

'Yes. I can't imagine how any man could be so callous about his own child.' Daniel made an obvious effort to collect himself. 'Anyway, the long and the short of it is that Claire had appointed me as Amy's guardian when she was born so naturally I took responsibility for her after the accident.

'I was working in London at the time but it was out of the question to uproot Amy and take her there to live. That's why I applied for the job at St Luke's when it came up and moved here to Clearsea. At least, Amy still has contact with her friends and is living in a place she knows.'

It must have meant a lot of sacrifice for him to give up his life in the city and move to the small town. Emma was filled with admiration for him and said so.

'Not many people would have done that, Daniel. You gave up your own life to come here and take care of your niece. It must have been hard.'

'Not at all.' His face softened as he looked at the child. 'So long as Amy has everything she needs then that's all I ask. My only aim is to make sure that she's properly cared for. It's what Claire would have wanted me to do and I won't let her down.'

It couldn't be easy, though, looking after a small child and keeping up with the demands of his job, Emma thought. She knew how hard all the registrars worked, and Max Dennison was a particularly hard taskmaster. Maybe it explained why Daniel had been so reluctant to socialise since he'd started work at the hospital. With Amy to look after, his free time must be extremely limited.

'I still think it's wonderful that you should put your life on hold for Amy,' Emma said sincerely.

'It isn't a problem.' Daniel shrugged dismissively. 'I was happy to do it and I get a great deal of enjoyment out of being with her as well. Amy is a great little kid, and she's been really brave since Claire died. That's why it's so important to me that she has a wonderful Christmas. It's bound to be hard for her because she misses her mother, but I'm trying to keep things as normal as they would have been if Claire had still been here.'

He sat back with a weary sigh. 'The trouble is that I'm not Claire. I just can't do the things she used to do for Amy.'

'Which is why you asked me if I could sew?' Emma looked expectantly at him and he grinned ruefully.

'Mmm, you catch on fast, Emma Graham. But, then, I've noticed that before at work. You seem to know what a patient wants almost before she knows it herself!'

Emma felt herself blush at the compliment. It meant a lot to her because Daniel was so good at his own job. 'Thank you. Anyway, exactly what is it that you need sewn?' she said hurriedly, not wanting to dwell on how it had made her feel to hear him say that.

'An angel costume.' Daniel rolled his eyes as he saw her stunned expression. 'I knew I shouldn't have asked!'

'Don't be silly! I was just a bit surprised, that's all. I was imagining something like sewing on a button or…or darning socks!' she explained faintly.

'Do people still darn socks in this high-tech world?' The

look on his face was so comical that Emma burst out laughing.

'I doubt it. And for your information, no, I'm sure I'd be a very *bad* darner! In fact, making an angel costume sounds a far better deal to me. Just tell me what you need it for.'

'The school nativity play. Amy is an angel, and although I've managed to put together some pretty nifty wings and a halo there's no way that I and a sewing machine see eye to eye.' Daniel paused as the waitress arrived with their pot of tea.

Emma picked it up. 'Shall I pour?' She filled their cups, adding a little sugar to her own cup before sliding the bowl across the table to him.

'Thanks.' He added three large spoonfuls to his tea and stirred it thoughtfully. Emma tried not to smile but she couldn't help it. 'What?' he asked with a frown.

'Three spoons of sugar?' she teased.

He grimaced as he picked up his cup. 'I know. I keep trying to cut down but...' His rueful laugh made her laugh as well.

He put the cup back on its saucer and sighed. 'Anyway, enough of my foibles. Back to this wretched costume. I had hoped to get a local dressmaker to make it but the poor woman has broken her arm. I'm absolutely desperate and I don't know where to turn.'

'When exactly is the nativity play?' Emma asked with a frown.

'The day after tomorrow,' he replied dryly.

'Thursday?' She looked at him aghast.

'I know. It doesn't give me much time. I only found out last night about Mrs Walsh's accident and I've been in a panic ever since, which is why I threw caution to the winds and accosted you!'

He laughed but Emma could tell how worried he was. No wonder. Finding someone prepared to make Amy a costume in such a short space of time would be an impossible task at this time of the year.

Emma took a deep breath but there was no way that she could refuse to help in the circumstances. 'I'm not the world's most brilliant sewer but I'll give it a go if you want me to.'

'Would you? Really?' Daniel could barely hide his delight. He reached over the table and squeezed her hand. 'I don't know how to thank you, Emma.'

'Is Emma your girlfriend, Uncle Daniel?' a small voice piped.

'No, I'm afraid not.' Daniel let go of Emma's hand and she let out the breath she hadn't known she'd been holding. Under cover of the table she ran her hand down her skirt, feeling the faint tingling sensation in her fingers. It bothered her that Daniel's touch should have left such an impression on her because she didn't understand it.

She fixed a determined smile to her face as Amy came and sat beside her. The child's face was tinged with disappointment as she looked from Emma to her uncle. 'Oh. I thought she was because you were holding hands. Jamie said that his mummy and daddy always hold hands 'cos they love one another.'

'I, um, well, that's nice, poppet.' Daniel looked a shade embarrassed. However, he soon recovered his composure. Maybe the thought of him being in love with her had thrown him for a moment, but it hadn't made any lasting impression, Emma thought, then wondered why the idea had stung a little.

She forced herself to concentrate as he quickly explained to his niece that Emma had agreed to make her costume.

'And it will be ready for the play?' Amy asked immediately. 'It's on Thursday…that's not tomorrow but the next day after tomorrow,' she explained carefully.

'I know. Which means that I shall have to set to work on it as soon as possible.'

'I don't suppose you could start tonight?' Daniel put in quickly. 'You could come home with us after we've finished here and then you could cut it out or measure it or whatever you need to do. Of course, you might already have plans for this evening,' he added as an afterthought.

'I haven't.' Emma took a deep breath because it felt as though she had just stepped onto a roller-coaster and was being hurtled along. Half an hour ago she had been on her way to do some shopping, before spending the evening watching television. Now it seemed that she was to spend the evening with Daniel and his niece!

She smiled as the waitress arrived with their meals. 'We'd better eat up. We have a lot to do this evening!'

Daniel's home was a surprise. When they pulled up in front of the modern little semi on one of the new developments on the outskirts of the town, Emma couldn't help thinking that it was the last place she would have expected him to live. However, she didn't remark on it as she got out of the car and waited while he helped Amy out of the back seat. Hunting in his pocket for his keys, he unlocked the front door.

'Come on in. And excuse the mess. Mornings are a bit hectic in this household and I haven't had time to clear up, with going into town,' he explained, leading the way along the hall.

Opening the door to the living room, he stepped aside. Emma went into the room and took a long look around, but if she'd hoped to find any clue as to what made Daniel tick through his surroundings she would have been sorely disappointed.

Daniel laughed softly as he followed her into the room. 'I think the best way to describe it is very *beige*.'

Emma chuckled at that. 'Well, it certainly seems to be the predominant colour! Do I take it that it's a favourite of yours?'

'No way!' Daniel rolled his eyes. 'I inherited it when I moved in. This was the show house so the furniture and fittings came as part of the package. If and when I ever get time I intend to paint the walls shocking pink or…or puce. Anything but this uniform beige colour!'

Emma smiled as she took another look round the small room. The walls were a pale shade of beige, the fitted carpet a darker shade. Even the suite was beige, although there were a few brightly coloured cushions scattered across it which helped to relieve the monotony.

'I imagine it's hard, finding time to decorate, with everything else you have to do,' she observed lightly.

'It is. There just aren't enough hours in the day, to be honest. Anyway, give me your coat then I'll find the material and show you what the costume is supposed to look like.'

He took her coat, shooing Amy upstairs to fetch the material. Emma sat on the sofa until they came back. She didn't have to wait very long.

'This is it.' Daniel shook out a length of white cotton fabric for her inspection then hunted a piece of paper out of the bag it had been wrapped in. 'And this is how the costume is supposed to look when it's finished.'

Emma took the paper from him and studied the design. It looked quite simple, thankfully enough, little more than a long-sleeved T-shirt from what she could tell, although it would need to be long enough to reach Amy's feet.

'That doesn't look too difficult,' she observed thoughtfully. 'It's pretty basic and shouldn't take long to make once it's cut out.'

'Won't it? Oh, that's great!' Daniel didn't try to hide his relief and Emma smiled.

'A weight off your mind, I can tell,' she teased.

'A ton weight and I don't mind admitting it.' He looked at Amy and his hazel eyes sparkled with laughter. 'Hopefully, you won't have to wear a bed sheet wrapped around you after all, sprog!'

'You wouldn't really have made me wear a sheet, would you, Uncle Daniel?' Amy asked worriedly.

He bent and hugged her. 'Of course I wouldn't! I was just teasing you. Now, will you go and fetch Mummy's sewing basket for Emma, please?'

He sighed as the little girl hurried away. 'I sometimes forget how literally children take things. I must be more careful what I say in future. I certainly don't want Amy worrying unnecessarily because of some chance remark I've made.'

'It must be hard, adapting.' Emma hurried on when he looked quizzically at her. She hoped that he wouldn't think she was being presumptuous but she didn't enjoy watching him blaming himself when there was no need. 'Bringing up a child isn't easy, especially when you have been thrust in at the deep end, so to speak.'

'No, I suppose not. I'm so aware of my responsibilities that I probably worry more than I should do about getting everything right.' He smiled. 'Thanks, Emma. I shall bear that in mind in future and not keep giving myself such a hard time. I want to be the perfect parent but I'm probably causing myself more headaches than if I took a more re-laxed approach!'

Amy came back just then so the subject was dropped. However, as she got out the tape measure, Emma couldn't help hoping that Daniel would do as he'd said he would. It was a shame if he was putting so much pressure on him-self when he was doing such a wonderful job.

She sighed as she jotted down Amy's measurements on a scrap of paper. She doubted if Daniel would appreciate her concern! He had always struck her as a man who was very much in control of his own life.

Once she had the measurements she needed, Emma rolled up the tape measure and put it back in the sewing basket. 'I think I've got everything I need now. Obviously, I'll have to make the dress then check that it fits properly, but we don't have a lot of time to spare before the play.'

'Maybe you could come here for tea tomorrow?' Daniel suggested promptly. He laughed when Amy clapped her hands. 'Obviously, Amy thinks it's a good idea as well.'

'Will you, Emma? Will you come again tomorrow?' Amy demanded eagerly.

'Well, yes, of course. If that's what you want.' Emma tried to temper the small glow of happiness with a large dose of common sense. Naturally, Daniel was eager to invite her to his home again when she had to make sure Amy's costume fitted her. However, when he smiled at her she couldn't help wondering if it was *only* because of her dressmaking skills that he'd issued the invitation…

'It is. If the costume doesn't fit then you'll be right here on the spot to make any alterations.' His tone was pleasant enough but it pricked her bubble like a pin stuck into a balloon.

Emma busied herself with fastening the sewing basket so that he wouldn't see how disappointed she felt. How silly of her to feel like that! Daniel had invited her here purely for his niece's sake. There had been nothing *personal* about the invitation. It had been purely practical.

'So, you're pretty confident that you can make the costume in time?' he asked as she stood up.

'I can't see it will be that difficult,' she told him quietly, hoping her voice wouldn't betray her disappointment. 'I'll cut it out when I get home and it shouldn't take more than a couple of hours to sew it all together.'

'Which means that most of your evening will be taken up doing it. Obviously, I shall pay you for your time and trouble, Emma,' he offered at once.

She shook her head, feeling a little bit hurt that he should imagine she wanted payment. 'Don't be silly. I'm happy to do it.'

'Are you sure?' Daniel persisted. 'I'm sure you can think of a lot better things to do with your free time rather than slaving over a sewing machine!'

'It isn't a problem. Really.' Emma quickly folded up the fabric and popped it back in its bag. 'Right, I think that's everything I need now.'

'I'll drive you home.' Daniel shook his head when she opened her mouth to tell him there was no need. 'No, I insist. It's the least I can do after you've been so kind.'

He went to fetch his coat so Emma didn't protest any further. Amy skipped down the path ahead of them and got into the car. Daniel made sure her seat belt was securely fastened then helped Emma into the passenger seat.

It didn't take them long to drive back into town. Emma's flat was on the top floor of one of the old Victorian houses facing the sea front. Daniel peered up at the house then looked across the road. The tide was coming in and they could hear it lapping at the shore now that the car had stopped.

'You must have a great view from here. I love these old houses. They are so full of character, aren't they?'

'Too full of it sometimes,' Emma replied ruefully. 'You try dealing with the quirks of ancient plumbing when you're in a rush to get ready for work! Take it from me, there's nothing to beat a nice modern bathroom with hot and cold water running *every* time you turn on a tap!'

'I shall bear that in mind! Maybe there's something to be said for modern houses after all.'

'Why did you choose to live where you do if you're not a fan of new houses?' she asked curiously.

'Because it's close to Amy's school and where all her friends live,' he replied simply. 'It made more sense to buy a property there.'

Even though it wouldn't have been his ideal choice if the circumstances had been different, Emma thought. It struck her once again just how much he'd been prepared to sacrifice for the sake of his niece. However, she didn't say anything as she opened the car door because she knew that he would be embarrassed to hear her praise him again.

'I'd better let you get home,' she said instead, stepping out of the car. She paused to smile at the child before closing the door. 'Bye, Amy. I'll see you tomorrow.'

'Thanks again for everything, Emma. I really do appreciate it, you know.' Daniel leaned over to speak to her. His face was lit by the glow from a nearby streetlight and Emma felt her heart roll over as she thought how handsome he looked as he smiled up at her.

She smiled back, praying that he wouldn't notice anything amiss. 'You're very welcome. I...I'll see you tomorrow, then.'

He raised his hand in acknowledgement then started the engine as she slammed the car door. Emma stood on the pavement and watched as he drove away. There was a funny bubbly feeling in the pit of her stomach, a sort of nervous excitement. She couldn't recall ever feeling anything like it before, apart from when she'd sat her final exams...

She gave a snort of disgust as she let herself into the house. Equating Daniel Hutton's effect on her with an attack of exam nerves just showed what a sorry state her life was in! It was her own fault, of course. She'd had her fair share of invitations from various male members of staff at St Luke's but, increasingly, she'd found herself turning them down. What was she holding out for? A knight in shining armour to come along on his white charger and carry her off to his castle? Huh!

Emma hurried up the stairs to her flat, annoyed with herself for the way she'd been behaving recently. Dropping her bag onto a chair, she went to haul out the sewing machine from the bottom of her wardrobe and set it up in the living room. The sooner she got this done, the better. Then she would start making a few changes to her life. She would do what most of her friends had done and settle for some pleasant man. No more waiting around for a knight to show up. They tended to be very thin on the ground!

Unbidden, a face sprang to mind and she sighed. Daniel Hutton would make a perfect knight in shining armour but he was way out of her league!

CHAPTER THREE

'WHAT were you up to last night? You must have been doing something to put those bags under your eyes, Emma Graham. Come on, tell!'

Emma sighed as she heard the speculation in Linda's voice. It was just gone seven and she was already late arriving for work. Taking a clean white uniform top out of her locker, she popped it over her head and smoothed it down over her trim hips. 'I stayed up late, sewing, if you must know.'

'Sewing?' Linda parroted. She folded her arms and stared at Emma. 'You can do better than that! Nobody looks like that after a night spent *sewing!*'

'They do if they've stayed up till one o'clock in the morning, trying to get it finished,' Emma informed her tartly. She quickly laced up her regulation shoes then headed for the door. 'Come on. Sister will have a fit if we don't get a move on.'

Linda shook her head. 'Oh, no, you don't! I intend to get to the bottom of this before we set one foot out of this staffroom. What were you sewing? And why did you need to stay up so late to get it finished?'

Emma sighed as she realised that she'd painted herself into a corner. Did she want to tell Linda that she'd stayed up late, making a costume for Daniel's niece? It would be bound to lead to more questions and the thought of betraying his confidence by telling Linda about his sister and everything was out of the question. If Daniel had wanted people to know about his private affairs, he would have told them.

'I just wanted to get it done, that's all,' she hedged.

31

'But it must have been something special.' Linda was like a dog with the proverbial bone as she scented a juicy story. 'What was it? A new dress for the dance, perhaps? I didn't think you were coming. Have you decided to go with Mike Humphreys after all?'

'I...um, yes.' Emma groaned as she was pushed into telling the fib. Mike Humphreys was a houseman on Max Dennison's team and he'd asked her to go to the Christmas dance with him a few days previously. Emma had been caught off guard and had ended up promising to think about it because she hadn't been able to come up with an excuse. Now she might have no choice but to accept Mike's invitation just to give credence to her lie!

'Good for you! It's about time you had some fun.' Linda was full of enthusiasm as they hurriedly made their way into the ward. Luckily, Sister Carter was busy in her office, taking an incoming call, so she didn't see them arriving. She was a tartar about time-keeping and woe betide any members of staff who didn't arrive at least five minutes before their shift was officially due to commence.

Emma began her round of the ward, checking the obs that the night staff had done. The patients had been given their breakfasts and Linda's first task of the day was to clear away the dirty dishes. She managed to do so and keep up with Emma as she made her way from bed to bed.

'So, what made you decide to go to the dance in the end?' her friend persisted, piling cups and bowls haphazardly onto the trolley.

'Oh, I just thought I may as well.' Emma shrugged, hoping that Linda would take the hint and not keep asking questions. It was a vain hope, of course, because her friend had no intention of letting the subject drop.

'Actually, Mike's quite fanciable if you like that little-boy-lost type. Of course, he isn't Daniel Hutton but, then, who is?' Linda whisked Jean Horrocks's cup and saucer off her locker and dumped them on the pile of crockery.

'Now, there's a man I'd stay up sewing for…or anything else for that matter!'

'You and me both, love,' Jean Horrocks put in. 'He's got those lovely come-to-bed eyes, hasn't he? Makes me go all shivery, just thinking about him.'

Emma had to bite her lip to hold back a snappy reproof. For some reason she resented hearing them talk about Daniel that way. She picked up Jean's chart then paused as it hit her that she might be jealous. Surely not. What right did she have to feel jealous about Daniel?

'Nothing wrong, is there, Staff? I did feel a bit woozy through the night and wondered if it was my blood pressure being too high. Or maybe too low. I read something in a magazine about that—it said it was really dangerous!'

Emma gathered her scattered wits as she heard the panic in Jean's voice. 'There is nothing wrong, Mrs Horrocks. Your blood pressure and everything else is fine. I…I was just checking that your notes were up to date, that's all.'

'And what could have gone wrong when you had dishy Daniel to do your op?' put in the irrepressible Linda.

'Nothing, of course. Silly of me to go worrying, wasn't it?' Jean Horrocks smiled at the mention of Daniel's name. 'I told him straight, I did, that I was more than happy to leave myself in his capable hands. Is he married, do you know, love?'

'No idea. Dr Hutton is the original mystery man and plays his cards very close to his chest,' Linda replied cheerfully. 'So if you find out anything about him, Mrs Horrocks, do let us know. We shall all be eternally grateful to you!'

Emma moved away. She was glad when Linda got delayed as Jean asked her another question. Maybe she was being overly sensitive but all this talk about Daniel's private life was starting to grate.

People should mind their own business, she thought crossly, then realised that it was natural curiosity which had prompted the speculation. She should see it as that and not get too defensive. After all, Daniel hadn't asked her to keep their meeting a secret so there was no real reason why she shouldn't have mentioned it. However, it felt wrong to start spreading gossip about him.

The morning flew past. There was a bit of panic just before break-time when an emergency case was sent up from A and E. Paula Walters, a woman in her mid-thirties, had been rushed in by ambulance when she'd started hae-morrhaging. She'd been at work when it had happened and was doubly distressed by the thought of her colleagues hav-ing witnessed what had gone on.

She'd lost a fair amount of blood and the staff in A and E had set up a drip. However, they'd been too busy to deal with the problem any further, which was why Paula had been sent straight to the ward.

Emma got her settled then checked that the intravenous line was working properly. Paula hadn't said much since she'd been brought to the ward. She seemed a little dazed by what had happened, which was no wonder.

Emma smiled reassuringly at her. 'You'll feel a lot better once your fluid level is back to what it should be. And the doctor will be here soon to examine you.'

'Can you get a message to my fiancé? I was supposed to meet him for lunch and he'll be worried.' Paula's eyes filled. 'We were going to the registrar's office to book our wedding, you see.'

'Of course. Can you give me a number where I can reach him?' Emma asked at once.

'In my diary…under Edmonds. Stephen Edmonds.' Paula pointed to her bag which was lying on top of her bedside locker. Emma opened it and found the diary. She made a note of the telephone number then put the diary back.

'I'll put your bag in this locker,' she told Paula. 'It's always safer not to leave valuables lying around.'

'Thanks. My engagement ring is in it so I don't want to

take any chances.' Paula managed a shaky smile. 'Stephen and I were taking it in to the jeweller's to have it made smaller as it's a bit loose.'

'Sister could put it in the safe in her office, if you'd prefer,' Emma offered immediately, but Paula shook her head.

'Thanks, but I'd like to keep it with me.' Tears welled into her eyes all of a sudden. 'I feel so awful about what happened. I was in the middle of this big meeting and I was the only woman there. How on earth am I going to face everyone again?'

'I shouldn't worry about that, Paula,' Emma said quickly. 'I know it must have been embarrassing for you, but it's just one of those things. Your main concern at the moment is to get yourself well again. Have you had any problems like this in the past?'

'Have I!' Paula sighed. 'I've come to dread the time when my period is due. It's got to the point where it lasts for a couple of weeks and it's so heavy that I live in fear of my clothes getting stained.'

Emma frowned. 'What has your GP said?'

Paula looked embarrassed. 'I haven't been to see him. I've been so busy with work that I don't seem to have the time to spare. I've just kept plodding on, hoping that a miracle would happen.'

'Unfortunately, miracles are rather rare,' Emma observed dryly, earning herself a rueful smile from the other woman.

'I know. I've been very silly but I've learned my lesson. I won't be such a fool about my health in the future, believe me!'

'Good. Now just try to relax. The doctor will be here very shortly to examine you.'

Emma drew the curtains around the bed. She sighed as she went to check what Sister Carter wanted her to do next. How many times had she heard a similar story since she'd started working on the obs and gynae unit? Far too many women dismissed the problems they were having because they were so busy trying to do a hundred jobs at once. When you were mother, lover, home-maker and wage-earner all rolled into one, it was hard to find time for yourself.

Max Dennison arrived for his ward round a short time later so he examined Paula. Sister Carter accompanied him but she'd asked Emma to make sure that the patient was ready, which was how Emma happened to be by the bed when the team arrived. She acknowledged Mr Dennison's curt nod then felt her stomach give a little jolt as she saw that Daniel was with him.

'Good morning, Staff,' he said formally, although there was a bit more warmth in his smile than she'd ever seen before.

'Dr Hutton,' she replied equally formally. She moved away from the bed as Mr Dennison went to take his place, holding the curtain open so that the others could follow him. Daniel hung back, letting Sister Carter and Mike Humphreys go ahead of him. There was a hint of concern on his face as he studied the dark circles under Emma's eyes.

'I hope you didn't stay up too late last night, sewing Amy's costume,' he said quietly, so that the others couldn't hear.

Emma shrugged. 'Not that late.'

He sighed. 'I feel awful now. It wasn't fair to put you on the spot like that.'

'Rubbish! If I hadn't wanted to help, I wouldn't have offered.' She caught Sister's eye and quickly moved out of the way, but she couldn't help smiling when she thought about how quick Daniel had been to spot the signs of tiredness on her face. Obviously, he noticed things like that about her...

Of course he did! He was a doctor, wasn't he? He was trained to spot symptoms and draw conclusions. The fact that he had homed in on her tiredness didn't mean that he took a *personal* interest in how she looked!

It was a sobering thought and it helped to show her how foolishly she was behaving. Daniel had asked for her help simply because there had been no one else to ask. She had to put what had happened into that context and not start spinning silly little fantasies around it.

She had managed to talk some sense into herself by the time she went for lunch. Linda went with her and she groaned as she read the day's menu chalked up on the board by the door.

'Fish pie! Oh, shoot the chef, someone…please!'

Emma laughed. 'Fish is good for you,' she teased. 'It's slimming, full of vitamins and wonderful brain food.'

'Maybe it is, but give me a nice big juicy burger and chips any day of the week!' Linda picked up a package of sandwiches and plonked it despondently on her tray. She suddenly brightened. 'Ah, there's Mike over there. Let's sit with him. Seeing as you're coming to the dance now, we could make up a foursome—you, me, Mike and Gary.'

'Oh, but…' Emma didn't get any further as Linda hurried away. She paid for her meal then slowly made her way across the canteen. It didn't help when she saw that Daniel was also sitting at the table. The thought of discussing her forthcoming date with Mike made her feel uncomfortable, although there was no reason why it should have done. Daniel Hutton had no claims on her, apart from needing her skills a seamstress!

'Hi, Em!' Mike grinned as she put her tray on the table. He hauled out a chair so that she had little choice but to sit next to him. However, she was deeply conscious of Daniel, watching her from across the table as she sat down.

She looked up but he avoided her eyes as he turned to Linda. 'So the four of you are going to make a night of it, then?'

'Yes. It should be good fun. The hospital dos usually

are.' Linda pretended to have been struck by a sudden wonderful thought. 'Why don't you come, Daniel? You could come with us then you wouldn't have to be on your own—not that you'd be short of a partner for long, I imagine!'

Linda treated him to a flirtatious smile and Emma snorted in disgust. She suddenly realised that everyone had turned to look at her and she coughed.

'A bit of a tickle in my throat,' she mumbled, blushing.

'Here, have a drink of this.' Mike passed her his glass of mineral water and she obediently took a sip.

'Thanks,' she muttered, passing the glass back to him.

'You're welcome.' He lowered his voice so that the other two couldn't hear him. 'I was really chuffed when Linda told me that you'd decided to come to the dance with me, Em.'

'I…um, yes. It was good of you to invite me,' she said, trying to inject a little enthusiasm into her voice. Fortunately, Mike didn't seem to notice anything amiss but, oddly, she could tell that Daniel was watching her closely.

Did he suspect that she wasn't as keen on the idea as Mike was? she wondered, then gave herself a mental shake. Of course not!

Mike's face split into a wide smile. 'I've been going to ask you out for ages, to be honest. Some of the guys warned me that you don't go out on dates so I've been a bit cagey. However, I wish I hadn't wasted so much time now.'

There was a note of triumph in his voice and Emma sighed. Did Mike see her acceptance as a sign that he'd succeeded where all the others had failed? Probably! Although he was pleasant enough, his attitude was still rather immature so she could well imagine that he enjoyed the thought of scoring points off his friends.

'I'd better be off.' Daniel turned to the younger man. 'Don't forget that Max wants you to check on Paula Walters again this afternoon. He's hoping to schedule her for surgery once he's had the results of the ultrasound scan.'

Mike groaned. 'Oh, save me from weeping women! I can't wait to finish my stint on Obs and Gynae. Why do they make such a fuss when most of these ops are purely routine?'

'Because they aren't routine to them.' Daniel's tone was icy. 'I suggest you bear that in mind, otherwise you could find yourself being moved sooner than you expected.'

There was silence after Daniel left. Mike shrugged but there was little doubt that he was embarrassed to have been told off like that. 'That's put me in my place, hasn't it? It must be wonderful to know that you're perfect, like our Dr Hutton obviously thinks he is!'

'I don't believe that Daniel thinks any such thing,' Emma said at once, immediately springing to Daniel's defence. 'He was just pointing out that you need to treat people sensitively.'

'And, obviously, you agree with him, Emma.' Mike looked annoyed. 'Maybe it isn't a good idea, you coming with me to the dance, if that's how you feel.'

He pushed back his chair and left. Linda sighed as she watched him storming out of the canteen. 'Not very tactful, Emma. You could have at least *pretended* to be on Mike's side, seeing as he'd asked you out.'

Emma shrugged as she unwrapped her sandwich. 'I was just being truthful. If Mike doesn't like it then it's his hard luck.'

'You were rather quick to take sides, though. Come on, confess; you have a bit of a thing about our Daniel, haven't you?'

'Of course not!' she denied, too quickly. She saw Linda's brows rise and moderated her tone. The last thing she wanted was her friend throwing out hints every time Daniel set foot in the ward! 'I just happen to agree with him in this instance, that's all.'

Mercifully, that seemed to bring the subject to a close. They finished their lunch then went back to the ward. Alison Banks was being sent home that afternoon and Emma helped her pack her bag. The girl was looking a lot happier than she had been, mainly, Emma suspected, because her husband had been granted compassionate leave and would be home for Christmas. Being on your own at Christmas could be particularly hard, as she knew only too well.

Mike barely looked at her when he came to the ward to check on Paula Walters. Emma ignored his ill humour as she accompanied him to the patient's bed. If Mike chose to behave like that, it was up to him. Paula's fiancé, Stephen, had arrived soon after lunch and he waited outside in the corridor while Paula was examined.

Emma tidied the bed after Mike had finished then went to fetch Stephen back in. She found him looking very distressed.

'Is anything wrong, Mr Edmonds?' she asked solicitously.

'I…I hadn't realised what it meant when Paula told me that she might need an operation.'

The poor man looked so dazed that Emma knew she couldn't let him return to the ward in such a state. She quickly led him into the office and closed the door. Sister Carter had been called away to deal with a query about supplies so there was nobody in there.

'Sit down, Mr Edmonds, and tell me what this is all about.' Emma waited until he had sat down. 'Obviously, it has something to do with your fiancée's operation.'

'Yes. That young doctor…Humphreys, was it?' He carried on when Emma nodded. 'Well, he just told me that Paula is going to need a hysterectomy. I hadn't realised that was what was going to happen, you see. I mean, we're planning on getting married and we both want a family but…but that won't be possible now.'

Emma could tell how distraught he was and no wonder. She felt very angry with Mike for telling the poor man something like that then just walking off. It was unforgivable, especially as she wasn't sure that it was even true.

According to Paula's notes, there was a strong suspicion that she was suffering from fibroids, benign tumours which grew within the uterus. Her symptoms—the excessive and prolonged menstrual bleeding and tenderness in the abdomen—pointed to that, although at this stage it wasn't possible to rule out other causes, which was why Max Dennison had ordered the ultrasound scan.

However, from what Emma had read, there had been no decision made about Paula undergoing a hysterectomy. Although in very severe cases it was often considered the best method of treatment, there were other options, like a myomectomy. Removing each fibroid separately from the uterus meant that a woman's fertility would be unaffected.

She decided that she needed to speak to either Max Dennison or Daniel so that they could explain the situation to Paula's fiancé. She certainly didn't want him upsetting Paula when there might be no need.

'I'll get one of the senior doctors to have a word with you, Mr Edmonds. Just bear with me while I have them paged.'

She put through a call to the switchboard. Sister Carter popped her head round the door then nodded when Emma mouthed that she wouldn't be long. Sister believed firmly in delegating responsibility to her staff so Emma wasn't worried about overstepping her authority. She was relieved when Daniel returned her call almost immediately.

'I wonder if you could come and have a word with Paula Walter's fiancé, Dr Hutton?' she asked calmly, although she couldn't ignore the jolt her heart had given when she'd heard his voice.

'Of course. Do I take it there is a problem, Emma?'

He'd never called her by her first name at work before

and she felt herself blush. It was an effort to keep her tone level, although she heard the slightly breathless note it held even if Daniel didn't.

'I think so.'

'I'll be up straight away.' He didn't question her further but hung up. Emma went to meet him at the lift, smiling when he appeared less than two minutes later.

'You were quick,' she teased.

'Your wish is my command, ma'am!' he replied with a light laugh. He glanced towards the office and sobered. 'So, what is this all about, Emma? I know you wouldn't have called me if you weren't worried.'

She quickly explained what had gone on and how upset Stephen Edmonds was. Daniel's face was grim by the time she finished.

'What a damned stupid thing to do!' He made an obvious effort to collect himself. 'I'm sorry. I know Humphreys is your boyfriend but he had no right to give out information like that. Quite apart from the fact that it's unethical to discuss a patient's condition with a third party, what he said isn't true. Max won't decide on the best course of treatment until he's seen the results of the ultrasound.'

'That's what I thought.' Emma grimaced. 'I hope Mike won't get into trouble…'

'Don't worry. I'll make sure he doesn't find out about your involvement,' Daniel said, curtly interrupting her. 'I don't want to make things awkward for you, Emma.'

That wasn't what she'd meant but there wasn't time to correct him as Daniel excused himself and went straight to the office. Emma went back to the ward and quickly explained to Sister Carter what had gone on. The older woman immediately agreed that she'd done the right thing. When Stephen came back into the ward a short time later, looking far less stressed, Emma breathed a sigh of relief. At least Daniel had been able to set the poor man's mind at rest.

The afternoon passed without any more hiccups. Jean Horrocks was discharged and left looking like a different woman to the nervous creature who had been admitted two days earlier. However, it didn't stop her making the most of the occasion. As she left the ward, Emma could hear Jean telling her husband that she wouldn't be able to do *anything* when she got home, not after her operation, so he'd have to do all the cooking and cleaning while she rested.

Emma exchanged a wry smile with Shirley Rogers as she went to strip Jean's bed. And why not? There had to be a few perks for being a woman!

The end of the shift arrived at last and they handed over to the night staff. Emma hurried to change out of her uniform. She wasn't sure which bus she would need to catch to get to Daniel's house so she would have to go all the way into town and ask at the depot.

'You're in a rush. Got a date, then?' Linda rolled up her uniform top and thrust it unceremoniously into a carrier bag.

'No, I've just got a lot to do, that's all,' Emma explained briefly.

'Not the dress again? Does that mean you and Mike have patched things up after that little episode at lunchtime?'

'I haven't spoken to him.' Emma closed her locker then picked up her bag. She had brought Amy's costume with her to save time. She mentally crossed her fingers that it would fit the child. She didn't have enough time to make another one and she couldn't bear to imagine the little girl's disappointment.

Linda accompanied her as they left the hospital via the staff entrance. It was obvious that she was still dying to know what Emma had planned for that night. 'Do you want a lift?' she offered guilelessly. 'If you're not going straight home, maybe I could drop you off somewhere.'

'No, it's fine, thanks. I'm going into town, as it happens,

and you don't want to get caught up in the rush, do you?' Emma hid her smile as Linda hesitated. However, common sense finally prevailed and her friend departed.

Emma set off down the path, hoping that she hadn't missed the bus that would take her into the town centre. St Luke's had been built on the outskirts of the town to allow for future expansion but it did mean that anyone working at the hospital had to travel there by bus or car. She'd almost reached the gates when she heard a car horn tooting behind her.

She looked round, expecting to see Linda, and was so surprised when she discovered that it had been Daniel trying to attract her attention that she just stared at him.

He wound down the window and stuck his head out. 'Come on, hop in. We're causing a traffic jam.'

Emma glanced up the path and flushed as she saw the cars which had needed to stop because Daniel had done so. She was very conscious of the interested glances being cast her way as she hurriedly got into his car. There was little doubt in her mind that the news would spread like wildfire through the hospital, and how would Daniel feel about that?

'What's wrong? You look as though you've lost the proverbial pound.' He paused and there was an oddly strained note in his voice when he continued. 'Humphreys hasn't been giving you a hard time about helping me with Amy's costume, has he? I was careful to keep your name out of the conversation when I spoke to him about Paula Walters but he wasn't pleased about being reprimanded by me twice in one day.'

'It's got nothing to do with Mike,' Emma declared. However, it was obvious that Daniel didn't believe her.

'Hasn't it? Look, Emma, the last thing I want is to cause problems between you and your boyfriend…'

'He isn't my boyfriend!' Emma saw Daniel look at her and grimaced as she realised how loudly she'd said that.

However, it was way past time that she set the record straight.

'Mike invited me to the Christmas dance, that's all,' she explained more quietly.

Daniel shrugged but his face was set as he slowed for the traffic lights as they changed to red. 'If you agreed to go to the dance with him then obviously you must like him.'

'Yes, I do. Well, I did before today. But it was sort of…of casual, if you know what I mean. Mike is just some-one I work with and he's always seemed pleasant enough…' She tailed off, wishing she had left well alone. Daniel probably now thought she was the sort of woman who accepted a date from just anyone!

'But he doesn't make your heart beat faster or rockets go off?'

She had to laugh at the droll note in his voice. 'Hardly! And as for accepting the invitation, well that was more by accident than design, I'm afraid.'

'Really? You can't leave it at that, Emma. I'm dying of curiosity now.' His smile was full of amusement and she felt her breath catch. Daniel was disturbingly handsome even when he wore his usual solemn expression, but when he smiled… Well!

She looked away, afraid that her own expression might be too revealing. 'It was a mix-up, that's all. Linda wanted to know why I looked so tired this morning and I told her that I'd stayed up late, sewing. Somehow she got it into her head that I'd been making a new dress for the dance.'

'And she knew that Mike had asked you to go with him and so it snowballed from there?' Daniel's tone was wry. 'It seems to me that I've caused you an awful lot of prob-lems, Emma. I'm sorry.'

'It doesn't matter. I could have told her the truth, of course, but I wasn't sure if you wanted people to know about your private affairs.' She shrugged when he glanced at her. 'You've kept yourself very much to yourself since you started at St Luke's.'

'I have. And that has been more by accident than design as well. I simply don't have time for a private life any more, with Amy to look after. It's easier not to get involved.'

Did that mean that he wasn't planning on getting involved in a relationship? The thought was unsettling, although it really wasn't any of her business. What Daniel did with his life was his affair. Yet it was one thing to know that and another to accept it.

'Anyway, I don't want you being put under pressure like that again, Emma. The fact that I am looking after Amy isn't a secret. People are bound to find out.'

They had reached the estate where he lived by then. He drew up in front of a semi very similar to his own and turned to her as he switched off the engine. 'Amy stays with a childminder after school. It's the same person Claire always used so she's quite happy with the arrangement. I'll fetch her then we can go home.'

'Fine.' Emma agreed. She watched as Daniel strode up the path and knocked on the door. It was a relief to know that she didn't have to keep everything a secret, although that didn't mean she intended to start spreading gossip, of course.

She sighed as she remembered all the curious eyes watching her as she'd got into his car that night. The gossip mill would already have started working if she knew anything about the hospital! Yet what was there to gossip about exactly? All she'd done had been to agree to make a costume for Daniel's niece. Once she'd checked that it fitted Amy, that would be that. Daniel wouldn't need her help any longer, would he?

She felt a sudden painful tug at her heart as she watched him coming down the path with Amy. She couldn't help wishing that she could be part of his life for a lot longer than just one day.

CHAPTER FOUR

'OH, IT'S beautiful! Look, Uncle Daniel…look at me!'

Emma smiled as Amy went rushing out of the room to find her uncle. The angel costume had proved to be a perfect fit and Emma was delighted that her hard work hadn't been in vain. She stood up as Daniel came into the room, smiling as she saw the astonishment on his face.

'How on earth did you manage to make it look so good in such a short time?' Daniel fingered the silver trim Emma had stitched so carefully around the neck and edges of the sleeves. 'It must have taken you hours of sewing.'

Emma shrugged modestly. 'It wasn't all that difficult. Once I'd got it cut out, it was just a question of stitching it all together. I still have to do the hem because I didn't want to take a chance on getting the length wrong.'

'Can I put my wings and hello on, Uncle Daniel… please?' Amy demanded.

'It's a halo, sprog,' he gently corrected her. 'You can try them on after we've had tea. It's almost ready now so why don't you take off your costume and set the table?'

Amy sighed. 'All right. But I can put it on again later, can't I? Promise?'

'Cross my heart!' Daniel made a cross over his heart and Amy laughed. She let Emma help her out of the costume then ran out of the room and they could hear the sound of cutlery clattering as she set about laying the table.

Daniel picked up the gown and examined the neatly sewn seams. 'I'm amazed. A dressmaker couldn't have made a better job than you have, Emma. Where did you learn to sew like this?'

'I taught myself.' She smiled reminiscently as she stowed

the offcuts of cloth back in the bag. 'I was so hard up when I left the home that I couldn't afford to buy any clothes so I made them instead. It was so much cheaper.'

'The home? What do you mean by that?' Daniel frowned as he carefully laid the costume over the back of a chair.

'I was brought up in care and lived in a children's home until I was sixteen,' Emma explained quietly, wondering how he would react to the information. People were usually curious when they found out about her background, wanting to know all the details.

'Really?' He captured her hands, holding them lightly as he studied her. 'That must have been hard for you. I imagine the worst thing of all is the lack of permanency in your life when you're brought up in care.'

Emma blinked because she'd never expected him to say that. The people who'd run the home had been kind enough and all the children living there had been well cared for. However, the staff had changed so frequently that there had been no question of forming a bond with any of them. It surprised her that Daniel had understood that so quickly.

'It was. I used to envy my school friends because they had mums and dads who were always there for them. Oh, they got told off sometimes but they knew that no matter what they did their parents would still love them.' She sighed softly. 'I envied them that, even though I'd never known what it was like to be part of a real family.'

Daniel was still holding her hands and she felt his fingers tighten. She had a feeling that what she'd said had touched him. 'So you never knew your parents, Emma?'

'No. I was a foundling, would you believe? I was left on the steps of a police station when I was a few hours old!' She laughed because she'd learned a long time ago that it was better to make a joke of the circumstances surrounding her birth. People were either embarrassed or overly curious when they found out, and she preferred not to have to deal with either if she could avoid it. However, surprisingly, Daniel seemed more upset than anything else.

'How awful! I can't imagine what would drive a woman to abandon her baby like that!'

His hazel eyes shimmered with concern and Emma felt her heart warm. She'd long since accepted what had happened, though it still hurt at times. However, it was good to know that Daniel genuinely cared.

'Maybe my mother had no choice,' she said softly. 'I try not to think about why she did it. I just focus on the thought that she must have cared otherwise she wouldn't have taken such trouble to leave me somewhere I'd be found.'

'You're right, of course.' Daniel smiled at her and his eyes were tender. 'Trust you to find something good about the situation, though, Emma. It's so typical of you.'

He let her go, obviously not expecting her to say anything. Emma was glad because she wasn't sure what she might have come up with. Had that been meant as a compliment?

A smile played around her mouth at the thought, although she knew that it was foolish to go reading too much into what had been probably just a passing comment. However, there was a definite spring in her step as she followed Daniel to the kitchen.

'Can I help?' Emma offered, sniffing appreciatively as she caught the waft of some deliciously spicy odour.

'Nope. You sit yourself down. You've done more than enough in the past twenty-four hours. It's time that Amy and I showed our appreciation!'

Daniel's tone was teasing as he drew out a chair with a flourish for her to sit on. Emma laughed as he draped a piece of kitchen towel across her knee in his best imitation of a waiter in a high-class restaurant.

'Well, if the food is as good as the service has been so far then I won't have any complaints,' she teased.

He waggled his eyebrows at her. 'You won't taste food

better than this anywhere in the whole of Clearsea. The chef is a genius. What he doesn't know about microwaving isn't worth mentioning!'

Emma shook her head. 'And here was I thinking that you'd been slaving over a hot stove, too.'

'Listen, it isn't easy, operating a microwave.' Daniel treated her to a stern look. 'First you have to read the instructions very carefully. Then you have to set the timer. Then you have to arrange the food on the plates…'

Emma held up her hands. 'I take it back! I can see just how difficult it is now.'

'We don't usually have plates,' Amy whispered conspiratorially. 'We usually eat our tea out of the plastic dishes 'cos Uncle Daniel says that it saves having to wash—'

'Shoo! Away with you, wretched child. Don't give away all our secrets!' Daniel scooped Amy up and threw her over his shoulder, making the little girl laugh uproariously. Emma joined in because there was no way she could resist. It was obvious that Daniel had a very close and loving relationship with his niece and that Amy adored him. She couldn't help thinking how lucky the little girl had been when her mother had died to have had Daniel to take care of her.

They lingered over the surprisingly tasty spaghetti Bolognese and salad that Daniel served. Amy had ice cream afterwards but Emma was too full to eat anything else so she just had a cup of coffee.

'That was excellent. My compliments to the chef…and his microwave.' She smiled as Daniel brought his coffee to the table and sat down. Amy had finished her ice cream and had gone into the sitting room to watch a cartoon on the video player.

'Thank you, although I think the microwave deserves more of the credit than the chef does.' Daniel sighed all of a sudden. 'Actually, joking apart, I do feel guilty that I don't cook more than a couple of times a week. Claire was always so careful about what Amy ate.'

'There was absolutely nothing wrong with the meal you served tonight,' Emma assured him quickly. 'You can't do everything, Daniel. You're doing your best and, from what I've seen so far, that's more than enough.'

'Think so?' He smiled when she nodded. 'Thanks. It's nice to hear you say that. It makes me realise how hard it must have been for Claire these past six years, bringing Amy up on her own.'

'She didn't meet anyone else after Amy's father left her?' Emma asked softly.

He shook his head. 'No. I think Claire was so hurt by what had happened that she didn't want to risk getting involved again. It was a shame because she was a lovely person.'

'Understandable, though,' Emma remarked.

'Mmm.' He stirred his coffee thoughtfully. 'A bad experience can put you off, can't it?'

Emma wasn't sure if that had been a general observation or not. Had Daniel had a bad experience with a woman in the past, perhaps? It made her wonder if his disinclination to socialise might not be solely because of his time being limited through taking care of Amy.

It was an intriguing thought but there was no way that she could question him about it. They drank their coffee, and while Daniel was clearing up she went into the living room and hemmed the angel costume. Naturally, Amy was eager to try it on again and this time she was allowed to put on the silver cardboard wings and halo as well.

Daniel stepped back and studied his niece. 'Perfect. You're going to be the prettiest angel in the play.'

Amy did a twirl so that the folds of the gown floated out around her and her wings fluttered. 'It's lovely. Thank you, Uncle Daniel.' She rushed over and kissed him then turned to Emma. 'Thank you, Emma.'

Emma gave the child a hug, taking care not to bend the wings. 'You're welcome, darling. I hope you have a wonderful time in your play tomorrow.'

'Will you come and watch me?' Amy's face had lit up as the idea had suddenly occurred to her. 'Please, Emma, will you?'

'Well, I don't know…' Emma began, not sure how to extricate herself without causing the child any distress. However, Daniel was quick to step in.

'What a lovely idea! Clever you for thinking of it, Amy.' He turned to Emma. 'Is there any chance at all that you could get the afternoon off?'

'I do have a half-day owing…' she began then shook her head. She really didn't want Daniel to feel that he *had* to ask her. 'But I'm sure you don't really want me to come.'

'Of course we do. Don't we, Amy?' Daniel laughed as Amy enthusiastically agreed. 'That's two against one, Emma. You're outvoted!'

She shrugged, although she couldn't stop her heart from swelling with happiness at the thought of spending more time with him and his adorable niece. 'All right, then. I'll ask Sister Carter in the morning if she can spare me.'

Daniel sent Amy upstairs to hang up her costume. He insisted on driving Emma home afterwards. She was a bit disappointed that he didn't ask her to stay longer until it struck her that he needed to put Amy to bed.

Emma spent the rest of the evening watching television but her mind was never far away from what was going to happen the following day. An afternoon with Daniel was something to look forward to and it delayed the moment when he wouldn't need her help any more. Funnily enough, she knew that she would really miss not being with him and Amy once the nativity play was over. How very strange.

Next morning Sister Carter was happy to agree to Emma's request to take the time owing to her that afternoon. In her usual way, she didn't question why Emma should want to take it at such short notice and Emma didn't volunteer the information either. Although Daniel had said that there was no need to keep things a secret, she simply didn't feel comfortable discussing his affairs. However, it soon became obvious that the gossip mongers had been at work.

'Come on, then—give. What were you doing in dishy Daniel's car last night, you dark horse?'

Jane Goodyear followed Emma into the kitchen when she went to fetch a fresh jug of water for Shirley Rogers. Shirley was in some discomfort that morning and they were waiting for Max Dennison to arrive and examine her. Consequently, Emma was a little distracted and not quite as quick as she might have been in thinking up an excuse.

'I…um…I was doing him a favour,' she muttered, picking up the jug and hurriedly making her way back to the door.

'Oh, I see.' Jane's tone was teasing. 'I wonder what sort of favour.' She glanced round as Linda walked past the door. 'Did you know that Emma here has been doing Daniel Hutton *favours?*'

'I certainly didn't! You sly thing, Emma Graham. I knew you were up to something last night! Now, come on—'

'If you could spare the time, Staff, I'd like to check on Paula Walters.'

Daniel's tone was so dry that Emma felt her face go red. Had he overheard what the other two had said? she wondered miserably as she handed the jug to Jane and followed him into the ward. However, there was no way she could ask him in front of a patient so she was forced to hold her tongue.

He greeted Paula in his usual courteous way then sat by the bed and explained that the ultrasound scan had shown several very large fibroids in her uterus. Paula began to cry before he'd got very far.

'I'll have to have a hysterectomy, won't I? That's what you're telling me, Doctor?'

'No.' Daniel smiled when he saw her surprise. 'Mr Dennison and I have talked this over very carefully and decided that we shall opt for a myomectomy. I explained what that was yesterday, if you recall?'

'You said that it meant removing the fibroids from my womb. So that means I shall still be able to have children— is that what you're saying, Dr Hutton?'

'Exactly. Normally we might have opted for a hyster-ectomy in a case like this. However, in view of your age and the fact that you're hoping to start a family, we shall carry out a myomectomy instead.' He shrugged. 'It will take a little more time but the end results will be worth it, won't they?'

'Oh, yes!' Paula smiled through her tears. 'Oh, I'm so relieved! I can't tell you how worried I was.'

Daniel laughed as he patted her arm. 'I think I can see that for myself. Anyway, we're scheduling the operation for tomorrow morning. As luck would have it, there's a free slot, so the sooner we get it over with, the faster you'll be back to your old self.'

With one last smile, he left Paula's bedside. Emma hur-ried after him but she didn't get chance to explain what had been going on as just at that point Mr Dennison arrived. It was all systems go after that as the consultant made his rounds in his usual imperious fashion. Mike Humphreys was with him but he cut Emma dead.

Mike was obviously still annoyed, she thought as she went to attend to a patient who was feeling sick after her pre-med. However, there was little she could do about it so she put it out of her mind for the rest of the morning. She was just getting ready to go off duty when Daniel phoned and left a message for her to meet him in the car park.

Linda took the call but mercifully she didn't get a chance to ask any questions as Sister called her away. However,

Emma knew that she would be given the third degree the following day. Still, it couldn't be helped so she would worry about it when she had to and not let it spoil the day. She was looking forward to it so much, and she knew that it wasn't just the thought of watching Amy in the play. Being with Daniel for a whole afternoon made it seem even more special.

He was waiting in his car for her and he opened the door as soon as she appeared. 'I thought we could stop off and have lunch beforehand,' he began, then stopped as his pager beeped. He checked the display and sighed. 'A and E. I'll have to go back in and see what they want.'

Emma stayed in the car, listening to the radio. Daniel came back a few minutes later, looking harried. 'We've had an emergency brought into A and E—an ectopic pregnancy, from the look of it. Max is tied up in a meeting at the moment so I'll have to deal with it. I'm sorry, Emma, but we're going to have to forget about lunch, I'm afraid.'

'Will you be finished in time for Amy's play?' she asked, her own disappointment forgotten as she thought how upset the child would be if Daniel wasn't there to watch her perform.

'I hope so, but I'm not sure how long this will take. The patient is in a pretty bad way, I'm afraid.' Daniel's tone was grim. 'Damn! Of all the times for this to happen. Still, at least you'll be there on time even if I'm late. You don't mind going on your own, do you, Emma? Only Amy will be so upset if there's no one there to watch her.'

'Of course I don't mind! Just tell me where her school is.'

Daniel explained then helped her out of the car. 'I don't know how to thank you for this, Emma. Really, I don't.'

He kissed her quickly on the cheek and his eyes were warm when he straightened. 'You're a real friend!'

Emma sighed as he hurried back inside the hospital. A friend, was she? Maybe she should have been satisfied to hear that but she couldn't help wishing that Daniel thought of her as more than just a friend, silly though that idea undoubtedly was. It would be nice to know that Daniel considered her to be special...very nice, indeed!

The school hall was packed when Emma arrived a little after two that afternoon. She found a seat near the back and looked around, but she couldn't see any sign of Daniel. Was he still in the operating theatre? She could only assume so.

Emma settled down to enjoy the performance as the curtains parted. There was a lot of shuffling as the children tried to spot their parents amongst the audience. Amy saw her and waved enthusiastically from where she was standing with the rest of the angels at the side of the stage.

Emma waved back, hiding a smile as she saw the little girl's tinsel halo had slipped to one side and was dangling over her right ear. All the angels were wearing the same costume and she was pleased to see that Amy's fitted in perfectly with the others. Mary was wearing a long blue gown with a pyjama cord tied around her waist, while Joseph and the shepherds were sporting what looked suspiciously like check teatowels on their heads. However, any shortcomings in the costumes didn't detract from her enjoyment. There was something very touching about watching the children perform their version of the Christmas story.

'Hi! I didn't think I was going to make it in time.'

Daniel quietly slid into the seat next to hers and Emma smiled at him. 'I'm glad you're here. Amy would have been so disappointed if you'd missed her performance.'

'So would I have been. I've been looking forward to this.' There was a note of pride in Daniel's voice which he didn't attempt to hide. Emma smiled as she realised just how much he loved his small niece. Daniel was making a wonderful job of looking after Amy in very difficult circumstances. She couldn't help thinking how few men would have devoted all their time and energy to bringing up a child, as he was doing. But, then, Daniel was a very special kind of man.

Her heart gave a small hiccup and she frowned, wondering why that thought should have disturbed her so much. However, it really wasn't the time to start worrying about it so she concentrated on the play instead. Nevertheless, she was very aware of Daniel sitting beside her, his large frame crammed onto the too-small chair.

When she breathed in she could smell the spicy fragrance of the soap he'd used, and when he leaned over so that he could get a better view of the three kings as they made their entrance—resplendent in someone's gold brocade curtains—she could feel the warmth of his body passing into hers. Suddenly her senses seemed to be heightened to an incredible degree, leaving her open to all sorts of emotions.

When the children began to sing 'Away in a manger' Emma felt tears start to trickle down her face. There was something so innocent and magical about the shrill little voices singing the beautiful old carol that it touched her heart.

'Here.' Daniel pressed a clean white handkerchief into her hand and his eyes were tender as he looked at her. 'It brings a lump to your throat, doesn't it?'

Emma nodded as she dabbed her eyes. 'It does.'

It seemed the most natural thing in the world after that when Daniel took hold of her hand and kept hold of it throughout the rest of the performance. It just seemed to add to the magic of the occasion. Emma couldn't remember when anything had moved her so much. It made no difference when two of the shepherds had a bit of a scrap because they each wanted to carry the toy lamb or that one of the wise men was so overcome with stage fright that he forgot his lines. The wonder and joy of that first Christmas was to be celebrated and who better to do that than the children?

58 A REAL FAMILY CHRISTMAS

Everyone clapped enthusiastically when the play ended. The children were very excited as they came racing down from the stage to find their parents. Amy's little face was aglow as she ran up to Emma and Daniel. Her halo was dangling over one ear and her wings looked very much the worse for wear, but it was obvious how delighted she was to have them both there.

'Did you see me? Could you hear me singing?' she demanded, hopping excitedly up and down.

'We could! And you were brilliant, sweetheart!' Daniel bent and hugged her. He exchanged a look with Emma and she smiled back. It was the sort of proudly amused look a lot of parents were exchanging, she thought, then felt her heart leap as it hit her what she was doing. She wasn't Amy's parent, for heaven's sake!

'What's wrong?'

With his usual astuteness, Daniel had homed in on her mood. Emma fixed a bright smile firmly in place, terrified that he might guess what she'd been thinking. It gave her hot and cold chills to imagine what his reaction would be.

'Nothing. What could be wrong after a brilliant performance like that? Well done, Amy. I really enjoyed it.'

'I told everyone you were coming,' Amy declared, catching hold of Emma's hand. 'My teacher and Ruth and Becky—they're my best friends—and the dinner ladies. Everyone! I told them *all* that you'd be here to watch me, Emma.'

'Did you, darling?' Emma was touched her presence should have meant so much to the child. She bent and kissed Amy, earning herself another huge smile. The little girl went racing off as one of her friends called to her just then.

'Thank you for sparing the time to come today, Emma. Having you here has made it all the more special for Amy.'

There was a pensive note in Daniel's voice. Emma frowned as she wondered what had caused it. However,

Amy came back at that moment so there was no opportunity to ask him. Amy insisted on leaving her costume on to go home in. Daniel had his car outside and they left the school together.

Emma hung back as he unlocked the car doors. She couldn't help feeling a little down at the thought that now the play was over Daniel would no longer need her help.

'Well, I'll see you both soon, I hope,' she said in a determinedly bright voice. 'And thank you again for asking me to watch your play, Amy. It was wonderful.'

'You aren't in a rush, are you?' Daniel asked as he turned to her. 'I was hoping that you'd come back and have tea with us.'

'Yes! Will you, Emma...please, please, please?' Amy added her invitation to Daniel's, making it hard for Emma to refuse, but she knew that it was foolish to delay the inevitable any longer.

'It's very kind of you both but I'm sure you don't really want me having tea with you *again*.' She laughed, making a joke of it because her heart was aching at the thought of this being the end of the road for the three of them. Maybe it was silly but she couldn't recall enjoying herself as much as she had these past two days, being a part of Daniel's and Amy's lives.

'Course we do! Don't we, Uncle Daniel?' Amy turned beseechingly to her uncle. Emma saw him frown and quickly stepped in. She didn't want Daniel being forced into doing something he didn't want to do out of politeness.

'No, really. I'm sure you must have a lot of things to do,' she began, but he shook his head.

'Nothing that can't wait.' He glanced at his niece and his face softened. 'Amy will be very disappointed if you don't help us celebrate her success, Emma.'

'Well...' Emma found herself wavering. What harm could there be in spending another couple of hours with Daniel and Amy? a small voice whispered seductively.

'That's settled, then. Good!' Daniel immediately took advantage of her hesitation. Whisking open the car door, he stepped back and bowed. 'Your carriage awaits you, ma'am!'

Emma shook her head. 'I give in. I can tell that I won't win.' She slid into the seat, smiling up at Daniel as he started to close the door. 'You can be very persuasive when you set your mind to it, Dr Hutton.'

'I try my best.' His hazel eyes sparkled with laughter as they held hers for a moment before he closed the door. Emma sank back in the seat, making a great performance out of fastening her seat belt as he got into the car. She took a deep breath but she could feel her insides wobbling. Did Daniel have any idea what he did to a woman's equilibrium when he looked at her like that?

She shot a sideways glance at him as he started the car, and sighed. He must have! He couldn't have got to this stage in his life and remained unaware of the effect he had on the opposite sex.

It was a sobering thought when she definitely needed sobering. To imagine that the look Daniel had given her had been meant only for her would be a mistake. Daniel wasn't at all interested in her in *that* way!

In the end they went to Emma's flat. She'd felt guilty about letting Daniel cook again so she'd offered to make them a meal. Daniel and Amy had been only too eager to agree to the suggestion and had made short work of the home-made cottage pie she'd taken from her small freezer and cooked for them. Now Amy was kneeling by the coffee-table, writing a letter to Father Christmas, while Emma and Daniel drank coffee.

'I like what you've done in here,' he said approvingly, looking around the room. 'That colour on the walls is beautiful and those stencils are wonderful. You must have a lot of patience!'

'Thank you.' Emma smiled as she looked at the warm, terracotta-coloured walls and the intricate border she'd stencilled so painstakingly around them. 'I have to admit that halfway through decorating this room I wondered if I'd taken leave of my senses. I was up a ladder at the time, trying to reach the ceiling and wishing that my arms were at least six inches longer. I don't think I would have been half as ambitious if I'd realised what hard work it would be!'

'But it was worth it, believe me. If you ever want to change careers then I have a house which is in serious need of decorating,' Daniel began.

'No way!' Emma held up her hands. 'I shall stick to nursing, thank you. It may be hard work but it beats being up a twenty-foot ladder any day of the week. And talking of work, how did you get on with that emergency ectopic?'

Daniel grimaced. 'It was pretty scary, I can tell you. The tube had ruptured so I had to remove it and she'd lost a lot of blood. Hopefully, we caught it in time but she's gone to ICU just to be on the safe side.'

'Fingers crossed, then,' Emma said quietly. Ectopic pregnancies—where a foetus developed outside the uterus—were always dangerous. Most were discovered within the first two months after conception but a few went undetected until they gave real cause for concern.

They let the subject drop as Amy looked up just then. 'Do you know where Father Christmas lives, Uncle Daniel? Mummy used to know 'cos she always posted my letters to him.'

'I think he lives at the North Pole,' Daniel replied seriously. 'I shall have to see if I can find his address.'

'Mummy had a book with addresses in,' Amy said at once. 'Maybe she wrote it down in there.'

'I'm sure she did. Your mummy was very clever about remembering to do things like that.' There was a catch in Daniel's voice as he said that. Emma sighed to herself as she realised that he still missed his sister a lot. It couldn't have been easy for him, coping with his own grief over Claire's death and having to keep up a front for Amy's sake.

Thankfully, Amy didn't appear to have noticed anything amiss. She got up and came over to them. 'Would you like to see my letter? It isn't a secret. Mummy said that Father Christmas didn't mind if mummies and daddies read the letters first,' she explained. 'So I'm sure he won't mind if you read it, Uncle Daniel.'

'Thank you, sweetheart.' Daniel took the letter from his niece and quickly read it. Emma was watching and she saw him tense. It made her wonder what the child had asked for.

Daniel cleared his throat but Emma could tell that he was having trouble controlling his emotions. 'That's a lovely letter, Amy,' he said quietly, although his voice grated.

Emma decided that he needed a moment to collect himself so she quickly turned to the little girl. 'If you go into the kitchen and look in the dresser drawer, you'll find a packet of envelopes, Amy. I have some stamps as well so you'll be able to post your letter to Father Christmas in the morning on your way to school.'

'Yes!'

Amy went rushing out of the room and they could hear her racing along the hall to the kitchen. Daniel took a deep breath as he ran a hand over his face.

'Thanks, Emma. I could feel myself getting a bit choked up and the last thing I want is to upset Amy. Take a look at what she's written and you'll understand why.'

Emma took the letter from him and read what the little girl had written in her best handwriting. She felt her own eyes mist with tears before she had got to the bottom of the page.

Dear Father Christmas,

My mummy has gone to heaven and I miss her a lot. My Uncle Daniel is looking after me now and he is very nice. I love him loads. I don't want lots of presents this year 'cept a Barbie doll with a sparkly dress. I just want Christmas to be special like it was when Mummy was here. We used to have a big tree with lots of lights and Mummy made mince pies and took me carol singing.

I don't know if you can make things like that happen but will you try.

Lots of love,

Amy Louise Hutton.

XXXXX

P.S. Please give Rudolph a big kiss from me.

'I don't know what to say, Daniel.' Emma took a tissue from her pocket and wiped her eyes. 'It doesn't seem a lot to ask, does it? All Amy wants is a really special Christmas, like all the other Christmases she's had.'

'I know.' Daniel stood up abruptly and went to the window. His back was rigid as he stood there, looking out. Emma ached to find the right words to comfort him but what could she say in a situation like this?

Daniel swung round and his face was filled with determination all of a sudden. 'If that's what Amy wants then that's what she's going to have. I'm going to make sure that child has a Christmas she will always remember, but I can't do it all by myself.'

He crossed the room in a couple of long strides and drew Emma to her feet. 'Will you help me, Emma? Will you help me make a little girl's dreams come true?'

CHAPTER FIVE

'ME? OH, but I'm not sure if I can.'

Emma saw Daniel's eyes darken. 'Why not? It's obvious how much Amy likes you...' He broke off and a look of chagrin crossed his face as he let go of her hands.

'Sorry. Of course, you already have plans for Christmas and you'll be far too busy to help me. I'm sorry, Emma, I shouldn't have put you on the spot like that. Forget I said anything.'

He picked up his coat from the back of the sofa and smiled politely at her. 'Thanks for the meal and for coming to watch Amy today. We both appreciated it.'

'It was my pleasure.' Emma knew she could leave it at that and Daniel wouldn't think any the worse of her. However, innate honesty refused to let him leave without telling him the truth.

'About what you said just now, well, you were wrong.' She hurried on when he looked quizzically at her. 'I don't have any plans for Christmas, to be honest.'

'You don't? Then why did you say that you couldn't help me?' He paused. 'There I go again. Maybe you simply don't want to get involved in this, Emma. That's up to you, of course.'

'Oh, but I *do!* I would love to help you give Amy a wonderful Christmas.' She saw his surprise and looked away in case her expression was too revealing. Would Daniel guess just how much the idea appealed to her? she wondered.

'I'm just not sure if I'm the right person to ask, you see,' she mumbled, disturbed by the thought. Why should the thought of spending more time with him make her heart sing? It didn't make sense.

'Why ever not?'

She could hear the bewilderment in his voice and bit back a sigh. However, now that she'd started, she had to explain.

'Because I've never had the sort of Christmas Amy expects. I have no idea what a real family Christmas should be like, actually. I usually spend Christmas day on my own if I'm not working.'

'Didn't you celebrate Christmas when you were in the children's home?' Daniel asked softly.

Emma shrugged. 'Yes, but it wasn't the same as spending Christmas with your family. The staff used to work split shifts and worked either morning, afternoon or evening. I always got the impression that they would have preferred to be at home with their own families rather than with us.'

'Then it's even more important that we make this year special.' Daniel came back across the room and his eyes seemed to blaze as he looked at her. 'For you, Emma, as well as for Amy!'

Emma looked away because she wasn't proof against the concern she saw on his face. Obviously, Daniel meant what he said and she appreciated it. However, she couldn't help thinking how hard it was going to be once Christmas was over and everything went back to normal again. Was it really wise to let herself get more deeply involved in his life when there could be no future in it?

Amy came back with the envelope just then so the subject was dropped. Emma helped the child address her letter to Father Christmas and found her a stamp. Daniel promised that he would check to make sure the address was correct as soon as they got home.

It was gone seven by that time and Emma knew that he must be anxious to take Amy home and put her to bed, so she didn't delay them. She accompanied them down the four flights of stairs to the ground floor, shivering as an icy wind whipped into the hall when she opened the front door.

Daniel quickly ushered his niece out to his car and got her settled then ran back to say goodbye. 'You look half-frozen, Emma, so I won't keep you standing there too long. I just want to say thanks once again for everything you've done and ask you to promise me that you'll think about spending Christmas with us.'

Emma smiled at him. 'You don't give up easily, do you?'

He laughed at that. 'Nope!'

He sobered abruptly and his eyes held an expression she found it impossible to define as he looked at her. 'I really hope you'll agree, Emma. I can't think of anything I'd enjoy more than the three of us spending Christmas together this year.'

He brushed her mouth with a kiss that was too fleeting to be more than a token. Emma watched as he ran back to his car and got in. He hooted then drove away.

Emma shut the door and went back upstairs, thinking about what had happened. Daniel had kissed her out of gratitude, of course. He'd been grateful for her help in making Amy's costume and he'd appreciated her going to watch his niece in the nativity play. He'd also wanted to thank her for providing them with their tea…

She sighed as she realised that she was listing all the reasons Daniel should have kissed her because it was the only way to stop her foolish mind running away with itself! Why bother?

She spent the rest of the evening weaving seductive little scenarios in which Daniel kissed her for a whole lot of *different* reasons…

'Paula Walters is first on this morning's list. Linda is just sorting out the paperwork.'

It was early on Friday morning and Emma had arrived to find that it was going to be another busy day. Sister

Carter was running through the schedule and it was hectic even by their standards.

'Shirley Rogers is going to be with us a bit longer than expected, I'm afraid,' Sister continued. 'Her temperature is still higher than it should be and Mr Dennison is worried about infection. I want you to keep an eye on her, Emma. I think hourly obs would be best until we see what's happening.'

'Of course, Sister,' Emma agreed, hoping that the problem would resolve itself given time and the appropriate treatment. Although strict controls were used during surgery, there were odd occasions when infection could set in. Hopefully, this setback would be only a temporary one in Shirley's case.

Once Sister Carter had finished going through her list, Emma went to check on Shirley. She found her looking rather dispirited that day, although in her usual way Shirley did her best to make light of what had happened.

'Seems you might have to put up with me a bit longer, love,' Shirley told her as Emma reached for the thermometer.

'So I believe. I don't know how we're going to stand all the moaning you do,' Emma teased, popping the thermometer under Shirley's tongue.

Shirley gurgled, hampered by the thermometer sticking out of her mouth. 'Wait till my hubby hears that he's got to put up with a few more days of his own cooking. He will be pleased—I don't think!'

'It will make him appreciate you all the more, won't it?' Emma replied with a laugh. She jotted the reading down on Shirley's chart. 'So how do you feel in general?'

'Oh, you know…as though one of our bulls has trampled me.' Shirley laid her hand on her stomach and winced. 'It's a bit painful where the stitches are, to be honest, love.'

'Let me take a look,' Emma offered immediately. She frowned when she saw how swollen the skin either side of the sutures looked. 'I think I'll ask Dr Hutton to take a look at that. He should be up in a moment to see Mrs Walters.'

'Whatever you think best, love,' Shirley agreed in her usual co-operative way. Emma couldn't help wishing that they had more patients like Shirley Rogers. Life would be so much easier then!

Afternoon came round and it was Emma's turn to work in the outpatients' clinic that day. Daniel was the doctor in attendance and he was already in his consulting room when Emma arrived after lunch.

She tapped on the door and went in, smiling as he looked up from the notes he'd been writing. Although she'd seen him in passing on the ward that morning, this was the first real opportunity she'd had to speak to him. She couldn't deny that her spirits seemed to lift at the thought of the next couple of hours they would spend together.

'From the look of the queue out there, it's going to be a busy session,' she announced cheerfully.

'As usual!' he replied dryly, tossing down his pen. He sat back in his chair and regarded her levelly. 'So, have you made up your mind yet?'

Emma didn't pretend that she hadn't understood. 'About Christmas? Yes, I have.' She took a quick breath, hoping that she wasn't making a mistake. She'd thought hard about what her decision should be, but at the end of the day she'd known in her heart that she couldn't bear to think of letting Amy down. 'If you want me to help you then I shall.'

'Great!' Daniel got up and came round the desk. He gave her a quick hug then let her go when there was a knock on the door. Smoothing his face into its customary expression, he bade the receptionist—who had brought the patients' files—to come in. However, Emma had seen enough to know how delighted he was by her decision.

She smiled to herself as she went to summon the first patient on the list. Obviously, Daniel was pleased because it would take some of the pressure off him, having her to help him get everything ready. However, she couldn't help hoping that he'd been pleased because it was *she* who would be working with him to give Amy a wonderful Christmas. For some reason that seemed more important than anything else.

'So, Mrs Dyson, how have you been since we last saw you?'

Daniel smiled at the elderly lady seated in front of the desk. Emily Dyson was a woman in her late sixties, a widow who had three grown-up children. She'd been referred by her GP a few months earlier when he'd noticed that she'd had a slight prolapse of the uterus.

An appointment had been made at the clinic and she'd seen Max Dennison, who'd recommended a ring pessary to hold the uterus in position. Unfortunately, the pessary had caused stress incontinence, which Mrs Dyson had mentioned at her second visit. A larger pessary had been fitted and today's appointment was to monitor the situation.

'Worse than ever, I'm afraid, Doctor.' Emily Dyson sighed wearily. 'The incontinence problem is really getting me down now. It's so embarrassing, you understand.'

'I'm sure it is.' Daniel looked at her notes again. 'To be honest, Mrs Dyson, I think we are heading towards surgery now. It's obvious that the pessaries aren't working so I really feel that a vaginal hysterectomy and repair would be your best option.'

'If that's what you think would be best, Doctor.'

Emma frowned as she heard the dispirited note in the elderly lady's voice. It was obvious that Mrs Dyson wasn't altogether happy with the thought of having an operation, even though she'd agreed with Daniel.

Daniel obviously had noticed it as well because he frowned. 'You don't sound too keen on the idea, Mrs Dyson. Why is that?'

'Well, it just seems as though things have all sort of

snowballed.' Emily Dyson clutched her bag. It was obvious that she felt uncomfortable about saying anything. However, Daniel urged her on, smiling to put her at ease.

'That sounds very intriguing! You can't possibly leave it like that and not explain what you meant.'

The elderly lady smiled and once again Emma thought how good he was with people. Daniel really cared about them as individuals, not just as *patients*. It just served to increase her admiration for him.

'I suppose I'd better, although I've not liked to say anything before, you understand. I know all the doctors I've seen have told me that I have a prolapse but it never caused me a bit of bother. I didn't know there was anything wrong until my GP mentioned it,' she explained.

'So that wasn't the reason why you visited your GP in the first place?' Daniel queried.

'Oh, no! I just went for a smear, you see. I'd never had one before—never seen the need, to be honest. But my daughter, Betty, well, she'd been on and on at me to go so I did. It was then that my GP discovered that I had a problem, although I'd had no idea that there was anything wrong up till then.'

'I see.' Daniel frowned. 'And the incontinence problem? When did that first crop up?'

'After I had that ring fitted. I'd never had a bit of trouble before that.' Emily Dyson sighed. 'And it's got even worse since they decided I needed a bigger one fitted.'

'And now I'm telling you that you need an operation. I can see why you would be so confused, Mrs Dyson. Here we are telling you that we can solve your problem this way or that when you didn't even *have* a problem to begin with!' Daniel's tone was wry. 'Why didn't you say something sooner?'

'Well, I didn't like to. I mean, it isn't for me to argue with a doctor, is it?'

Emma barely managed to hide her dismay. The poor

soul! Fancy getting swept along in the system because she hadn't felt that she had the right to question what was happening.

'What would you say if I suggested that we went right back to the beginning, Mrs Dyson? We can remove that ring pessary and see how you go from there,' Daniel suggested gently.

'And I won't need an operation?' Emily Dyson's face broke into a relieved smile. 'Oh, that would be lovely, Doctor. Thank you so much!'

It was a very happy woman who left the clinic a short time later. Emma sighed as she watched the old lady walking purposefully down the corridor. 'Incredible, isn't it? That poor woman would have gone through with an operation rather than say, Hang on but I don't want this.'

'It is. But a lot of older people feel the same way—that they can't question what their doctor tells them.' Daniel grimaced. 'I just wish that someone had picked up on the problem—or, rather, lack of one—sooner, instead of putting that poor woman through so much unnecessary worry and discomfort. In some instances it's better to leave well alone rather than try to do anything!'

'That's a lesson we should all learn,' Emma said thoughtfully. 'I shall be a lot more aware of it in future.'

'Oh, I think you're already very quick to pick up on problems,' Daniel observed lightly. 'I could tell that you'd sensed something wasn't quite right with our Mrs Dyson. Nurses like you, Emma, are worth your weight in gold.'

'Try telling that to the management. Maybe they'll give me a pay rise!' she retorted lightly, because the comment had meant such a lot to her.

'I doubt it. They'd be bankrupt if they had to pay all the nursing staff what they're really worth!'

Her pleasure dissipated a little as she realised that he must view all the nursing staff in the same favourable light. However, she shrugged off the feeling of disappointment by telling herself how silly it was. They worked their way through the rest of the list and then it was five o'clock and time to go home.

Emma gathered together the files to take them to the office but paused as Daniel called to her.

'Just before you go, Emma, are you free tomorrow by any chance?'

Emma looked round, trying to quieten the noisy thundering her heart was making. 'Yes, as it happens. It's my long weekend.'

'Great! Then how about making a start on the Christmas preparations?' Daniel picked up his pen and slipped it into the top pocket of his white coat. He accompanied Emma from the room.

'Fine by me. What did you have in mind?'

'It's knowing where to start, isn't it?' He grimaced as he ran his hand through his hair. 'I'm a novice at all this, I'm afraid. If I wasn't working then I used to spend the day with Claire, and if I was working I'd still not need to actually *do* anything. I had Christmas dinner in the staff canteen and simply bought a few presents and left it at that!'

Emma laughed at the rueful note in his voice. 'Snap! We're a right pair, aren't we?'

'Well, at least there are two of us and you know what they say about two heads being better than one.' Daniel's smile was warm and Emma couldn't help smiling back.

'Mmm, I'll reserve judgement on that, thank you! Maybe we should compile a list to make sure that we don't forget anything?' she suggested. 'It would be a start.'

'Good idea! Why didn't I think of it? Mind you, I do know the first thing we need because Amy has been nagging me for days now—a Christmas tree. Why don't we buy that tomorrow then do as you suggested and make a list of everything else that needs doing?'

Emma frowned. She didn't want Daniel to think he had

to ask her to accompany him and Amy everywhere. 'Are you sure you need me to come along?'

'Of course! This is your Christmas as much as it's Amy's and mine.' He sounded so surprised that any reservations she'd had instantly disappeared.

'Very well, then. I'd love to come with you. The only question now is where shall we go for a tree? There are still some left in the shops in town, I expect.'

Daniel shook his head. 'No. The best of them will have been sold by now. We want this tree to be extra-special, don't we? Tell you what, I'll check out the best place to buy a Christmas tree and you just be ready bright and early in the morning. OK?'

'OK,' Emma agreed. Daniel sketched her a wave then hurried off. He was obviously anxious to collect his niece from the childminder's house.

Emma took the files to the office then went back to the ward to collect her coat. Linda and Jane were just leaving and they paused as they saw her stepping from the lift.

'So how did it go? You and Daniel have a nice afternoon together, did you?' Jane asked pertly.

'I don't know about nice but it was busy,' Emma replied noncommittally. She took off her uniform and slipped into her outdoor clothes. Linda and Jane were still waiting and she sighed as she realised that she was going to have to explain what was going on at some point.

'Well, I never! Just imagine, Daniel has been looking after that little girl all by himself and none of us knew a thing about it,' Linda declared after Emma had finished.

'I don't think he wanted it broadcasted, although he did say that he hadn't been deliberately trying to keep it a secret.' Emma shrugged on her coat and headed for the door. 'So don't go spreading it all round the place, you two.'

'Oh, you can trust us, Emma!' Linda claimed, looking hurt. 'Anyway, it does explain why you weren't too worried about falling out with Mike. You have bigger—and better—fish to fry!'

'It isn't like that! I'm just helping Daniel out over Christmas,' she declared. 'There isn't anything, well, *romantic* about the situation.'

'Come on! This is me you're talking to, kiddo.' Linda placed a friendly arm around Emma's shoulders and winked at Jane. 'You can tell us till you're blue in the face that you're only doing this for the most altruistic reasons, but I won't believe you. No woman worth her salt is immune to Dr Delectable Hutton!'

Emma sighed as Linda and Jane both laughed. She knew that it was pointless, trying to convince them they were wrong. It would have been a lie anyway, she acknowledged as they all walked to the lift together. She wasn't helping Daniel *only* for Amy's sake, but for her own as well. Prolonging the time she could spend with him was part of the attraction...

Saturday was cold and windy but mercifully dry. When Emma left her flat just before eight to buy some milk, she was glad that she'd dressed in her warmest clothes. Across the road, the waves were bouncing against the breakwaters, sending up plumes of spray which sparkled in the frosty air. It would be high tide that night, and if the wind kept up there was a very real danger that some parts of the coastline might be flooded. There had been a lot of erosion in the area and the local council had been trying to get government funding to repair the damage. Only last winter a house had fallen into the sea when a section of the cliff face had broken away.

Emma hurried home with her pint of milk and made coffee and toast which she ate standing by the window. Daniel hadn't said what time he would be coming for her and she didn't want to miss him. It was barely eight-thirty when she saw his car pulling up and she waved as she saw him looking up at her window.

Emma hurriedly collected her bag, shooting a glance in the mirror as she passed it to check her appearance. She'd decided on denim jeans and a chunky blue sweater which made her grey eyes appear even greyer by contrast. The sweater had a roll neck which would keep out the chill and it went well with her padded jacket which was a deeper shade of blue.

She'd brushed her short hair until it gleamed like spun gold as it curled around her heart-shaped face. Her make-up consisted of a lot of moisturiser to protect her skin, a little mascara and a slick of pale bronze lipstick. However, she felt quite pleased with the overall effect, if she was honest. Daniel shouldn't be ashamed to be seen with her at least…

She cut short that silly thought and quickly ran down the stairs. This outing wasn't a date! It was simply a first step towards making sure that Amy had a wonderful Christmas. However, it was impossible to curb the way her heart lifted when Daniel leaned over to open the door for her.

'Hi, there. I was hoping it wasn't too early to collect you but someone—naming no names, of course—couldn't wait any longer!'

He shot a meaningful glance in the rear-view mirror and Emma laughed. 'I wonder if I can guess who that someone is?' She turned and smiled at the little girl strapped into the back seat.

'Are you excited about choosing your tree, Amy?'

'Yes! I told Uncle Daniel that you wouldn't mind what time we came for you. You don't, do you, Emma?' the child asked uncertainly.

Emma smiled at her. 'Of course not! I'm looking forward to it.' She turned to Daniel and in her haughtiest tone instructed, 'Get a move on, my good man. We have a tree to buy. Don't spare the horses!'

'Yes, ma'am!' Daniel treated her to a mocking salute then started the car. Emma sank back in the seat, smiling to herself. It felt so good to be able to tease him like that, so *right*. It made her wonder what it would feel like to be able to do it on a permanent basis.

She sighed. Sometimes it was better not to wish for too much. That way you didn't run the risk of being disappointed.

'Amy, are you sure that's the one you really want?'

Daniel's tone was tinged with disbelief as he studied the scrawny little Christmas tree his niece was pointing to. He'd brought them to a garden centre several miles outside the town. The place was obviously extremely popular because the car park had been packed when they'd arrived. Daniel had managed to find them a space then, at Amy's insistence, they'd headed straight to where the trees where being sold.

Emma had been amazed by the number of spruce trees which were piled up in the enclosure. There were many different varieties as well, making it even harder to choose. However, Amy had taken one look at the wilting little tree with its twisted branches, standing on its own in a corner, and had made up her mind.

'Yes, that one,' she insisted. 'It looks so sad and lonely, Uncle Daniel. We have to buy it and take it home with us.'

'I don't believe this. What do you say, Emma?' He turned imploringly to her. 'After all, this tree is supposed to be for all of us.'

Emma exchanged a conspiratorial smile with Amy and tried not to laugh. 'Well, if we don't buy it then I'm sure nobody else will.'

'I give up! I can't win, can I? It's two against one.' Daniel shook his head but Emma could tell that he wasn't the least bit annoyed. He paid for the tree and dryly asked the young assistant if he would put it to one side while they went into the shop to buy some decorations. Amy went racing on ahead while Emma and Daniel followed at a more sedate pace.

'Well, I don't think we need worry that anyone will try to gazump us and buy that tree while we're gone,' he said drolly. 'Did you see that boy's face when I told him which tree I wanted? He obviously thought I'd taken leave of my senses!'

Emma laughed. 'Maybe he thought you had poor eyesight and couldn't see the gaps where branches are missing.'

'Don't! Can you imagine how much tinsel it's going to take to make that tree look halfway respectable?' Daniel shook his head in despair. 'Why did Amy have to choose *that* one?'

'Because she has a kind heart, like her uncle,' Emma teased, and earned herself a rueful look.

'Remind me to make some changes to my attitude, will you?' he replied, opening the door for her. 'There's being kind and being *kind!*'

The next couple of hours passed so quickly that Emma could hardly believe it when she saw what time it was. Sitting in the garden centre's bustling café with a steaming mug of hot chocolate in her hands, she realised that she'd never had so much fun as she'd had that morning.

They'd filled numerous carrier bags with decorations, which ranged from the tasteful to the downright hideous, but they'd had a wonderful time. Now Amy had gone to watch the animated display which had been set up in a corner, a moving tableau of elves and fairies helping a harassed-looking Santa.

Daniel took an appreciative swallow of his drink. 'Oh, boy, do I need this! I had no idea that shopping could be so tiring.'

'You've obviously led a charmed life,' Emma teased. 'Anyway, we've just about finished now, haven't we?'

'I hope so.' Daniel picked up one of the carriers and poked around inside it. 'Have you see some of this stuff? I hope you weren't expecting an elegant Christmas tree, Emma, one of those done in a few tasteful colours.'

He withdrew a thick coil of purple tinsel from the bag and draped it around her neck then added another in a particularly virulent shade of red. 'Mmm, it's going to be different, I can say that for it.'

'It will be lovely,' Emma declared firmly. 'And I hate those designer-done trees. Who wants only silver decorations on their tree when they can have all these lovely colours, anyway?'

'You're as bad as Amy! Am I the only one with any taste around here?'

Emma laughed as she took the tinsel from around her neck and threw it at him. 'Cheek! Just you wait and see, Daniel Hutton. This tree will be a positive work of art after we've finished with it.'

'From the Picasso school, no doubt,' Daniel retorted as he fielded the tinsel. He put it back in the bag then leaned towards her. 'You've got tinsel in your hair now.'

'Have I?' Emma raised her hand to her head but Daniel got there before her. She felt his fingers gently plucking the glittering strands out of her hair and her breath caught.

'That's it… Oops, no. There's another bit.' He bent closer as he spotted another strand of tinsel. Emma felt as though her lungs were going to burst at any moment. She wanted to breathe out and then breathe in, to act naturally, but it seemed to be beyond her to do that when Daniel was so close to her.

Perhaps her tension communicated itself to him because he suddenly glanced down. His hazel eyes met hers and she couldn't have done anything to stop what happened next even if she'd wanted to.

'Emma…'

Her name was the merest whisper on his lips before they

found hers. His mouth was warm and gentle yet it held a hunger she'd never expected. Daniel kissed her not just because the moment was right and the opportunity was there but because he wanted to. Knowing that, it made her heart lift with joy.

He drew back and smiled at her. 'That's better.'

'Better…' she repeated huskily.

'All the tinsel has gone now.' His hand brushed over her hair one last time before he picked up his cup. However, Emma could see that his hand was trembling when he raised it to his lips.

She looked away, afraid of what might be on her face at that moment. That Daniel had been as affected by that kiss as she had been made her feel more mixed up than ever. Had he asked her to help him just because he wanted to give Amy a marvellous Christmas? Or had there been another reason?

It was impossible to know what the answer was without asking him and she couldn't bring herself to do that. It was something of a relief when Amy came back. Whilst she was concentrating on the little girl there was no room to start wondering about matters which might be best left alone.

They left the garden centre not long after that, stowing the decorations in the boot and fastening the tree securely to the roof-rack. Amy was obviously tired out by all the excitement and quickly dozed off in the back of the car. Daniel put a tape into the stereo and Emma let her mind drift as she listened to a selection of light classics. It was better not to think too hard about what had happened. That way she wouldn't be disappointed if she'd misread the situation.

It was already growing dark when they drew up in front of Daniel's house. The wind was even stronger now, making it difficult to stand upright when they got out of the car. Daniel handed Emma his keys.

'You and Amy go inside and I'll bring in the tree.'

Emma took tight hold of the child's hand as a sudden blast of wind threatened to blow her over. 'Are you sure you can manage?'

'Quite sure,' he replied firmly.

Emma hurried up the path and unlocked the front door. Amy went to take off her coat but Emma waited by the door. She grabbed hold of the tree when the wind caught it as Daniel tried to manoeuvre it through the door.

'Thanks. Looks like we're in for a real storm, doesn't it?' He carried the tree into the living room and propped it up in the corner of the room then went back outside for the bags of decorations.

Emma frowned as she watched him struggling to close the boot. The storm was getting worse and she couldn't help wondering how she would get home later. She didn't want Daniel having to drive her home in the middle of a gale.

By the time he came back inside, she'd made up her mind. 'Look, Daniel, I think I should get off home now. This storm is going to get really bad soon and I don't want to end up stranded.'

'Nonsense! You can't leave now. We have a tree to trim, remember?'

Emma shook her head. 'You and Amy can manage perfectly well without me. It's better that I go now. I don't want you having to drive me home later. I wouldn't have a minute's peace, worrying about you two being out on the roads in weather like this.'

'And I wouldn't have any peace, thinking about you taking the bus.' Daniel folded his arms. 'If the storm gets that bad then there's an easy solution, Emma. You can stay here.'

CHAPTER SIX

'HERE?' Emma echoed.

'Uh-huh. There's a spare bedroom so it isn't as though we don't have enough room. Anyway, you could treat it as a practice run, couldn't you?'

Emma was having trouble following what Daniel was saying. Her brain seemed to have stalled on the thought of staying the night under his roof and wouldn't oblige her by moving forward from that. She ended up by once again repeating what he'd said, and inwardly groaned as she realised that he must think her a complete idiot!

'Practice run?'

'Yes.' He frowned as he looked at her. 'Obviously, you'll be staying here on Christmas Eve, Emma.'

It may have been obvious to him. However, it most certainly hadn't been obvious to her. Emma took a deep breath, but before she could explain that she hadn't thought about it Amy came racing back down the stairs.

'Can we start decorating the tree now, Uncle Daniel?' she demanded eagerly.

Daniel smiled as he turned to his niece. 'Of course we can! You take that stand into the living room and we'll get the tree safely set up before we do anything else.'

'Yes!' Amy picked up the metal supporting stand which they'd bought at the garden centre and carried it into the living room. She set it down in the centre of the room then looked around. 'Here? Then we can see it properly.'

Daniel treated Emma to an amused look and she forced her thoughts into some semblance of order. It would serve no purpose, creating a fuss. She would simply tell Daniel that she didn't think it was a good idea if she stayed at his house on Christmas Eve, although what reason she could give was open to question. She just knew in her heart that it wouldn't be wise.

'Maybe we should put the tree nearer to the window,' Daniel suggested tactfully. 'That way everyone will be able to see it when they walk past the house.'

Amy nodded solemnly. 'Then if they haven't got a lovely tree like ours they can still feel Christmassy?'

'Exactly!' Daniel gave his niece a hug then moved the stand closer to the window. 'Right, now that we've decided where to put it we can make a start. Can you unpack the bags, please, Amy, while I fix up the tree?'

Amy happily began to unload the carrier bags, arranging each item carefully on the sofa. Emma shook her head in amazement as she saw the amount of decorations. 'I didn't realise that we'd bought so much.'

Daniel grinned as he picked up the little tree. 'Think it will hold all that lot?' he teased. 'Maybe you two are starting to wish that you'd bought a proper tree?'

Emma and Amy looked at one another then shook their heads. 'No way!' Emma stated firmly.

'This is going to be the best tree ever, Uncle Daniel!' Amy declared. 'You'll see!'

Daniel rolled his eyes. 'I give up!'

'Right, stand back, you two. Here we go!'

Emma held her breath as Daniel slid the plug into its socket. They had spent a couple of hours trimming the tree and its puny branches were sagging under the weight of all the baubles. They had left testing the lights until the very last moment and now it was time to see if they worked.

'Wait a minute, Uncle Daniel!' Amy raced across the room and turned off the central light, plunging the room into darkness. 'Now you can switch it on.'

'Oh, how lovely!' Emma exclaimed in delight as Daniel flicked the switch and the fairy lights came on. They'd decided on a set of tiny white lights and she thought how lovely they looked, shimmering amongst the branches like miniature stars.

'It really is the best tree ever!' Amy's small face was filled with wonder as she stared at the tree. 'Emma and I told you it would be beautiful, didn't we? And it is!'

Daniel laughed as he put his arms around his niece and hugged her. 'You did, sweetheart. I shouldn't have been such a doubting Thomas, should I?'

'Who's Thomas?' Amy asked, frowning up at him.

'It's just a rather silly saying, poppet,' Daniel explained, exchanging a wry look with Emma. 'It means that I should have believed you two when you told me that this tree was going to look wonderful. I shouldn't have had any doubts.'

'It's all right, Uncle Daniel,' Amy said generously. 'Emma and I don't mind. It's 'cos you're a boy and boys don't know about things like that, you see.'

Daniel laughed. 'Obviously not! Anyway, let's get this mess cleared up then we can have something to eat. Have you seen what time it is?'

He grimaced as he checked his watch. Emma was surprised when she realised how late it was. She'd been having so much fun that she'd lost track of the time. She was just about to suggest that it was time she left when Daniel spoke.

'If you'd mind Amy, I can pop out and buy some fish and chips, Emma.'

'Fish and chips?' Amy clapped her hands in delight and Emma didn't have the heart to refuse and spoil the treat. However, she made up her mind that she would leave as soon as they'd eaten the meal. She and Amy cleared up all the wrappings from the tree decorations while Daniel went to get their supper. They had the table set by the time he came back.

'I just heard on the car radio that there's been a flood warning. Evidently, they're expecting the sea to breach its defences because of this storm,' he informed her as he took off his coat.

'I did wonder if it might happen,' Emma replied, quickly unpacking the steaming hot fish and chips and arranging them on the plates. 'It's high tide tonight as well, you see, so that could cause extra problems.'

'Then why don't you stay here? There doesn't seem any point in taking unnecessary risks.' He frowned. 'Heaven only knows what the roads will be like in a couple of hours' time.'

'You can sleep in my room if you want to, Emma,' Amy told her quickly. 'Then if you get scared by the storm we can snuggle up in bed together. Mummy used to let me snuggle up with her if I was scared.'

Emma's heart ached at the wistful note she'd heard in Amy's voice. It was obvious that Amy still missed her mother a lot. 'Thank you, sweetheart. That's very kind of you but I think it would be better if I went home. I've a lot of things to do in the morning, you see.'

'Oh. All right, then.'

Thankfully, Amy didn't sound too disappointed as she started to eat her supper. However, when Emma glanced at Daniel she could see the pain in his eyes. She knew that he must be thinking about his sister, and her heart went out to him.

Without stopping to think, she touched his hand. He smiled as he gave her fingers a gentle squeeze. It was a moment of sadness made bearable because they'd shared it. It made Emma feel very close to him, closer than she'd felt to anyone ever before.

'So the two little elves stayed at the North Pole and helped Santa make all the presents for the children.'

Emma closed the book and quietly turned off the bedside lamp. Amy had begged Emma to read her a bedtime story before she left and she hadn't been able to refuse the child's pleas. One story had led to another but Amy had finally fallen asleep.

After tucking the quilt around the little girl, Emma crept from the room and went downstairs. It was almost nine and way past the time she should have left. She went to find Daniel to ask him if she could ring for a taxi and discovered that he was in the living room. He'd turned off the light so that the room was lit only by the fairy lights on the Christmas tree.

'Is she asleep at last?' Daniel must have heard her coming downstairs because he turned towards the door. Emma couldn't help thinking how handsome he looked in the soft glow from the tree lights. It was warm in the house so he'd shed his sweater and was wearing only a thin white polo shirt. When he stood up she felt her heart bump heavily as she saw how it clung to his powerful torso, emphasising the perfect conformation of muscles.

'Yes.' She heard the thickness in her voice and cleared her throat. 'It took three stories before she gave in, though.'

Daniel laughed softly. 'I should have warned you that Amy would have you reading until you were hoarse if you let her. In fact, you sound as though your throat is a bit dry, so how about a glass of wine to lubricate it?'

'I…I was just going to ask if I could phone for a taxi, actually.' Emma was glad of the darkness because it hid her blush. Obviously, Daniel had heard that husky note in her voice but mercifully put his own interpretation on its cause.

'Another few minutes won't make much difference surely? And it isn't that late. You should be home by ten even if you stay for a glass of wine.'

Emma laughed at the unashamedly wheedling note in his voice and it helped dispel the tension. 'All right, then. But just one glass and I really must go home.'

'Just one glass it is. Scout's honour!'

He gave her a smiling salute as he left the room. Emma

went and sat on the sofa, resting her head on the cushions. It was so quiet in the room after all the bustle of the day that she found herself sinking deeper into the cushions. She could hear Daniel moving about in the kitchen but the sound was too muted to disturb her...

She jolted awake as she felt her eyelids drooping. Whether it was because of the warmth in the room or the fact that they hadn't stopped all day long, she could barely stay awake. When Daniel came back a few minutes later with the wine she had to force her eyes open once again.

'Sorry it took so long. The wretched cork broke...' He stopped and looked at her. 'Were you asleep?' he asked silkily.

'Um, no, of course not.' Emma sat up straighter and tried to look suitably alert. However, the effect was somewhat spoilt when she felt an enormous yawn creeping up on her.

Daniel laughed as he handed her one of the glasses. 'I believe you although thousands wouldn't! Just try to stay awake long enough to drink that wine. I hope you like white, by the way, because that's all I've got.'

'It's fine. Thank you.' Emma took a sip of the wine while he filled a second glass for himself. He sat down beside her and she flinched as she felt his thigh brush hers.

Burying her face in the glass, she took another swallow of the wine while she tried to control the rush of sensations which had assailed her. It wasn't easy, however. When Daniel bent down to put the bottle on the floor next to the sofa and his arm touched hers, she felt her nerves tauten. Maybe it was the fact that it was dark in the room that made her senses seem hyperactive all of a sudden, but she was so deeply aware of him sitting beside her that it was an effort to behave naturally.

'Not bad, although I can't claim to be an expert.' Daniel smiled at her over the rim of his glass. 'I know if I like a particular wine and that's about it, I'm afraid.'

Emma summoned a smile, pleased that the conversation

had turned to such impersonal topics. If she could concentrate on discussing the relative merits of the wine, she wouldn't be nearly as conscious of him, she reasoned.

'Me, too. Seeing as my budget only stretches to a bottle of whatever is cheapest at the supermarket that week, I don't think I'm going to become an expert either!'

'You mean you don't go in for all that tasting and spitting?' Daniel feigned surprise, making her laugh.

'I most certainly don't! When I buy a bottle of wine I certainly don't waste any of it!'

'Ah, a woman after my own heart.' He grinned at her and Emma couldn't help smiling back. There was a moment when they looked at one another while they shared the joke, and then the mood seemed to shift with a speed that left Emma reeling. She wanted to look away yet she felt incapable of doing that when Daniel's gaze seemed to have mesmerised her.

'Has anyone ever told you how pretty you are, Emma Graham?' he asked softly, his voice grating so that she shivered.

'N-not really,' she muttered. She nervously wet her lips then shivered again when she saw his eyes following the movement of her tongue. Suddenly the atmosphere in the room seemed to crackle as though the air had been charged with electricity. She could feel her body growing tense in response to it, feel the jolt her heart gave when Daniel took the glass from her hand and put it on the floor next to his.

Her grey eyes were enormous as she watched him turn to her once more. She knew that he was going to kiss her and she knew also that he was giving her time to decide if it was what she wanted. Was it? Yes! No! She wasn't sure!

'They must be mad,' he whispered, his warm breath stirring the curls by her ear as he put his arms around her. 'Mad or blind, maybe.'

'Who?' she murmured, struggling to follow what he was saying. It wasn't easy because her brain had so many other things to deal with. Was it wise to let him kiss her? Would she regret it? If only she could decide!

'All those men who haven't told you how beautiful you are, of course.'

Daniel's voice was rich with amusement but there was nothing playful about his kiss. Emma felt the confident way his mouth closed over hers and knew the decision had been taken for her. She closed her eyes and simply gave herself up to the pleasure of being kissed by an expert. It was like a master-class in what a kiss should be, and when it ended she was breathless and shaking. Oddly enough, so was Daniel.

He rested his forehead against hers and his tone was rueful. 'Wow! Did anyone ever tell you what a great kisser you are, Emma Graham?'

'No.' She smiled because the conversation was so ridiculous. 'I'll be getting big-headed if you carry on like this. I'm pretty and a great kisser? Oh, boy!'

He laughed at that. Drawing her into the crook of his arm, he brushed his mouth over the top of her head. 'You're also kind to helpless males and young children.'

'Please!' She grinned up at him, feeling happier than she'd ever felt at that moment. 'I don't know if I can take any more compliments! Anyway, if you were referring to yourself when you mentioned ''helpless males'' then I think that's exaggerating things a little too much. You don't strike me as at all helpless, Dr Hutton!'

'Maybe not in my professional capacity. However, I'm not sure about in my private life.'

There had been the strangest note in his voice when he'd said that. Emma frowned as a chill ran through her. Had it been a reference to something that had happened in the past? Once again the thought surfaced that Daniel had been in a relationship which had gone wrong. She was on the verge of asking him to explain what he'd meant when the telephone rang.

'I wonder who that can be. I'd better answer it before it wakes Amy.'

Daniel hurried from the room, turning on the main light as he did so. Emma blinked as she looked around the room. Suddenly, the magic which had been in the air a few moments earlier seemed to have disappeared. Why *had* Daniel kissed her just now? Because he was a normal, healthy male, programmed to respond when there was a young and obviously willing female beside him?

The thought was perhaps a little too close to the truth. Emma stood up abruptly, hating herself because it had hurt so much to realise it. It was an effort to hide how she felt when Daniel came back. However, one look at the grim expression on his face told her that there must be something seriously wrong.

'What's happened?' she demanded anxiously.

'That was Max on the phone to tell me that there's been an accident on the outskirts of town. Evidently, the high tide has washed away a section of the coast road and the rescue services aren't sure how many people may have been injured.

'They've managed to rescue six so far but there's every chance that there will be more casualties. The hospital has declared it a major incident and are asking for all staff to report for duty.'

'We'd better get into work, then...' Emma stopped in dismay. 'What about Amy?'

'Max said that if I couldn't find anyone to mind her, I should bring her with me.' Daniel shrugged. 'It isn't ideal to take her but I can't think what else to do. There's nobody I can leave her with at this time of the night and she can't stay here by herself, that's for sure.'

Emma thought rapidly. 'I could make up a bed for her in the office. She would be safe enough in there and I could keep an eye on her to make sure that she doesn't wander off.'

'Would you?' Daniel looked relieved. 'At least I'd know she was in safe hands with you there, Emma. Heaven knows where I'll be needed and I might not get chance to keep checking on her.'

'You don't need to worry, Daniel. I'll take good care of her,' she assured him.

'I know you will.'

His voice was very deep as he said that. Emma wasn't sure if there had been something behind it but there was no time to ask questions. While Daniel woke up Amy and explained what was happening, Emma put together a bag of toys which she thought the little girl might need. It might be noisy in the ward if they were having to admit patients and it was doubtful if Amy would get much sleep.

Still, at least she'd be there to keep a watchful eye on her, Emma thought as she followed Daniel and Amy out to the car. For some reason that seemed very important. Taking care of Daniel's niece was something she was only too pleased to do…for many reasons.

'We've managed to stop the contractions but she's going to need monitoring closely for the next twenty-four hours.'

Daniel's tone was curt but Emma knew that it was because he was worried. She glanced at the young woman who had been sent up to the ward from the casualty department. Maria Carstairs was twenty-two weeks pregnant with her first child. She had been a passenger in one of the vehicles involved in the RTA and had been rushed in by ambulance because she was threatening to miscarry.

Daniel drew Emma aside while one of the night staff got Maria settled. The extra nursing staff had been deployed wherever they were needed most throughout the hospital. Emma had stayed in her own ward as they were expecting the bulk of the admissions. Beds were at a premium so it was a question of finding places for the injured even though

they would need to be moved at a later date. It had meant
a lot of juggling around but they were coping.

'The ultrasound shows that the baby is still alive so we
just have to keep our fingers crossed, basically. I've put her
on salbutamol as a uterine muscle relaxant and that seems
to have worked.'

'I'll put her down for half-hourly obs,' Emma assured
him. 'How is it down in A and E?'

'Pretty grim, but we're getting there. The police seem to
think that they've found all the casualties now, which is
something to be thankful for.' He looked round and
frowned. 'How's Amy been? I can't imagine that she's
been asleep with all the comings and goings tonight. I hope
she hasn't been a nuisance?'

'Of course not!' Emma laughed. 'When is she ever a
nuisance, Daniel? She's been quite happy in the office,
drawing a picture.'

'So long as you haven't been tearing your hair out, trying
to look after her and work as well.' Daniel sighed. 'I really
didn't mean to offload my responsibilities onto you, Emma.
You must be regretting the day you took pity on me and
agreed to help.'

'Rubbish! I'm only too happy to help any way I can.'

'Really? You aren't just saying that?' There was a note
in his voice which told her that her answer was important
to him. She couldn't help wondering why he should doubt
that she'd been telling him the truth.

'No, I'm not,' she said firmly, knowing that it was neither the time nor the place to start worrying about it. Even
now she could hear the lift arriving, undoubtedly bringing
yet another patient to the ward. 'I mean it, Daniel. I really
enjoy being with Amy.'

And with you, she added silently, only she thought it
better not to mention that fact out loud. However, it did
appear that he was reassured.

'Thanks. I don't feel so guilty now—' He stopped as his

pager beeped. 'Looks like I'm wanted again. I'll see you later. Wait for me in the foyer when we're given the all-clear so that I can run you home.'

'You don't need to…' she began, but he was already hurrying towards the lift. He waited until the porters had wheeled out the trolley then disappeared.

Emma smiled to herself as she went to meet the new patient. It was all systems go but it was good to be part of the team and feel needed. Was that why she was enjoying helping Daniel make this Christmas special for Amy?

It was a simple enough explanation yet Emma knew in her heart that the answer was far more complex than that. She frowned as she tried to work it out but it was rather like one of those maths problems—if you added A to B then added C, what did you get?

She tried substituting names for the letters to see if that made it any clearer.

Daniel plus Amy plus herself equalled…what?

A happy family?

Of course not! No wonder maths had been her worst subject at school if that was the kind of answer she came up with!

CHAPTER SEVEN

IT WAS almost two a.m. before the all-clear was given. It had been a hectic night and Emma was glad that it was over. There had been fourteen casualties brought into the hospital but, amazingly, only two were in a critical condition. All in all, it could have been an awful lot worse, she reflected as she went to collect a tired-looking Amy.

'Can we go home now, Emma?' the little girl asked as soon as she saw her.

'We can, indeed. We have to meet Uncle Daniel downstairs. He'll be waiting in the foyer for us so let's go and get our coats.'

Emma led Amy to the staffroom. She smiled as she opened the door and saw Linda leaning against the lockers with her eyes closed. 'No sleeping on the job, Nurse Wood!'

'I'm bushed.' Linda didn't bother opening her eyes. 'I've been on autopilot for the past hour. To think I'd planned to spend the evening in front of the telly, watching that new hospital drama.'

'But instead you found yourself playing a starring role in our very own version,' Emma teased. 'Who says that real life doesn't mirror fiction, or is it vice versa?'

'I dunno. I'm too tired to care anyway.' Linda opened one eye and stared blearily at her. 'I've no idea why you're so perky at this time of the night.'

'Oh, I could hazard a guess.' Jane had arrived back from the A and E unit where she'd been helping to register the casualties as they'd been brought in. She shot a pointed look at Amy and grinned. 'They say that love overcomes all obstacles so maybe that includes bad backs and aching feet!'

Emma blushed furiously, although she didn't say anything. She quickly took Amy's coat from her locker and helped the child to zip it up.

'Anyway, your Daniel was a huge hit in A and E, Emma.' Jane was in the process of shedding her uniform and her voice was muffled as she dragged the top over her head. 'I think he's added several more members to his fan club tonight.'

'He isn't *my* Daniel,' Emma corrected her, conscious that Amy was listening to what was being said. 'I told you that I'm just helping him out.'

'Hmm, well, there's helping and then again there's *helping,* isn't there?' Jane teased, pulling on her sweater.

Emma rolled her eyes. 'I give up! Think what you like. I know what the truth is!'

She headed for the door then paused when she saw Mike Humphreys standing there. He gave her an odd look but carried on along the corridor without saying anything. Emma sighed as she realised that Mike still appeared to be nursing a grudge. She didn't want to fall out with him but there was no way that she was going to apologise when she didn't believe she'd been at fault.

'Hold on! I'm coming with you.'

Linda caught up with them and they went down in the lift together. There were a lot of staff milling about in the foyer. Emma looked round but she couldn't see any sign of Daniel.

'Daniel said to tell you that he's been held up.' Ruby Jones, one of the senior staff nurses on A and E, tapped Emma on the shoulder. 'He said that he'd be grateful if you'd take Amy home with you and he'll collect her as soon as he can.'

'Oh, right. Thanks, Ruby.' Emma sighed as the other

woman hurried away. 'I suppose I'd better see if I can find a taxi.'

'Don't be daft. I'll drop you off on my way,' Linda offered immediately.

'Would you? Oh, thanks, Linda. I'd appreciate it.' Emma turned to Amy with a smile. 'It looks as though you'll be staying at my flat until Uncle Daniel can leave the hospital. Is that OK?'

Amy nodded solemnly. 'Does that mean I can sleep in your bed, Emma?'

'You'll have to, seeing as I only have one bed. Still, it's a big bed so there'll be plenty of room for us both.'

Emma took hold of the child's hand as they left the building. The wind had died down now that the storm had passed. It was still raining, however, so she quickened her pace as they hurried to where Linda had parked her car.

'Where will Uncle Daniel sleep? Is your bed big enough for him as well?' Amy asked in all innocence.

'Out of the mouths of babes, eh, Emma?' Linda teased as she unlocked the car doors.

Emma pretended that she hadn't heard the remark as she helped Amy into the car. 'Don't worry about that now, Amy,' she said firmly. 'Let's just concentrate on getting home.'

Thankfully, Amy let the subject drop. Linda didn't mention it again either, although Emma knew that it wouldn't have been forgotten. She sighed as she fastened her seat belt. When would people accept that she was only helping Daniel as any friend would have done?

Maybe when *she* believed it herself, a small voice whispered silkily.

Emma's lips compressed. She didn't intend even to think about that!

It didn't take long to get Amy ready for bed. The child was almost asleep on her feet. Emma found one of her T-shirts for the little girl to wear in the absence of any proper night-wear. She tucked Amy up in one side of the big double bed then quickly undressed and slid beneath the quilt. She, too, fell asleep almost as soon as her head touched the pillow and didn't stir until the sound of the doorbell ringing woke her just before nine.

Emma struggled out of bed and dragged on a dressing-gown. Amy was still fast asleep so she took care not to wake her. She ran down the stairs and opened the front door to find Daniel on the step. He looked grey with fatigue, his shoulders slumping tiredly as he propped himself against the wall.

'Hi. Sorry it took so long to get here. I ended up in Theatre, dealing with an abruption of the placenta,' he explained. 'Fortunately, the baby was viable so we were able to do a Caesarean, but the mother was very shocked.'

'Will she be all right?' Emma asked worriedly. When the placenta suddenly separated from its bed it could cause a lot of problems. The main risk was to the baby because of the interruption to the blood supply it received via the placenta. Shock and blood loss were the most dangerous side effects for the mother and always required urgent hospital treatment.

'I think so, but it was touch and go at one stage which is why it took so long. Anyway, I decided that I might as well collect Amy on my way home rather than come back for her later.'

'She's still asleep, I'm afraid. Look, why don't you come in and have a cup of coffee?' Emma offered immediately.

Daniel hesitated. 'I don't want to disturb you, although it's probably a bit late to worry about that. Were you asleep as well when I rang the bell, Emma?'

He sighed when she nodded. 'Sorry! I feel really guilty about waking you up now. Look, you go on back to bed. You can phone me whenever you're ready and I'll come back for Amy.'

He started to leave but Emma stopped him. 'Don't be silly. I'm up now so there's no point in me going back to bed. Come in and have that coffee. You look as though you need it, quite frankly.'

'Well, if you're sure...?' Daniel shrugged. 'OK. You've talked me into it. Actually, a cup of coffee would be great. I've just about reached the point where my eyes are open but the rest of me has gone to sleep!'

'Then you certainly shouldn't be driving in that state!' Emma said firmly. 'Or it will be you having an accident if you're not careful.'

Daniel laughed. 'Yes, Staff!'

Emma laughed with him then led the way upstairs to her flat. 'Go into the sitting room and make yourself comfortable while I make the coffee. Could you manage some toast to go with it?'

'Please.' Daniel sighed ruefully. 'It seems an age since we had those fish and chips, doesn't it? I'm starving.'

He ambled into the sitting room, leaving Emma to hurry to the kitchen to make coffee and toast. She loaded everything onto a tray then took it through to the sitting room, pausing when she discovered that Daniel was sprawled out on her sofa, fast asleep.

Emma quietly put the tray on the coffee-table and went to fetch a blanket to cover him with. He murmured as she tucked it around him but he didn't wake up. Emma smiled as she studied his sleeping face. He was obviously worn out after the hectic night and would probably sleep for hours if he got the chance.

She poured herself a cup of the coffee then sat down while she drank it, watching Daniel while he slept. It felt right to have him here in her flat just as it felt right to know that Amy was asleep in her bed. Funny how important Daniel and his niece had become to her in such a short time. It made her realise how hard it was going to be once Christmas was over. She'd promised Daniel that she would help him give Amy a very special Christmas, but it was a gift which came with strings attached. It wasn't going to be easy to cut them and walk away afterwards.

Amy awoke a short time later. Emma went to the bedroom as soon as she heard the little girl moving around.

'Good morning, Amy. You had a nice long sleep, didn't you? Are you hungry?'

Amy nodded sleepily. 'Can I have my breakfast here with you, Emma, before Uncle Daniel comes?'

'Uncle Daniel is already here, darling. He arrived a few minutes ago but he was so tired that he's fallen asleep on the sofa.' Emma smiled as Amy giggled. 'Shall we try to be very quiet so that we don't wake him up?'

The child thought it was a marvellous game, tiptoeing around the flat. Emma took her into the kitchen and gave her a bowl of cornflakes and some orange juice then sent her to get washed and dressed. Daniel was still fast asleep when Emma checked on him so she decided there was no point in waking him up. She wrote him a brief note to let him know that she was taking Amy to the shops then they set off.

They spent a very pleasant couple of hours, pottering around the shops. With there being only a week or so to go before Christmas, most of the town's traders had decided to open that Sunday. Emma bought a few small gifts for her friends at work then helped Amy choose a present for Daniel. It wasn't easy, finding something the child thought would be just right for him, but in the end Amy decided on a bright blue tie patterned all over with bells and holly. Emma couldn't help smiling as she pictured Daniel wearing it with one his elegant suits!

It was almost noon when they arrived back at the flat. Emma let them in then crept into the sitting room, expecting to find Daniel still asleep. However, the only sign of him was the neatly folded blanket on the sofa, and she frowned. Had he decided to go home when he'd discovered that she and Amy had gone out?

'Hi, there. Have you two had a good time, then?'

Emma spun round as Daniel suddenly appeared. She felt her eyes widen as she took in what he was wearing, which was very little! He must have just got out of the shower, and one of her pink towels wrapped around his hips was all he had on.

Emma felt her mouth go dry as she was presented with the sight of his muscular body. In a fast sweep her eyes took note of the tanned skin drawn tautly over those well-honed muscles, the thick, dark curls which covered his broad chest. Droplets of water sparkled in his hair. As Emma watched, a bead of water dropped onto his shoulder and began to trickle down his chest. Her eyes seemed to be mesmerised as she followed its progress...

She turned away, feeling shaken by the way she was behaving. She had seen other men naked before—it would be amazing if she hadn't, considering the job she did! However, there was no way that she could compare how she'd felt on those occasions with how she felt at that moment, her body aching in a way she barely understood.

'Emma? Are you OK?' Daniel asked. He paused and she heard the faint uncertainty in his voice when he continued, 'You didn't mind me taking a shower, did you?'

'Of course not! Don't be silly.' Her tone was a shade too bright and she saw his eyes darken with puzzlement. She hurried on, wanting to distract him before he worked out why she was behaving so strangely. It was bad enough knowing how Daniel affected her, without him realising it as well!

'I was just a bit surprised when you appeared like that. When I saw that you weren't in the sitting room I assumed that you'd gone home.'

'I've only just woken up,' he explained quietly. 'I read your note so I thought I'd take a shower while you and

Amy were out. Then I'd be ready to take her home when you got back.'

He turned to his niece and Emma had the funniest feeling that it was just an excuse to avoid looking at her. Why? What was it that Daniel didn't want her to see?

'So, what have you bought, then? Aren't you going to show me?'

She pushed the thought to the back of her mind as Amy shook her head. 'I can't tell you, Uncle Daniel, 'cos it's a secret!'

'Oh, is it, indeed? A secret, eh? I wonder what *sort* of a secret,' he teased the little girl.

'It's a present for you but you have to wait till Christmas Day to see what it is!' Amy couldn't quite manage to keep it to herself and Emma laughed.

'Don't tell him anything else, Amy! It won't be so much fun if you spoil the surprise.'

'Whose side are you on, you wicked woman?' Daniel's tone was dry as he turned to her. 'I thought you were a nice kind person but here you are encouraging this little horror to torment the life out of me. I don't know if I can last till Christmas Day without knowing what my present is!'

'Tough!' Emma declared unsympathetically. 'You'll just have to learn to be patient, won't you? Anyway, it's only just over a week until Christmas Day. I'm sure you can wait that long!'

'I suppose I shall have to, seeing as you two females have ganged up on me.' Daniel tried to look suitably pathetic but failed miserably. He gave a heavy sigh when Amy giggled. 'I can see that I'm not going to persuade you two to take pity on me so I may as well get dressed. But it's tit for tat, don't forget. If you won't show me my present then I won't show you yours!'

Emma laughed as he stalked away. 'Isn't he naughty, trying to get you to show him his present, Amy? I tell you what, why don't you wrap it up before he comes back? That way he won't get chance to peek at it.'

She found the child some colourful Christmas paper and helped her to wrap the tie. Amy insisted on using several sheets of paper and yards of sticky tape. Emma chuckled as she looked at the lumpy package. 'Well, I don't think there's much danger of Daniel managing to undo that in a hurry.'

'What are you up to now?' Daniel came back into the room, fully dressed now. He laughed as Amy ran to show him the present. 'Can I just have a little squeeze?' he wheedled. 'Maybe I can work out what it is…'

'No! That's naughty, Uncle Daniel.' Amy whipped the present out of his reach and turned appealingly to Emma. 'Tell him he's not to do that, Emma.'

'You most certainly mustn't. Father Christmas takes a very dim view of people who try to peek at their presents before Christmas Day,' she warned him solemnly, trying not to laugh.

'I shall bear it in mind. I don't want to wake up on Christmas morning and find my stocking is empty. All right, I promise that I'll behave from now on,' he replied with suitable solemnity, although his eyes were sparkling with laughter. 'Anyway, it's time that Amy and I were on our way. We've taken up enough of your time one way and another, Emma. Thanks for having Amy to stay last night and for looking after her while I was in A and E. I really appreciate it.'

'It was my pleasure,' she told him sincerely. She gave the child a hug when Amy came running to her. 'You must come and stay here again some time. Would you like that?'

'Oh, yes!' Amy turned to Daniel. 'Emma has a really big bed, Uncle Daniel, so you could stay, too,' she explained guilelessly.

'Mmm, I think it's time we left,' Daniel declared. There seemed to be more amusement in his voice than anything else, Emma noticed. There certainly wasn't any indication that he found the idea of spending the night in her bed tempting!

Emma didn't know why she should feel disappointed. However, she did her best to hide her feelings as she saw him and Amy out. Daniel paused on the step. 'Thanks again, Emma. I really do appreciate everything you've done.'

He kissed her lightly on the cheek then hurried to his car. Amy waved as they drove away and Emma waved back. She closed the door as the car disappeared from sight and went back upstairs. She had a lot to do that day—washing, ironing, cleaning—all the hundred and one jobs which accumulated while she was out at work. However, her mind was only partly on what she was doing as she started loading the washing machine. Her thoughts were mainly of Daniel and what had happened in the past week.

She sighed as she added detergent to the machine. How had he become such a major part of her life in such a short time?

Most of the extra patients had been moved from the ward by the time Emma arrived for work on Monday morning. However, Maria Carstairs, the patient who'd been threatening to miscarry, was still there.

Fortunately, Daniel's prompt treatment appeared to have worked and there was a good chance that Maria's baby would go to term. She was staying in the ward for a few more days as a precaution, but everyone was cautiously optimistic that the danger had been averted. Emma went to speak to her in the middle of the morning and found Maria looking a lot better than when she'd been admitted on the Saturday night.

'No need to ask how you are,' she said cheerfully, automatically checking Maria's chart. 'You look a lot better than the last time I saw you.'

Maria frowned. 'I'm sorry, I don't seem to remember you. It was all such a nightmare, you understand. I was so scared that I was going to lose the baby.'

'It must have been awful for you,' Emma sympathised. 'It's no wonder you don't remember everyone's faces. I was here when Dr Hutton brought you up from A and E.'

'I remember Dr Hutton. How could I forget him?' Maria's face broke into a warm smile. 'He was so kind to me. Rob, that's my husband, well, Rob said that if it hadn't been for Dr Hutton we would have lost the baby. Is that right?'

'Oh, I think it's fair to say that,' Emma said lightly, feeling a little rush of pride at the thought of the role Daniel had played in helping to save Maria's baby. 'He's a wonderful doctor and all the patients like him.'

'Obviously, you think very highly of him, Nurse,' Maria observed, and Emma blushed. She hadn't realised how revealing her comments had been.

'We all do,' she explained carefully, and excused herself as she saw that Sister Carter was trying to attract her attention to warn her that the ward round was about to begin.

She hurried to fetch the patients' notes because she knew how Max Dennison hated to be kept waiting, but when she came back with the trolley it was to find that Daniel was taking the round that day. He had Mike with him, as well as Tina Majors, the obs and gynae junior registrar. Sister Carter took her aside and quietly explained that Mr Dennison was off sick that day so Daniel was standing in for him.

Emma left them to carry on because there was always a lot to do throughout the day. However, she couldn't help wondering how it would affect Daniel's schedule if he had to step in for his chief for a prolonged period. That it might have repercussions on the amount of time he could spend with Amy was another worrying thought.

She made up her mind to have a word with him and

offer to help in any way she could. Amy would be breaking up from school in the next few days so that could cause a problem. And there was all the shopping still to be done— the food and all the other things which needed to be bought. With Christmas now less than a week away there was an awful lot to get ready.

Emma had no chance to speak to Daniel after the ward round because Sister Carter was keen to discuss the adjustments that had been made to various patients' treatment. Shirley Rogers's temperature was still causing some concern and Daniel had increased the level of antibiotics she was receiving. It meant that Shirley would be staying with them a bit longer and the poor woman was very disappointed. Emma found her close to tears when she stopped by her bed after Sister Carter had disappeared into the office with Daniel and his entourage.

'Why did I have to get this stupid infection?' Shirley demanded, blowing her nose on a very damp tissue. 'I thought I would have been discharged today and now it looks as though I might still be here on Christmas Day! I don't know what my Ron and the boys are going to do without me there to cook the dinner for them.'

'There's still time for you to be allowed to go home, Shirley, although I have to say that it would be very silly of you to go rushing around,' Emma warned. 'Surely your husband and sons can manage for once?'

'Oh, I don't know about that…' Shirley shook her head. 'I can't see any of them setting to and stuffing a turkey, can you, love?'

Emma laughed at that. She'd met Shirley's husband and sons and could understand her concerns. All four of the Rogers men were very down to earth but she doubted that they'd seen any need to learn how to cook when they had Shirley to do it for them.

'No, I can't, I'm afraid. It's your fault for spoiling them, Shirley.'

'I can't help it. I think I must just be made that way. I enjoy looking after them, although I know that isn't the politically correct thing to say.' Shirley laughed. 'I suppose I must seem very old-fashioned to a young woman like you.'

Emma shook her head. Her tone was unconsciously wistful as she thought about how much she was enjoying looking after Amy and, in a way, Daniel. 'No, I don't think that at all. I imagine it's very satisfying to take care of the people you love. But don't forget that it works two ways. Maybe Ron and the boys would enjoy having the chance to look after you for once.'

Shirley nodded thoughtfully. 'You could be right at that. Thanks, love. You've cheered me up a bit.'

'My pleasure,' Emma declared with a grin, before she went to prepare a patient who would be going to Theatre shortly. All the time she was running through the familiar routine, her mind kept playing with the thought of how hard it was going to be after Christmas when there was only herself to look after. Being part of a family, even if it was only for a short time, was something to treasure.

In the end it was Daniel who sought Emma out. She'd not had time to speak to him because he'd been due in Theatre after leaving the ward. She was on her way to the canteen for lunch when he caught up with her by the lift.

'Can you spare a minute, Emma?' he asked, nodding pleasantly to Linda and Eileen.

'Of course.' Emma turned to her friends, trying to ignore the knowing looks they were giving her. 'I'll catch you up in a minute.'

'Don't rush. We'll save you a seat.' Linda treated her to a wicked smile and Emma groaned as she realised that she would be in line for the third degree when she did join them! However, there was no point worrying about it right then so she put it out of her mind and followed Daniel into the television lounge, which was empty at that moment. He looked so harassed, anyway, that her main concern was what might be wrong.

'Problems?' she asked, perching on the arm of a chair.

'How did you guess?' He sighed as he sank heavily onto the chair opposite. 'You know that Max is off sick. Well, evidently, he's been having chest pains for several weeks but has ignored them. However, it got so bad last night that his wife had to call his GP.

'Anyway, the outcome of it all is that Max is suffering from angina and he's been told that he has to take time off work while they sort out his treatment.'

'Really? He always seems so fit. He certainly rushes around like a man half his age,' Emma exclaimed.

'I know, although I've noticed on a couple of occasions that he appeared to be in some sort of discomfort. He passed it off when I asked him if he was all right, said that it was indigestion. Obviously, it was more serious than that,' Daniel explained dryly.

Emma sighed. 'Sounds about right. Medical professionals are the world's worst at admitting that there might be anything wrong with them!'

Daniel laughed. 'Amen to that! But it does mean that with Max off my workload is going to virtually double, and that's going to create no end of problems at the moment.'

'You know that I'll do anything I can to help,' Emma offered immediately.

'Thanks. I was hoping you'd say that, even though I feel guilty for putting on you like this.' Daniel's smile was warm and Emma shrugged, not wanting him to guess how it affected her. Just a smile and her heart was singing arias. Crazy!

'Don't be silly. Just tell me how I can help you.'

'Well, first off is the shopping. I had been planning on taking a couple of days off this week to get everything done, but that's out of the question now. Is there any chance I can leave it to you, Emma?'

He ran his hand through his hair and sighed. 'It's not only the food that needs to be bought but Amy's presents as well. I just haven't had chance to get round to doing it, you see.'

'I'll be happy to get anything you need. Luckily I'm off from the twenty-third right through till after Boxing Day so I'll have plenty of time to do it.'

'Are you sure? I don't want you spending all your free time on this. You must have other things planned, apart from Amy's Christmas!'

Daniel laughed ruefully and Emma smiled. 'Nothing that can't wait, believe me. No, I'm happy to do it, Daniel. Honestly, I am.'

He took a deep breath and his eyes shone with something she found impossible to understand. 'Thank you, Emma. I just don't know what I would have done if you hadn't offered to help me.'

'You'd have managed somehow,' she said, smiling at him. 'Anyway, I'm looking forward to it. I want it to be a very special Christmas, too!'

'Oh, it will be. I don't have any doubts about that.' Daniel glanced round as the door opened. His smiled faded when he saw Mike Humphreys. 'Did you want me?' he asked coolly.

'Max is on the phone. He needs to speak to you urgently,' Mike told him flatly.

Daniel got up at once. 'I'd better see what he wants. He won't do himself any good if he keeps worrying about what's going on here.' He glanced at Emma. 'I'll catch you later, Emma. OK?'

He hurried away as Emma got up and went to the door. Mike was still standing there and he looked quizzically at her. 'You two seem to be getting very pally of late. Linda said that you're helping Hutton with his niece or something.'

Emma quelled the urge to tell him to mind his own business. Maybe this was the opportunity she'd been looking for to smooth over their differences. 'That's right. Daniel asked me if I'd help him get everything ready for Christmas.'

'It's a shame, isn't it? I feel sorry for the poor kid.' Mike hurried on when she looked at him. 'It must be hard on her, losing her mother at such a young age, I mean.'

Emma smiled more warmly at him. Maybe Mike wasn't quite as insensitive as she'd thought him to be. He was obviously concerned about Amy and that had to be a point in his favour. 'It is a shame. Amy is only six and it must have been a huge wrench for her, losing her mother. Still, Daniel's making a marvellous job of looking after her.'

'I'm sure he is.' Mike smiled easily when she shot him a sharp look. She couldn't help wondering if there had been a trace of sarcasm in his voice. However, she couldn't see any sign of it and immediately felt guilty that she should keep misjudging him all the time.

'Look, Em, you and I seem to have got our signals crossed somehow or other. I hate to think that we can't be friends so can we forget what happened the other day?'

'If that's what you want, of course we can, Mike,' she agreed immediately, feeling worse than ever when she saw how anxious he looked. Obviously, her friendship meant a lot to him.

'Oh, that's great!' He gave her a wide smile. 'It's a weight off my mind, I can tell you. So, to prove that we're friends again, will you come to the staff dance with me after all?'

'Oh, well, I'm not sure—' she began, but Mike didn't let her finish.

'Come on, say you will! I was so looking forward to having you as my partner and I won't feel that we've cleared the air unless you agree,' he added persuasively.

Emma sighed because she wasn't sure what to do. She didn't want to fall out with Mike again by refusing, but she wasn't sure if she had the time to go when there was so much to do.

'Maybe you've had a better offer.' Mike sounded disappointed. 'I don't blame you if you'd prefer to go to the dance with Daniel Hutton.'

'That isn't it at all,' she said quickly, wanting to stem any rumours before they had chance to circulate. 'I'm helping Daniel with his Christmas arrangements, but we certainly aren't going *out* together.'

'Then say you'll come to the dance. I don't expect you to stay all night if you have things to do, but it would mean a lot to me, Em.'

Emma's tender heart went out to Mike as he pleaded with her. What harm would there be in spending a couple of hours at the dance? She would have plenty of time to help Daniel. All he wanted her for was to help him make Amy's Christmas perfect. It wasn't as though he wanted her company for any other reason.

The thought was so deflating that it spurred Emma into making up her mind. It was about time she started trying to build up her social life. Once Christmas was over with there would be a big gap in her life. She would have to find a way to fill it one way or another.

'All right, then, I'll come. But I might not be able to stay all night.'

'Oh, don't worry about that. So long as you come, that's all I'm interested in.'

Emma frowned as Mike quickly said goodbye and hurried away. Was it her imagination again or had there been something behind that last statement?

She sighed as it struck her that she was in danger of misjudging the young house officer once again. Or was it that she was in danger of judging him against Daniel?

Could any man bear such a comparison and come out on top? she wondered as she went for her lunch. Unlikely. Highly unlikely. Daniel Hutton was head and shoulders above any other man she knew. It would be very hard to find anyone to measure up to him.

Her mouth curved into a sad little smile. The thought of spending her life looking for someone to match up to Daniel wasn't an appealing prospect at all.

CHAPTER EIGHT

DANIEL was waiting for Emma when she left the hospital that evening. He drew her aside out of the way of the flow of people making their way in and out of the building.

'I won't keep you long,' he told her quickly. 'I just thought it might be useful if I gave you this.'

He handed her a key. 'It's a key to my house. It seems pointless, you having to haul bags of shopping home to your flat and then me having to collect them later, doesn't it? You may as well take them straight to the house.'

'It would be a lot easier, if you don't mind,' Emma agreed.

'Of course I don't mind! You just go in whenever you need to, Emma. You don't need to check with me before-hand either.'

'Right, I'll do that.' Emma sighed. 'I could do with a list of the things you want me to buy, though, Daniel. I don't mean the food and stuff like that, but the presents you want me to get for Amy.'

'I've already thought of that. Here you are.' He handed her a list, grinning when she frowned. 'Sorry about the writing. I wrote it in a bit of a hurry.'

'I can tell. What does this say? Chocolate monkey?' Emma pointed to a line of the scrawled black script and Daniel laughed out loud.

'Chocolate *money!* You know, those foil-wrapped choc-olate coins you get in a little net bag. Amy loves them and I remember that Claire always used to make a point of buying her some each Christmas.' Daniel shook his head. 'If there's a *monkey* around here, it's you, Emma Graham.

111

You're a real cheeky monkey for being so rude about my handwriting.'

'Rude? I was being honest.' Emma laughed up at him. 'A spider with its legs dipped in ink could have made a better job of writing this! Typical doctor's handwriting, though. I have no idea how you lot ever pass any exams when nobody can read your writing.'

'Oh, the rot only sets in *after* you've passed all your exams. It's pressure of work, you see—something you nurses know very little about…' He held up his hand when she opened her mouth. 'Just teasing. Honest!'

'I should hope so, too,' Emma declared loftily, although she could feel a smile playing around her lips. It was such fun to swop banter with Daniel like this. It was hard to remember that only a week ago their conversation had been nothing more remarkable than a discussion about a patient's progress! They had come a long way in a very short time, it seemed. But, then, necessity had been the deciding factor for the change in their relationship. Daniel had needed her help and that was why his attitude towards her had changed so dramatically.

It was a sobering thought because it brought it home to her how ephemeral their present relationship was—it would probably revert to normal once Christmas was over. Emma suddenly knew that she was going to miss these engaging exchanges they had but, then, she was going to miss a lot of other things as well. Being part of Daniel's life had given an added meaning to her own life. It wasn't going to be easy to go back to how things had been before all this had happened.

She realised that Daniel had said something while she'd been daydreaming. 'Sorry? I didn't catch that.'

'I was just checking that you would be in this evening around six-thirty,' he explained. 'I've arranged for one of the local garages to bring a car round to your flat and thought that would be the most convenient time for them to call.'

'A car?' Emma repeated, not sure that she'd heard him correctly.

'That's right. I don't want you trying to lug all this shopping about on the bus, Emma. It's far too heavy for you. I've arranged for you to have a hire car for the next week which should help.'

'That's really kind of you, Daniel. Are you sure, though? I never expected anything like this.' She couldn't hide her surprise and she saw his eyes darken. He half reached towards her then stopped and looked around as though he'd suddenly remembered that they were standing in full view of anyone going in or out of the hospital. And when he spoke his voice held a note which made Emma's heart catch as though it had suddenly forgotten how to beat.

'I know that you didn't expect it, Emma. I doubt if you even thought about the inconvenience it would cause you, having to go rushing about with heavy shopping bags. Putting other people first seems to come naturally to you. It's about time that someone put you first for a change.'

He gave her the most gentle smile that she'd seen on anyone's face. Her heart gave a small hiccup then it was off and running, sending the blood shooting through her veins and making her feel dizzy. Emma managed to smile back but it was an effort when what she really wanted to do at that moment was cry her eyes out. To know that Daniel cared about her this much seemed to have touched a raw spot inside.

How many times had she longed to have someone to care about her, to look after her, to love her? How many times had she longed to have someone to care for, to look after, to love? Could that someone she'd been looking for all her life be Daniel?

Someone jostled her arm and she took a shaky breath. Her head was spinning and her mind was too crowded to think of pleasantries, yet anything else would have been unthinkable. Daniel was just trying to be kind. It would be foolish to let herself read more into his actions than might have been intended.

'I…I appreciate your thoughtfulness,' she told him flatly, because she was desperate to keep any trace of emotion out of her voice. 'It will be a great help, having a car to use. I'll be able to go into Bournemouth and get some of the shopping there. There's a much better selection in the shops there than there is here in Clearsea.'

'Good. So long as it makes life easier for you.' Daniel's tone was brisk once more as he dug into his pocket and pulled out an envelope. 'I don't want you having to pay for the shopping yourself so take this, Emma. And promise me that you'll tell me if you need more money.'

Her eyes stung as she slid the envelope into her pocket without even glancing at it. It hurt to have their relationship reduced to a simple business arrangement, though she knew that it wasn't what he'd intended to do. Daniel was just trying to make life as easy as possible for her, and yet…

'I'll let you have a receipt for whatever I buy,' she told him, refusing to let herself go any further. She shook her head when it looked as though he was going to object. 'I'd prefer it, if you don't mind.'

'Of course, it's up to you.' Daniel's tone was emotionless. Nevertheless, Emma shot him a look from under her lashes, wondering why she had a feeling that he was annoyed. However, there was no trace of anything on his face to reinforce that idea so she dismissed it.

Stick to the facts, Emma! she told herself firmly. The fact is, you're helping Daniel out of a difficult situation. He's grateful to you so naturally he wants to be as helpful as possible, which is why he's arranged for the car and given you the money. Easy when you think about it, isn't it? So stop looking for problems!

'I won't detain you any longer. I'd offer you a lift only

I have to finish some paperwork that Max hadn't got round to doing.' Daniel sighed as he glanced at his watch. 'Hopefully, I should have it done by six so I won't need to leave Amy with the childminder too much longer.'

It was on the tip of Emma's tongue to offer to fetch the little girl but she decided against it. She didn't want Daniel thinking that she was overstepping the line and trying to take on too big a role in his life.

She said goodbye and hurried away to catch her bus. She was just in time because it arrived as soon as she got to the stop. Emma climbed aboard and paid her fare then sat staring out of the window as it trundled through the town.

The streets were ablaze with Christmas lights and it seemed that every house she passed had a tree in its window. With six days to go, the excitement was mounting. Emma realised that she felt excited about it herself, although she'd never really enjoyed Christmas before. This year was different, of course, because she wouldn't be on her own and would have someone to share it with. However, there was a bitter-sweetness to the thought.

One glorious and very special day then it would be over. Daniel and Amy wouldn't need her after that.

Emma arrived at work the following day to find the ward in a state of chaos. Paula Walters had discovered that her engagement ring was missing and so far nobody had been able to find out what had become of it.

'The silly woman. Fancy leaving an expensive ring like that lying around.'

Sister Carter's tone was scathing but Emma knew that it was because she was worried that the finger of suspicion might point to one of the staff. It was rare for anything to go missing but whenever it had happened in the past it had left a nasty taste in everyone's mouth. It wasn't pleasant to wonder if someone you'd been working with might be a thief.

'I did offer to put the ring in the office safe,' Emma said sadly. She saw Sister Carter's surprise and hurried to explain, wondering why she felt guilty all of a sudden. That was another horrible side effect when something like this happened—it tended to make *everyone* feel on edge.

'Paula asked me to find her fiancé's phone number in her diary and happened to mention in passing that her engagement ring was in the pocket of her bag. I offered to put it in the safe but she said that she preferred to keep it with her.'

'I see. I wonder if anyone else heard what she said? Can you remember, Emma?' Sister Carter sighed. 'The puzzling thing about this is that only the ring is missing. Paula's bag was still in her locker and she swears that she hasn't taken the ring out of it since she's been here.

'I couldn't understand how anyone knew it was there but perhaps this explains it. Maybe someone overheard your conversation? Or maybe Paula told someone else as well?'

Emma frowned. 'I honestly don't remember anyone else being around at the time. Paula is in the end bed next to the folding doors so there may have been someone visiting a patient in the obstetric unit.'

'Possible. Although surely we would have noticed a stranger poking around in Paula's locker?' Sister Carter shook her head in exasperation. 'I don't know what the answer is. We'll have to leave it to the police to see if they can find out what's happened to it. It could turn out that the wretched ring is in Paula's house and she simply *thought* that she'd brought it with her.'

'Let's hope so,' Emma replied quietly, because she couldn't help thinking what an awkward position it put her in if she was the only one who had known about the ring being in Paula's bag.

There was little time to dwell on the matter, however, as the day got off to yet another busy start. The ectopic pregnancy patient Daniel had dealt with a few days earlier was moved down to the ward from the IC unit. The woman's name was Fleur Simmonds, a pretty redhead in her early twenties. Emma got her settled in after her transfer to the ward.

'It's nice to be out of that place,' Fleur declared as Emma finished straightening the bedclothes. 'It's really scary when you wake up and find yourself surrounded by all that equipment.'

'It must be. But the IC unit is the best place to be when a patient is very ill, like you were, Fleur. You received individual nursing care, which is impossible to give on the average ward.'

'Oh, I know that. And I'm really grateful for it, too,' Fleur said quickly. 'I know that it was touch and go at one point and that if I hadn't had such a wonderful doctor and nurses to look after me I might not have made it.'

She shuddered expressively. 'I never guessed that there was anything wrong with me until it happened. Surely I should have realised something wasn't quite right?'

'Sometimes it happens that way with an ectopic pregnancy,' Emma assured her. 'There are no indications at all until a woman suffers severe abdominal pain and bleeding. All the symptoms of being pregnant are just the same as if the pregnancy were normal so there's no reason to suspect anything is wrong. That's why it can be so dangerous.'

'Dr Hutton explained that he'd had to remove one of my Fallopian tubes because it was badly damaged.' Fleur looked sad.

Emma knew what she was thinking and hurried to re-assure her, even though she knew that Daniel would have explained what it could mean. However, sometimes a woman needed to be told more than once that it wasn't all doom and gloom.

'That's right—but it doesn't mean that you won't be able to conceive again, Fleur. Naturally, it does slightly reduce the chances of you getting pregnant, but most women who've had ectopic pregnancies do go on to have another baby.'

'That's what Dr Hutton told me. I shall just have to look on the bright side, won't I?' Fleur said positively.

'You will,' Emma agreed with a smile. 'I bet it won't be long before you're booking into St Luke's again, only it will be into the maternity unit next time!'

Fleur laughed at that. Emma left her to rest because she knew that Fleur must still be feeling weak after what had happened to her. Shirley Rogers was looking a lot better that morning because her temperature had come down. When Emma stopped by her bed she was full of what might have happened to the missing engagement ring.

'I can't understand it going missing like that, can you, love? I mean, there's nobody here who'd take it!' Shirley declared forcibly.

'I agree. I just hope it turns up soon, though.' Emma grimaced. 'It's not nice, feeling that you're under suspicion.'

'I wonder if Paula imagined that she had it in her bag,' Shirley said *sotto voce*. 'I've done things like that myself more than once, I can tell you—imagined that I've done something or other and I haven't. I mean, Paula was in a right state when she was brought in so it would be easy to get a bit confused, wouldn't it?'

'It would. Fingers crossed that the ring turns up at her home, safely tucked in a drawer!' Emma declared. 'Anyway, how are you feeling this morning?'

'Fine. I've got my fingers *and* my toes crossed that I'll be allowed to go home soon, although how I'm going to get all my shopping done I have no idea!'

'I would write out a list and send one of your sons to do it, if I were you. Tell them that Christmas is cancelled if they don't play Santa's little helpers!'

Shirley laughed then clutched her stitches. 'Santa's little

helpers, indeed. The three of them are over six feet tall and built like rugby players!'

Emma left Shirley still chuckling at the idea. Eileen Pierce was off sick that day so they were busier than ever with one member of staff short. She was ready for a break by the time lunchtime came around.

Linda went with her to the canteen and they queued up for their lunch. Emma loaded a portion of cottage pie onto her tray then added a bottle of fizzy mineral water. She looked round for a place to sit, while Linda debated the merits of the cottage pie or the chilli, and couldn't help noticing that people seemed to be looking at her.

'Do you ever have the feeling that you've got a smut on your nose or something?' she murmured to Linda as they made their way to an empty table. 'Why is everyone staring like that?'

'Probably stunned by your beauty, Emma!' Linda laughed as she plonked her tray on the table. 'They say that a woman in love has a certain *glow* about her.'

Emma rolled her eyes. 'I won't even dignify that with an answer!' She unloaded her tray then shot a wary look over her shoulder, but nobody seemed to be looking their way.

'Must be getting paranoid,' she muttered, picking up her fork and digging into the lukewarm meal.

'Maybe. Or maybe everyone is speculating about you and Daniel. Come on, Em, you don't honestly expect folk to believe that there's nothing going on between you two.'

'There isn't. I'm just helping him out, that's all.' Emma forked up another mouthful of the cottage pie and chewed it slowly, though it tasted just a degree better than atrocious.

'Then I despair. What are you, a woman or a mouse? How can you let a gorgeous hunk like Daniel Hutton slip through your fingers without trying to do something about it?' Linda glared her displeasure. 'You're a disgrace to womankind, Emma Graham!'

Emma laughed. 'And you're a complete idiot. Anyway, it takes two to tango, as the saying goes. I...I don't get the impression that Daniel has any ideas about me *that* way.'

'But you'd like him to, wouldn't you?' Linda leaned across the table. 'I can tell I'm right, Emma. You do fancy him, don't you?'

Emma shrugged. 'Maybe, but I don't think Daniel is in the market for a relationship and if he was, why would he choose me?'

'Why? Take a look in the mirror and you'll see.' Linda sounded exasperated. 'Your trouble is that you don't realise just how gorgeous you are. If you knew how many men in this place have lusted after you, I'm sure you'd be shocked! No wonder Mike is cock-a-hoop that you're going to the Christmas dance with him.'

'You're exaggerating.' She frowned. 'I only agreed to go to the dance with Mike because I felt so guilty about us falling out. I hope he isn't reading too much into it.'

'I don't know about that but I'm sure it's given his standing in this place a bit of a boost. He's letting it be known that he's snatched you out from under dishy Daniel's nose!'

Emma was incensed to hear that. 'It wasn't like that at all! Daniel hasn't even asked me to go to the dance with him. I don't think he's even thought about going, with having Amy to look after.'

'You know that and I know that, but the rest of the people around here don't appear to,' Linda observed wryly. 'Maybe you should set Mike straight before Daniel hears the rumours. I still live in hope that you two will get your act together.'

Emma didn't say anything to that but she couldn't help wondering what she should do. It was wrong of Mike to go spreading stories like that. She decided to have a word with him as soon as she got the chance. Maybe it would be better if she didn't go to the dance after all, because it seemed to be causing no end of problems.

She had the opportunity to speak to him sooner than she'd expected. She was in the staffroom after lunch, combing her hair before going back on duty, when Mike came in and she decided that there was no time like the present to set matters straight.

'Can I have a word with you, Mike?'

'Sure. Any time, any place, anywhere,' he agreed, giving her a smile that set her teeth on edge. He laid a possessive arm around her shoulders and looked into her eyes. 'What is it, my sweet?'

Emma pointedly removed his arm. 'I believe that you've been telling everyone that you beat Daniel Hutton to it by getting me to agree to go to the dance with you.'

Mike shrugged. 'So what? It's more or less true, isn't it?'

'No, it isn't true. Daniel has never mentioned the dance to me. You're giving everyone entirely the wrong impression.'

'Oh, come on, Emma! What does it matter?' Mike grinned at her. 'If Daniel didn't ask you then I'm not treading on his toes, am I?'

'I still don't like the idea that you're turning this into something it isn't. I only agreed to go with you because I didn't want to refuse after you'd tried to make amends for what happened last week,' she retorted.

'Oh, did you?' Mike's face darkened. 'Well, it may interest you to know that I wasn't trying to make amends. I saw it as the perfect way to put Hutton's nose out of joint! I've had it up to here with his preaching, I can tell you!'

Emma felt sick. 'Then all I can say is thank heavens I found out what you were up to. Find yourself another partner, Mike, because I won't be going with you!'

Emma left the staffroom. She could feel herself trembling and had to stop when she reached the office to take a deep breath. Ridiculous though it was, she felt deeply hurt that Mike had tried to use her to score points off Daniel like that.

'Emma? Are you OK? Is something wrong?'

She hadn't realised that Daniel was in the office, using the phone, and jumped as he spoke. His face darkened into a scowl as he came to the door and took hold of her arm. He led her into the room and closed the door.

'Tell me what's been going on.'

'Nothing!' She gave a shrill little laugh which wouldn't have convinced anyone she was telling the truth. It certainly didn't convince Daniel because his mouth compressed.

'You're a rotten liar, Emma. I can see that you're upset and I want to know why.'

She shook her head. 'It's nothing, really—just something Mike said.'

'Humphreys?' His tone was grimmer than ever. Emma had never heard Daniel sound like that before and looked at him in surprise.

'Would I be wrong to suggest that whatever he said or did had something to do with me?' He must have seen from the way the colour swept up her face that he had been right because his expression turned even grimmer.

'I want to know what's been going on, Emma. I promise you that I won't do anything to embarrass you in front of Humphreys. If he's still concerned because you're helping me, there's an easy solution. I won't keep you to your promise to help me arrange Amy's Christmas if it's causing you problems in your personal life.'

'It isn't!' Emma was horrified that he should have imagined that. 'I've told you before that Mike isn't my boyfriend. He's just someone I work with.'

'So what's the problem, then? I can't understand if you won't explain.' Daniel sounded exasperated and Emma realised that she was just making the situation worse.

'Mike had a word with me the other day and asked me

if I would still go to the Christmas dance with him.' She shrugged, feeling uncomfortable about pouring the whole story out to Daniel. 'He told me that he was sorry that we'd fallen out and wanted us to be friends, and I believed him.'

'Only he had an ulterior motive for asking you?' Daniel smiled thinly. 'Why doesn't that surprise me?'

'Y-yes.' Emma rushed on, wanting to get it over with as quickly as possible. 'Evidently, Mike saw it as a way to get one over on you. If...if I was going to the dance with him then I couldn't go with you.' She tailed off, wondering if she should have told Daniel the truth or not. It was hard to tell because his expression revealed very little about his feelings.

'I see. I imagine the fact that you'd agreed to go with him would also have increased his standing amongst his friends.' He gave her a dry look. 'It's widely known that you're very discriminating when it comes to accepting dates, Emma.'

'It's a shame I wasn't discriminating in this case, then, wasn't it?' she replied, trying to lighten the mood. Daniel looked rather scary, she decided, studying the grim set of his mouth. That he was annoyed on her behalf went without saying, and her heart warmed at the thought that he cared about her being used by Mike for his own miserable ends.

'It was. Humphreys isn't fit to lick your boots,' he declared softly. Emma felt her heart leap into her throat as he looked at her. His eyes were lit by some inner fire yet she knew that it wasn't simply anger that made them glow that way. When he reached out and touched her cheek she felt her breath catch, though it had been the lightest of touches.

His voice seemed to have reached new depths as he added softly, 'Any man who earns your love, Emma, would be fortunate indeed.'

What might have happened next was anyone's guess. However, the sound of someone tapping on the door broke the spell and reminded them both of where they were.

'Come in.' Daniel swung round, his face smoothing into its customary noncommittal expression as Sister Carter came into the office with a message for him.

Emma excused herself and hurried back to the ward, but all afternoon she found her thoughts returning to what had happened—the way Daniel had looked at her and what he'd said. It felt as though something had changed in their relationship but she was too scared to let herself wonder what it might be. If she didn't think about it, maybe it would happen...whatever *it* was!

'Mike's been in a foul mood all afternoon. What did you say to him, Em?'

They were in the staffroom, collecting their coats at the end of the day, when Linda asked the question. Emma sighed but there was no reason why she should keep what had happened a secret from her friend.

She briefly explained what had gone on, without going into detail, and heard Linda sigh. 'Uh-oh! You'll have to watch out. Mike isn't a person I'd like to cross so be on your toes, Em. It won't sit easily with him when everyone finds out that you dumped him for Daniel.'

'But I didn't!' Emma protested.

'I know that, but that isn't how it will look to everyone else. You know how folk love a good gossip so they'll put their own spin on the story once it gets round. Mike isn't going to be a happy bunny so just watch your back. OK?'

Emma nodded miserably, wishing she could erase the whole unpleasant episode. It was going to be pretty miserable, working with Mike, if he was determined to pay her back. She hauled her coat out of her locker, glancing down as something dropped out of her pocket.

'Here you go... My, my, someone's in the money!' Linda grinned as she shoved a wad of ten-pound notes back into the envelope. Her brows rose as she turned it over and read the logo printed on the back. 'Wilkins Jewellers. What have you been doing, Em, selling the family silver?'

'How did you guess?' Emma laughed as she took the envelope from her friend and put it in her bag. It was the money Daniel had given her the previous night to buy the Christmas shopping—she'd forgotten about it being in her coat pocket.

She left it at that, not wanting to have to explain to Linda that Daniel had given it to her. It didn't feel right, discussing every detail of their arrangement with a third party, to be frank. Linda didn't mention it again as they left the hospital together. Emma had brought the hire car with her and her friend's brows rose when she saw it.

'A car as well? Forget the family silver—you must have won the lottery.' Linda looked round as her boyfriend, Gary, beeped his car horn. 'Have to go. It's the big day today. Gary's taking me into town to buy my engagement ring.'

'How lovely. Have fun!' Emma waved them off then got into the car. It was one of the latest models and it was a pleasure driving it, she thought as she set off for a super-market on the outskirts of town. She rarely had the chance to go there to shop so it was a treat to be able to go that night. She had a list of everything she needed, food-wise, for Christmas and intended to get the bulk of it done so that she would have more time to spend looking for Amy's presents.

Armed with the list, she spent a couple of hours loading her trolley with goodies. The size of the bill made her blanch but she consoled herself with the thought that she would offer to split the cost of the food with Daniel. After all, she would be eating a lot of what she'd bought so it was only fair.

She left the supermarket and headed back towards town, pausing when she came to the junction. If she turned left she could be at Daniel's house within ten minutes. It would make more sense to take the shopping straight there.

Her heart lifted at the thought of seeing him again even if was only for a few minutes. She parked in front of his house then went and knocked on the door. He'd given her a key but there was no way that she wanted to use it when he was at home. It didn't seem right.

His face broke into a welcoming smile when he saw her. 'Emma! What a lovely surprise. Come in.'

'Actually, I've only called to bring the shopping,' she explained, warmed by his greeting.

'I'll fetch it inside. You go on in. Amy's in the sitting room. She'll be thrilled when she sees you.'

Daniel took the car keys from her and headed down the drive. Emma watched him walk to the car while a lump came to her throat. What a normal everyday kind of event, to arrive home with bags full of shopping. Millions of women—and men—performed the very same task week in and week out yet for her it was a special moment to treasure.

It was what being part of a family must be like—performing all the humdrum tasks and sharing them with someone else. It was a taste of a life she'd never known, a life she wanted so much she ached...

Or did she ache because it was Daniel she wanted, his life she wanted to be part of, his future she wanted to share?

Emma took a deep breath as he turned and smiled when he saw her standing on the step. Maybe there should have been bells ringing or rockets going off at that moment. That was how it happened in films when a woman discovered that she was in love.

There were no bells or rockets for her, however, just a boot full of shopping. It didn't make any difference, though. She was in love with Daniel. How funny to realise it at that moment. How sad not to be able to run out into the street and tell him. Until she knew how Daniel felt about her, there was no way she could run the risk of embarrassing him by declaring her feelings.

Emma went inside the house and her heart was brimming over with joy and sadness. Could Daniel ever love her? Did he ever wish that Christmas could last for ever so that she could be a permanent part of his life?

She just didn't know!

CHAPTER NINE

'EMMA!'

Amy came racing across the room. Emma forced away the lingering sadness as she hugged the little girl.

'What a greeting! It makes me doubly glad I came.'

'What was the first reason?' Daniel paused by the door, his arms loaded with carrier bags. He grinned wickedly when Emma looked blankly at him. 'You said that you were *doubly* glad that you came to visit us.'

Emma laughed, glad of the moment of lightness because it helped ease the ache inside her. 'Doctors can be very pedantic at times! If only their handwriting was as good as their grasp of the English language, eh?'

'Ouch! Not that it's answered my question, of course. If doctors are pedantic then nurses are very adept at prevaricating.' Daniel's eyes glinted with amusement and Emma smiled back at him.

'I dispute that. Nurses are just *tactful*. That's an entirely different thing. Anyway, Dr Pedantic, I meant that I was glad to come because it means you can unload all that shopping.'

He rolled his eyes. 'And here I was thinking you were pleased to see me.'

He carried on down the hall, mercifully sparing her the need to answer. Emma sighed, thinking to herself that if he knew how glad she was to see him that would definitely alter things! Daniel might want to run a mile if he knew how she really felt about him...

'Emma, you're not listening!'

She jolted back to the present as Amy shook her arm.

'I'm sorry, darling. I was wool-gathering. What did you say?'

'I was telling you that Uncle Daniel and I are going carol-singing tonight. Will you come with us, Emma? Please!'

'Oh, I'm not sure…' Emma sighed when she saw Amy's face fall. 'Let's see what Uncle Daniel says, shall we?'

Daniel had finished bringing in the shopping and was standing in the kitchen, staring bemusedly at the amount of goodies Emma had bought. He looked round and grinned when they came into the room.

'We could feed an army with this little lot!'

Emma flushed. 'I'm sorry. Maybe I have gone a bit over the top…' she began apologetically.

'Nonsense!' Daniel came round the table and hugged her. 'We wanted a Christmas with all the trimmings and that's what we're going to have. Anyway, we can always throw a party to use up any food we haven't eaten.'

Emma's heart sang as he included her in his plans so naturally. Maybe it was foolish to read too much into it but she couldn't help it. She loved him so much that the thought of having even an extra day with him was like being given a wonderful gift.

'Uncle Daniel, can Emma come carol-singing with us?'

Amy, with a child's eye for the priorities, returned the conversation to what was uppermost in her mind. Daniel shrugged, looking faintly surprised that she'd asked him such a question.

'Of course she can.' He released Emma and went to make a start on putting away the food. 'It's Amy's Sunday school class who are carol-singing, although there'll be lots of parents going along as well. Evidently, it's something of a tradition and Amy and Claire have always gone along. I thought it would be nice if we went this year, too.'

He picked up the turkey and stowed it carefully in the bottom of the—thankfully large—refrigerator. 'It would be great if you came as well, Emma. It would make it all the more special.'

Emma smiled, although she could feel the excitement coiling tightly in her stomach. There had been something in Daniel's voice when he'd said that, a note which had told her he'd meant it. Daniel wanted her to go with them that night and not just because it would please Amy.

'Then I'd love to come.'

'Good.' The smile Daniel gave her was so gentle that it brought a lump to her throat.

'Yes!' Amy's shout of pleasure cut short the moment. Emma took a small breath before she turned to the excited child.

'Let's help Uncle Daniel get all this shopping put away then we can get ready.'

Amy set to with great gusto. With the three of them working together, it didn't take long to fill the fridge and freezer, not to mention the cupboards. Daniel folded up the plastic carriers and stowed them in a drawer then sent Amy upstairs to fetch her coat.

'Have you got a scarf with you, Emma? It will get cold out there tonight. Did you know that they're forecasting snow in the next twenty-four hours?'

'Really? Oh, wouldn't it be marvellous if we had a white Christmas? It would make it extra-special!'

'It's going to be extra-special with or without the snow.' Daniel caught her hand and pulled her towards him. His hazel eyes shimmered as he looked into her face. 'This is going to be the best Christmas ever, Emma—for all of us.'

His lips were warm as they closed over hers. Emma simply gave herself up to the pleasure of having him kiss her. When he drew back there was a faintly bemused expression on his face but, then, she guessed that there was a matching one on hers!

'I suppose we'd better go and get ready,' he suggested with such reluctance that she couldn't help smiling.

'I suppose we should.'

Daniel's grin was a trifle crooked as he raised her hand to his mouth and kissed her fingertips. 'You're the best thing that could have happened to me and Amy. I want you to know that.'

'Thank you.' She managed to smile, although she could feel the emotions welling inside her. Maybe it was foolish to let herself get carried away but she couldn't help hoping that he meant that in the way she wanted him to.

Amy came clattering down the stairs just then, her coat all askew, her hat rammed down over her eyebrows. Emma chuckled as she set about sorting her out and soon had the little girl ready to leave the house.

'Here, put this on.' Daniel wound a thick, cherry-red woollen scarf around Emma's neck. He made sure that it was snugly fastened to keep out the cold air then drew her hood over her head. 'I don't want you getting cold tonight.'

Emma smiled because her heart was overflowing with happiness. Nobody had ever taken such care of her as Daniel did. She stepped out onto the path and looked up at the frosty sky. There were a lot of stars out that night and one in particular was very bright.

She closed her eyes and made a wish, wondering if there was any truth in the saying about wishes coming true if you wished on a star. She hoped so. She really did. She didn't want to lose what she had at this moment. She wanted it to go on and on for ever!

'I'm afraid this will have to be our last performance, everyone.' The vicar smiled as there was a chorus of groans. 'I know. It's been a wonderful evening. Thank you all for coming.'

'It has been fun, hasn't it?' Daniel grinned at Emma as the band of carol-singers headed down the road. 'I can't remember when I last went carol-singing, can you?'

'I can't.' Emma clutched hold of the songsheet as the

wind tried to whip it out of her hands. It was difficult to hold onto it because she was wearing a pair of thick woolly mittens. She looked up in surprise when something plopped onto the paper. 'It's snowing!'

Daniel laughed. 'So it is! Wowee!'

He sounded all of ten years old at that moment and Emma couldn't help laughing. 'No one would ever believe that you were usually so poised. There are two sides to you, Daniel Hutton, did you know that?'

'I refuse to answer on the grounds that it might incriminate me,' he declared loftily. Whipping the errant song-sheet out of her hand, he took hold of it instead. 'Come along now. No loitering. Our superb voices are needed.'

Emma chuckled as he led her down the street to where the group had assembled outside some bungalows. The area was part of the town's sheltered housing scheme for elderly people and one of the regular ports of call on the yearly carol-singing route. Emma could see that most of the old folk were standing in their windows, watching.

Daniel made space for her beside him with the rest of the adult singers. Amy and the other children were gathered at the front. The vicar had brought along a lantern and the scene was like something from a Christmas card, Emma thought as she looked at the children's smiling faces in the lamplight.

The snow was coming down harder now, turning the pavements and gardens white. She stuck out her tongue and caught an icy snowflake on the tip of it then smiled at her own childishness. She glanced at Daniel to see if he'd seen how silly she was being and felt her heart stop when she saw the expression in his eyes. Obviously, Daniel didn't think it had been at all childish...

It was an effort to concentrate as the vicar announced the first carol and everyone began to sing. However, Emma was soon caught up in the singing. One carol flowed on to

another as they worked their way through the whole rep-
ertoire and ended with the ever-beautiful 'Silent Night'.

Emma knew that she wasn't the only one who was sorry
when they finished and the vicar announced that it was time
to go home. It had been a magical, wonderful night and
one she would remember for ever.

'Right, time to go home, sprog.' Daniel lifted a tired
Amy into his arms as they walked back up the street. The
little girl snuggled against him, yawning.

'It was fun, Uncle Daniel. Just like when Mummy and I
used to go carol-singing. I know Mummy's in heaven but
d'you think she knows what we've been doing tonight?'

Daniel smiled at Emma over the top of his niece's head
and Emma could see the sadness in his eyes. 'I'm sure she
does, sweetheart. I bet she's really pleased that you had a
lovely time, too.'

'Spect so,' Amy said trustingly. She snuggled closer to
Daniel, her eyelids drooping. She was asleep by the time
they reached the end of the road and didn't wake until they
arrived home.

'Here, I've got a key.' Emma quickly unlocked the door
because Daniel was hampered by the child in his arms.

'Thanks. Look, I'll take Amy straight up to bed. I won't
be long. Will you wait, Emma?'

For ever! she wanted to say, but merely nodded. 'Shall
I make us a drink? Tea or coffee perhaps?'

'Whichever you prefer.' Daniel gave her a quick smile
before he carried Amy upstairs.

Emma went into the kitchen and took off her coat and
scarf, draping them over the back of a chair. She filled the
kettle then stared out of the window. The snow lent the
garden a fairy-like prettiness. It was that kind of night when
there seemed to be magic in the air—unless it was just how
she was feeling.

She felt a bubble of excitement floating beneath the surface of her mind, a frisson of anticipation as though some-

thing wonderful was going to happen. She could sense it, feel it, and it both scared and exhilarated her. When Daniel came into the kitchen she didn't turn round because she was afraid that the bubble would burst and she didn't want that to happen yet.

'Emma?'

He said her name softly, questioningly, and she had to turn, though it took her a moment to find the courage. She loved him so much that it seemed to drain the strength from her limbs as it hit her how empty her life would be without him in the future.

'Emma.' He said her name again, softer still, aching with tenderness, throbbing with passion. It seemed that she'd never heard the word before, never known that it could sound that way—so beautiful, so full of emotion.

Her eyes lifted to his face, caught by the myriad emotions she could see on it. Maybe she should have tried to decipher them but she didn't have the strength. It was easier to stand there while Daniel took a couple of steps until he was so close that she could touch him.

His body felt warm and hard as she laid her hand against his chest, so vital and alive that Emma murmured yet she wasn't aware of making any sound. She could feel the rhythmic beating of his heart beneath her palm, feel the tremor which ran through him all of a sudden. He said her name again, softly yet with a need in his voice which made an answering yearning awake inside her. She was already moving towards him when he pulled her into his arms.

Their bodies met with a small jolt, like the aftershock of a huge seismic eruption, even though nothing had gone before. Daniel's mouth was hungry as it claimed hers, but hers was just as greedy. There was nothing poised about this kiss, nothing practised or perfect about the urgent meeting of their mouths. Their desire for each other was too raw to worry about polish and performance. Daniel wanted her and she wanted him. That was all that mattered.

He was breathing heavily when he raised his head. 'Tell me now if this isn't want you want, Emma.'

She heard the roughness in his voice and knew how hard it had been for him to stop when what he'd wanted had been to carry on. That was what she wanted, too—to lose herself in this passion, to lose herself in Daniel. It touched her heart and her soul to know how much he cared about her feelings.

'I do want it, though, Daniel.' She went on tiptoe, punctuating her words with kisses, feeling his heart racing almost out of control as it beat against her breasts. 'I...want...it more...than...'

She didn't get chance to finish. She didn't need to. Daniel knew what she was telling him. He drew her back into his arms and his eyes blazed.

'You won't ever regret this, Emma. I promise you that!'

Emma closed her eyes, letting the words sink deep into her soul. She wanted to believe them so much and maybe she should. There had been magic in the air tonight so maybe wishes could come true.

Daniel kissed her again, his mouth drawing a response from her that Emma hadn't known herself capable of. Her body felt as though it were on fire, the blood almost too hot as it flowed through her veins. She was trembling when the kiss ended but so was Daniel. He cupped her face between his hands as he stared into her eyes, and his voice was so husky that she *felt* as much as heard the words he ground out.

'Will you stay the night with me, Emma?'

'Yes.' Oddly, her own voice sounded so normal that she smiled. Funny that on such a momentous occasion she could feel so confident and carefree. But maybe it wasn't strange when she thought about it. She loved Daniel so showing him how she felt was the most natural thing in the world.

He kissed her once more then took hold of her hand and

led her upstairs to his bedroom. Emma looked round the drably painted room and smiled. 'Beige again.'

He laughed softly as he closed the door then came up behind her and slid his arms around her waist so that he could nuzzle her neck. 'The colour my life was until you came and brightened it up, Emma.'

She smiled at that, letting her head fall to the side as his mouth worked its way towards the curve of her ear. 'You have a nice line in patter, Dr Hutton,' she teased him.

'You think so?' He turned her round to face him and the expression in his eyes made her breath catch. 'Maybe you should sample some action next. I wouldn't want you thinking that I was all talk…'

He didn't quite finish the sentence as his desire got the better of him. Emma murmured incoherently as his mouth claimed hers in a drugging kiss which seemed to steal her ability to think. Why think when you can feel, anyway? her heart murmured, and she took its advice.

Daniel's hands moved to the hem of her sweater so that he could draw it over her head. He tossed it aside with barely a glance because his eyes were locked to what it had revealed. Emma felt her nipples harden as his eyes ran over her full breasts, barely concealed by the lacy black bra she was wearing.

'You're beautiful, Emma, very, very beautiful…'

He trailed a finger almost reverently over the full curve of one breast. Emma bit her lip to contain her gasp of pleasure but somehow it still escaped from her lips. The excitement she had felt before seemed to have increased tenfold so that she was trembling with it…

Or perhaps the truth was that she was trembling with desire. She had never felt like this before so she couldn't judge and didn't try. It was enough to know that Daniel wanted her and that what she saw in his eyes was for her and her alone. Even if Daniel couldn't love her for ever she knew in her heart that he loved her at that moment!

'Emma. Sweet, beautiful Emma.'

She went into his arms willingly, trustingly, knowing that whatever happened later she would never regret what was happening now...

The light was so bright that Emma had to shade her eyes. She looked round the unfamiliar room, at the light pouring in through the window, and frowned. It took her a moment to remember where she was and her heart lurched as she realised that she was in Daniel's bed.

She rolled onto her side, feeling the flurry which ran through her as her thigh brushed his. He was still asleep, his long lashes painting shadows on his cheeks, his breathing slow and steady.

Emma smiled as she lay there absorbing all the tiny details, like how a night's growth of beard had darkened his jawbone, how the tiny lines that fanned from the corners of his eyes were so much paler than the rest of his skin. It was what an artist had to do before he painted a portrait—absorb the details, fine-tune his mind to assimilate the insignificant as well as the more important features.

She already knew how Daniel looked—if she'd had the skill she could have painted his portrait from memory without any trouble. But it wouldn't have had all the minuscule details that would have made it true to life. She wanted to store up all those details, build up in her mind a complete picture of this man she loved...

'I'm getting a complex, lying here. You *do* remember who I am, I hope?'

She jumped, the colour sweeping up her cheeks when she realised that Daniel was watching her from under his lashes. He gave a deep laugh as he rolled onto his side and propped himself up on his elbow.

'You seemed so intent when you were looking at me that I was beginning to wonder if you'd forgotten my name.'

Emma laughed because it was impossible not to find his teasing funny. 'Not at all. It's David, isn't it?'

'It most certainly isn't!' He clamped a strong arm around her waist and scooped her towards him so fast that she didn't have time to draw breath. 'Think you can tease me like that and get away with it, do you?'

His punishment was a very thorough kiss, which left Emma reeling. Daniel looked decidedly smug when he saw her expression. 'So, what's my name, woman?'

'Daniel…' She cleared her throat and repeated it. 'Daniel.'

'That's better!' Rolling onto his back, he drew her into the crook of his arm and his tone was gentle all of a sudden. 'Are you OK, Emma?'

She knew what he meant and nodded, feeling her cheek rubbing against his warm skin. 'I'm fine.'

He turned to look at her and his eyes were dark, questioning. 'No regrets? Honestly?'

'None.' She took a deep breath then plucked up her courage. 'How about you, Daniel? H-have you any regrets?'

'No. I—' He broke off as the sound of footsteps pattering along the landing alerted him to the fact that Amy was awake. Sudden indecision crossed his face and Emma knew at once that he was concerned about his niece's reaction if she discovered them in bed together.

'Why don't you get Amy ready for school?' she suggested softly, not wanting to cause problems for him. 'I'll pop into the spare bedroom so that Amy will think I spent the night there.'

'You don't mind?' Daniel frowned. 'I just don't want Amy getting the wrong idea, you understand. Children are so impressionable, aren't they?'

Emma nodded, although a dull little ache crept into her heart as she wondered what kind of *wrong* impression his niece would have received. Was he afraid that Amy might think that Emma was going to be a permanent addition to their lives? And was that something he didn't foresee happening? Suddenly she was awash with doubts so that it was hard to maintain her smile.

Daniel seemed not to sense that she was upset, thankfully enough. Snatching up the robe from the end of the bed, he dragged it on then smiled at her. 'Thanks, Emma. For everything.'

He hurried from the room but it was a few seconds before Emma could force herself to get up. She shivered as she dragged on her clothes then quickly straightened the rumpled bed. Why had Daniel thanked her like that? Because she'd stayed the night with him?

The thought was another black cloud on her bright horizon so that her happy mood slowly dissipated. What might have meant the world to her might not have meant nearly so much to Daniel. She had to face that now. Just because she loved him, it didn't mean that he felt anything for her.

Amy was eating breakfast when Emma went down to the kitchen ten minutes later. The little girl smiled when she saw her, although she didn't appear surprised.

'Hello, Emma. Uncle Daniel said that you were asleep so I had to be quiet,' she explained, spooning cereal into her mouth.

'You were like a little mouse!' Emma gave the little girl a hug then glanced round as Daniel picked up the teapot.

'Fancy a cup? There's toast as well.'

She shook her head, not wanting to prolong what was turning into an awkward situation, or at least it was awkward for her. Daniel didn't appear at all fazed by it, she noted, and that thought made it hurt all the more.

'No, thanks. I'd better get a move on or I'll be late for work.'

She headed for the door but Daniel was right behind her. 'I'll see you out.'

He followed her down the hall, politely taking her coat

off the hook and holding it out for her. However, when Emma tried to move away his hands clasped her shoulders.

'I get the distinct impression that something has upset you, Emma.'

She shook her head. 'Don't be silly. Of course I'm not upset. Why should I be?'

He turned her to face him. 'Because this isn't the way last night should have ended. It isn't how I would choose to have it end, believe me. But I won't do anything that might…well, might upset Amy. Where she's concerned, I have to be one hundred per cent certain that what I am doing is right.'

There was an odd note in his voice but Emma barely noticed it. Her mind had homed in on the thought that Daniel didn't believe it was *right* to have her in his life! Somehow she managed to conceal her pain because it was unthinkable to let him know how hurt she was when that had never been his intention.

'I'm sure you're right, Daniel. Amy's welfare must be your main priority.'

His eyes darkened. 'It is. I won't do anything that might cause her more pain. Amy's had enough heartache in her young life as it is.'

There wasn't anything Emma could say to that. In her heart she knew that he was right to take such a stand. However, it didn't make her feel better to know how easily he could cut her out of his life.

She gave him a quick smile, aware that tears were only a blink away from falling. 'I'd better be off. I'm not due in till eleven today but there are things I need to do.'

'I've got meetings most of the day so I doubt if I'll see you.' Daniel sighed. 'With Max off I'm having to stand in for him and it isn't easy, trying to do things the way he would do them. I'm very much aware that I could be treading on his toes if I'm not careful.'

'Tricky situation, but I'm sure you'll do what you think best,' Emma said lightly.

'Mmm, but best for one person might not be best for another,' he replied quietly.

She didn't ask him to explain that rather cryptic remark as she hurried out to the car. There were many ways to interpret it. Daniel might have considered it a good idea to ask her to help him give Amy a wonderful Christmas but it might not be *his* idea of the best way to spend it.

Emma closed her mind to that unhappy thought as she made her way up the path. There was a thick layer of snow on the ground and more snow still falling, making it difficult to keep her footing. She hunted her keys out of her pocket and unlocked the car then glanced round when Daniel called out to her.

'Drive carefully, Emma.'

It was an effort to smile as she got into the car. Emma's hand shook as she started the engine. She knew that in years to come she would picture him standing there at the door. Her mind had taken a mental snapshot of the scene. It was one more memory to add to all the memories they'd made the previous night, something to look back on when Daniel was no longer part of her life. It seemed all too little to ward off the loneliness of the coming years.

Emma arrived at the hospital just before eleven. She was heading for the staffroom to change into her uniform when Sister Carter stopped her.

'Emma, can you come into the office, please? The police are here and they'd like a word with you about Paula's ring.'

'It hasn't turned up, then?' Emma sighed when Sister Carter shook her head. 'Oh, dear.'

She went straight to the office where she was interviewed by the two policemen, who wanted to know exactly what had happened the day Paula had been admitted. Emma repeated what she'd told Sister Carter then left the office. However, the nagging feeling that maybe she was a suspect didn't sit easily with her. It wasn't nice to know that anyone would think she was capable of such a horrible deed.

Linda was working the late shift as well that day and had been delayed because of the snow. She came rushing into the ward almost half an hour after the time she should have been there.

'The buses were cancelled along my route so Gary had to take the car this morning. I was hoping they'd be running again by the time I left, but no such luck. I ended up having to walk, and it took me ages!'

Emma smiled sympathetically. 'What a drag! You should have phoned me and I could have picked you up.'

'I'd forgotten about you having transport. Drat!' Linda rolled her eyes as she stopped beside Paula Walters's bed. 'I think you must have a money tree at home, Em. Between that envelope full of tenners and a new car!'

Emma laughed. 'If only! No, Dan—' She broke off as Paula suddenly let out a shriek and turned to her in alarm. 'Paula, are you all right?'

'That's my ring! She's wearing my ring!'

Emma's mouth dropped open as she realised that Paula was pointing at Linda. It was only then that she realised her friend was wearing an obviously expensive sapphire and diamond engagement ring.

'I don't know what you're talking about!' Linda looked horrified. 'Gary and I bought this ring last night at the jeweller's in town.'

She turned appealingly to Emma. 'You remember me saying that we were going in to town to buy my engagement ring, don't you? We bought it from Wilkins, that jeweller's in the high street.'

'It's my ring! I know it is.' Paula was becoming more and more agitated. 'Stephen had it made specially for me. I have the designer's drawings at home so I can prove it!'

Both women were obviously upset and no wonder. When Sister Carter came hurrying from the office to see what was going on, Emma quickly explained. Sister decided that she had no option but to call the police and asked Linda to wait in her office until they arrived.

The police arrived a short time later and took a statement from Linda. They also took away the ring, which upset her even more. Paula's fiancé had been summoned and he, too, had identified it as being the ring he'd had made for her. He'd brought with him the designer's drawings and they seemed to prove that the ring was the one that had gone missing from Paula's bag.

Between trying to console Linda and keep the ward running smoothly, Emma had little time to think properly. It was a relief when it was time to go home because the atmosphere in the ward had been dreadful all day long.

Emma breathed a sigh of relief as she let herself into her flat. With a bit of luck everything would have been sorted out by the following day and they could get back to normal. Although how the ring had ended up in the jeweller's possession was anyone's guess. Still, there had to be a logical explanation for it.

It was another late shift the following day, the last one before her Christmas break. It was busy as usual so that Emma was glad when break-time came around. Linda had been very subdued at first but she cheered up as the day had worn on. Gary had phoned to say that he'd been to the police station with the receipt and the police now accepted that the ring had been bought in good faith, which was something to be thankful for.

Of course, the story had spread like wildfire through the hospital. However, it wasn't until break-time that Emma realised the full extent of the rumours that were circulating when she happened to overhear two nurses from a different ward talking while she was in the ladies' cloakroom.

'Evidently, the finger is pointing at Emma Graham,' one

nurse told the other, unaware that Emma was in one of the stalls. 'I heard that she was the only one who knew that the ring was in the woman's bag. Obviously, she was ideally placed to take it.'

'I know. I didn't want to believe it at first. I mean, Emma, of all people! But then I heard that she had all that money in an envelope with the jeweller's name on it.' The second nurse sighed. 'It does seem suspicious, doesn't it…?'

Emma didn't hear the rest of their conversation as the two women left the cloakroom. She didn't want to. What she'd heard already made her feel sick. Where on earth had those ugly rumours sprung from? She couldn't believe that Linda was responsible but someone must have started them.

Her heart lurched painfully. What would Daniel think when he heard them? Would he believe them? If people she'd worked with for several years were ready to think so badly of her then surely he would have doubts?

She felt her eyes fill with tears and angrily brushed them away. What Daniel believed was up to him but she had to put a stop to what was being said!

She left the cloakroom and hurried back to the ward. Her heart seemed to lurch to a stop when she got out of the lift and saw Daniel and the two policemen standing by the office. He turned when he heard her footsteps and his face was set into such a grimly uncompromising expression that she shivered. Daniel was angry, very angry indeed, but who with? Her? Surely he couldn't believe that she was capable of stealing from a patient?

'Would you come into the office, please, Emma?' he asked her flatly. 'The police need to speak to you about Paula's ring.'

Emma took a deep breath but it felt as though something inside her had just died. It would make no difference even if she proved her innocence. To know that Daniel didn't have enough faith in her to *know* that she wasn't guilty was too much to bear!

CHAPTER TEN

THE next half-hour was a nightmare. Emma repeated what she'd told the police the previous day. She was aware that Daniel was sitting at one side of the room, listening to every word. She glanced at him but there was nothing in his face to tell her what he was thinking.

The senior of the two police officers checked his notes. 'Mr Wilkins from the jeweller's has given us a description of the young woman who sold him the ring. He describes her as being in her early twenties, of medium height, with short blond hair.' The policeman looked up.

'Obviously, there must be a lot of young women who fit that description in this town, Miss Graham. However, it has been brought to our attention that you had in your possession quite a considerable sum of money in an envelope bearing the jeweller's name and address. Can you explain where you got it from?'

'I think I can answer that question, sergeant.' Daniel's expression was grimmer than ever as the two policemen looked questioningly at him. Emma took a deep breath but the feeling of sickness didn't go away. Even if Daniel explained about the money and the police believed him, it wouldn't alter the fact that he'd believed her capable of theft.

'Miss Graham kindly agreed to help me with the preparations for Christmas. I withdrew three hundred pounds from my bank account on Monday and gave it to her to pay for the shopping and various other items that I'd asked her to buy.'

'I see.' The policeman frowned. 'I imagine that you must have a record of this cash withdrawal?'

'Certainly. And I'm sure my bank will be happy to verify it as well,' Daniel confirmed.

'How did you happen to have one of the jeweller's envelopes in your possession, Dr Hutton? I am assuming that it was you who put the money in the envelope?' the policeman queried.

'It was. Whilst I was in town, withdrawing the cash, I went into the jeweller's to collect an item of jewellery that was being repaired. Mr Wilkins wrapped it in one of his envelopes. I had the envelope in my pocket and put the money into it before I gave it to Miss Graham. I'm sure that Mr Wilkins will be able to confirm that as well.'

Daniel's tone was clipped, as though he resented being cross-questioned about his actions. Would that be another point against her? Emma wondered sadly. The fact that Daniel had been dragged into this unpleasant affair? He would be bound to resent it, and resent her for causing him all this trouble.

Her spirits had sunk so low that they didn't rise even when the policeman closed his notebook. 'Well, that seems to have cleared up a few points. I'm sorry to have troubled you, Miss Graham. I hope you understand that we have to follow up every lead we get.'

Emma forced herself to smile as the two policemen got up to leave. 'I understand. I wish that I could have been more help but I have no idea who took Paula's ring.'

'Before you go, sergeant, you mentioned something about being given a lead. Was it someone from the hospital who contacted you?' Daniel asked, standing up as well.

Emma frowned, wondering what he wanted to know that for.

The sergeant shrugged. 'I'm afraid that I'm not at liberty to say, sir. I'm sure you understand.'

He nodded politely to them then left. Emma stood up as the two officers disappeared. She saw Daniel look at her but she didn't look at him in case he saw the hurt in her eyes. It felt as though her heart had been ripped apart to know that he'd suspected her even if it had been only for a few minutes.

'I'd better get back to work,' she murmured, hurrying to the door.

'Emma, wait! Look, I think we need to talk about this, don't you?' he began, but she didn't let him finish.

'No. Quite frankly, I can't see that there's anything to talk about! I'm only sorry that you didn't feel able to trust me, Daniel.'

'What do you mean?' He sounded so stunned that for a moment her foolish heart grasped at the idea that she'd made a mistake. But she'd seen the look on his face, hadn't she? What further proof did she need?

'You know what I mean. At the very least I would have expected you to give me the benefit of the doubt before you found me guilty of stealing Paula's ring! Still, why should you have done that when the rest of the staff in this hospital evidently believe that I'm a thief?'

'Emma…!'

She didn't wait to hear what he had to say. She didn't want to hear it. It was easy to apologise after the event but that didn't change a thing. Daniel should have *known* in his heart that she wasn't capable of stealing the ring!

Emma went back to the ward, feeling as though she were weighed down by despair. When Linda came hurrying over to ask what the police had wanted, she flatly explained.

'Someone tipped them off that you had that money? I hope you don't think it was me, Em,' Linda exclaimed in horror. 'It never crossed my mind that you had anything to do with Paula's ring going missing. You wouldn't do a thing like that!'

'I'm glad someone believes in me,' Emma said with a shrug when Linda looked at her. She didn't want to bring Daniel's name into the conversation because it was too painful.

'I overheard a couple of nurses talking about what had gone on. It appears that a lot of people in this hospital believe I'm the thief. They've heard about the money and put two and two together, it appears.'

'No!' Linda looked really upset. 'Oh, me and my big mouth. Why on earth did I mention it? It was just a joke, honestly. I made some crack about you being loaded. Everyone just laughed and I thought no more about it. I'm sorry, Emma. Really, I am.'

'It isn't your fault. Someone must have become suspicious and contacted the police. I suppose they thought it was the right thing to do.'

'But that's horrible! I can't remember exactly who was there when I was telling the tale, but to imagine one of your friends grassing on you like that is just awful!'

Emma laughed hollowly. 'Not really a friend, I'd say.'

They let the subject drop after that. Emma guessed that Linda was feeling guilty about her unwitting part in the events. All she could hope was that word would soon get around about her having been cleared by the police. However, that didn't compensate for the fact that Daniel had believed her guilty even if it had been only fleetingly.

It made Emma realise that there was no way that they could continue with their present arrangement. She made up her mind to explain that she wouldn't be able to help him after all as soon as she got a chance, but he didn't return to the ward as the afternoon wore on.

Shirley Rogers was being discharged that day and two of her sons arrived to collect her in the middle of the afternoon. Shirley hugged Emma before she left.

'Thank you for everything, love. I know it's probably not the right thing to say, but I've rather enjoyed being here!'

Emma laughed. 'Not many of our patients say that! Anyway, look after yourself, Shirley.' She turned to Shirley's eldest son, Martin, a strapping young man in his twenties. 'Don't go letting your mother do too much, will you?'

'No chance of that.' Martin winked at his brother. 'Ma is banned from the kitchen for the next month. We've set up a rota and got it all worked out as to who will be doing the cooking. Mind you, it's a test of endurance when it's Dad's turn. I never knew that you could make gravy so thick that you have to chew it!'

They all laughed. Shirley wiped her eyes as she let her son help her to her feet. 'The mind boggles at the thought of their dad cooking a meal. It will be the first time he's done it in thirty years of married life!'

'It just shows how much he cares, then, doesn't it, Shirley?' Emma said softly so that Shirley's sons couldn't hear.

'It does indeed. When you find a good man like my Ron, you're surely blessed.'

Emma smiled a little sadly to herself as Shirley left the ward with her sons. Shirley was right—it was a blessing to find a man who loved and cared for you for all those years. She couldn't help thinking about Daniel at that point before she realised how fruitless it was. Daniel wasn't going to be part of her life for much longer so there was no point in thinking about him in that context.

The day finally came to an end and Emma was glad when eight o'clock came around so that she could go home. It wasn't just the late shift or the amount of work she'd done which had left her feeling so tired. She was so dispirited by what had happened that day that it had cast a pall over everything.

It had stopped snowing but the night was very cold. A thick layer of frozen snow crunched beneath her feet as she made her way to the hire car. She got in, thinking how good it was to be able to drive home, instead of waiting at the bus stop on a night like this, although she wouldn't be able to enjoy such luxury for much longer.

She would phone Daniel in the morning before he left for work and explain that she'd decided that it would be better if they cancelled their arrangements for Christmas. Naturally, she would tell him to ask the garage to collect the car. She felt guilty about letting him down at the last minute but it would be for the best.

It didn't take Emma long to drive home. She parked outside her flat and got out of the car. She was halfway across the pavement before she saw the man standing by her front door. She came to a stop, wondering what Daniel was doing there at that time of the night.

'Hello, Emma. I know it's late but we need to talk.' He held up his hand when she opened her mouth. 'I know what you're going to say but I intend to get this cleared up right now. I'm willing to stand here all night if need be but I won't go away until you've heard what I have to say.'

'You'd better come in, then.' Emma walked stiffly up the path and unlocked the door. She simply didn't have the heart to argue with him. It would be easier to let him say his piece and then tell him what she'd decided.

She led the way up to her flat and let them in. The central heating was on but the air felt chilly. Leading the way into the living room, she lit the gas fire, aware that she was simply putting off the moment when Daniel would tell her why he'd come.

Did he want to tell her that he no longer needed her help? The thought was painful, even though she'd been going to tell him that she didn't think she would be able to help him any longer.

She swung round to confront him, not wanting to draw out the agony any longer. 'Look, Daniel, I'm tired so if you have something to say, please, get on with it.'

His mouth thinned. 'Very well. Obviously, you believe that I thought you'd stolen Paula's ring. Well, you're wrong. It never crossed my mind that you were responsible for it going missing!'

'No?' She gave a sceptical laugh. 'Come on, Daniel. I saw your face when I stepped out of that lift. You were angry, and the reason for it was because you were worried that you might have invited a thief into your life!'

'Yes, I *was* angry. But it certainly wasn't because I thought you were a thief.' His hazel eyes blazed as he glared at her. 'I was furious that anyone in his right mind should have imagined that you would do such a thing, Emma!'

'Oh!' She stared at him in confusion and heard him sigh roughly.

'Look, I may as well be honest and admit that I'd heard the rumours that were going around about you being involved in the theft of the ring. That was bad enough. However, until the police questioned you, I had no idea that I was partly responsible for them. If I hadn't given you that envelope full of money, there would have been no reason for people to start speculating.'

She heard the agony in his voice and knew that he was blaming himself for what had happened. 'It wasn't your fault, Daniel. I don't suppose it was anybody's fault, really. People just added two and two and came up with the wrong answer.'

'Maybe. Although those rumours must have started somewhere. Also, someone must have contacted the police and given them your name, otherwise they wouldn't have interviewed you.'

Emma shrugged, although it wasn't pleasant to imagine that someone she worked with had contacted the police even if it had been with the very best of intentions. 'Perhaps they felt they had to tell the police what they knew.'

'Perhaps.' Daniel suddenly sighed. 'I suppose you're right but I doubt that I could be so forgiving in your shoes, Emma.'

'So long as people accept that I'm not to blame then that's all I care about.' She hesitated but there was something she had to say, despite how difficult it was. 'Look, Daniel, I'll understand if you would prefer to forget about Christmas.'

'What do you mean—forget about it?'

'It's just that it may be, well, awkward for you, having your name linked with mine at the moment.' She gave a short laugh, trying to make light of it all. 'You know how mud sticks, and I certainly wouldn't want you getting a bad name as well as me!'

'Don't be daft!' He took hold of her hands and gave her a gentle shake. 'I don't care a jot what people are saying, Emma. I know that you're innocent. And I most certainly don't intend to spoil our wonderful Christmas because of malicious gossip.'

She felt tears fill her eyes and looked away, but not quickly enough. He drew her into his arms and held her tight. 'Oh, Emma, don't let it upset you. It really isn't worth crying over. Give it a couple of days and then all the gossip will have died down. Anyway, your friends know that you wouldn't have stolen Paula's ring and that's what matters.'

He tilted her face up and kissed her gently. His lips lingered for one second…two…

He sighed as he reluctantly drew back. 'I wish I could stay longer and convince you that none of this makes a scrap of difference, but I have to get back. I asked a neighbour to sit with Amy so that I could come here and I don't want to be gone too long.'

He gave her a last kiss then set her away from him. 'Anyway, the other reason I came was to ask you if you would do me the honour of being my partner at the dance tomorrow. I know it's short notice but I didn't think I'd be able to go. However, Amy has been invited to a sleep-over party at her friend's house so it means that I have a whole evening to myself. So will you come, Emma? Please.'

'Are you sure?' she began, but he interrupted her firmly.

'Quite sure. So if you're still worrying about what people

are saying then forget it. We're going out on the town to-morrow and we're going to do it in style!'

Emma laughed at that. 'Mmm, you haven't been to a staff dance before, have you?' she teased. 'It's usually a lot of fun but as for stylish… Well, you'll see what I mean soon enough. I hope you're good at silly party games.'

'I'll soon learn if I'm not! Does that mean you'll come?' He grinned when she nodded. 'Great! The dance starts at seven so I'll pick you up at a quarter to if that's OK?'

'Fine.' She paused then hurried on. 'And you still want me to help with the Christmas arrangements, Daniel?'

He kissed her quickly. 'Yes! So stop worrying. This Christmas is going to be the best one we've ever had!'

He left straight after that. Emma sighed as she took off her coat. It might be the *best* Christmas ever but once it was over then that would be that. Daniel had made no mention of what would happen afterwards.

The next day flew by. Emma drove into Bournemouth and spent several hours shopping for presents for Amy. Top of her list was the Barbie doll with its sparkly dress. She added several other items to her basket, including a jigsaw puzzle in the shape of a pot-bellied pig—which was sure to appeal to the little girl—some colourful crayons and a thick pad of artist's paper.

She was flagging by the time one o'clock came round so she headed for a well-known department store which fronted the town's square. It was full of shoppers and the mood was very up-beat. Christmas songs were playing softly in the background and every department had been decorated with tinsel and baubles.

Emma made her way to the café on the top floor, stop-ping off on the way to visit the children's department where she bought a sweater for Amy in a lovely shade of blue. It struck her that she hadn't bought anything for Daniel as yet so she wandered through the homeware department, looking for something that would appeal to him. She didn't want to buy him anything too personal and decided that it might be better to give him something for the house.

The department was beautifully set out with arrangements of glass and china, silver and linen. It was hard to decide but in the end Emma opted for a glass paperweight which he would be able to use at home or in his office. It was quite expensive but she knew that Daniel would love the twisting patterns of purple and black glass embedded in it.

It was almost five when she arrived home so she just made herself a cup of tea, conscious of the fact that she had to get ready. Daniel would be arriving to collect her in less than two hours' time and she was going to need every minute to prepare!

Almost two hours later, Emma stood in front of the mirror and studied her reflection. It was the moment of truth. Would Daniel think that she looked all right?

Her eyes swept over her gleaming blond hair. She had decided on a new style that night but it suited her, she decided. With the silky strands tucked behind her ears she looked far more sophisticated than she usually did. She didn't have much jewellery but the sparkling diamanté studs she wore in her earlobes caught the light whenever she moved her head.

Her usual light make-up had been enhanced by shimmery face powder which gave her skin an added glow. Soft grey eye shadow and daringly black mascara made her eyes look huge and rather mysterious, while the plum-toned lipstick she'd bought in the summer sales and never dared wear before made her full mouth look little short of luscious.

Her increasingly confident gaze moved to her new black dress. As soon as she'd seen it in the window of that high-class boutique that afternoon, she'd known that she'd had to try it on. It had fitted perfectly so she'd taken a deep breath then told the assistant that she would buy it. It had made a big hole in her savings but, as she studied her reflection, Emma knew that it had been worth every penny.

It was a classic shift style that made the most of her slender curves. From the front it appeared almost staid, with its high neckline and rather severe lines. However, it was an entirely different story from the back!

Emma smiled as she twisted round so that she could see the lace insert which dipped in a V shape almost to her waist. There was no doubt that the dress was guaranteed to attract a second or even a third glance! Ridiculously high-heeled, black suede sandals—another impulsive buy in the sales—completed the picture of sophistication. All in all, she didn't think that Daniel would be too disappointed.

The sound of the doorbell made her jump. Emma pressed her hand to her racing heart as she made her way downstairs to let Daniel in.

'You look wonderful, Emma.' His hazel eyes swept over her with such undisguised appreciation that she laughed.

'So do you. Very handsome and distinguished, in fact.'

She was pleased to hear that her voice sounded light, though she meant every word. Daniel was wearing a well-cut dinner suit with a snowy white shirt and black bow-tie, and he looked absolutely stunning.

'Reckon it beats the white coat, do you?' he asked with a grin.

'Just!' Emma laughed when he glowered at her. 'Don't go fishing for compliments then you won't be disappointed.'

'Would I do such a thing? *Moi?*' he declared, in all innocence.

'Yes! Anyway, I'll just fetch my coat, otherwise we'll be late.' Emma ran back upstairs to fetch her coat and bag. Daniel had the door open when she came back down. He cast an assessing look at the snowy pavement then an equally assessing one at her feet in the strappy sandals.

'Well, in the absence of a cloak…' He swept her up into

his arms, grinning when he saw the surprise on her face. 'You'll get frostbite, going out into the snow in those shoes, Emma.'

He dropped a kiss on the tip of her nose then stepped out of the door. 'Hang on tight! And no wriggling. I don't want to drop you!'

'Oh, my hero!' Emma teased, hanging on for dear life as he slid and slipped his way to his car. He managed to open the door and deposited her on the passenger seat. 'Who says the age of chivalry is dead?'

'Anyone who doesn't want a hernia!' Daniel retorted with a wicked grin. He ducked when she reached for a handful of snow. 'Only joking—honest! You're as light as a feather.'

He slammed the door then made a great performance of clutching his back as he walked round to the driver's side. He stamped the snow off his feet before he got in, grinning at her as she rolled her eyes. 'I can see you aren't impressed by my acting so I may as well give it up as a bad job. Let's get going. This is going to be a night to remember, and we don't want to waste a minute of it!'

And it was a night to remember. From the moment they arrived, Daniel went out of his way to make sure that Emma was having a good time. Emma knew that they were the object of many curious pairs of eyes as they danced the night away, but she didn't care what people were thinking.

Mike Humphreys was there, partnered by a new nurse from A and E. He glowered at Emma as she and Daniel danced past but even that didn't spoil her enjoyment. Just being with Daniel, that made the whole evening special. She felt as though nothing could spoil it for her.

There was a buffet supper served at ten o'clock and they joined the queue waiting to be served. Outside caterers had been hired for the occasion and the food was delicious— smoked salmon, ham, beef, turkey and wonderful salads.

Linda and Gary were just ahead of them, waiting to be served, and Linda groaned when she saw the magnificent spread.

'Oh, bang goes my diet! I'm going to look like a meringue, walking down that aisle, if I'm not careful!' She gave Emma a cheeky smile. 'Not something you'll need to worry about on your wedding day, Em.'

Linda shot a pointed look at Daniel and Emma flushed. She could cheerfully have throttled her friend for saying that. She had no idea what Daniel must be thinking so hurried to limit any damage that might have been caused.

'I'm not planning on getting married for a long time to come, so you can stop throwing out hints, Linda. Just because you're eager to tie yourself down doesn't mean that we're all like you!'

Linda laughed good-naturedly as she took her turn at the buffet table. Emma shot an anxious look at Daniel but he wasn't looking at her. He was staring into the distance and there was an expression of such pain on his face that her heart ached.

'Is anything wrong?' she asked him softly, driven to ask.

He shook his head and it seemed as though a mask had fallen over his face all of a sudden. 'Of course not. What could be wrong?'

He smiled but there was no real warmth in it. Emma shivered, though she couldn't have explained why she felt chilled all of a sudden. It was their turn to select from the buffet so she didn't say anything else. However, the episode seemed to cast a shadow over the evening. Nothing was quite the same after that, although Daniel was as attentive as he had been earlier. When he suggested that they leave just before midnight, Emma agreed at once.

He drove her home without saying very much. He seemed to have a lot on his mind and Emma didn't know how to start up a conversation. When they stopped outside her flat, she noticed that he didn't switch off the engine.

'Would you like to come in for coffee?' she invited, hoping that he would accept. Maybe it was silly but she *knew* that something was wrong. Perhaps she could get him to talk about it over coffee.

'I won't, thanks. You've had a busy day and I'm sure you must want to get to bed.' He kissed her cheek but the kiss was so impersonal that Emma felt her eyes mist with tears. It was like one of those social kisses strangers bestowed on one another, completely devoid of meaning.

It was an effort to behave as though nothing was wrong. 'I'll bring Amy's presents round to your house tomorrow so that you can wrap them. What time would suit you best?'

'I have the afternoon off as it's Christmas Eve. Would two o'clock suit you? Say if it isn't convenient.'

How polite he sounded! They could have been two strangers for all the emotion he showed. Emma couldn't bear it any longer and reached for the handle.

'Fine. Two o'clock it is, then.'

She heard the taut note in her voice and knew Daniel must have heard it, too, because his hands tightened on the steering-wheel, although he didn't say anything else.

Emma got out of the car and carefully picked her way across the pavement, thinking back to what had happened earlier when Daniel had carried her to his car. What had gone wrong? Why was he so distant all of a sudden?

Daniel waited only long enough to see her safely inside before he drove away.

Emma went straight up to her flat and into her bedroom. Her sandals were probably ruined from their soaking in the snow but she didn't care. She stood in front of the mirror, thinking back to how she'd felt a few hours earlier. All the excitement had gone and all the anticipation along with it. What a fool she'd been to hope for more than she could ever have. What a fool to hope that Daniel might ever come to care for her!

CHAPTER ELEVEN

IT WAS almost one a.m. when Emma was woken by the sound of someone ringing her doorbell. Tossing back the bedclothes, she hurried to the window and peered down into the street but she couldn't see who it was. She was tempted not to answer but the thought of the people in the other flats being woken made her decide that she couldn't ignore it.

Fastening her dressing-gown around her, she ran downstairs and was shocked to find Mike Humphreys standing on the step. It was obvious from the way he was swaying that he was very drunk.

'Ah, Emma…pretty, scheming, little Emma,' he slurred, lurching towards her.

Emma pushed him away, feeling her stomach heave when she caught the smell of alcohol on his breath. 'What do you want, Mike? Have you any idea what time it is?'

He peered blearily at his watch then shook his head. 'Nope! Still, it's not that late, is it? Aren't you going to invite me in for a cup of coffee, Em, seeing as I've come all this way to see you?'

Before she could stop him, he'd stepped inside and closed the door. He leered as he noticed her dressing-gown. 'Oops, did I wake you up? I hope I didn't wake his lordship as well. That will have really blotted my copybook, won't it? Mind you, it's so full of blots now that I don't suppose it will make much difference.'

He laughed loudly at his own joke. Emma shook his arm as she saw a light come on in the ground-floor flat. 'Shh! You'll wake everyone up. Look, Mike, you're drunk so the best thing you can do is to get yourself off home.'

'So I don't interrupt your little party?' He shook his head so hard that he staggered against the wall. 'No, now I'm here I'm staying. It wouldn't be sociable if I didn't pay my respects to my revered boss.'

'Daniel isn't here if that's what you think,' Emma told him shortly. She shook her head when Mike opened his mouth. 'I mean it, Mike. Now, come along. It's time you went home.'

She steered him to the door but he resisted her efforts to usher him out. 'So Hutton didn't get any further with you than the rest of us have? Oh, dear, he wouldn't have liked that.'

Emma felt sick as she realised what he meant. 'My relationship with Daniel—or anyone else for that matter—is none of your business. Now, I want you to leave.'

She pushed him out of the door then paused when she saw his car parked in the road. 'You didn't drive here!' she exclaimed in horror.

Mike shrugged then had to grab hold of the wall to stop himself falling over. 'Course. Why not?'

'Because you're drunk, that's why!' Emma held out her hand. 'Give me the car keys—now!'

He took a bit of persuading before he finally handed them over. Emma shoved them in her pocket then realised that now she was faced with the problem of how he would get home. Finding a taxi at this hour could be difficult. Clearsea didn't boast much in the way of nightlife so there were few taxis running after midnight.

She sighed as she realised that she had no choice but to drive Mike home herself. She certainly couldn't take the risk of him wandering about on such a cold night in that state.

'Stay there.'

She ran back to her flat and dragged on jeans and a sweater. Mike was sitting on the step when she arrived back downstairs. He had his eyes closed and was snoring loudly as the effects of the alcohol caught up with him. It was a struggle to wake him and get him into the car. Emma muttered under her breath as she started the engine. The last thing she felt like doing was driving across town at this time of the night!

It was almost two before she arrived back home. Mike's flatmate had taken some rousing but she'd finally been able to hand over the young houseman into someone else's care. She switched off the engine then gasped as the car door was wrenched open.

'Where the hell have you been?'

Emma blinked, not quite able to believe that her eyes weren't deceiving her. What on earth was Daniel doing here?

'I…um…I went to Mike's. He—'

Daniel didn't let her finish. 'Forget it. I don't want to know what you've been up to because it isn't any of my business. Hurry up. I've wasted enough time waiting around here as it is.'

He turned and strode to his car. He had the engine running before she'd even got out of hers. Emma ran over to the car but Daniel didn't even look at her.

'Get in.'

'Why? What's happening? Look, Daniel, what is this?'

'Amy's been hurt. She's in hospital and she's asking for you.' He looked at her then and his eyes were as hard as pebbles. 'That's the only reason I'm here, because Amy wants you.'

Emma got into the car without another word. She could feel her heart hammering with fear. There was also a burning pain in her chest but she didn't allow herself to think about it. It was Amy who mattered now, not what Daniel thought about her. Just Amy. For now…

'The good news is that the scan is clear. There is no obvious damage to Amy's skull.'

'But there could be bruising to the brain, couldn't there?'

Daniel was as taut as a coiled spring. Emma ached to comfort him, only she knew that he wouldn't thank her for her concern. He'd briefly explained what had happened on the drive to the hospital. Evidently, Amy and the rest of the children at the sleep-over party had crept out of bed while her friend's parents were asleep and had gone into the garden to play with snowballs.

Unfortunately, Amy had slipped on a patch of ice and had hit her head on the edge of the patio. Daniel had arrived back from the dance to find a message on his answering machine, telling him that Amy had been taken to hospital. Emma knew that he must be tormenting himself with the thought that he should have been there and that it had added to his distress.

'I'm not going to lie and say that it isn't a possibility.' Lee Brennan, the young Casualty doctor on duty that night, shrugged. He was doing his pre-registration training and it was obvious that he was a little in awe of Daniel so was being very careful about what he said.

'You know enough about head injuries, sir, to understand that it's always a concern. However, we're hopeful that Amy has suffered nothing more serious than concussion, so let's try to be positive.'

Lee turned to Emma with relief when Daniel didn't say anything. 'Amy has been asking for you, Emma, so why don't you go and see her? We want to keep her as quiet as possible for the next twenty-four hours.'

'Of course.' Emma didn't look at Daniel as she hurriedly made her way to the side room where Amy had been taken. The little girl had her eyes closed, a huge bruise on her right temple telling its own tale about her exploits that night.

Emma felt a lump come to her throat as she looked at the small figure in the bed. She had grown to love Amy as though she were her own and it hurt to see her lying there, looking so ill.

'Emma…you came. Uncle Daniel promised that you would…'

Emma sat down by the bed and took hold of the little girl's hand as Amy opened her eyes. 'Of course I came. What was that I heard about you cracking a flagstone with your head?' she teased, earning herself a wan smile.

'I slid over in the snow and it hurt.' The little girl raised her hand to her head but Emma gently stopped her. Amy was attached to a drip and she didn't want her pulling out the IV line.

'I know. You've got a wonderful bruise on your forehead. It's every colour of the rainbow.'

Amy smiled. 'Is it? Can I see?'

'Maybe later. You just lie there nice and still and it will make you feel better.' Emma looked round as Daniel came to join her. He barely glanced at her, however, as he drew up a chair to the other side of his niece's bed.

'Hi, horror. How do you feel now?'

Amy smiled. 'Better 'cos Emma's here.'

Daniel glanced across the bed and for a moment his expression was unguarded. Emma inwardly recoiled when she saw the pain in his eyes. Surely she wasn't responsible for putting it there?

It was impossible to tell, of course. However, when Daniel turned away she heard the rough note in his voice and knew in her heart that she was right.

'Emma cares a lot about you, poppet. That's why she came. Now, you be a good girl and rest then you'll soon be better.'

'Will you stay…both of you?' Amy clutched tightly to their two hands.

Daniel looked at Emma and she nodded, although she couldn't help wondering why he'd needed to ask. Surely he must know that she would stay with Amy for however long the little girl needed her there?

She sighed. Maybe not. It seemed there was a lot that Daniel didn't know about her.

It was a long night. Amy became increasingly fretful because she was tired. Emma knew that the child couldn't understand why the nurses kept waking her. However, it was imperative that they checked for any deterioration in her condition. By the time morning came, all three of them were worn out.

Daniel stood up and stretched as a different nurse came in with a drink for the little girl. His face was grey with fatigue, contrasting with the white of his evening shirt. He must have rushed straight to the hospital as soon as he'd heard the message, and Emma couldn't help thinking how awful it must have been for him.

He beckoned her over to the window as the nurse ran through the obs once more. 'There's no point in you staying any longer, Emma. Why don't you go home? You can come back later if you want to.'

It was said so indifferently that Emma had to bite back a retort. Daniel was tired and worried so it was neither the time nor the place to make a fuss, though it hurt to have him speak to her that way.

'I'd rather stay,' she said flatly. 'I don't want Amy getting upset because I'm not here.'

'Fine. That's up to you, of course.'

He went back to the bed, smiling as he bent to speak to his niece. Emma felt herself choke up with emotion because it was obvious that Daniel was deliberately trying to cut her out. She couldn't understand why he was behaving that way but there was little she could do about it. She certainly wouldn't risk upsetting Amy by causing an argument! However, when the duty doctor arrived to check on the little girl, she took the opportunity to slip away to the canteen for a cup of coffee. The atmosphere in the room was so oppressive that she simply had to take a break.

There were few people about at that time of the morning. Emma paid for her drink and also bought a croissant, though she really didn't feel hungry. She had just sat down when Mike Humphreys appeared at her table.

He held up his hands placatingly. 'I know what you're going to say, Em, and you're well within your rights. I behaved abominably.'

'Well, you said it.' Emma picked up her cup, wishing that he would go away. She certainly didn't want to speak to him after what had happened the previous night. However, he pulled out a chair and sat down.

'I'm not going to make excuses because there aren't any. I just want to say thanks for what you did last night by driving me home.' He ran his hand over his face and sighed. 'I can't believe that I was actually going to drive in the state I was in.'

'It was stupid.' Emma had no intention of letting him off the hook. 'You could have killed yourself or, worse still, you could have killed somebody else.'

'I know, I know. I've been acting like a complete idiot of late. I just wanted you to know that I'm sorry, both about last night and everything else.'

'What do you mean?'

Mike shifted uncomfortably. 'It was me who started those rumours about Paula Walters's ring, Em. I was peeved because you'd made it obvious that you weren't interested in me.' He laughed hollowly. 'The old ego got the better of me, I'm afraid.'

Emma stood up because she didn't want to spend another second in his company. 'That was a horrible thing to do, Mike! Now, if you'll excuse me, I'm needed elsewhere.'

'I heard about Hutton's niece. How's she doing?' Mike grimaced when he saw her sceptical expression. 'Look, I don't wish any harm to come to the kid.'

'She's fine.' She turned away, leaving most of her coffee and all the croissant untouched.

'You really are keen on Hutton, aren't you? I hope he appreciates how lucky he is.'

Emma didn't pause as she hurriedly left the canteen. There was a bitter pain in her chest as she thought about what Mike had said. She doubted very much if Daniel would appreciate how she felt about him after the way he'd been behaving in the past few hours!

Amy was asleep when she got back to the room and Daniel was slumped in a chair. Emma thought at first that he was asleep as well but he suddenly looked up.

'The doctors are hopeful that she'll be allowed home later today,' he announced flatly.

'That's good. At least she'll still be able to enjoy her Christmas.'

Daniel smiled thinly. 'Yes, that's another thing to be grateful for. At least all your hard work won't have been in vain, Emma.'

There was a certain harshness in his voice, though he'd spoken quietly so as not to disturb the sleeping child. Emma frowned.

'What do you mean by that, Daniel?'

'Nothing. Forget it.' He stood up, motioning Emma to follow him from the room. His tone was devoid of expression as he continued.

'I'm going to be tied up here most of the day so I was wondering if you would mind wrapping up Amy's presents and getting things ready for tomorrow. I take it that you still intend to carry on as we arranged?'

'Of course.' She didn't ask him why he thought that she might have changed her mind. It was obvious that Daniel was deliberately trying to put their arrangements on a solely businesslike footing so she wasn't going to make the mistake of letting personal feelings creep in. However, that didn't mean she wasn't hurt by his attitude or that she understood it.

Last night at the dance had been so wonderful. Then there had been that night she'd stayed at his house. That had been even more wonderful! Yet it was hard to believe that she'd shared either experience with this man who now spoke to her so coldly.

'Then I can safely leave everything to you, Emma. Thank you.'

He turned and went back into his niece's room without a backward glance. Emma took a deep breath. She wouldn't make a fool of herself by breaking down. That would be unforgivable. She would carry on as they'd planned—make sure that Amy had the most wonderful Christmas Day. Then she would slip quietly out of Daniel's life…

That was it! Everything was wrapped.

Emma sighed in relief as she studied the mound of gaily wrapped parcels stacked on the end of Daniel's bed. She'd decided to wrap Amy's presents in his bedroom in case he brought his niece home earlier than expected. He'd rung to say that they should be home by four but Emma knew enough about hospitals not to take that for granted.

Now she picked up two of the presents and took them downstairs to the sitting room where she placed them under the Christmas tree. There were a few other parcels there already and she smiled when she recognised one as being Amy's present to her uncle. What *would* Daniel make of that tie?

Her smile faded when it struck her that she wouldn't be around to know if he wore it very often. Once Christmas Day was over Daniel and his niece wouldn't need her in their lives any longer. What they did wouldn't be any of her concern, and although it was bitterly painful to know that, it would be foolish not to face the facts.

The sound of a car drawing up warned her that Daniel

and Amy were arriving. Emma fixed a smile to her face as she went to greet them.

'Hello, there! How do you feel, Amy? Is your head still sore?'

'A bit, but the doctor said I could come home. I was glad 'cos I was worried in case Father Christmas didn't know where to find me,' Amy explained seriously.

'Oh, I'm sure Santa would have found out where you were,' Emma assured her. 'He always manages to deliver presents to the boys and girls who have to stay in hospital over Christmas.'

'He must be really clever, mustn't he?' Amy said, obviously impressed.

'Oh, he is!' Emma took the little girl's coat and led her into the sitting room. She was very aware that Daniel hadn't said a word since he'd entered the house. She shot him a wary glance but he avoided her eyes as he made his niece comfortable on the sofa.

'Now, remember what the doctor told you, Amy? That you have to be a good girl and rest.' He smiled at the child. 'Then you'll be well enough to enjoy yourself tomorrow. OK?'

'OK.' Amy agreed obediently.

She looked worn out, poor little mite, Emma thought, seeing the shadows under the little girl's eyes. She felt suddenly sick with relief that Amy hadn't suffered any worse injuries. She knew how dangerous knocks to the head could be…

'Emma?'

She looked up with a start when she realised that Daniel was speaking to her. 'Yes?'

'I just asked if you wanted a cup of tea,' he said politely.

'I'll make it,' Emma offered immediately, conscious of the way he was looking so intently at her.

She hurried from the room and went into the kitchen to fill the kettle. She didn't realise at first that he'd followed

her, and jumped when she turned and saw him standing by
the table.

'Are you all right?' he asked flatly.

'Of course. Why shouldn't I be?' she snapped back,
stung into replying that way by the indifference in his
voice. Did he have any idea how it hurt to have him speak
to her like that? Probably not! Why should Daniel care
about her feelings?

'Because you're acting so strangely, of course. You were
miles away just now. You had no idea I was speaking to
you.'

He paused and his tone was clipped all of a sudden.
'Maybe you were wishing that you didn't have to waste
time here when you could be spending it with someone
who's really important to you. Well, don't let us keep you,
Emma. Amy and I can manage perfectly well without you!'

'Fine! If that's how you feel, I may as well leave.' Emma
hurried towards the door. She was so hurt that he could say
such a thing that all she wanted to do was leave before she
broke down. Tears filled her eyes and she let out a gasp of
pain as she walked into the end of the table and banged
her hip.

'Careful!'

Daniel was beside her in an instant. He swore softly
when he saw the tears running down her face. 'You've hurt
yourself. Here, sit down...'

'No!' Emma pushed him away when he tried to guide
her to a chair. 'I'm fine. Don't waste time worrying about
me, Daniel. I know you don't want me here so I'll leave.'

'What do you mean—*I* don't want you here? It's you
who wants to be somewhere else. I can hazard a guess as
to where as well. Tell Humphreys that I'm sorry for taking
up so much of your time of late but that it won't happen
again!'

He pointedly stepped aside but Emma didn't move. 'I
don't know how many times I need to repeat this before it

sinks in,' she bit out through clenched teeth, 'but Mike Humphreys hasn't any claim on my time!'

'Oh, no? Look, Emma, it isn't my business, so—'

She didn't let him finish because she was sick and tired of hearing him speak to her in that…that *know-it-all* tone! 'You're right, Daniel. It isn't any of your business. You've made it clear that you don't want it to be *your* business! However, for your information, there never has been, nor will there ever be, anything going on between Mike and me. Got the message now?'

She started to walk past him but his hand fastened around her wrist and drew her to a halt. Emma felt her breath catch because there was an expression on his face that she'd never seen there before. Why did Daniel look so…so scared all of a sudden? She had no idea but it certainly scared her!

'Do you really mean that, Emma? I know you've told me before that you and Humphreys weren't involved, but last night…' He broke off.

Emma could see the struggle he was having but there was nothing she could do to help him. It would be wrong to read more into what was happening than Daniel might mean, even though her foolish heart was already writing whole chapters about it!

'What happened last night, Emma? I must have phoned you a dozen times from the hospital. I was so worried when I couldn't get an answer that I went to your flat to see if you were all right. I was ready to rouse everyone in the whole house after I rang your bell and didn't get a reply. Then, lo and behold, you appeared and told me that you'd been with Humphreys. What was I to think?'

'I've no idea. Maybe you should have given me chance to tell you that when Mike turned up drunk at my door I confiscated his car keys. Then I could have explained that it meant I'd had to drive him home myself. That's what happened, you see, Daniel. Not very exciting, was it?'

'Oh, Emma, I'm sorry! I'm such an idiot, aren't I? If only I'd given you chance to explain!'

'Uh-huh.' She gave him a tight little smile. 'You are an idiot, Daniel!'

He chuckled. 'I can see that you aren't going to let me off too lightly. I don't blame you. I did rather jump to conclusions. I was so keyed up with everything that had happened that I wasn't thinking rationally. Will you forgive me?'

How could she refuse when she heard the entreaty in his voice? 'There's nothing to forgive. It was a misunderstanding. So long as you accept that I'm not interested in Mike, and certainly not after what he told me this morning.'

'What do you mean?'

Emma quickly explained about Mike having started the rumours, and she saw Daniel's face darken. 'I bet it was Humphreys who contacted the police as well. I wondered who was responsible for that.'

'Probably.' Emma shrugged. 'I didn't ask him. I was so sickened by what he told me that I didn't want to hear any more.'

'Why did he do it, though?' Daniel frowned. 'If he was keen on you, it was a funny way of showing how he felt.'

'I think he was trying to get back at me for refusing to go out with him,' Emma explained.

'Also, he was probably annoyed because I was taking up so much of your time. Humphreys and I haven't seen eye to eye since I started working at St Luke's. I don't like his attitude and he knows it.' Daniel sighed. 'I seem to have caused you a lot of problems, Emma. I bet you're sorry you ever agreed to help me.'

'That's where you're wrong. I've enjoyed every minute. I'm only sorry that once Christmas is over it will have to end.' She hadn't meant to say that and wished she could take it back when she saw him look sharply at her.

'Because you'll miss being with Amy?' Daniel's voice

was flat. 'I know that you've grown fond of her, Emma, and I know how fond she is of you. However, it wouldn't be fair to expect you to give up any more of your time, nor would it be fair to Amy to let her grow even more attached to you. I know you aren't interested in that kind of commitment.'

'Why do you think that?' she asked quietly, although her heart was thumping so hard that it was difficult to think straight.

'Because of what you told Linda last night. You were quite honest about not wanting to get tied down just yet, and who can blame you?'

'I know what I told Linda. I know why I said it as well.' Emma coloured. 'Linda was throwing out hints about you and me, and I didn't want her embarrassing you.'

'But you must have meant it, surely?'

She heard the uncertainty in his voice and her hands clenched. Why did she have a feeling that her answer was important to him? 'Not really. I'm certainly not trying to avoid commitment, if that's what you thought.'

'I see.' He turned away, picked up the kettle then put it down again with a thud. Emma saw his shoulders rise and fall as he took a deep breath before he suddenly swung round to face her once more.

'I swore that I wouldn't say this but what you've just told me has changed everything. Having you in my life these past weeks has been the best thing that has ever happened to me, Emma. I go cold thinking about what it's going to be like when I can no longer use Christmas as an excuse to be with you.

'I promised myself that I would *never* use Amy as an inducement, but I can't help myself. I know that you enjoy being with her. I know that you would agree to continue being part of our lives for her benefit. I'm desperate enough to use all of those to my own ends, though it doesn't make me feel proud of myself for doing so.'

Emma's head was swimming. She could barely take in what he was saying. 'Wh-why are you so desperate to have me in your life, Daniel? I don't understand.'

'Because I'm head over heels in love with you, of course! Surely it's obvious?'

He sounded so amazed that Emma laughed out loud. 'Not at all. I can honestly say that I had no idea how you felt about me!'

Maybe he sensed something from her tone because his expression suddenly lightened. 'Well, if it's a surprise then I have to say that you're taking it extremely well. You don't look as though you're about to turn tail and run.'

'Don't I?' She smiled as he came and stood in front of her, and wondered how she could tease him at such a momentous time in her life.

'No. In fact, if I were a betting man I'd say that there was a greater than even chance that the idea never crossed your mind.' His smile was slow and sexy, a growing confidence creeping back into his voice.

'You could be right. Of course, you really need to study form before you place a bet.' Emma was enjoying herself now. There was something deliciously enticing about drawing out the moment when she would tell him how she felt.

'Oh, I'm fairly confident that I'm on a winner.'

'So you don't want to know what odds I'm offering?'

'Well, I suppose it can't hurt.' He smiled at her. 'So, what are the odds on you not running out of here?'

'Oh, a hundred to zero against...'

Emma didn't manage to finish. Daniel obviously had other things on his mind by that point! He swept her into his arms and kissed her so thoroughly that Emma wasn't capable of standing upright let alone running.

His eyes were full of wonder as he gazed at her. 'I can't believe this. You are sure, Emma? I mean, you're sure how you feel about me and it isn't just that you love Amy...?'

'Shh.' She pressed her fingers against his lips. 'I know how I feel, Daniel Hutton. I love you.'

He closed his eyes and she felt him take a huge breath. 'Thank heavens for that! I've been dreading this Christmas as much as I've been looking forward to it.' He opened his eyes and looked at her with a wealth of love. 'Now I know that Christmas is the beginning, not the end as I feared it would be.'

Emma smiled as she reached up and kissed him. 'I think that's very appropriate, don't you? Christmas should be a time when wonderful things start to happen.'

Daniel smiled back at her. 'You're right. I love you, Emma Graham. I wish I could show you how much only there's a small girl in the sitting room who's bound to be wondering where we've got to—'

He broke off when, on cue, there was a shout from the other room of, 'Uncle Daniel, Emma, where are you?'

Emma laughed as she slid out of his arms. 'It appears that we're wanted. I think we shall have to leave the demonstrations for now, don't you?'

CHAPTER TWELVE

IT WAS well past nine before Amy settled down to sleep. Daniel came downstairs after tucking her up in bed and flopped down onto the sofa.

'Thanks heavens for that! I thought she would *never* give in.'

Emma laughed as she snuggled against him. 'She's so excited, isn't she? Did you see her face when we were arranging the glass of sherry and mince pie for Santa?'

'I did.' Daniel laughed softly as he looked at the mantelpiece which now bore Amy's offerings. 'Isn't it lovely when a child believes so fervently that there's a Father Christmas?'

'You mean there isn't one?' Emma feigned surprise. Daniel laughed as he pulled her closer and kissed her lingeringly.

'Let's just say that I'm beginning to have second thoughts on the subject,' he replied rather thickly several, highly satisfying minutes later. 'A couple of weeks ago I would have stated categorically that Santa didn't exist but after what's happened recently I'm not so sure. There has to be some explanation for why I've received such a wonderful gift.'

'And what gift would that be?' Emma asked smugly, already sure what the answer would be.

'You. As if you needed to be told!' Daniel kissed her again in loving punishment for her temerity. 'Knowing that you're going to be a permanent fixture in my life is the best present I could have hoped for, Emma. Have I told you how much I love you, by the way?'

'I think you did mention it but that was *hours* ago. It

wouldn't hurt to tell me again because I certainly won't get tired of hearing you say it.'

'Good.' He took her face between his hands. 'I love you, Emma. You have made my life complete, though I had no idea there was anything missing from it before you came along.'

She laughed a little shakily because she was so touched by the depth of emotion in his voice. 'So you thought that you had everything you wanted before my advent into your life, did you?'

'I did.' He sighed softly as he pulled her back into his arms and held her close. 'I had my job and I had Amy—that seemed enough. Oh, I've had relationships in the past but they were just temporary affairs in all senses. I'd never met anyone I wanted to spend my life with.'

'Me, too. Or is it me neither? Whichever. What I mean is that I'd never met anyone I wanted to share my life with before I met you, Daniel.'

'I'm glad. It makes what we have all the more special, doesn't it? As though we each have been waiting for the other to come along.'

'It does. And we have Amy to thank for it happening. If you hadn't been desperate enough to ask me if I could sew, we might never have got together,' she said wonderingly.

'Oh, I don't know about that.' Daniel's tone was so wry that she shifted slightly so that she could look at him. He kissed the tip of her nose then grinned. 'I was very much aware of you, Staff Nurse Graham. You had impinged on my consciousness in a big way.'

'I had? But you never said anything…' She took a deep breath. 'You never *showed* how you felt either!'

'Mmm, discretion being the better part of valour and all that.' He laughed deeply. 'I'd heard that you were very choosy about who you dated and I was scared of getting turned down. It wouldn't have done much for my ego, I can tell you!'

He sobered. 'Also, I was very much aware that my first duty was to Amy. I didn't have the time for a relationship and couldn't imagine any woman wanting to get herself lumbered with looking after someone else's child.

'I'd been dating someone when Claire died and she made it clear that she didn't intend being a surrogate mother to Amy. Not that there was *any* chance of me asking her to be, I might add. However, it did bring it home to me that most women would take a very dim view of taking responsibility for someone else's child.'

It explained a lot, Emma thought. She hurried to reassure him. 'I'm not them, though, Daniel. I love Amy. I can't think of anything I want more than to be able to play a part in bringing her up, if you'll let me.'

'I can't imagine doing it alone now. I've seen how Amy has blossomed under your care, Emma. She needs you as much as she needs me. Together we shall be able to give her all the love and stability that Claire would have given her.'

Emma felt humbled to hear him say that. She kissed him quickly. 'We shall. We'll try our best to be good parents to her, Daniel.'

'And to our own children as well.'

Emma heard the question in his voice and smiled at him. 'And for them as well.'

It seemed pointless wasting time on words at that point. Emma wasn't sure how much time had passed when Daniel finally raised his head. She loved him so much that the world seemed to stop when she was in his arms! However, a glance at the clock on the mantelpiece showed her how late it was and she reluctantly stood up.

'Much as I hate to break up the party, it's time I left.'

'You're going home? But I thought you'd stay the night here?' Daniel's voice betrayed how he felt about the idea of her leaving.

'I don't want to leave but I was worried about what Amy

might think if I stay here again—' she began, but he cut her off.

'We shall explain the situation to Amy in the morning if she asks,' he stated firmly. 'Once she knows we're getting married she'll understand.'

'Married?' Emma gulped. She saw Daniel smile as he stood up and took hold of her hands.

'Uh-huh. You will marry me, won't you, Emma? I know it's an old-fashioned idea in today's world but it's what I want more than anything.'

'Then I suppose I must be an old-fashioned sort of woman because it's what I want, too. Yes, Daniel, I will marry you.'

'Great!' He swung her off her feet and twirled her round.

'Has Father Christmas been?' a hopeful little voice demanded from the doorway.

Daniel chuckled as he set Emma back on her feet and turned to his niece. 'Not yet, sweetheart. But I'm sure he's on his way.'

'Oh! Then why were you and Emma so excited?' Amy asked, looking sleepily from Emma to her uncle.

'Because Emma and I are getting married.' He picked up the little girl and kissed her. 'Which means that Emma is going to be living here with us soon. Won't that be nice?'

'Mmm.' Amy smiled her delight then suddenly frowned. 'You'll have to make sure that Father Christmas knows that you're going to live with us, Emma, or he might not be able to bring you your presents.'

Emma laughed as she kissed the child's cheek. 'I'll do that! Now it's time you went back to bed. Father Christmas won't bring your presents unless you're fast asleep.'

'Will you take me?' Amy asked.

Emma lifted the little girl out of Daniel's arms and hugged her. 'Of course I will.'

She looked at Daniel over the top of Amy's head as she carried her from the room. She could see in his eyes everything that she was feeling. They would share their lives and their love with this precious child and become a family. It seemed her wish had come true after all.

Christmas Day passed in a whirl from the moment they were woken by Amy's excited cries when she discovered her presents. Both Emma and Daniel went into the little girl's room and watched her unwrap them.

Amy was thrilled with everything, particularly the doll and the pot-bellied pig puzzle. Emma's help was enlisted as she tipped the pieces of puzzle onto the floor.

That took a couple of hours, although Amy did break off several times to play with the doll and draw some pictures with her new crayons. Daniel made them all tea and toast then it was time to unwrap the presents under the tree.

Amy loved her sweater and insisted on wearing it right away. Emma helped her put it on then watched as the child solemnly presented Daniel with his present.

'It's wonderful,' he declared, immediately putting the tie round his neck and knotting it under the collar of his dressing-gown. 'It's the best tie I've ever had!'

'I knew you'd like it,' she said happily, then dug through the parcels and produced one for Emma. 'Uncle Daniel helped me choose this. He said that you'd like it.'

Emma unwrapped the many layers of paper and was touched to find a bottle of her favourite perfume inside. 'It's my favourite! How did you know?'

'Oh, it took a lot of sniffing and testing before we tracked it down, didn't it, Amy?' Daniel winked at his niece. 'I think the lady in the shop was glad when we finally decided which one it was!'

'I can imagine!' Emma laughed as she handed him the present she'd bought for him. 'I hope you like this.'

'It's beautiful!' Daniel placed the glass paperweight in pride of place on the mantelpiece. 'I could even use those colours when I decorate in here.'

Emma and Amy exchanged horrified looks. 'I think we prefer *beige* to shocking pink, don't we, Amy?'

Daniel laughed. 'Spoilsports! Anyway, now it's your turn to see what I bought for you. I hope you like it, too, Emma.'

He handed her a small package wrapped in gold paper. Emma frowned as she worked the sticky tape away from one end. She had no idea at all what it could be. She gasped when she opened the velvet box and discovered a beautiful gold locket inside.

'It's gorgeous, Daniel. I don't know what to say.'

'I'm glad you like it. Look inside.'

Emma carefully unfastened the tiny clasp and opened the locket to reveal photographs of Daniel and Amy. She was so touched that she couldn't say a word because she knew in her heart what it symbolised. Daniel was giving her himself and Amy as her Christmas present, and she knew that she could never have been given anything more wonderful or more special than that.

'I came downstairs and put the pictures in it while you were asleep last night,' he explained, drawing her aside as Amy started playing with some of her new toys. 'The locket was my mother's and I had the jeweller fit a new chain because the old one was broken. I was going to give it to you empty, but after last night I realised that the locket was just a token and that the gift I really wanted you to accept was Amy and me.'

He drew her round to face him. 'I know I've asked you this before, but will you marry me, Emma?'

'And I've told you before but I don't mind saying it again—yes, I'll marry you, Daniel. There couldn't be a better, more wonderful gift than the one you've given me.'

Emma knew he understood that she didn't mean just the locket. He kissed her gently then looked up when Amy sighed heavily.

'I suppose this means that you two will be kissing and stuff all the time, doesn't it?'

'Very possibly,' Daniel replied, completely deadpan. 'Why? Is it a problem, Amy?'

'S'pose not. But I'm never going to kiss a boy. It's really yucky!'

Emma laughed. 'We'll remind her of that in a few years' time, shall we?' she asked softly as Amy went back to her toys.

'Don't! Can you imagine what it's going to be like when boyfriends appear on the horizon?' Daniel's expression was horrified.

'We'll cope,' Emma assured him. 'We'll be fully quali-fied parents by that stage.'

'I'll remind you of that when the time comes,' he growled, obviously not convinced.

Emma just laughed then suddenly caught sight of the time. 'Look at the time! Why didn't you say something?'

'Say what? What's wrong?' Daniel demanded in alarm.

'What's wrong is that I have a turkey to get in the oven and it had better be soon otherwise we'll be eating Christmas dinner at midnight!'

She rushed out of the room, smiling when she heard Daniel laugh. She set to work in the kitchen and he joined her a short time later, helping her peel the vegetables and get everything ready. It was obvious that he wanted it to be special as well, and it would be. It was going to be their first Christmas dinner together, the first of many to come!

'So I opened this cracker and there was a ring. Gary had been back to the jeweller's and bought it for me because he knew how disappointed I was.'

Linda held out her hand so that they could all admire the dainty diamond solitaire she was sporting. It was their first day back after the Christmas break and they were all gath-ered in the staffroom, getting ready to go on duty and swop-ping stories about what they had done.

'It's beautiful, Linda. Wasn't that a lovely thing for Gary to do?' Emma said.

'It was. He can be quite thoughtful at times.' Linda smiled. 'Then he can be a real pain at others! Still, he's my pain and I love him.'

'Oh, she's getting soft in her old age,' Eileen Pierce remarked with a laugh.

'Not at all,' Linda denied swiftly. 'It's just an overload of Christmas spirit. Anyway, how was your Christmas, Em? Did you enjoy it as much as you thought you would?'

'It was even better than I'd hoped,' Emma replied dreamily. She coloured when she heard the others chuckle but there was no way she could keep what had happened a secret. She was dying to tell everyone her news.

'Daniel and I are getting married.'

'What! You are? Why, you dark horse, you! Mind, I knew there was something afoot. I could smell it in the air!'

Linda hugged her hard as the others offered their congratulations. Emma laughed.

'I still can't believe it. I feel as though I'm walking on air!'

'I really am pleased for you, Emma,' Linda told her as the other two left the room. 'I could tell that you were crazy about Daniel the night of the dance and that he was just as smitten.'

'Really?' Emma shook her head in amazement. 'I had no idea, although Daniel seemed to think that I knew how he felt.'

'Well, I'm just glad that you had such a wonderful time. You deserved it, Emma, after all the rotten things that happened.' Linda paused. 'Did you hear that the police have found out who stole Paula's ring? The jeweller told Gary when he went to buy me this. Turns out it was Alison Banks—remember her?'

Emma frowned. 'Alison Banks...not the young girl whose husband was in the army!'

'That's right. Evidently, she overheard Paula telling you about the ring and took it on an impulse while Paula was having her scan.' Linda shrugged. 'I don't think she was thinking clearly at the time because she was so upset about her miscarriage. She told the police that she sold it and used the money to buy food and presents for Christmas. Her husband couldn't understand where all the stuff had come from and made her tell him what had happened. Then he took Alison to the police.'

'Oh, the poor girl! Grief does some very strange things to people. I do hope the police take that into account,' Emma said sadly.

'I'm sure they will.' Linda looked up as Daniel suddenly appeared. 'Oh, time I was on my way. Two's company and three's definitely one too many!'

Emma shook her head in despair as Linda left. 'She really is incorrigible!'

'I'd say that she showed a rare degree of sensitivity,' Daniel replied, coming into the staffroom and firmly closing the door behind him. He took Emma in his arms and kissed her thoroughly.

'That's better. I was starting to get withdrawal symptoms.'

Emma laughed. 'It's only ten minutes since you last saw me!'

'And that's far too long.' He kissed her again then sighed when his beeper began to trill. 'Why does that always have to happen at the most inopportune moments? Anyway, I'll see you later.'

One last kiss and he was gone, leaving Emma smiling. She seemed to be floating as she made her way to the ward, and the feeling didn't go away for the rest of the day. Daniel was waiting in the foyer for her when she finished work. Emma stepped from the lift and smiled as she saw him, her own walking, talking, *loving* Christmas present. Santa had really pulled out all the stops this year!

'Ready to go home?' he asked, taking hold of her hand. Emma knew that everyone in the hospital now knew that they were getting married, thanks to Linda and the grapevine. She saw a lot of looks being cast their way and smiled. She loved Daniel and he loved her—she wanted the whole world to know how they felt!

'More than ready. Let's go and collect Amy, shall we?'

They left the hospital and drove through the town. The lights were still on even though Christmas had been and gone. Soon it would be time to take down the decorations for another year.

Emma smiled as she looked at Daniel sitting beside her. This had been the best Christmas ever, and the best thing of all was that it was going to last for ever. They were going to be a *real* family all year round, not just for Christmas!

Modern Romance™
...seduction and
passion guaranteed

Tender Romance™
...love affairs that
last a lifetime

Medical Romance™
...medical drama
on the pulse

Historical Romance™
...rich, vivid and
passionate

Sensual Romance™
...sassy, sexy and
seductive

Blaze Romance™
...the temperature's
rising

27 new titles every month.

Live the emotion

MILLS & BOON®

PENNINGTON

BOOK SEVEN

Available from 2nd January 2004

Available at most branches of WHSmith, Tesco, Martins, Borders,
Eason, Sainsbury's and most good paperback bookshops.

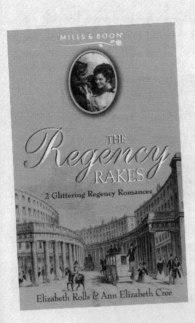

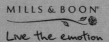

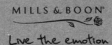

MILLS & BOON®

Live the emotion

Tender Romance™

THE FRENCHMAN'S BRIDE by Rebecca Winters

Hallie Linn can't fall in love with gorgeous Frenchman Jean-Vincent Rolland – it's too complicated, too difficult – it would change her life for ever. Vincent also has reasons for not getting involved with Hallie – but he does want her – as his bride...

HER ROYAL BABY by Marion Lennox

Tammy is guardian of her orphaned nephew, Henry, who will one day be Crown Prince of a European country. Marc, the darkly handsome Prince Regent, wants Henry brought up as royalty – but Australian Tammy has no time for titles. As she and Marc clash, the passionate charge between them becomes impossible to resist!

HER PLAYBOY CHALLENGE by Barbara Hannay

Jen Summers has no idea how she'll juggle being temporary mum to her little niece and holding down a glamorous new job – and then a sexy stranger decides to give her a helping hand! Harry Ryder is used to helping women into bed – not with small children. But Jen is caring, shy, and he just can't help himself...

MISSION: MARRIAGE by Hannah Bernard

Lea is turning thirty and the alarm on her biological clock is ringing. But how does a woman with just one ex-boyfriend learn to find Mr Right? Tom is a serial dater, with no interest in settling down – but he's perfect as a dating consultant! Except their 'practice date' leads to more than one 'practice kiss'...

On sale 2nd January 2004

Available at most branches of WHSmith, Tesco, Martins, Borders, Eason, Sainsbury's and all good paperback bookshops.

1203/02

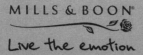

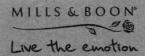

MILLS & BOON®

Live the emotion

Medical Romance™

THE REGISTRAR'S WEDDING WISH *by Lucy Clark*

Annie Beresford is a talented surgeon and trainee consultant – but her wish is for marriage and children before it's too late. She knows that falling for her new boss, Hayden Robinson, is a bad idea – but he might just be the one. She knows they can't be happy without each other – even if he won't believe her...yet!

THE DOCTOR'S RESCUE *by Kate Hardy*

When GP Will Cooper rescues a toddler from a busy road and ends up in hospital himself – with a broken arm and leg – he also discovers a beautiful stranger, Dr Mallory Ryman, by his bed! And then Will asks her to be his locum – and live in his house to care for him while he recovers!

THE GP'S SECRET *by Abigail Gordon*

GP Davina Richards is content with her life, caring for the Pennine community she grew up with – until her sexy new boss arrives! Dr Rowan Westlake has eyes only for Davina, but he has a secret, and she's not going to like it. His only hope is that facing the past will allow them to face the future – together!

On sale 2nd January 2004

Available at most branches of WHSmith, Tesco, Martins, Borders, Eason, Sainsbury's and all good paperback bookshops.

1203/03b

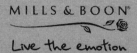

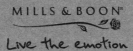

MILLS & BOON®

Live the emotion

Sensual Romance™

THE MIGHTY QUINNS: LIAM by Kate Hoffmann

Photographer Liam Quinn can't believe his luck when he gets paid to spy on sexy suspect Eleanor Thorpe. But he can't help thinking she's innocent. And when he saves her from an intruder Liam comes dangerously close to blowing his cover – when what he really wants is to get under Eleanor's!

THE CHOCOLATE SEDUCTION by Carrie Alexander

Thanks to a bet she made with her sister, sex is off the menu for feisty Sabrina! So to satisfy her cravings she indulges herself with chocolate desserts – made by sexy chef Kristoffer 'Kit' Rex! Kit knows Sabrina's got great will-power, and that she loves chocolate, so what better way to tempt her than with a skilfully sweet seduction . . .?

WICKED AND WILLING by Leslie Kelly

Sassy Venus Messina is wary when she discovers she's the long-lost granddaughter of a millionaire. But soon the bad girl finds herself lounging in luxury and *in lust* with Troy Langtree, her grandfather's new business partner. Now that Troy's met Venus all he wants is to have his wicked way with the racy redhead. And, if he's lucky, Venus will be as bad as she looks . . .

LOOK, BUT DON'T TOUCH by Sandra Chastain

When photographer Cat McCade meets Jesse Dane, she can't get him out of his clothes fast enough and they share one night of sizzling sex. But when Jesse discovers his new job is as Cat's bodyguard, he knows she's strictly off limits. However, how far is Cat willing to go to get her body *back* in Jesse's bed . . .?

On sale 2nd January 2004

Available at most branches of WHSmith, Tesco, Martins, Borders, Eason, Sainsbury's and all good paperback bookshops.

1203/21